Erin's Blood Royal

Also by Peter Berresford Ellis published by Constable

Celtic Inheritance
The Celtic Revolution
A Dictionary of Irish Mythology
The Celtic Empire
A Guide to Early Celtic Remains in Britain
A Dictionary of Celtic Mythology
Celt and Saxon
Celtic Dawn
The Druids
Celtic Women
Celt and Greek
Celt and Roman
The Ancient World of the Celts

Erin's Blood Royal

THE GAELIC NOBLE DYNASTIES OF IRELAND

PETER BERRESFORD ELLIS

CONSTABLE · LONDON

First published in Great Britain 1999
by Constable and Company Limited,
3 The Lanchesters,
162 Fulham Palace Road,
London W6 9ER
Copyright © Peter Berresford Ellis 1999
ISBN 0 09 478600 3
The right of Peter Berresford Ellis to be identified as author
of this work has been asserted by him in accordance with
the Copyright, Designs and Patents Act 1988

Set in Linotron Janson 10½pt by
Rowland Phototypesetting Limited
Printed in Great Britain by
St Edmundsbury Press Ltd,
both of Bury St Edmunds, Suffolk

A CIP catalogue record for this book
is available from the British Library

I am a ghost upon your path,
An ethereal wisp.
But you must know one word of Truth
Can give a phantom breath

Aisling-thruagh do mhear meisi
(A sorrowful vision has deceived me)
by Donal IX MacCarthy Mór (d. 1596)
last regnant King of Desmond

Note

As this book was being prepared for press, the *Sunday Times* (Ireland, 20 June 1999) reported that the Chief Herald of Ireland was to take the unprecedented step of withdrawing his office's 'courtesy recognition' of the title of MacCarthy Mór, Prince of Desmond, who contributes the Foreword to this book. The Chief Herald's office had originally given such recognition nine years ago following a process of investigation lasting six years. The *Sunday Times* suggested that such recognition would probably be granted to a great nephew of a retired judge who had, in 1921, adopted the form 'MacCarthy Mór' as a name by Deed Poll. Details of this judge's claims are given on p. 127.

The conflict between the Chief Herald's office, insisting on primogeniture recognition and those maintaining that Gaelic titles originate and can only descend by Brehon successional law, of whom MacCarthy Mór has been the most outspoken advocate, is detailed in Chapter 6. This chapter also discusses the international judgements handed down in 1998 supporting Gaelic successional law and criticising the insistence of the office of the Chief Herald for continuing to maintain that its recognition can only be on concepts which arise from the very law system which abolished Gaelic titles between 1541 and 1610.

Contents

Part One
THE 'EXTINCTION' AND SURVIVAL
OF GAELIC ARISTOCRACY

Part Two
THE FAMILIES

Part Three
RANK AND MERIT

List of Illustrations

between pages 148 and 149

The President of the Irish Republic receives some of
the survivors of the old Gaelic aristocracy.
Three of the four heirs to the High Kingship
Donal IX MacCarthy Mór, King of Desmond, 1568
Heirlooms of the Royal House of MacCarthy Mór
Leopoldo O'Donnell, Duke of Tetuan, 1954
Hugo O'Donnell, Duke of Estrada, 1997
The MacCarthy Mór, Prince of Desmond
The MacMorrough Kavanagh, Prince of Leinster
The Countess of Clandermond with The O'Brien,
Prince of Thomond, 1996
The Maguire, Prince of Fermanagh
The O'Ruaire, Prince of Breifne
Desmond O'Conor, tanist (heir-apparent) to O'Conor
Don
The O'Morchoe and his wife
The O'Grady at Cashel
The O Dochartaigh of Inishowen
The O'Carroll of Ely
The O'Donovan
The O'Callaghan
The Fox
The MacCarthy Mór, Prince of Desmond, welcomes
Irish President and her husband, 1996
The Standing Council of Irish Chiefs and Chieftains,
1994

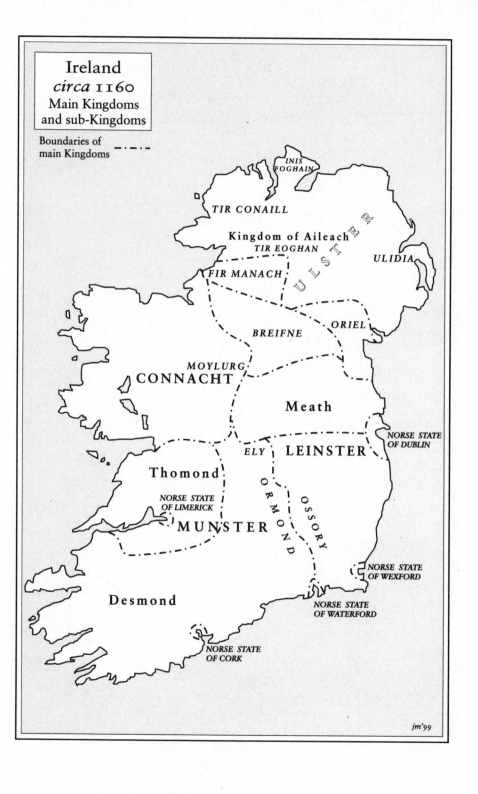

Ireland
circa 1160
Main Kingdoms
and sub-Kingdoms

Boundaries of
main Kingdoms — · — · —

INIS
FOGHAIN

TIR CONAILL

Kingdom of Aileach
TIR EOGHAN

ULSTER

ULIDIA

FIR MANACH

BREIFNE

ORIEL

MOYLURG

CONNACHT

Meath

ELY

LEINSTER

NORSE STATE
OF DUBLIN

Thomond

NORSE STATE
OF LIMERICK

ORMOND

OSSORY

MUNSTER

NORSE STATE
OF WEXFORD

Desmond

NORSE STATE
OF WATERFORD

NORSE STATE
OF CORK

jm'99

Foreword

by
The MacCarthy Mór, Prince of Desmond

Gaelic chiefship is dead; only its poor spirit still lingers on! It died as a
real institution, possessing cultural and political significance, the very
embodiment of two thousand years of unbroken native culture, a century
and a half ago in the wake of the Great Hunger. But long before that
catastrophic tragedy overwhelmed Ireland, it was a dying institution.
Aodhagáin Ó Rathaille (1670-1728), the last great native poetic genius
of Eóghanacht Munster, understood this fact. Surveying the destruction
of the Gaelic aristocracy in the wake of the Cromwellian genocide, the
Williamite Wars, the 'Flight of the Wild Geese' and the implementation
of the Penal Laws, he cried out to the Godhead in an agony of prayer:

> I beseech the Trinity, most August, Holy,
> To banish this sorrow from them altogether –
> From the descendants of Ir, of Conn, of Eibhear –
> And to restore the Gaels to their estates.[1]

But God, who has His own purposes, heard not the prayer, brought
back not the exiled Gaelic princes, nor restored their estates. And so
Gaelic chiefship died a lingering death. But the soul, freed from the
corpse, lived on, not merely as a shadow of the substance, but as its true
spiritual counterpart, vibrant with energy. Neither the viciousness of
the Penal Laws, nor the Williamite confiscations, and the systematic
degradation of the Gaelic gentry by the 'Irish' parliament in Dublin,
could destroy it entirely, nor exorcise it from the hearts and minds of
the Irish people. Chiefly families, who came to be known as 'the rare old
gentry', often reduced to penury, lived on among their people, loved by

their people, and suffering with their people. Some, it is true, converted to the Established Church to save their lands, and forswore allegiance to the exiled King James III. They secured their social positions in the Protestant Ascendancy at the price of meriting the utter contempt of the bardic class. On one such convert, Muirchertach O'Griffin, the poet Ó Rathaille pronounced his curse:

> Since thou didst condemn the race of Eibhear of perfect fame,
> And didst turn thy back on the fair company of the clergy,
> Since thou didst desert the son of James by means of an oath,
> Thou serpent of evil, I grieve not that thou art in hell![2]

Such 'English chiefs' were disowned by their people, excommunicated from Gaelic society, and taunted as counterfeit Irishmen by the bards. 'Síol mBríain dearbh na nGaillaibh le tréimhse!'[3] It is true that these outcasts represented a small minority, but unlike their Catholic counterparts they had money, power and influence, and actively collaborated with the English administration. They were the 'unacceptable face' of Gaelic chiefship. At a later tragic period of Irish history, during the Great Hunger, a legend grew up that the Protestant clergy had offered food to starving peasants at a price – their conversion. This oral tradition has survived in a 'skipping song' which includes the line: 'They sold their souls for penny rolls and slabs of hairy bacon!' But the chiefly 'converts' of the seventeenth and eighteenth centuries had infinitely less excuse for apostasy than the starving peasants of mid-nineteenth-century Ireland. And they were infinitely better paid for their pains in the form of army commissions, appointments in the diplomatic corps, bishoprics, fat rectories, and the social approval of Dublin Castle and the Vice-Regal Lodge. These 'chiefs' lost the Gaelic language, they lost the brogue, and many of them, it is to be feared, lost their souls. But it was a price that they were content to pay, for who was to judge them? The Brehons had been driven into exile and there was no law but English law! It was not of them that Ó Rathaille was thinking when he implored God 'That those of them who are alive with us may thrive after them'[4] nor when he wrote:

> O Christ, restore betimes to the Gaels
> All their estates, rescued from the dire bondage of foreign churls;
> Chastise the vile horde, behold, our country is faint,
> And Erin's nursling, weak, feeble, subdued, beyond the sea![5]

But, through a long and ever darkening twilight, Gaelic chiefship continued to exist in its true and best sense. At Belanagare O'Conors

acted as patrons of the bards, MacDermots observed the protocol of
their long-forgotten princely state at Coolavin, and MacCarthys,
O'Donoghues, O'Callaghans and O'Longs fed and protected clerics,
bards and *ollamhain* alike. This 'secret kingdom', ignored or unsuspected
by the Anglo-Irish Ascendancy, was lauded by Ó Rathaille. In his elegy
on the death of The O'Callaghan (24 August 1724) he explicitly refers
to him in the traditional role of a Gaelic chief:

> By his death the friars are wounded to the quick
> Untold destruction has come upon the clergy;
> Behold it was a signal for the ruin of bards,
> By reason of the storm that rushes through heaven.[6]

Such truly Gaelic chiefly households were few and far between in the
bleak landscape of early Georgian Ireland. Again and again Ó Rathaille
returned to his most constant theme, the destruction of his class, one
which had existed in a symbiotic relationship with the Irish Princes.

> The truly wet night seems long to me, without sleep, without snore,
> Without cattle, or wealth, or sheep, or horned cattle;
> The storm on the wave beside me has troubled my head,
> And I was unused in my childhood to [eat] dogfish and periwinkles.
>
> If the protecting Prince from the bank of the Laune were alive,
> And the band who were sharers with him, – who would pity my
>   misfortune? –
> Ruling over the fair, sheltered regions, rich in havens, and curved,
> My children should not long remain in poverty in the land of
>   Duibhnigh.
>
> The great, valiant MacCarthy, to whom baseness was hateful,
> And MacCarthy from the Lee, enfeebled in captivity without
>   release,
> MacCarthy, Prince of Kanturk, with his children in the grave –
> It is bitter grief through my heart that no trace of them is left.[7]

For perhaps a century and a half, between the débâcle of 1690 and the
Great Hunger of the mid-1840s, the spirit of Gaelic chiefship lingered
on. Chiefs, who were the 'fathers of their clan' and 'protectors of the
bards and priests', still existed. Then came the potato blight and everything rotted; the tubers in the fields, the people in their cabins, and the
Gaelic language at the behest of Daniel O'Connell ('The Liberator').
To paraphrase Yeats, 'a terrible ugliness was born'. An almost totally

Anglicised Ireland! And a chiefless Ireland. The spirit of Gaelic chiefship survived the Great Hunger but only in the empty form of titles divorced from cultural significance. The very essence and spirit of chiefship had died. In truth, it had starved to death with the people from whom it derived its sole force and legitimacy. 'Chiefs' of a sort continued to exist but without clans, without responsibilities, without hospitality, without religion, and without a trace of Irishness. They entered the British army, they served as Privy Councillors, and one even presumed to dignify the coronation of a German prince as King of Ireland by 'carrying the banner' of St Patrick, a shameful act of which his descendants still boast. These were 'chiefs' without shame or any sense of 'pride of race'.

And yet, as if to emphasise its very Gaelicness, the spirit of chiefship not only refused cultural exorcism but was reborn. At first it appeared to be but 'a ghost upon' the path of Ireland's history; 'an ethereal wisp' but 'the word of truth' gave the 'phantom breath'.[8] An O'Donoghue of the Glens entered the Imperial Parliament at Westminster, but only to bid defiance to it on behalf of the Irish people; an O'Neill of Clanaboy, in exile, donated money towards arming the Irish Volunteer movement through the good offices of his friend, Sir Roger Casement; a MacDermot fought for the republic in the General Post Office in Dublin during 1916; whilst a MacCarthy Mór, and his French kinsmen, plotted the restoration of an independent 'Gaelic social-monarchy' with emissaries from the Irish Republican Brotherhood. Improbable as the latter project may now seem, it should be remembered that as late as Easter 1916, during the shelling of the General Post Office, Dublin, by the British army, the founding fathers of the 'first Republic' were actively discussing the restoration of a Gaelic monarchy.[9]

Although it is the involvement of The O'Rahilly in the 1916 Insurrection which is chiefly remembered by Irish historians, the papal Marquis MacSwiney, de jure The Mac Suibhne, presided at Irish Volunteer reviews in Dublin in the period prior to World War I, whilst the teenage son and heir of The Maguire of Fermanagh acted as a messenger for the Irish Republican Army during the War of Independence (1919-21). Madam Maguire stored weapons in a secret passage constructed in her bedroom especially for that purpose. Other chiefs may also be cited as having played a fundamental role in bringing Irish independence to fruition. The then MacMorrough Kavanagh sat as a Nationalist member in the Irish Convention of 1917-18 while The MacGillycuddy of the Reeks served as a member of the Irish Senate from 1928 to 1943. In almost every sphere of politics or diplomacy, chiefs eagerly sought to assist at the birth of the Irish State. In 1919, following the declaration of the Irish Republic, The O'Kelly was sent as Envoy Extraordinary and Minister

Plenipotentiary by President de Valéra to the League of Nations. Afterwards, he assisted in the formation of the Irish Diplomatic Service. But
none of these sacrifices and services, rendered spontaneously by the chiefs
concerned, are now remembered. Most Irish historians suffer from that
malignant and untreatable disorder known as SRA – 'selective republican
amnesia'.

Those chiefs known to have participated directly or indirectly in the
movement to create an independent Ireland shared a common aspiration.
They actually believed in the ideal to which Eamon de Valéra, the architect of the modern Irish republic, paid mere lip service; namely that
Ireland would be 'not free merely, but Gaelic as well'. They did not see
their goal attained in their lifetimes. Nor did their sons or grandsons.
The dream faded, and a nightmare took hold. Part of Ireland was free,
but it remained essentially English for what else defines the soul of a
nation if not its laws? The Irish Free State retained English common law
as did its successor state, the Republic of Ireland. This fact, the continuance of 'English law', now lies at the heart of the discordance between
the Standing Council of Irish Chiefs and Chieftains and the Office of
the Chief Herald of the Republic of Ireland.

The Chief Herald, a civil servant appointed without regard to qualifications in heraldry or genealogy, apparently seeks to enforce the principle
of primogeniture on the descent of Gaelic chiefly titles. The fact that
several of the current chiefs were not recognised on that basis, nor ever
claimed their titles under that particular English law, does not appear to
deter the Office of the Chief Herald. How are we to address the fact
that not a single MacCarthy King of Desmond, or MacCarthy Mór, was
the primogeniture head of his family? Problems arise even from the
period of King Dermod I (1144-85). Irish law set aside his eldest son,
Cormac Liathanach, from the succession. Yet Cormac's descendants were
still flourishing in the early twentieth century. How is the Herald to
accommodate the fact that The O'Donoghue of the Glens, O'Callaghan,
Maguire and other chiefs have appointed as *tánaiste*, or heirs-designate,
individuals who are not their heirs by primogeniture? It is rather sad,
some might say pathetic, that after eighty years of *de facto* independence,
and as we enter the third millennium, the Genealogical Office seemingly
seeks to revive the mid-Tudor policy of 'surrender and regrant' rather
than acknowledge that the descent of Gaelic chiefly titles may only be
determined by the law code which gave them birth, the Laws of the
Fénechus, more popularly called the Brehon laws. If the Chief Herald's
will prevails, then Gaelic chiefships will only be acknowledged as valid
if their present incumbents accept the principle of English common law
inheritance as the sole mechanism governing their succession, an idea

balked at even by the English Norroy and Ulster King of Arms! The Italian courts have declared that such a policy is null and void in international law, and the Castile and Leon King of Arms of Spain has simply ignored it, recognising that in international law, and by force of logic, a Gaelic title can only exist and descend by tanistry.

All that is left of Gaelic Ireland, in a real sense, is the language and the chiefs. The language has already suffered Anglicisation by the adoption of the 'English' alphabet. Now, it would seem, the chiefs are to be similarly Anglicised. In direct contravention of international law, of their express wishes, of academic opinion, and every concept of natural justice, the Genealogical Office appears determined to impose the English common law principle of primogeniture on the Irish chiefs as a condition of their continuing to accord them 'courtesy recognition'. As a class, or more accurately, as a caste, we have nothing left to lose by refusing to submit to this dictate. Nothing, that is, but dignity and our honour. The vast majority of our ancestors when faced by an almost identical situation in mid-Tudor times preferred to lose their lands and their lives rather than abandon the very principle now at issue. We, their heirs, have little left to forfeit by comparison if we keep faith with the laws of tanistry. We have neither broad acres which may be confiscated nor castles which can be burnt. Our clans cannot be destroyed by genocide as once were the O'Moores, and few of us, if any, own herds of cattle which can be driven off to leave our dependants starving in midwinter. What then can we lose? Only our self-respect.

Throughout this Foreword, I have deliberately used the expression 'Gaelic chiefs' in preference to 'Irish chiefs'. It is a fact of history that some of our dwindling number are not 'Irish' but Spanish, Portuguese, American, Welsh and even English! Irish is a nationality but Gaelic is a concept. We are Gaelic chiefs! Our chieftainships are defined by Gaelic perceptions, by Milesian descent, patronage of the arts, promotion of our Gaelic language and culture, but – above all else – by our adhesion to the Brehon law of succession. That is the touchstone of our legitimacy.

Erin's Blood Royal tells the remarkable story of some twenty families over a period of twenty centuries. It will either serve as an epitaph of Gaelic chiefship or, more hopefully, as the manual of its revivification. If 'one word of truth can give a phantom breath' then Peter Berresford Ellis has provided us with a veritable lung transplant. For Gaelic chiefship to die now it must perish by suicide, drinking from the poisoned chalice of primogeniture. The sole reward held out to the Standing Council for taking such a course of action is that the death certificate of our order will be handsomely scrivened on vellum, embellished with coats of arms which we will no longer own, sealed with a blob of red wax, and duly gazetted in *Éire Iris Oifigiúil* (the Irish Government gazette). *Dia ár sábháil!* God between us and it!

MacCarthy Mór,
Feast of St Ruadhán of Lorrha
15 April 1999

Introduction

This is essentially the story of twenty families of the old Gaelic aristocracy whose ancestors were kings, princes and nobles in Ireland before the English Tudor conquests of the sixteenth century. The heads of these families still maintain their Gaelic titles and are given 'courtesy recognition' by the modern Irish state as 'chiefs'.

The Irish Gaelic aristocracy are the most ancient in Europe; written genealogies survive from the seventh century and were transcribed from oral traditions handed down for a thousand years before Christianity reached Ireland. The history of these families, therefore, can be said to encompass three thousand years of Irish experience and folklore. These families have survived today as a last link with an ancient civilisation that has been pushed to the verge of extinction. Indeed, the 'utter extinction' of that culture was the declared colonial policy of England from 1541 onwards. The history of the practical application of that policy is one that makes uncomfortable reading.

Surprisingly, the history of the native Gaelic monarchy of Ireland and its destruction is one which is barely acknowledged in modern Ireland where the popular perception of history generally begins with the 1798 uprising and the republican struggle for independence. The concept of Gaelic kingship is one that is only vaguely acknowledged and barely understood. Many years ago, at a lecture on Irish kingship in Dublin, a student, apparently wishing to demonstrate his support for the policy of egalitarianism, interrupted the professor by declaiming the popular Irish saying: 'But we are *all* kings' sons!' The lecturer responded irritably: 'That may be; but we can't all prove it!'

In Ireland, any history of kings and princes, albeit native ones, is generally an unfamiliar territory. Modern Irish historiography, with a few notable exceptions, seemed geared either to proving its impeccable republican credentials or to demonstrating that republican ideology was not a popular Irish philosophy and that Ireland would have been content with domestic self-government remaining within a United Kingdom framework. The latter school, popularly called 'Revisionist' during the last decade, has not become part of the mainstream historical doctrine. The history of Ireland is seen either from the anti-imperialist pro-Irish standpoint or from the pro-British Unionist one. In both approaches, however, monarchy in Ireland has become synonymous only with English monarchy.

Sometimes, in what appears to be almost a conscious attempt to keep to a republican 'purity', the Irish state bureaucracy expunges references to native monarchy in the most unlikely places, to the point of ignoring the provenance of many of the great art treasures of Ireland. Some years ago, a catalogue, describing the twelfth-century 'Shrine of the Book of Dimma', mentioned in passing that an inscription on it 'refers to Thaddeus O'Carroll, who died in 1152'. The catalogue passed hurriedly on without explaining that this inscription was actually an acknowledgement that the shrine was made on the instructions of King Tadhg Ó Cearbhaill (Thaddeus O'Carroll) of Ely.

The same catalogue, describing the now world-famous 'Processional Cross of Cong' from the twelfth century, detailed everything about it except that it bore the name of King Tairrdelbach Ua Conchobhair (O'Conor) of Connacht, also High King (d. 1156), who commissioned the great artwork. In referring to the fifteenth-century Cross of Lislaughtin, it stated that 'the O'Conor family built a Franciscan monastery at Lislaughtin', yet failed to add that this family, who endowed the monastery and financed the construction of the cross, were the royal dynasty of Connacht.

There is a popular perception, which has its origins in the propagandists of Tudor England, that the kings and princes of Ireland were quaint, barbaric chiefs of small warring tribes, mainly famous for being cattle rustlers. Even Charles J. O'Donnell of Carndonagh, himself the descendant of the princely house of Tirconnell, who endowed the prestigious O'Donnell lectures at Oxford and other universities, could suggest that to mention the idea of kings in Ireland was 'an ignorant practice'.

It has become almost a cliché to state that without a knowledge of the past, we cannot understand the present nor create a sound springboard to the future. Cliché or not, it is still a truism.

The story that follows is of a much neglected area of Irish history. No assessment of the history of Ireland can ever be complete without a consideration of the story of those dynasties which ruled the country for at least two thousand years prior to the English Tudor conquests. It is the story of a struggle against a foreign empire, of survival against incredible odds, of confiscations, the destruction of books and records, genocidal warfare, deliberately created famines and an enforced dispersal of the princes and their people throughout the world in a manner as poignant as the Jewish Diaspora.

It is a story made vivid by the personalities of the individual members of these aristocratic families. Some inevitably sold out under the pressure; some went down fighting; some merely vanished 'underground', continuing to live in Ireland surrounded by loyal countrymen, who did not betray them to the new authorities. Others were forced to flee into exile where their progeny gave of their remarkable talents to other nations. They became presidents of France, Chile, Argentina, Mexico, the United States. A descendant of the princes of Tirconnell became a prime minister of Spain. Three were High Chamberlains of Austria, the equivalent of first minister under the emperor. Numerous others rose to be generals and admirals not only in the armies and navies of Europe but in many other quarters of the world. Some exiles married into other European royal dynasties. Even Elizabeth II of England can, perhaps ironically, boast the O'Brien kings of Thomond in her ancestry. Many were compensated in their exile with foreign honours, awards and titles.

The stories of these families encapsulate the Irish experience, not only prior to invasion, but in the aftermath of conquest. They are representative of how the Irish, in differing ways, came to terms with the conquest of their country. The surviving Gaelic aristocratic dynasties, whose titles were 'abolished for ever' by the conquerors in the sixteenth century, preserve a fidelity to an ancient and highly civilised culture that went down in a holocaust of blood, flame and famine under the ruthless colonial policy of an unsympathetic alien power.

A NOTE ON NAMES

Readers may wonder at finding variant spellings for what appear essentially the same name. This is not merely the result of sixteenth- and seventeenth-century English administrators straining to render Irish names into English phonetics. The many various attempts to render Irish sounds into English certainly cause confusion. The name Ó Dochartaigh has been rendered, with or without the 'O', as Doughtery, Doherty, Dockerty, Daughtery, Dorrity, Dogherty and so on. Ó Domhnaill may be rendered not only as O'Donel, but with almost as many 'n's and 'l's as you like. However, there is also the problem of grammatical cases in Irish. If the name was heard in the vocative form, it might be regarded as a different name. The most obvious example of this is the name Séamas; this becomes Shéamais, phonetically Hamish, which is accepted now as a separate proper name. Additionally, if Éilidhe had a grandson, he would become known as Ó hÉildhe, Anglicised as Hely. Conchobar may equally be found as Conchobhair and Conchúir (pronounced kru-húr) and rendered into Anglicised form as Conor or Connor. I have tried to maintain some standardisation wherever possible.

PART ONE

The 'Extinction' and Survival
of Gaelic Aristocracy

1

The Gaelic Aristocracy

The indigenous Gaelic aristocracy of Ireland is, without doubt, the most ancient in Europe. Most of the families have pedigrees which stretch back more than 1500 years; and, if we accept the validity of the ancient genealogical records, some can date their ancestry back three thousand years. The Irish royal houses have genealogies, contained within these early records, tracing their descent, generation by generation, from the sons of Golamh, otherwise known as Milesius or Míle Easpain (soldier of Spain) who invaded Ireland, traditionally, at the end of the second millennium B C.

Many scholars are unhappy at placing complete faith in these early genealogies based on oral transmission to the early Christian period. Thomas O'Rahilly even rejected placing any reliance at all on the oral traditions: 'The fact is that no trust can be placed in the pedigrees of pre-Christian times.' Some of his contemporaries disagreed. Eoin Mac-Neill was more cautious and believed that they 'are probably fairly authentic in the main as far back as 200 B C.' In recent years, scholars have come to a better understanding and acceptance of the accuracy of oral traditions. We must also remember that these family pedigrees were being maintained in written form at least from the seventh century A D.

Whether we accept pre-Christian oral traditions or not, the fact remains that the antiquity of the Irish royal houses is rivalled only by that of the royal Bagration family of Georgia who trace their descent from the Armenian (Bagratuni) nobles of the third century A D and are considered 'the most ancient family of the old Christian East'. According to the *International Edition of The Royalty Peerage and Nobility of Europe* (1997), commenting on the modern bearers of Gaelic titles: '. . . despite these facts, their existence is largely unknown to all except academic historians and genealogists'.

[15]

The bulk of the early Irish collections of genealogies is impressive. The earliest material comes from the seventh century AD when, having adopted the Latin alphabet, the Irish were committing their extensive knowledge to written form. Among the oldest fragments of Irish poetry collected by Kuno Meyer were four genealogical poems, one of them giving a genealogy of the Munster king Cathal II Cú-cen-máthair (d. AD 641) and the others of Leinster kings.[1] These poems were known as *forsundud*, praise poems to princes of Irish dynasties which extolled their ancestry. Myles Dillon has pointed out that the *forsundud* is the oldest surviving form of Irish poetry and is comparable to other ancient Indo-European poetic forms such as the Sanskrit Vedic *narasamsyah* songs in praise of princes and their ancestry. Dillon writes: 'I would now suggest that these oldest Irish quatrains are true *narasamsyah*, that is to say stanzas composed by the bard to be recited on the occasion of a king's inauguration . . .'

The *forsundud* were handed down orally for a thousand or more years, being added to with each generation, before finally being committed to writing. It was a poetic form still being used when the chief bard of Ó Ceallaigh of Hy-Maine (d.*c.* 1375) wrote such a genealogical poem about the Eóghanacht dynasty of Munster. The word *forsundud* implies illumination, casting light upon a matter. The same root is found in *fursaintid*, the order of the third degree of wisdom of the study to become an *ollamh*, the highest qualification of learning and now the modern Irish word for 'professor'.

The earliest surviving complete genealogical manuscripts date from the early twelfth century. Although many genealogical books have been lost or destroyed, a large number remain. There has been an attempt to print these remarkable manuscripts; the first volume in the projected series, edited by M.A. O'Brien as *Corpus Genealogiarum Hiberniae*, appeared in 1962.

At the time of the Anglo-Norman invasion of Ireland in the late twelfth century, the island was divided into a number of provincial kingdoms. Giraldus Cambrensis, in his *Expugnatio Hibernica*, reported that Ireland was a pentarchy of Munster, Ulster, Connacht, Leinster and Meath, as the seat of the High Kings.

Prior to the late tenth century, the principal Irish kingdoms consisted of Munster (royal house of MacCarthy), Ulster (royal house of O'Neill), Leinster (royal house of MacMorrough) and Connacht (royal house of O'Conor). Within these kingdoms were many petty 'kingdoms' whose rulers were akin to princes, dukes, counts and barons, but all giving allegiance, though sometimes unwillingly, to the king. There was also a theoretical High King elected by and from the ranks of the provincial dynasties, enjoying what the heraldic expert Gerard Crotty has described as a 'precedence of honour' rather than an executive position. The position of the High King was a symbolic acknowledgement of the common origin and unity of the Irish peoples. Until the late tenth century, the High King was chosen from either the Uí Néill (O'Neill) and their kindred clans or the Eóghanachta (MacCarthys) and their kindred clans. After the Christian period, the Eóghanacht seemed to lose interest and the High Kingship was simply a struggle between northern and southern Uí Néill dynasties.

The High Kingship was centred in the 'middle kingdom', Midhe, from which Meath gets its name, and consisted of Meath, Westmeath and parts of adjoining counties. In the twelfth century Midhe was no more than a petty kingdom and its position will be discussed in Chapter 2.

This High Kingship, together with the Irish legal system, a fairly standard written language and a common mythology and religion, marked a sense of unity which was not present in many other lands with a multiplicity of kingdoms, such as the Iberian and Italian peninsulas, or the territory which is now known as France, or even England itself prior to its tenth-century unification under Athelstan, who melded the Anglo-Saxon and Danish kingdoms into one.

The Uí Néill and the Eóghanachta, acknowledged as the only original legitimate claimants to the High Kingship at this time, claimed their descent from the two sons of Milesius, Eremon and Eber Fionn, who were the progenitors of the Gaels in Ireland and who divided Ireland between them – Eremon ruling in the north and Eber Fionn in the south.

However, in the tenth century another dynastic family was able to seize the High Kingship. The rulers of a rebellious clan in northern Munster (Thomond, or Tuaidh Mhumhain), called the Dál gCais (descendants of Cas, and later to become known as the O'Briens), managed take possession firstly of the throne of Munster and then of the High Kingship itself by means of force. The most famous member of the Dál gCais dynasty was Brían Bóroimhe (Anglicised as Brian Boru, d. 1014); hence the name of O'Brien or descendant of Brían. Under his rule the High Kingship became, for the first time, a centralised, executive power over the kingdoms. It would be wrong to say that the seizure of kingship by force was meekly accepted by the other dynasties. The Eóghanachta in Munster challenged the Dál gCais in arms, not just over their claim to the High Kingship but over the Munster throne itself. The Eóghanachta were pushed back on the territory of Desmond (Deis Mumhan – South Munster) which was to remain their kingdom until the Elizabethan conquests.

Later in the twelfth century, another powerful dynasty seized the High

Kingship by similar military means. This dynasty was the Uí Briúin or O'Conors of Connacht. To further secure their power base, by the Treaty of Glanmire in 1118, the O'Conors forced the Dál gCais and Eóghanachta to accept the partition of the kingdom of Munster into the kingdoms of Thomond (North Munster – O'Brien) and Desmond (South Munster – MacCarthy). Thus, at a stroke, the O'Conor High Kings weakened the power of these rival dynasties. But before the O'Conors could further assert a strong centralist power over the other kingdoms, King Dermot MacMorrough of Leinster had gone abroad to seek help from the Angevin emperor, Henry II, in order to secure his kingdom against the High King, Ruaidri Ua Conchobhair (Rory O'Conor).

In the twelfth century, the kingdoms of Ireland, with their new centralising High Kingship, were already under threat from the rapidly expanding Norman empire which we retrospectively call the Angevin empire.

What sort of places were the kingdoms ruled over by the Gaelic kings at this time? If an equitable social order, if literacy and advancement in the arts and known sciences are yardsticks by which to judge civilisation, then Ireland had produced one of Europe's outstanding cultures. The kingdoms had become Christianised during the fifth century. From this time the Irish intellectual class turned from a centuries-old orally transmitted culture to committing their vast wealth of knowledge, poetry and legends to written form. Seizing the impetus of the new faith with enthusiasm, the Irish religious of both sexes took their learning and literacy to many other peoples. Singly and in groups, they brought Christianity to the pagan Anglo-Saxons and taught them the art of writing. They spread their foundations further, as far east as Kiev in the Ukraine, north to Iceland and the Faroes, and through France, Germany, Spain and Italy. And the peoples of Europe were welcomed to the great centres of learning in Ireland itself. Durrow, in the seventh century, boasted students from eighteen different nations.

Even the Viking raids, beginning in AD 795, did not upset the Gaelic order. The Vikings settled down in seaports and set up their own petty kings to rule their settlements. Dublin was formed in 841 under King Olaf. The Irish managed to contain the warlike ambitions of these Vikings. The Munster king, Ceallacháin I (c. 944–52), whose campaigns are recorded in the twelfth-century romance *Caithreim Cheallacháin Chaisil*, broke Viking power in his kingdom and made them acknowledge his rule. More famous is the final breaking of Viking territorial ambitions in Ireland by the High King Brían Bóroimhe, who defeated the combined Viking army at Clontarf in 1014. But even before this the Viking city colonies had already begun to merge into an Irish cultural ethos, with their petty rulers acknowledging the Gaelic kings.

The Irish kingdoms were rich in agriculture, in pastoral farming, in mining – even gold was mined and worked in several parts. There was regular contact with Europe, especially in intellectual exchanges. Imports and exports flourished. The fortresses and the castles, and architecture in general, were more than merely functional. Standing in the Gallarus oratory, on the Dingle peninsula, two and a half miles east of Ballyferriter, one cannot help but be impressed by its construction. It is one of the best examples of corbel pattern building, its construction of dry stone masonry arranged to slope slightly downwards and outwards to throw off the rain. When one considers that this is probably over 1200 years old and that, in spite of its being constructed without any mortar, not a drop of rain has entered the building in that time, then one must acknowledge the expertise of those early Irish builders. The Irish round towers, built as defensive structures against Viking raids, with conical caps, such as the one at Ardmore, Co. Waterford, are further examples of advanced building techniques. King Cormac's Chapel at the old Munster capital of Cashel built in 1127–34 remains another fascinating demonstration of how architecture was developing under the patronage of the kings.

The Irish kings ruled rich courts and patronised both artists and artisans. The illuminated gospel books, the amazing book shrines, such as that for the Book of Dimma and the Domnach Airgid, the processional Cross of Cong and the processional Cross of Lislaughtin, Co. Kerry, the Shrine of St Patrick's Bell, the Ardagh Chalice, the Derrynaflan Chalice and other masterpieces of Irish metalwork leave one gasping in amazement at an artistic and technical brilliance which remained unsurpassed in succeeding centuries. Many of these pieces were commissioned by the Irish kings and nobility. The fascinating Shrine of St Lachtin's Arm carries an inscription asking for prayer for Cormac III MacCarthy, King of Munster; the Shrine of the Book of Dimma is inscribed as commissioned in the twelfth century by The O'Carroll of Ely and the fifteenth-century Ballymacasey Cross as commissioned by The O'Connor Kerry; the Derrynaflan hoard includes a stag device, the symbol of the Eóghanachta dynasty who had connections with Derrynaflan. The royal courts were havens of patronage and hospitality for the Irish artists. The popular notion that their work was solely the product of support by the Irish ecclesiastical centres is incorrect. Kings did, in fact, endow ecclesiastical centres but also encouraged secular colleges and personal patronage.

Also at the royal courts were lawyers; theologians and philosophers;

medical men, for medical practice was highly advanced as well as the laws governing it; historians or chroniclers; poets, musicians and astronomers. Musical manuscripts survive from the twelfth century; Cashel Diocesan Library contains a treatise on music written by a musical scholar at Cashel during the reign of Dermod I (1144–85) and dated 1168.

With regard to astronomy, Dan MacCarthy of Trinity College has recently examined twelve of the Irish annals and chronicles. He collated and examined, for the first time, all observations made of astronomical phenomena between AD 442 and 1133. What emerged was a record of eclipses, comets, aurorae and even a supernova, all carefully and accurately set down. MacCarthy checked some ninety astronomical observations using a computer and found that between 627 and 1133 some thirty observations were found only in these Irish records. No other European textual evidence has been found. But the references corresponded precisely to non-European (mainly Chinese and Japanese) sightings.

In 1054 the Italians recorded what appeared to be a supernova in the Crab Nebula, dating it 19 April, the date of the death of Pope Leo IX. But Irish astronomers placed the supernova nearly eight weeks later. Who was right? A comparison with the Chinese and Japanese records proved that the Irish astronomers were accurate. The Italians had altered the observation to make it coincide with the death of Pope Leo.

Left to themselves, the Irish kingdoms could perhaps have continued developing as the great intellectual centres of Europe. But the one thing the Irish had not developed was a ruthless military capability. For the Irish, like their fellow Celts, took an attitude to warfare which had not altered in a thousand years. Combat was still a matter of personal honour and often an entire battle could depend on a single combat between two champions. Warriors were individuals and not merely part of some mindless killing machine. True, as we shall examine later, there were élite warrior groups, but these were generally royal bodyguards. There were no standing armies in Ireland such as had developed in Rome, nor was warfare held in the same cultural esteem in which the Germanic peoples held it. Therefore, the Irish had no centralised, trained force to withstand an assault by a more ruthless foe. And in the twelfth century they were faced with just such an enemy.

Viking Norsemen had settled in the area which was to be named after them – Normandy – and in 991 Charles III, King of the Franks, had ceded control of the territory to the Norse chief, Rollo, whom he recognised as 1st Duke of Normandy. These Normans quickly merged their lifestyle into that of the Franks, another people of Germanic origin. Both were thirsty for the conquest of new lands. By the twelfth century the Norman empire had grown considerably and consisted of Normandy, Brittany,

Maine, Anjou (from which the name Angevin empire derives), Touraine, Aquitaine, Gascony, England and Cornwall, with a tenuous overlordship of parts of Wales and Scotland. It was obvious that Ireland would be the next step for the Norman expansion.

In 1066 William of Normandy conquered England and although he claimed the title 'King of England' his dominions were primarily in the south. Indeed, after his conquest, he remained in England barely three months, leaving it to his half-brother Odo to attempt to secure Norman domination. He returned for a military campaign a year later and spent a few years in the country. England, therefore, was merely one province of the empire centred in Anjou, the main residence of the Norman kings. This was the position in 1169 when the first Norman lords invaded Ireland. It was not, as some misrepresent it, an English invasion.

When King Dermot arrived at Henry's court in Aquitaine, Henry was not particularly keen to gather an army to invade Ireland. However, he did not put any obstacle in the way of any of his Norman liegemen who might like an adventure. So King Dermot found an ally in Richard FitzGilbert, Earl of Pembroke and a member of the de Clare family, descended from the Dukes of Normandy. He has taken his place in Irish history as 'Strongbow'. Dermot promised him his daughter's hand in marriage, and Strongbow thought this meant he would inherit the kingdom of Leinster. He was in for a rude awakening for primogeniture had no status in Irish law. Troops were sent with Dermot to Ireland in August 1167 but were defeated by the High King and his ally Ó Ruairc of Breifne. Another band of Normans and Flemings landed in Wexford on 1 May 1169, and on 23 August 1170 Strongbow himself arrived. The initial victories, followed by the death of King Dermot on 1 May 1171 and Strongbow's claim to be king (a position the Irish could not accept under their laws of succession), caused Henry II to reconsider his position. He doubtless feared that Strongbow might make himself king of Ireland and become a threat to him. So, on 17 October 1171, Henry II landed near Waterford with his army as much to keep the original adventurers in obedience to his feudal authority as to conquer Ireland. The result of this military campaign was that the High King, Ruaidri Ua Conchobhair, having abdicated his position under law, and acting only as king of Connacht, signed the Treaty of Windsor on 6 October 1175. By this treaty, Ruaidri recognised Henry II as his paramount lord; but Henry II went further and declared himself paramount lord of (all) Ireland. It is true that Henry had received several submissions from the Irish kings and nobles during his months in the country. Among the major rulers who submitted were King Dermot MacCarthy of Desmond, King Donal O'Brien of Thomond and O'Ruairc of Breifne.

One of the great debating points of this history is the Bull Laudabiliter, granted by Pope Adrian IV (1154–59), which gave Henry II, of the Angevin empire, full permission and support to 'enter the island of Ireland in order to subject its people to law and to root out from them the weeds of vice'. In return for this papal approval, Henry II agreed to pay an annual tribute to Rome of one penny for every household in Ireland. The Bull is thought to have been issued about 1155, many years before the invasion. In Norman terms, the Bull Laudabiliter was seen as the 'legal' basis for the invasion of Ireland.

It became almost fashionable for many nineteenth-century Irish Catholic nationalists either to claim that the Bull was forged, or to emphasise that Pope Adrian IV was one Nicholas Breakspear, an 'Englishman'. He was, indeed, the only Anglo-Saxon to become Bishop of Rome. However, why should the fact that Adrian was an Anglo-Saxon, whose people had after all recently been conquered by the Normans, be of any significance? Henry II was born in Le Mans, in Maine, died in Anjou, was buried at Fontevrault Abbey, and was the French-speaking ruler of a predominantly French-speaking empire. The Anglo-Saxons were not yet assimilated into that empire and conflict was still erupting between Norman overlords and their Anglo-Saxon vassals throughout England. Any conclusion that Adrian's cultural background had *per se* some 'national' bearing on the issuing of the Bull is illogical.

The eighteenth-century *Généalogie de la Royale et Serenissime Maison de MacCarthy* reported the tradition that when Donnchadh O'Brien was deposed from the throne of Munster he went on a pilgrimage to Rome where he died in 1064 and 'made a present of his crown of massive gold and other regalia to the pope'. It has been suggested that this was interpreted by the popes, in their role as feudal princes, as an act of submission giving them the right to dispose of Ireland. Was Donnchadh's crown the same crown sent by a later pope to Henry II in 1186 to confirm his fiefdom in Ireland?

The fact was that in the nineteenth century many Irish Catholics found it hard to accept that the Church of Rome, as a temporal and feudal institution, was not a friend to the Irish nation. It was forgotten that the Church in Ireland, at this time, had been in conflict with Rome for many centuries. It disagreed on several fundamental matters of theology with Rome but, most importantly, it stood in opposition to the social system espoused by Rome. In this fact, more than theology, lay the reason for Rome's enthusiastic advocacy of an invasion and conquest of Ireland.

In their *Short History of the Irish People* Mary Hayden and George Moonan explained:

Each clan had its own bishop, and its own priests . . . The clan allotted to its clergy, for their support, certain lands . . . looked after by an officer who was generally a layman. The clergy of a clan mostly lived in communities under their bishop, so that the church was both tribal and monastic.

In other words, the Irish Church, while it was building up its own ecclesiastical laws, called the *Penetentials* and generally inspired by Roman custom, still found itself constrained by the Irish native law, popularly called Brehon law, and the social system it generated. Irish law was ancient. It is regarded by scholars as the oldest surviving codified law system in Europe and, in Chapter 2, we will examine its Indo-European origins and its parallels with the Hindu Laws of Manu. The Irish had an amazing respect for the law and their ancient literature contains many references to the high regard that they gave their Brehon (judge) and *ollamhain* (professors). An *ollamh* could even speak before a king, and kings and princes had to obey the judgement of the Brehons.

Under this social system, there was no such concept as inheritance by primogeniture. Kingship was electoral although within the same families. There was no absolute ownership of land, nor right of alienation of the land. Kings were not law-makers but only officers of the law established, and could be deposed by being forced to abdicate if they became either negligent or despotic. Women's rights were protected under the law and offences against women, even sexual harassment, are listed in native Irish law. Women could aspire to office in all the professions and, in certain exceptional circumstances, might become head of a clan during their lifetime and a leader in battle. There was even a 'medical health service' which was highly advanced whereby sick maintenance (including curative treatment, attendance and nourishing food) had to be made available to all who needed it no matter their station in life. The exceptional working of the Irish system was undoubtedly due in large part to the clan system.

William E. Montgomery felt the clash between the Irish system and the crushing slavery of feudalism then emerging out of Europe was inevitable.[2] He points out that the original system was undergoing change, first by the contact with Christianity and secondly by contact with the Danes who had formed several city states on the coast of Ireland. There is no denying that from the start of the eleventh century a system of territorial lords was arising, particularly in Munster. The fifty or so territorial lordships were clearly feudal in essence and were at the bestowal of the king. In 1588 Sir Warham St Leger compiled a report for Elizabeth's Privy Council in which he enumerated the major territorial lordships subject to Donal IX MacCarthy Mór as king of Desmond. It was judged, in an international nobiliary court in 1998, that these territorial lordships were still the 'ideal property' of the current MacCarthy Mór to bestow and bequeath as he saw fit. There is little evidence of this practice, the equivalent of an English 'Lord of the Manor', outside Munster.

What was happening has been described by William E. Montgomery as 'the steady march of time' which 'advanced the feudalisation of the land, which in Aryan races seems always to have gone hand in hand with increase of population.'

Laurence Ginnell has commented:

The idea of private property in land was developing and gathering strength, and land was generally becoming settled under it. The title of every holder, once temporary, was hardening into ownership, and the old ownership of the clan was vanishing, becoming in ordinary cases little more than a superior jurisdiction the exercise of which was rarely invoked.

However, by the time of the Norman invasion the change was only beginning in Munster and not in the other kingships to the same degree. Even in Munster it was a new idea that one could have a feudal relation with the king. Doubtless, left to themselves, the Irish might have developed their own feudal ideas slowly over the centuries. As Montgomery says: 'the growth of the power of the Chief, the idea of landlord and tenant was still strange to the Irish mind and its compulsory imposition on an unwilling people [by the Norman invasion] was probably a fatal mistake'. The persistence of the native equitable communal laws against the complete feudal system of the Anglo-Normans is without parallel and the reason for this was imposition by force rather than the continuance of natural development. This natural development, starting probably a century before the Norman invasion, was certainly not fast enough for the temporal princes of the Roman Church. Montgomery comments:

The Church lands were in the first place probably granted by the tribe from the common stock, and the Brehon Law recognises to a very remarkable extent the claim of 'the tribe of the Saint' to support. The most important influence exerted by the Church on the system of land holding is that it undoubtedly did much, from more or less selfish ends, to aid free alienation of land. The *Corus Brescna* shows that, in the cause of acquisitions, the Church had made great inroads on the restrictions imposed on alienation by the tribal system; and that even

in allotments a succession attack had been made on the original inviol-
ability of tribal possession as far as regards alienation to the Church.

He further observes: '... at the end of the 10th or beginning of the
11th Century the Irish people were in a state of transition from common
property to several ownership, the Brehon writers themselves favouring
the theory of private property.' However, attempts to change the Irish
social system were generally unsuccessful before the Norman invasion.

Rome had long been dismayed at the lack of a centralised Irish political
state ruled by a strong autocrat. This was why the emergence of the
O'Brien and O'Conor dynasties was encouraged by the agents of Rome.
Rome, as a feudal power, sought to extend that feudal power to Ireland
where feudalism was still generally an alien concept. The Irish Church's
most zealous reformer was Maelmaedoc Ó Morgair (St Malachy) born in
Armagh in 1095. He paid two visits to Rome in the early and mid-twelfth
century. One can argue that St Malachy was the real architect of the
invasion by convincing Rome that its feudal policies could only be
brought about by a strong outside force. Even Malachy's friend,
St Bernard of Clairvaux, with whom he stayed, seemed surprised at the
invective with which Malachy denounced his fellow Irishmen, calling
them 'beasts, not men'. 'In all the barbarism which he had yet encountered, he had never met such a people so profligate in their morals, so
uncouth in their ceremonies, so impious in faith, so barbarous in laws,
so rebellious in discipline, so filthy in life ...' Was it with irony that
St Bernard wondered how 'so saintly and lovable man could come of
such a race'?

It must be remembered that the Bishops of Rome of this period
regarded themselves as temporal princes, with more feudal power than
most emperors, and that they often led their own armies into battle to
assert that power and reap tribute from those they subjugated.

When Henry II finally took his armies to Ireland and began to force
the Irish kings to submit to him, Pope Adrian's successor, Pope Alexander
III, wrote to him; three of his letters are extant, confirming that Henry
II was recognised by him as 'Lord of Ireland'. The excuse of nationality
could not be levelled against Alexander III. He was one Rolando Bandi-
nelli from Sienna, and his concern for Ireland was simply to exercise his
feudal rights and claim the financial tribute from Henry II.

Many of the Irish clergy followed the leadership of St Malachy. The
Irish bishops and abbots 'concluded that the defects and backward state
of their Church and nation were justification for subjecting their native
land to a foreign king as one destined by Heaven and the Vicar of Christ
to reform otherwise hopeless abuses.'[3] During the winter of 1171/72 a

council of Irish bishops convened in Cashel, the Munster capital, passing several decrees which were submitted to Henry II for confirmation. As well as covering purely ecclesiastical affairs, some of the decrees attacked the Irish social system and sought to bring it in line with feudalism, freeing all Church property from the jurisdiction of the clan assemblies and placing all clergy, for the first time, above the law, excusing them from paying fines if found guilty of transgressing the law, even if they committed homicide. Cashel decided 'the divine offices shall be celebrated according to the forms of the Church of England' (that is, still the Roman Church at this date). 'The bishops indeed went the whole way to oblige Henry and, if we are to believe reputable chroniclers of the next century, each of them gave him a letter with his seal attached, confirming to Henry and his heirs the kingdom of Ireland.'[4]

The Irish Church now came in line with Rome and all the Irish were ordered to pay feudal tithes to the parish priests, each clan territory now becoming a parish. Henry II wrote to Alexander III in 1173 acknowledging the pope's feudal superiority; this letter is found recorded in Thomas Rhymer's *Foedera*. The annual payment for Ireland, as a vassal state, was duly paid by Henry II to the pope.

John of Salisbury, in his *Metalogicus*, recorded that the pope, in return, sent Henry a golden ring adorned with an emerald to be worn to symbolise his authority, on Rome's behalf, over Ireland. So it is quite clear that when Ireland became the newest province of the Norman empire, with several of its kings having submitted to Henry II as *Dominus Hibernia* (Lord of Ireland), it had, constitutionally, became a papal fiefdom with the Angevin emperors merely as middlemen. The Bishops of Rome had conspired in the conquest of Ireland, asserting themselves as feudal lords of all the lands of Europe and even beyond, taking their feudal authority from God, whom they represented on earth. In this position they were able arbitrarily to give Ireland into the charge of Henry II in return for payment.

Henry II, in a passing fit of generosity, thought to bestow the 'Kingship of Ireland' on his nineteen-year-old son John in 1186. He had already crowned his eldest son, Henry, as 'King of England' in June 1170, demonstrating the fact that England was regarded only as one of the provinces of the empire. But 'young Henry' died in Turenne on 11 June 1183. Enthusiastically, Henry II even sought permission and papal sanction from Urban III for the use of the title 'King' instead of 'Lord'. Urban III, naturally, demanded more money for the proposed change of title and sent three papal legates to Henry II bearing a crown of peacocks' feathers set in gold for the inauguration ceremony. Was this the crown the deposed O'Brien king had presented to the pope a century earlier?

However, 1186 turned out to be a bad year for Henry. His son Geoffrey, now heir to the throne, was killed in a tournament in Paris and there was a growing dispute between his sons Richard and John over their claims to the empire. Henry changed his mind about John, deciding that he might became too big for his boots! Three years later Henry II was dead.

Richard I spent even less time in England than his father. Few of his subjects even noticed when he died, contrary to the romantic myths centred around Robin Hood. Although 'King of England' for ten years, he spent only six months there. Apart from his crusading period, he preferred to spend his time in the duchy of Aquitaine. 'The English, in their usual way of preferring the legend to the facts, have long cherished the memory of a man who, in fact, had no interest in England other than as a source of revenue, and who was a ruthless fighting machine who made enemies of most of the royalty of Europe.'[5]

Henry II's next surviving son, John, became the new Angevin emperor on 2 June 1199. John turned his attention to securing his power as king by murdering his nephew Arthur, son of his older brother Geoffrey, who had a superior claim for the throne under the primogeniture system. John proceeded to lose most of the empire in what is now France. In fact, in 1204, the heartland of Normandy was captured by the Franks. He fell back on England and it is only then, although dominated by its Norman ruling class, that England begins to emerge as an independent kingdom rather than merely a Norman province.

John was excommunicated by Pope Innocent III but then, as now, money talked. On 15 May 1213, at the House of the Templars at Ewell, near Dover, John assigned the 'kingdom of England' and the 'lordship of Ireland' to the pope. Innocent III then regranted the kingship of England and lordship of Ireland to John on condition that John acknowledge, for himself and his heirs and successors, Rome's temporal feudal authority. John and his heirs agreed to pay the Bishop of Rome an annual tribute of 700 marks for England and 300 marks for Ireland.

This act was solemnly ratified in St Paul's Cathedral, London, on 3 October 1213, in the presence of Nicholas, Cardinal Bishop of Tusculum, and sealed with a golden Bull on behalf of Innocent. Ireland, therefore, continued to be a papal fiefdom at the whim and gift of the Bishops of Rome but with the Norman kings of England, emerging from the chaos of Henry II's Angevin empire, still as middlemen. And, under the new papal deal, the Irish kings and princes were instructed, on pain of excommunication, to obey the authority of the English kings as their paramount lords.

By now the kings of England were trying to destroy the Irish legal system. In 1246 Henry III decreed that 'all the laws and customs which are observed in the realm of England should be observed in Ireland'. Edward I asked his Justiciar in Ireland, Robert D'Ufford, to report in 1277 on the possibility of extending English law to Ireland. Edward II issued a royal order to admit the Irish to 'the protection of English law' in 1321.

In the face of this, the Irish kings appealed directly to the pope. 'The Remonstrance of the Irish Princes to Pope John XXII' was sent in 1317:

> Let no one wonder that we are striving to save our lives and defending as we can the right of our law and liberty against cruel tyrants and usurpers, especially since the said King, who calls himself Lord of Ireland, and also the said Kings, his predecessors, have wholly failed in this respect to do and exhibit orderly government to us and several of us.

The Statutes of Kilkenny of 1366, declared by the English administration in Ireland, tried to abolish native Irish law and encroach on the authority of the Gaelic kings and princes. However, the Statutes in effect recognised that the chiefs were still a strong power and stipulated that those 'who continue to live under their own chiefs by Brehon law are regarded as outside the protection of English law and liberty.'

The fact was that English law prevailed only in a few isolated areas in Ireland where the colonists had established themselves. Irish law continued in the territory governed by the Irish kings. Indeed, most of the colonists, from 1169 onwards, had found the Irish law more equitable, and had adopted the Irish language, law, customs and dress. Families like the Barry family, Blake, Brown (Le Brun), Burke, Butler, Cusack, Dillon, FitzGerald, Joyce, Nugent, Plunkett, Roche, Taafe and Walsh, all became indistinguishable from the Gaelic Irish.

It was mainly towards these 'degenerate English', as the Gaelicised families were termed, that the legislation for spreading English law and language was aimed, especially the Kilkenny Statutes. Intermarriage was forbidden; the adoption of Irish forms of names, the use of the language, the toleration of Brehon law, still more submission to its judgements, were considered high treason by the English administration.

Perhaps the most fascinating thing about the Statutes of Kilkenny was that they in effect recognised not only the continued existence of the Gaelic kingdoms but the existence of a 'middle nation', the Anglo-Irish who had merged themselves into Irish culture. What is more to the point, they demonstrated that the English administration had little control over the colonists.

Even the kingdom of Leinster, which had been the first area entered by the Normans and settled, was by no means conquered. When Richard II landed with his army in Waterford on 1 June 1399, accompanied by the Dukes of Exeter and of Albemarle and the Earl of Gloucester, he was faced with a formidable foe in Art Mór Mac Airt (MacMorrough Kavanagh), King of Leinster (1375–1416). Art Mór had already defeated the army of the Viceroy, Roger Mortimer, *de facto* heir to the English throne, at Kelliston near Carlow. Mortimer was slain in the battle. King Art Mór was an exceptional commander who would not be drawn into a battle until conditions favoured him and similarly he did not respond to offers of negotiation on unfavourable terms, showing that he had astute political acumen.

When a frustrated Richard II demanded his surrender, Art Mór replied, according to the *Annals of Loch Cé*: 'I am rightful King of Ireland [*sic*], and it is unjust to deprive me of what is my land by conquest.' Before Richard could do anything further he had to hurry back to England: Henry Bolingbroke had invaded the country with ten ships and 300 men and seized the throne as Henry IV. The result of the English regnal power struggle was that Ireland, for a century afterwards, continued to be ruled by its own Gaelic kings and princes, secure in their kingdoms, with the Gaelicised Anglo-Norman lords, protected in their earldoms and estates and baronies. Indeed, the Ó Raghaillighs of Lough Oughter, Co. Cavan, were so unassailable that they were issuing their own coinage through the fourteenth century.

Under the settled conditions of the Irish kingdoms there was a new flowering of Irish learning, much influenced by the new Arabic ideas permeating the European universities. The Irish language contains the largest corpus of medical literature written in any one language prior to 1800. There was a new outpouring of literary endeavours and a new school of courtly poetry. Many manuscript books were composed and recopied from older books during this period before the coming of printing technology. Even new studies on the law system were produced and the *Senchus Mór* was rewritten with careful glosses. In addition, Irish scholars were translating avidly from Greek, Latin, Hebrew, Arabic, French and English. During the fifteenth century Arthurian tales became popular and many versions were produced in Irish.

The position of the Irish kings and the aristocracy continued unchanged until the reign of the Tudor King Henry VIII who was crowned in 1509, aged eighteen. In many ways, until this time the English Crown's relationship to the native kings and princes of Ireland paralleled that in India under the British Raj. Until Indian independence in 1947, the English Crown had made treaties with many of the native kings and princes of the Indian sub-continent. One has to remember the vastness of India and that it was never a homogeneous unit. Some fourteen major languages and 1500 dialects are spoken there.

Under British rule, native kings and princes still ruled a major part of the sub-continent. There were some 600 of them ranging from the powerful Nizam of Hyderabad, whose principality was the size of Italy with a population of fourteen millions, down to the Siem of Nongliwai in Assam whose authority extended over a few hundred people in an area of a few hundred acres. While these princes had absolute authority over internal affairs in their states, British Residents 'advised' them, acting on behalf of the Viceroy in the name of the 'King-Emperor of India', the English Crown.

During the 1920s, as India began approaching independence, there was an attempt to set up a 'Council of Princes'. One policy favoured by the English Crown was to create a union of the nations of the sub-continent by means of a federation of the princely states. However, Congress, the then Indian independence movement, and especially Gandhi, believed that the Indian princes, in accepting British suzerainty, had merely become India's 'badges of slavery'. Although the English Crown had solemnly signed treaties with these princes, guaranteeing their autonomy, political 'expediency', the standard morality, caused the Crown to discard the treaties unilaterally. The princes were told that they must take their states either into the new state of India or into Pakistan.

The Nizam of Hyderabad, a Moslem with a large number of Hindu subjects, tried to keep his state independent. The Hindus rose up, demanding to join India, and troops marched in: the ancient capital Hyderabad is now in Pakistan while southern areas of the kingdom are in India. The Maharajah of Kashmir, a state the size of Ireland, decided to join India. His people were mixed Moslem and Hindu. A state of conflict still exists in a partitioned Kashmir. The power of the Indian princes was eventually abolished by the Republic of India but 'courtesy recognition' is still given to their titles and most still own their personal palaces and estates.

Between 1175, with the Treaty of Windsor, and the accession of Henry VIII, the Irish kings and princes stood in almost the same position as those Indian princes, still ruling their ancient kingdoms and principalities, and theoretically deferring to the suzerain authority of the English Crown as a paramount lordship.

In 1533, Henry VIII began his break with the Church of Rome and declared himself head of a separate Church of England. The most important aspect of this separation was that Henry VIII was breaking with

Rome not simply on religious matters but on the feudal level and that meant a loss of revenue to the papal coffers.

As early as 1515, and again in 1533, Henry VIII had ordered accounts of the 'State of Ireland, and Plan for its Reformation' to be compiled. The 1533 assessment reported that there were 'more than 60 countries, called territories (*regionis*) in Ireland, inhabited with the King's Irish enemies . . . where reigneth more than 60 chief captains, whereof some calleth themselves Kings, some Kings' peers, in their language, some princes, some dukes, some archdukes . . . and obeyeth to no other temporal person . . .'[6]

The report lists the names of these holders of Gaelic titles and says that there are also 'more than 30 great captains of the English noblefolk that followeth the same Irish order'. The report goes on to show that the Gaelic kings and Anglo-Irish nobles still ruled most of Ireland, two-thirds of which was under the native kings and one-third under the Gaelicised Anglo-Irish. Only in a few tiny pockets, cities and walled towns, particularly on the coast, did the native Irish law hold no sway at all. It was pointed out to Henry VIII that 'all the English folk of the said countries be of Irish habit, of Irish language, and of Irish conditions, except the cities and walled towns'. And even most of the municipal governments of these cities and walled towns paid tribute to the Gaelic kings. The inhabitants of Cork city, for example, paid The MacCarthy Mór £40 per annum.

The King's Council in Ireland was asked to send some recommendations to John Alen, Master of the Rolls, as to how Ireland might be incorporated as an indistinguishable part of England. The recommendations were simple.[7] It was pointed out that in reality England was in control only within the Pale, a small area around Dublin. The term Pale, from which the expression 'beyond the Pale' comes, is from the Norman-French *pal*, a stake used to make a fence as a limit or boundary. Calais was called the 'English Pale' until 1558 when the English Crown finally lost this last piece of the former Angevin territory. It was then feared that, at any time, the Dublin Pale could follow Calais' example and revert to the Irish.

The recommendations submitted to Henry argued that the temporal lords of Ireland had been long opposed to the rule of the kings of England. 'Item, another hurt is, the committing the governance of this land to the lords, natives of the same . . .' John Alen considered the matter for some time and in 1537 wrote a letter advising Henry VIII's Commissioners in Ireland that it would be better for Henry to be recognised as 'King of Ireland' and 'then induce the Irish Captains' (Gaelic kings and nobles) 'as well by their oaths as writings, to recognise the same which things shall be, in continuance, a great motive to bring them to due obedience . . .'[8]

In 1541 Henry VIII ceased to use the title *Dominus Hiberniae* (Lord of Ireland) and thus became the first English king to style himself *Rex Hiberniae* (King of Ireland). Ireland's constitutional position now changed from being a papal fiefdom in which the kings of England, as Lords of Ireland, had accepted the Bishops of Rome as paramount lords and had ruled Ireland exercising 'but a governance under the obedience of the same'.[9]

From the Irish viewpoint, it could be argued that Henry VIII, in ceasing to acknowledge the feudal dues of the Bishop of Rome, had freed the Irish kings and princes from their feudal dues to Henry, for their ultimate authority was the Bishop of Rome. They therefore had no further obligation to acknowledge any English king's jurisdiction in Ireland by a claim to European feudal law. The point was certainly recognised at once by the papal administration of Pope Paul III (1534–50) who realised that Henry VIII of England was 'stealing' the papal fiefdoms not only of the 'Kingdom of England' but of the 'Lordship of Ireland'. Pope Paul III wrote to the king of Ulster, Conn Bacach O'Neill, in 1538, addressing his letter 'To Our most Dear Son in Christ, Conn O Neale, the Greater, Our Noble King of Our Realme of Ireland'. The pope revoked the grant made by Adrian IV's Bull Laudabiliter, confirmed by letters of Alexander III and Innocent III, and formally released all the Irish princes from the feudal duty of obedience to the English king as 'Lord of Ireland'.

A report dated 17 April 1539 from the O'Conor king of Connacht claimed that Conn Bacach O'Neill had plans to march an army to Tara and there have himself proclaimed King of Ireland, with the support of FitzGerald, Earl of Desmond.[10] O'Neill and Aodh Dubh Ó Domhnaill did join with FitzGerald, but before any formal inauguration was made the Irish army was defeated by the English forces of the Lord Deputy at Belahoe, recorded in the *Annals of Connacht* for 1539.

The new policy of the Bishop of Rome was to re-establish a dynasty in Ireland which would recognise him as feudal prince of the country. On 24 April 1541, Pope Paul wrote to Conn Bacach O'Neill, saying that he had 'heard with grief how that Island is, by the present King, reduced to such impiety and devastated with such cruelty'. He 'exhorts the whole Irish people to persevere in the Faith they received from their fathers'. He goes on to say that he 'holds that Ireland specially dear, as these Nuncios, John (Codurious) and Alphonsus (Salmeron) and Raymond will report'.

A mission of these three papal nuncios had been sent to the king of Ulster. What was the purpose of that mission? What did they communicate to the Irish kings? Was their purpose to ensure that the kings rejected

Henry VIII's new claim to the kingship of Ireland and the abandonment of Ireland's status as a papal fiefdom? Indeed, Pope Clement VIII (1592–1605) later endorsed the struggle to maintain the papal fiefdom of Ireland against the authority of Protestant England. He did so in response to an appeal by The O'Neill, Florence MacCarthy Mór, MacDonagh MacCarthy of Duhallow and James, the Earl of Desmond. On 18 April 1600 Clement VIII issued a Bull of Indulgence to 'archbishops, bishops, prelates, Chiefs, earls, barons and people of Ireland'. Clement acknowledged that the Irish 'have long struggled to recover and preserve your liberty ... to throw off the yoke of slavery imposed on you by the English ... we grant to all of you ... plenary pardon and remission of all sins, as usually granted to those setting out to the war against the Turks for the recovering of the Holy Land'.[11]

However, Pope Paul's intercession with King Conn Bacach O'Neill proved fruitless because the Ulster king became one of the first to offer his submission to Henry VIII in 1542, surrendering his Gaelic title and taking from Henry an English title as Earl of Tyrone.

From 1541 Ireland was to constitute a separate realm called the Kingdom of Ireland, but with the English king as head of state. This position remained until 1 January 1801, when the Kingdom of Ireland became part of the United Kingdom of Great Britain and Ireland.

On 26 June 1541 the Lord Deputy, Sir Anthony St Leger, wrote to Henry VIII telling him that a parliament had been summoned in Dublin at which Henry's claim to be king of Ireland was endorsed.[12] There were attending, says St Leger, two earls, three viscounts, sixteen barons, two archbishops, twelve bishops, and Donough O'Brien, the king of Thomond, a doctor named O'Nolan, and a bishop and deputies assigned by O'Brien to represent him in parliament. The Ó Raghailligh Mór and many other Irish nobles had attended. In fact, the 10th Earl of Ormond, James Butler, had to volunteer his services to translate the words of Henry VIII's emissary to the parliament from English into Irish; not so much, it has been pointed out, for the Gaelic lords attending but for the Anglo-Irish lords who did not speak any English.

In the wake of Henry VIII's assumption of the kingship of Ireland came the announcement of the policy which was to 'utterly abolish' all Gaelic titles, the native law system, the social system and methods of land-holding in Ireland. As a Master of the Court of Wards, Sir William Parsons, was to state: 'We must change their course of government, apparel, manner of holding land, language, and habit of life. It will otherwise be impossible to set up in them obedience to the laws and to the English Empire.'

The first step on that road to bring the Irish nation into obedience to

England was that all holders of Gaelic titles were to be asked, with threat of force, implied or real, to surrender their titles and clan lands to the English Crown; if they took an oath of allegiance to the same Crown, they would be granted English titles and returned such portions of their former estates as was deemed fit, to hold by feudal tenure from the English Crown. Any such surrenders, of course, meant an acknowledgement of the new religious order in which the English king, and not the Bishop of Rome, was now Head of the Church.

2

Gaelic Dynastic Laws of Succession

What made it difficult for the Normans, and subsequently the English, to establish control over Ireland? Had the kingship laws and the social order, with the system of land tenure, been close to the English feudal law system and the concept of the divine right of kings, where the king and the law were inseparable, then the nature of the conflict might have been different. However, the Irish law system and the government of kings was so different to the Anglo-Norman system that struggle, and eventual dominance of one system over the other, was inevitable. As soon as Henry VIII made himself king and demanded the surrender of the Irish kings on a feudal basis, unaware of the intricacies of the laws which governed them, war became unavoidable.

According to the ancient chroniclers it was an eighth-century BC High King, Ollamh Fódhla, who ordered the laws of Ireland to be gathered. They were called the Laws of the Fénechus, or Féini, the tillers of the land. He is also said to have founded the great Féis Temhrach or Festival of Tara, held every three years, at which the laws were discussed and revised. The laws are now popularly called the Brehon laws deriving from the word *breitheamh*, a judge.

The laws were the result of many centuries of transmission by oral tradition and show fascinating parallels both with the Vedic Laws of Manu in India and with the Welsh law system, the Laws of Hywel Dda, named after King Hywel ap Cadell who ruled Wales between AD 910 and 950. He decreed that the laws of Wales be gathered and examined by an assembly presided over by Blegwywrd, archdeacon of Llandaff, and set down in a single law book.

The first known codification of the Irish law system was in AD 438 when the High King Laoghaire established a nine-man commission to examine the laws, revise them and set them down in writing. Three leading Brehons, or judges, of the day, Dubhtach maccu Lugir, Rossa and Fergus, sat on the commission. Dubhtach is referred to in other sources as King Laoghaire's Chief Brehon and Druid. Laoghaire sat on the committee with Dara, King of Ulster and Corc, King of Munster, indicating the importance of these two kings above the other kings of Ireland. In deference to the new faith, three Christian advisers sat on the committee, Patrick, Benignus and Cáirnech.

The committee eventually codified the laws into the *Senchus Mór*. The Cáin law applied to all Ireland and the Urradus law was specific to a particular province. The criminal law was set down in the *Book of Acaill*. Even in the fifth century the 'law language' or *Bérla Féini* was already archaic, demonstrating how old the Brehon system was. The codification is said to have produced no *new* laws but was a setting down of those already in use with some addition of scriptural or canon law. The introduction to the *Senchus Mór* states:

> What did not clash with the word of God in the written Law and in the New Testament, and with the conscience of the believers, was confirmed in the laws of the Brehons by Patrick and by the ecclesiastics and the Kings of Erin; and this is the *Senchus Mór*.

The earliest surviving record of the laws in their most complete form is found in the *Leabhar na hUidre* (Book of the Dun Cow) dating from the eleventh and twelfth centuries.

The Brehon system is unique and what makes it one of the most fascinating ancient law codes in world jurisprudence is that the basis of the system of criminal liability was compensation for the victim or victim's family and rehabilitation for the perpetrator; it was not merely a system of vengeance. Compensation was more important and the provision of compensation by the transgressor was paramount. The culprit or his family had to contribute to the individuals and to the society they had wronged.

The laws and their language, so comparable to the Vedic Laws of Manu, and the similarity between Old Irish and Sanskrit are demonstrable proof of their common Indo-European origin. Calvert Watkins pointed out that 'Old Irish represent[s] an extraordinarily archaic and conservative tradition within the Indo-European tradition ... The classical Old Irish nominal and verbal system of the eighth century of the Christian era is a far truer reflection of the state of affairs in Indo-European than is the Latin system of more than a thousand years before ... the structure of the archaic Old Irish sentence can be compared only with that of the sentence in Vedic Sanskrit or the Hittite of the Old Kingdom.'

D.A. Binchy, examining the oldest records of the Irish law tracts, in particular the *Bretha Nemed*, says they indicate, in language and law, a system harking back to Indo-European times. Much has now been written on the Vedic-Old Irish similarity, especially by Myles Dillon. In terms of kingship even the terminology is related: the Irish *rí* (*gh*) is similar to the Gaulish Celtic *rix*, the Latin *rex* and the Sanskrit *rajan* (Hindi, *raj*). Certainly, the English 'king' from the Gothic *kunnings* has quite a different root, but the English words 'rich' and 'reach' hark back to the ancient Indo-European concept that a king *reached* forth his hand to protect his people. In Old Irish *rige* was the word not only for kingship but also for the act of reaching. So in many Indo-European cultures, from India to Ireland, we have the concept of a deity with a 'long hand' who reached it out to encompass his people – Lugh Lamhfada (Lugh of the Long Hand) has his Vedic equivalent in Dyaus. Oenghus Olmuchada of the Long Hand is said to have ruled Ireland in 800 BC. The Uí Néill's ancient symbol of the Red Hand doubtless stems from this concept. It is the hand of a just ruler.

The Irish word *aire* for noble is related to the Sanskrit *ayra*, from which the word Aryan comes, now much perverted by Nazi philosophy. Similarly *nemed*, rendered as a name and word for privilege in Irish, is cognate with the Sanskrit *namas*, a sacred person. The Indians had a form of election of their kings (*parisad sam iti*), as did the Irish, and both cultures shared the condition that a king had to be without physical blemish. Another fascinating point in the cultural tradition of both peoples was the idea of the division of the nation into five kingdoms (the Irish word for a province still remains *cúige*, from the Old Irish *cóiced*, a fifth). A central kingdom exerted a theoretical control over the others; in Ireland this kingdom was designated *Midhe* (the origin of Meath, still sometimes referred to in memory of the kingship as 'Royal Meath'), meaning 'middle', while in Sanskrit the Hindu kingdom was designated *Madhya* which has exactly the same meaning.

Central to the clash between the Irish and their invaders were these laws reflecting an entirely different social concept and philosophy of life. More significant were the different successional laws and the constraints put upon an Irish ruler. While an Irish king had to be of the 'blood royal' he also had to be elected to office by his family. His succession relied on his *derbhfine*, or kinship electoral college.

Irish society, being kin-based, was categorised in law in the following manner. The *innfine* were the male great-great-grandchildren of the original head of the family. That five generations could be alive at one time was so unusual as to be discounted, although their rights are listed in law. The *iarfine* were the male great-grandchildren, a generation whose rights to be part of the electoral college and heirs to any property, real or ideal, were negligible. The *derbhfine* were the male grandchildren, and they formed the usual basis of the electoral college. The *geilfine* were the male children of an existing ruler. The *Book of Acaill* frequently mentions the *derbhfine* as 'seventeen' in number. Probably the idea of seventeen male grandchildren existing at any one time and capable of taking part in an electoral college was not beyond the realms of possibility. This number is mentioned in the tract 'On Succession' quoted in the *Ancient Laws of Ireland* (Vol. IV, p.373 *et seq.*).

So the head of a family, a chief of whatever degree, and the king himself were all elected by an electoral college consisting of the sons, grandsons and even great-grandsons of a common ancestor. According to the law a king was appointed *do thaobh a ghlun ngeineamha*, by virtue of his ancestry. A king of whatever rank was also a member of his *derbhfine* and on his death his title became a heritable property within the limits of his *derbhfine*. In modern law we might call this title an 'ideal property' of the *derbhfine*.

As Eoin MacNeill points out, succession was a combination of the elective with the hereditary principle and was a logical application of the Irish laws of inheritance.[1] But the decisive criterion for election to kingship was *febas*, or personal ability and standing. Part of that standing could be the *febas* of a candidate's father and grandfather, so if they had both held the kingship, his claim would be strengthened. T.M. Charles-Edwards points out: 'Seniority is a rejected principle unless other considerations should be equal.'

Election was often confined to one of the three generations of the *derbhfine* but this was not an unbreakable rule. Donnchadh Ó Corráin made a survey of the Uí Cheinnselaigh dynasty within a given period, and found that their succession could be expressed in these percentage figures:

54% were sons of kings, though not necessarily the eldest son, and of these only a small number (he lists six) succeeded directly after their father. With the majority, other relatives intervened in the kingship.

16% were grandsons of kings.

3% were great-grandsons of kings.

20% were great-great-grandsons and further removes.

7% were of unknown lineage.[2]

In the kingdom of the northern Uí Néill, specially between AD 879 and 1260, the figures were: 66% sons of kings, 15% grandsons, and 3% great-grandsons.

However, it was not unusual to find candidates elevated to kingship

outside the confines of the *derbhfine* and outside the normal five generations. Among the Eóghanacht, for example, the famous Cormac II mac
Cuilennáin (d. 908) was eleven generations removed from his last regnant
ancestor while Dub-dá-Bairenn mac Domhnaill (d. 959) was sixteen generations from his. However, at least half the kings elected were the sons
of previous kings and they were usually chosen by three generations of
the family.

It was a principle of Irish law that all the *derbhfine* of a king or chief
must be of suitable age. The male *aimsir togú*, or age of choice, was
seventeen years. No one under that age could succeed to a title or, indeed,
inherit property. For a female, the *aimsir togú* was fourteen years. To be
elected to office, kings had to possess the necessary accomplishments;
they had to be of sound mind and body. Value was put on their intellectual
powers although military prowess was also important. As potential heirs
to a title, particularly to a kingship, they were styled *Rígdamnae (Materies
Regis)*, kingship material. This title implied their eligibility to the kingship
by being within the requisite degree of kindred. James Hogan has pointed
out: 'In short a Rígdomna was a prince whose father, grandfather, or
great-grandfather had been a king'.

The electoral college of the *derbhfine* did not, of course, have to wait
until the title had become vacant to meet and vote for the successor
among themselves. Certainly from the twelfth century, the practice was
to appoint an heir apparent, *tánaise*, Anglicised as tanist, during the life
of the king. The king or chief could make the nomination himself from
any member of his *derbhfine*. Any debate among the *derbhfine* could then
take place during the lifetime of the king or chief so that his successor
was able to assume his title without challenge.

Indeed, in the law tract *Críth Gabhlach*, the term for the royal heir
apparent, *tánaise ríg*, is explained by the sentence 'because the whole clan
looks forward to his kingship without opposition to him'. David Greene
has shown that the word derives from the past participle of *to-ad-ni-sed*
and translates as 'the awaited one'. Only as it developed later did it come
to mean 'second in respect of dignity and function'.[3]

To sum up the important point of difference between the Irish kingship
succession and that of the Anglo-Normans, we may quote Lawrence
Ginnell:

> An eldest son did not succeed merely because his father had been king,
> if there was an uncle, nephew, brother, cousin or other member of
> the *Damhnae Ríg* better fit for the position; and the Tanist was usually
> such a relative, and not a son. The same rules applied to the election
> of sub-kings . . .[4]

However, the law did not expressly forbid the succession of the eldest son, providing he was qualified and had the support of the electoral college. Because of this, some scholars have mistakenly argued that the law of kingship succession was naturally evolving away from the original method in favour of primogeniture.

In *Gaelic and Gaelicised Ireland in the Middle Ages*, Kenneth Nicholls, K. Lydon and M. MacCurtain pointed out:

> In practice it often happened if a Chief was long lived and survived all his younger brothers, his son would qualify (for the succession) thus introducing a form of pseudo-primogeniture which has led some writers to the mistaken conclusion as to the existence of true primo-geniture among such families as for example, The MacCarthy Mór, where son followed father for six generations between 1359 and 1508. Simply because no MacCarthy Mór during the period was outlived by a younger brother or at least one strong or able enough to take the lordship.

Some years later, however, delivering his May 1976 O'Donnell Lecture at University College, Cork, 'Land, Law and Society in Sixteenth-Century Ireland', Nicholls broke ranks with his academic comrades by stating:

> While admitting that conclusions in this field are open to contro-vertion, my impression is that the difference in forms of land holding between the lordships of purely Gaelic origin and those of the Gaelicised Anglo-Normans, had, by the sixteenth century, become of little significance, at least so far as Connacht and the west midlands were concerned. In Munster a residue of feudal practice still survived along with the rule of primogeniture succession ... In Gaelic Tho-mond, too, we find a recognition of primogeniture in the rule which gave children of a deceased elderly brother preference in partitions over their senior but cadet uncles.

This was indeed a highly controversial suggestion and was immediately dismissed by his colleagues.

We may admit that there were cross-influences between the Irish and English law systems by the sixteenth century. Even in vocabulary we find departures from ancient law terms and borrowings such as *turnae*, attorney, *seicdedúir*, executor, *réléas*, release, and hybrid terms such as *oighridhe agus sighinoighridhe* for 'heirs and assignees'.[5] However, can we accept the thesis that the Brehon law of succession had altered to one of primogeniture? I share the view of James Hogan, an expert on Brehon kingship and successional law, expressed in his study 'The Irish Law of Kingship with special reference to Ailech and Cenél Eoghan'. He had already pointed out that for certain periods the eldest male heir succeeded to the throne of an Irish kingdom, sons succeeding their fathers. He also pointed out that this was not forbidden under Brehon law, that the eldest son could succeed his father, being a member of the *derbhfine*, providing he was not challenged by that *derbhfine*.

This pattern of succession was noticed among the Uí Néill kings after the death of Domhnall Ua Néill in 1325. Hogan stressed: 'The Uí Néill kings failed to substitute a lineal, that is, hereditary kingship, for the traditional succession of collaterals by election.' Father to son inheritance was not contrary to Brehon law, merely highly unusual, and certainly did not replace the earlier successional law.

The custom of 'non-opposition' or 'opposition' to the heir apparent became very significant in the period after the abolition of Gaelic titles. For it can be argued that Gaelic titles have survived during the three hundred years after their abolition by two means: succession by a passive tanistry (*tánaise cen fresabra*) and succession by an active tanistry (*tánaistecht gnímarthach*).

In both active and passive tanistry the eldest son could certainly succeed to the title, and often did so when Brehon law continued to hold sway, but not simply by virtue of the fact that he was the eldest male heir. If the title did pass down via the eldest male heirs, among the aristocratic families, following the abolition of those titles through conquest, it could well have done so on the basis that he was not challenged by any member of the *derbhfine*, that no challenger (*agóideoir*) presented an opposition (*an fresabracht*) or that such a challenger did not receive the approval of the *derbhfine*. So the eldest male heir could inherit if he had the tacit approval of the *derbhfine*.

The most important point is that no holder of a Gaelic title could, at any time, declare the Brehon law of succession to be invalid. The law stood above them as expressed in the *seanfhocal* (proverb), *Is treise dli ná tiarna*, The law is stronger than a lord. The Irish kings, unlike the kings (and queens) of England, were not law-makers nor were they the embodiment of the law. This was central to the mistakes of the Tudor politicians in their dealings with Ireland.

English kings were the embodiment of the English law and are still so symbolically considered: all prosecutions in the United Kingdom are carried out as 'the Crown versus . . .' whoever the defendant is, by virtue of the Crown's unique place *above* the law of the land. In republics it is usually the 'state' or the 'people' in whose name prosecutions are made.

But the Irish kings were hemmed in and constricted by Irish law to the point where they could only promote the common wealth of their people, for they, too, could be brought to account by law. A king was merely an officer of the law *established*. The law texts demonstrate quite clearly that the king was subject to the law in the same manner as the lowliest member of his *tuath* (people). In the *Críth Gablach* comes an admonition: *Is treise tuatha ná tiarna*, A people are stronger than a king or lord. It goes on to ask why this is so and states very clearly that it is because the people ordain the king, the king does not ordain the people.

Kings sat as judges in the courts but always with a *juris peritus* or Brehon and a scribe. While the judgement of the king's court might be given in the name of that king, it is clear, from the extensive and technical corpus of law, that the king consulted with his Brehon before reaching any verdict. Indeed, it was an essential part of the king's household to support the Brehons and the *ollamhain*.

It is clear from the law that if the king, or any chief, attempted to surrender his title on behalf of his heirs and successors, he simply could not do so. He could surrender his body, he could make a treaty, within certain parameters, and he could abdicate office for himself, as many Irish kings did. But there are plenty of examples to demonstrate that no king could abrogate the law or any part of it, especially the successional system.

Should the *derbhfine* ever become deadlocked regarding the succession of a candidate, an appeal could be made to the overlord of the clan. For example, in Tudor times, The O'Donel was recognised as overlord of northern Connacht at a time when the chieftainship of the Burkes was in question. Aodh O'Donel, while in Mayo, was asked to arbitrate in the matter. In Munster during the Tudor period, MacCarthy Mór was acknowledged as overlord of O'Sullivan Mór and O'Sullivan Beare and had the sole right to present them with the white rod of office. So each major king was responsible for any deadlocked succession within his territory.

Before leaving the subject of successional law, it will inevitably be asked, could a woman inherit a title? It is certainly true that women feature prominently in Old and Middle Irish literature and we have the famous example of Queen Medb. Her traditions may well be interlinked with those of a sovranty goddess but in the 'Ulster Cycle', as well as in the histories and genealogies, she appears as a real person. She is given as the daughter of a High King, Eochaidh Feidhlioch, and is said to have had several husbands and lovers. Her most famous husband was Ailill Mac Máta, who was the handsome commander of her royal bodyguard. Medb ruled Connacht in her own right and not as the consort.

The only woman, however, to appear on the 'High King Lists' is Macha Mong Ruadh, listed as the 76th monarch of Ireland, daughter of Aodh Ruadh and said to have reigned from 377 BC for seven years. She was an Ulster queen, of the line of Ir son of Míle, so not of the usual Uí Neill lineage from Eremon son of Míle. Macha is said to have founded Emain Macha (Navan, Co. Armagh) and, indeed, Armagh itself (Ard Macha, Macha's Height). She succeeded on the death of her father, who had ruled jointly with his brothers or cousins, Dithorba and Cimbaeth. It is more likely that they were cousins as Macha is reported to have married Cimbaeth. She is frequently confused with other Machas, of whom we can point to at least five in the ancient texts; one was undoubtedly a war goddess, while another is also clearly a legendary figure being the wife of the mythical invader Nemed.

We have many examples of female rulers in Celtic society, although mostly outside Ireland. Onomaris, Cartimandua and Boudicca were famous queens in their own right. Within Irish society several women leaders commanded their clans in battle, including Étain ní Fínghin Már Mac Carthaigh, who led a wing of the army of the Desmond king at the victory of Callan in the thirteenth century, and Éabha Ruadh ní Murchú, who wound iron bars into her hair and refused to take any English prisoners.

The twelfth-century collection of genealogical lore about women, the *Banshenchas* (History of Women), would suggest that women were entitled to achieve positions of power under Brehon law. The explanation might lie in the *Cáin Lánamna* that if there is no male heir, a woman may be called the *banchomarbae* (female heir) and, like any male, have the right to make formal legal entry into her inheritances. If she married a landless man or someone from another *tuath* (tribe), she made the decisions and paid his fines and debts: indeed, as Medb was clearly doing for Ailill. But, after her death, the rights and properties of a *banchomarbae* normally reverted to her own kin, her father's *derbhfine*, and did not pass to her husband nor to any sons that she may have had by him.

The obvious objection, in a system of law such as the clan system, to female succession is that it naturally leads to the alienation of the title and lands of the *tuath* by intermarriage with people from outside the *tuath*. Thus we also see in the *Cáin Lánamna* the provision that after the female's life her inheritance rights revert to her father's family.

The female heir is here referred to who has had the father's and grandfather's land, and though she should desire to give it to her sons, she shall not give it unconditionally.

We are told that this right was confirmed by the female judge, Brígh Briugaid, in the legal tract *Uraicecht Bec* which arose when the Brehon, Sencha Mac Ailella, gave a wrong judgement on female rights.

Technically, the woman did not pass into the *fine* of her husband for the purposes of inheritance but remained in the *fine* of her father. But her children did pass into the *fine* of her husband. The only property, in land, she could transmit to her heirs was property acquired for services rendered (*orba cruib ocuss sliastal*) or by gift (*ar dúthracht*). If she did become a chief, she could not appoint one of her own children as tanist, and the title remained with her father's *derbhfine* presuming, at the time of her death, a suitable candidate had emerged from that *derbhfine*. The period of her chiefship was considered only a lifetime 'stop-gap'.

The circumstances in which a female heir was necessary would arise so infrequently that this would explain why so few female rulers are recorded in ancient Ireland.

Women's rights in all other aspects of Brehon law were far superior to the constraints suffered by their English sisters. The Irish laws gave more rights and protection to women than any other Western law code at that time or until recent times. Women could and did aspire to all professions as the equals of men. They could be political leaders, military commanders, physicians, local magistrates, poets, artisans, lawyers and judges. Women were protected by laws against sexual harassment, discrimination and rape; they had the right of divorce on equal terms from their husbands with equitable separation laws and could demand part of their husband's property as a divorce settlement; they had the right of inheritance of personal property and were entitled to sickness benefits.

This was the system which Henry VIII and his administrators in Ireland now faced, a social order that they set out methodically to destroy. They knew that, unless it was eliminated, it would be hopeless to attempt to bring Ireland into the growing empire of England. Without an understanding of the Irish social order and law system, it is impossible to comprehend the turmoil into which Ireland was about to be plunged.

3

The 'Utter Abolition' of Gaelic Titles

The first Gaelic noble to surrender himself under Henry VIII's new 'surrender and regrant' policy was Turlough Ó Tuathail of northern Wicklow.[1] Ó Tuathail surrendered his title and clan lands because he was threatened by aggressive military policy from the English Pale which his lands bordered. His clan was domiciled in northern Wicklow, adjacent to Dublin. Henry, writing to his Lord Deputy and Council in Dublin, was aware of the military situation.[2]

> The lands of O'Reilly, O'Connor and Kavanagh etc. we take to lie so upon the danger of our power, as you may easily bring them to any reasonable conditions, that may be well desired of them. The other sort, as O'Donnell, MacWilliam, O'Brien etc, we think to lie so far from our strength there, as, without a greater force, it will be difficult to expel them out of their country, and to keep and inhabit the same with such as we would thereunto appoint; albeit we may easily correct and punish any of them as the case shall require ... We think that you may easily bind all them which lie upon our strength, to all the conditions whereunto Turlough O'Toole is bound.

Henry VIII had an astute eye for strategy. Those Gaelic kings and nobles whom his armies could dominate by military strength were to be approached first. Turlough Ó Tuathail had agreed to surrender his 'chiefship' and his 'lands'; in return, the lands were, in part, regranted to him as King Henry pleased, to use under English law and habits, and he promised to bring his children up to speak English. He would no longer use the title 'The Ó Tuathail'. However, The Ó Tuathail was still leading his clan one hundred years later during the 1641 uprising. His successor was forced to flee to France and joined the Irish Brigade of the French army in which eight of his sons served. In 1944 Charles Joseph Antoine Thomy O'Toole, Comte O'Toole de Leinster, living in the Avenue des Champs Elysées, Paris, claimed to have succeeded his father in 1889 as The O'Toole of Fer Tire and his pedigree was accepted by the Irish Genealogical Office.

Within a short time, the new English policy had succeeded in netting some important members of the Irish nobility including Conn Bacach O'Neill, King of Ulster, Murrough O'Brien, King of Thomond, and an Anglo-Irish 'chief' Ulick na gCeann Bourke, The MacWilliam Uachtar. Conn Bacach O'Neill surrendered his title at Henry's palace at Greenwich on 1 October 1542. We will return to him shortly.

The next most important 'catch' was Murrough O'Brien, 57th King of Thomond, who surrendered to Henry VIII at Greenwich on 1 July 1543. He was rewarded with the title of Earl of Thomond. Now we find an interesting recognition of the Brehon law of succession by Henry VIII. Under tanistry, Murrough's nephew, Donough O'Brien, was his heir apparent. Yet Murrough had a son who, by English rules, should have succeeded him as Earl of Thomond. Donough, however, was created Baron Ibrickan and it was agreed that he would succeed his uncle as 2nd Earl of Thomond and the title would thereafter descend through his heirs male. To square their consciences under primogeniture, Murrough's son would take the title of Baron Inchiquin.

Sir Thomas Cusack, acting as Lord Justice, wrote gleefully to the Duke of Northumberland on 8 May 1553 that the policy of forcing the Irish kings to surrender to Henry VIII was working out very well. 'The making of O'Brien an Earl made all that country obedient ... Irishmen were never so weak, and the English subjects never so strong as now.'[3]

The next 'catch' was the powerful Gaelicised Anglo-Norman lord, Ulick na gCeann, The MacWilliam Uachtar (Upper) of Galway, who surrendered his chiefship to became Earl of Clanricade on the same day as O'Brien. Although an Anglo-Norman lord, MacWilliam Uachtar and his cousin MacWilliam Iochtar (Lower) of Mayo governed their families, and those dependent on them, as Irish clans, spoke Irish and obeyed Irish law. Now MacWilliam Uachter took the English title and promised to obey English law and speak English.

The surviving documentation setting out the terms and conditions for the submissions of the Gaelic kings and aristocracy shows precisely what was intended by Tudor policy. The Gaelic titles, and the laws of tanistry under which they were passed down, were to be totally abolished. The essential condition of surrender was the acceptance of the English common law and the primogeniture system. The Articles of Submission for the king of Ulster, Conn Bacach O'Neill, included the demand that

'He utterly forsake the name of O'Neill'. The abolition of this title was confirmed in a speech by Sir John Davies, when he was appointed Speaker of the Commons in the Dublin parliament of 1613. Sir John said: 'What was the principal cause that Sir Henry Sidney held a Parliament in the eleventh year of Queen Elizabeth but to extinguish the name of O'Neill and entitle the Crown to the great part of Ulster?' In both instances, of course, it is not a surname that is being discussed, but the Gaelic title *The O'Neill*. The text of the Elizabethan Act of Attainder of Shane O'Neill makes clear that it is the title The O'Neill which 'shall henceforth cease, end, determine, and be utterly abolished and extinct for ever'. Constantia Maxwell points out that Elizabeth I, by this Act, declared the title of The O'Neill abolished and her Crown entitled to the whole of Ulster.

Indeed that Act makes clear that 'what person soever he be that shall hereafter challenge, execute, or take upon him that name of O'Neill, or any superiority, dignity, preeminence and jurisdiction, authority, rule, tributes, or expenses, used, claimed, usurped, or taken heretofore by any O'Neill, of the lords, captains, or people of Ulster, the same shall be deemed, adjudged and taken high treason against your Majesty, your crown and dignity . . .'

When King Murrough, The O'Brien, of Thomond, surrendered his title, the first item of the submission was: '1, Utterly to forsake and refuse the name of O'Breene [*sic*], and all claims that he might pretend to by the name; and to use such name as it should please the King to give unto him.'

In Leinster, King Caothaoir Mac Airt, MacMorrough Kavanagh, who had succeeded in 1547, was persuaded to surrender his title and on 8 February 1554 he was created Baron Ballyanne. One wonders why he was not given the greater carrot of an earldom like O'Brien and O'Neill and later MacCarthy Mór. We know that the colonial administration 'persuaded him' by taking two of his sons as hostages to ensure his surrender. Yet he was removed by his *derbhfine* within a year of surrendering and died four years later. Caothaoir was succeeded to the kingship not by his sons but by a cousin, Murchadh Mac Muiris. This cleaving to Brehon law obviously presented the English administration with problems but they persuaded the new MacMorrough Kavanagh, Murchadh, to surrender also and replace his title with that of Baron of Coolnaleen. The last to claim the title of King of Leinster was Domhnall Spáinneach mac Donnchadha in 1595. He chose to abdicate after the general Irish surrender in 1603, rather than surrender the kingdom, and he died in 1632.

In Connacht, the way was made easier by the split in the O'Conor royal dynasty into three separate houses – O'Conor Roe, O'Conor Don and O'Conor Sligo. O'Conor Sligo surrendered his title in 1567 and, it is said, was offered an earldom, which he declined. No evidence of this appears in the State Papers. But the kingship of Connacht was contested between O'Conor Roe and O'Conor Don and Connacht had been partitioned between the two branches. It had been reunited in the fourteenth century under O'Conor Roe but soon split again. By the mid-sixteenth century it was again a single kingdom ruled by Dermot, The O'Conor Don. In 1568, Tadhg Buidhe O'Conor Roe had surrendered his title for a knighthood. However, King Dermot O'Conor Don proved the more difficult 'catch'. Finally, the English 'President of Connacht', Sir Edward Fytton, invited King Dermot to his castle for 'talks' in 1571. For the Irish, and, indeed, all the Celts, the laws of hospitality were sacred. Fytton did not respect such niceties and made King Dermot a prisoner.

In the following year, King Dermot's tanist, Aodh (Hugh) O'Conor, together with the son of O'Conor Roe, led a rescue party to Fytton's castle and succeeded in releasing King Dermot. War erupted in Connacht. But, by 1576, the English forces were achieving the upper hand. The forces of Aodh O'Conor, who appeared as commander of King Dermot's army, managed to hold out until 1581 before surrendering to Lord Deputy Sir John Perrott. King Dermot died in 1585, the year in which 'The Composition of Connacht' was agreed and the titles of O'Conor Don, O'Conor Roe and O'Conor Sligo were 'abolished and made extinct for ever'. The O'Conor titles were to be exchanged only for English knighthoods, presumably in retaliation for King Dermot's refusal to submit immediately.

Another major problem, so far as the English administration was concerned, was the kingdom of Desmond. The king of Desmond, Donal VIII (1516–c.1558) had toyed with the new proposals and in 1552 he obtained a grant of 'English liberty' for himself, his younger son and tanist Donal and his daughter, as a means of ensuring the inheritance of either his son or daughter to the ownership of his estates and personal property. This was in violation of Brehon law. However, sometime between 1552 and 1558 Donal VIII died and Donal IX The MacCarthy Mór came to the throne. Donal IX was a strong leader and was concerned with protecting his kingdom by diplomacy first and by force if there was no other choice. He was an Irish poet of considerable merit; several of his poems survive, including *Aisling-thruagh do mhear meisi* (A sorrowful vision has deceived me) and *Och an och! a Mhuire bu de* (Alas! Alas! O benign Mary). He was married to Honora FitzGerald, daughter of the 13th Earl of Desmond.

Although the kingdom of Desmond had been compressed back by this time in Co. Cork and Co. Kerry, by the encroachments of the palatine earldoms of Desmond (FitzGerald) and of Ormond (Butler), Donal still ruled a sizable kingdom; Sir Warham St Leger reported that he controlled at least fourteen 'countries', ruled by petty chiefs and several lordships which paid him rents and services. Having been pressed to surrender his title as king, Donal seemed expert at avoiding the issue and there is no reference to any such surrender during the reigns of Henry VIII, Edward VI or Mary, nor in the first years of the reign of Elizabeth I.

Perhaps a demonstration of how frustrated the Tudor administration became with Donal lies in the fact that in 1565 David Roche, Lord Fermoy, organised the kidnapping of the king. He was taken as a prisoner to London where, under duress, he was forced to accept the title of Earl of Clancare. But Donal IX MacCarthy Mór was, as previously said, an astute politician. When in 1760 Sir Isaac Heard, then Norroy King of Arms (later Garter King) and Ralph Bigland, then Clarenceux King of Arms, compiled a history of the royal house of MacCarthy for the Muskerry MacCarthys entitled *Généalogie de la Royale et Sérénissime Maison de MacCarthy*, they had this to say about the incident:

> Donal MacCarthy Mór, King of Desmond, being taken prisoner by David, Lord Roche of Fermoy, Sir Henry Sydney, then Lord Lieutenant of Ireland, mistrusting the rebellious intentions of Gerald, the last Earl of Desmond, sent Donal MacCarthy Mór to England, to the intent that by Her Majesty Queen Elizabeth's good usage to him, he might be made an instrument against the said Desmond. Her Majesty did so effectually prevail on him by Royal gifts and fair promises that she engaged him to surrender into her hands his Kingdom of Desmond and to take it back from the Crown by English tenure. She paid his expenses of his journey, conferred many ample privileges on him, *left him in full possession of all his royalties*, and power of appointing Sheriffs at will in his territory, at the same time she created him Earl of Clancarré and Baron of Valentia by letters patent bearing date the 7th year of her reign, *anno* 1565. Donal on his return to home was so much despised by his vassals and followers for his new titles that he rejected them immediately, and after the example of O'Néill in Ulster, took to arms in the South, assumed the title of King of Munster and sent ambassadors to the Pope and King of Spain for assistance . . .

The English heralds compiling this account admit that Elizabeth left him in 'full possession of all his royalties' for Donal had actually managed to get the compiler of the letters patent to refer to him by the royal title MacCarthy Mór so that he was both Earl of Clancare and, simultaneously, MacCarthy Mór. In the Gaelic context, MacCarthy Mór embodies the royal status as head of the Eóghanachta, just as in the time of the Roman empire the surname Caesar was adopted by the emperors as the title of imperial dignity.

Donal IX, once safely back in his kingdom, proclaimed that he was still king of Desmond. The mayor of Waterford, in 1569, complained to Sir William Cecil about 'MacCarthy Mór, who refuses the new titles of Earl, and is offended with any one that calleth him Earl of Clancar.' The war between King Donal and the English lasted until 1569 when he was again forced to surrender and make submission to Elizabeth. This time, his only son, Tadhg, had been taken to Dublin Castle to be held as a hostage for Donal's good behaviour. Donal still remained Earl of Clancare in English eyes but documents showed that he never used the title and simply stuck to the Gaelic form as MacCarthy Mór, thus still implying his continued royal status and supported in this by his letters patent. When he died in 1596 he went into history as the last regnant king of Desmond for Tadhg, Lord of Valentia, though he had escaped from Dublin Castle, died in France before his father. There was no clearly appointed tanist and the title was disputed in the chaos that followed the devastating conquest of Munster, then being subjected to plantation by a new wave of English colonists.

In the wake of initial surrenders in 1541–43, there came the surrender of members of the lesser aristocracy. The Mac Giollaphádraig (MacGilpatrick) of Ossory, then chief of an area in Upper Ossory, surrendered. MacGilpatricks had been petty kings of Ossory, once a sub-kingdom of Leinster at the time of the Anglo-Norman invasion. It had stretched from Waterford in the south to the Slieve Bloom mountains in the north, along the west bank of River Nore (An Fheoir). It was a kingdom which Strongbow had seized by conquest. Donal MacGiollaphádraig (d. 1185) was the last king of all Ossory. The territory had then shrunk to the Upper Ossory ruled by The MacGilpatrick of Tudor times. He submitted on the terms laid down:

> First, the said MacGilpatric doth utterly forsake and refuse the name of MacGilpatric, and all claim which he might pretend by the same; and promiseth to name himself, for ever hereafter, by such name as it shall please the King's Majesty to give him.

There was a further essential item.

> . . . the said MacGilpatric, his heirs and assignees and every other the inhabiters of such lands as it shall please the King's Majesty to give unto him, shall use the English habits and manner, and, to their knowledge, the English language, and they, and every of them, shall to their

power, bring up their children after the English manner, and the use of the English tongue.

There followed the surrender of The O'Grady of Clan Donghaile, The MacNamara of Clancullen and The O'Shaughnessy, each of whom received English knighthoods although it had initially been recommended that they could 'swap' their Gaelic titles for the title of Baron. The O'Kennedy of Ormond, The O'Carroll of Ely, The O'Meagher of Iker-rin, The MacMahon of Cocobaskin, The O'Conor of Corcoro, The O'Loughlin of Burren, The O'Brien-Arra, The O'Brien of Oghonagh, The O'Dwyer of Kylenemana and 'The O'Mulrion de When' are all listed as coming forward to declare they would each surrender their names and titles. 'William O'Carroll' of Ely later surrendered personally all his estates into Chancery on 2 August 1578, and was granted a small portion of these lands back to hold as an estate for 'a knight's fee'.

The surrender of the king of Ulster, Conn Bacach O'Neill, was a major step forward in the process. Hogan does not agree.

The submission of Conn Bacach in 1542, in common with most of the native princes, is an event the significance of which has been somewhat overrated. It is certain that the Irish kings did not regard their submission as involving the abandonment of the old order. It did not enter their heads that their own immemorial social and political scheme of life was suddenly to disappear because they recognised the English King as overlord. But even the partial introduction of English land tenures was bound to antagonise a people so closely wedded to custom and tradition, and it was this feeling of antipathy that enabled Seán (*an Diomais*) to come forward as the champion of the native order against the feudalising and Anglicising programme for which, at the time, his own father Conn (Bacach) seemed to stand; and, again, towards the close of the century a similar racial resurgence carried Aodh Ua Néill away from his English ideas and leanings, and moved him to seek for himself the traditional inauguration accorded to the Kings of his line at Tulach Óg.

It is hard to imagine that the Irish kings were as naïve as Hogan suggests. Whatever their expectations, the conditions of their surrender seem unequivocal. The intention of the 1570 Act, according to Sir John Davies, James I's Attorney General for Ireland and Speaker of the Dublin parliament, in his *A Discovery of the True Causes Why Ireland was Never Entirely Subdued* (1612), was that the clan system and all chiefships were to be totally abolished. And whether the Irish aristocrats knew the results of their surrenders, most of the intellectuals of Ireland were perfectly aware of what was going on and would have advised the kings.

Aonghus mac Daighre Ó Dálaigh (*c*.1540–*c*.1600) was poet to The O'Byrne of Wicklow. In a poem called *Dia Libh a Laochradh Ghaoidheal* (God be with the Irish host) he states:

> Torment it is to me that, in the very tribal gathering, foreigners proscribe them that are Ireland's royal chiefs, in whose own ancestral territory is given to them no designation but that of a lowly outlaw's name.

For 'outlaw' he used the term which translates as 'wood-kerne' but which the English used as a general name for all Irish outlaws. The poem became well known and is first recorded in the *Leabhar Branach* (Book of the O'Byrnes). That the bards and *ollamhain* were effective in advising against surrender is attested by a letter from Lord Justice FitzWilliam, writing to William Cecil (Lord Burghley), complaining that plans for Anglicisation were being frustrated by them. He speaks of 'the discountenance of heraldry and the prevalence of rhymers who set forth the beastliest and most odious of men's doings.'

We may be sure that one of the main pressures on the Irish kings and princes for their initial surrender was the fear of the use of greater force against their peoples and territories. A few years before the first surrenders, in 1536, Lord Leonard Gray (afterwards Viscount Graney), then Lord Deputy, had marched an army throughout Ireland. It was then that Donal Mór, The O'Morchoe, described as a 'chief captain of Ireland', being of the cadet line of the kings of Leinster, surrendered to Lord Grey, and agreed on 10 May 1536 to hold his country and 'lordship' from the English Crown.

Sir John Davies pointed out that the result of the Lord Deputy's display of force was that 'the principal septs of the Irishry, being all terrified, and most of them broken in this journey, many of their chief lords, upon this Deputy's return, came to Dublin and made their submissions to the Crown of England, namely, the O'Neills and O'Reillys of Ulster, MacMororough, O'Byrne and O'Carroll of Leinster and the Bourkes of Connacht'.

Several of the lesser nobility were persuaded to surrender in the expectation of bettering their own positions. Sir John Davies says:

> Hereupon the Irish captains of lesser territories, which had even been oppressed by the greater and mightier – some with risings out, other with bonaght, and others with cuttings and spendings at pleasure –

did appeal for justice to the Lord Deputy, who upon hearing their complaints, did always order that they should all immediately depend upon the [English] King, and that the weaker should have no dependency upon the stronger.

A bonaght, from the Irish *buannacht*, was the tax levied upon a district for the wages and provisions of soldiers who were protecting it. By extension, it eventually became a word for a mercenary soldier.

English diplomacy used the argument that if these lesser chiefs and chieftains surrendered to the English king, he would then 'protect them' and give them greater independence than if they continued their allegiance to their native princes. Greed thereby entered into the argument: the English documentation shows that the administrators emphasised the 'iniquities' and 'injustice' of the native Irish taxation system to these petty chiefs. It was, of course, no more unjust than any other taxation system whereby public moneys had to be raised for the welfare and defence of the people. How many of these petty chiefs were fooled into thinking they would escape payment of taxes, not realising that they were going to be infinitely worse off under Tudor taxes, is not known.

Some of the petty chiefs did initially manage to work the system to their advantage, according to Davies. In stating that James I had to clear up some of these ambiguities of the previous Tudor administration, he admits that in Elizabeth I's reign 'there were many Irish lords who did not surrender, yet obtained Letters Patent as the captainships of their countries, and of all the lands and duties belonging to those captainships; for the Statute which doth condemn and abolish these captainries usurped by the Irish doth give power to the Lord Deputy to grant the same by Letters Patent'. Therefore, some letters patent actually acknowledged certain nobles as 'captains of the nation'. James I had sent two special Commissions to Ireland to clear up any anomalies in case the letters patent could be construed as confirming the Gaelic titles.

Davies was referring mainly to the letters patent issued on the direction of Lord Deputy Sir Henry Sidney. In fact, there was little ambiguity in Sir Henry's letters patent. On 11 February 1570, Sidney had signed an agreement with Faghne O'Farrell, The O'Farrell of Annaly, Co. Longford, who was chief of the Clan tSédin, one of the two branches of the O'Farrells. The O'Farrell surrendered to Sir Henry and agreed that 'the captainship of that portion of the said county . . . shall from henceforth be utterly abolished . . . and that the said Faghne O'Farrell shall receive and take, by Letters Patent from the Queen's Majesty . . . the names and styles of seneschal'. Therefore it is clear that The O'Farrell had given up his Gaelic title and agreed to adopt the English designation.

Davies speaks of Sir Henry Sidney's policy in this manner:

For, the first to diminish the greatness of the Irish lords, and to take from them the dependency of the common people, in the Parliament which he held eleventh of Elizabeth, he did abolish their pretended and usurped captainships and all exactions and extortions incident thereunto. Next to settle their seignories and possessions in a course of inheritance according to the course of the Common law, he caused an Act to pass whereby the Lord Deputy was authorised to accept their surrenders and to regrant estate unto them, to hold of the Crown by English tenures and services.

It depended on the degree of one's Gaelic title what English title was offered in its place. These ranged from an earldom for most provincial kingships to a barony for The Maguire of Fermanagh, and a knighthood for The Ó Raghailligh of Cavan. Some of the Gaelic aristocrats were considered of less significance and given such titles as the now defunct seneschal, major domo, serjeant and esquire – titles of dignity and authority below a knight.

It is interesting to note that Dr John O'Donovan, writing to Morgan William O'Donovan on 25 October 1841, comments: 'I am satisfied that none of the name of O'Donovan ever had a title; never! not even that of knight! . . . It does not appear that any of that family ever got a title under the Crown of England except Sir Owen, who fought at Kinsale 1601–2.' It may be that Dr O'Donovan was not considering seneschal, serjeant or esquire as a title of lesser gentry, which they were at that time.

Donal na gCroiceann (of the Hides) had been inaugurated as The O'Donovan by The MacCarthy Reagh, Prince of Carbery, in 1560. He died in 1584. It is not clear who was The O'Donovan for the next seven years. However, in 1591, the son of Donal na gCroiceann received the white wand of office from MacCarthy Reagh. In spite of his acknowledged fealty to his rightful prince, the following year, on 12 February 1592, the English Lord Chancellor, Adam Loftus, received his surrender. In 1608 Donal O'Donovan surrendered the lands of Clan Cathail against native law. Dr O'Donovan, in a subsequent letter to Morgan William O'Donovan, believed that Donal was then unsuccessfully challenged under Brehon law by his second son Teige for the chiefship. Donal received a regrant of his real estate in 1613 and seems to have accepted a mere 'esquire' in place of his Gaelic title.

Many of the lesser chieftains, such as The O'Molloy, The MacMahon and The O'Hanlon, were given grants of land to hold on a 'knight's service' or as 'serjeant'. Certainly it was made clear in a letter of 1 December 1587, granting some land to 'Ogie' O'Hanlon, that the grant was made 'provided that no person shall have any title claiming as O'Hanlon or tanist, which titles are abolished'. In a grant of February 1571 it is clearly stated that any fees which were formerly paid to a chief and his tanist were now to be paid to the persons holding the English titles, 'these customs not to be called by Irish names but to be known as the fees of the Chief Serjeant and Under Serjeant'.

Gradually, the Tudor 'Kingdom of Ireland' was emerging with feudal titles of manorial and baronial jurisdiction, reaching their height in the palatine earldoms of Desmond and Ormond. There was now a system of chartered boroughs, with the capital at Dublin deemed a royal borough, and with lords' towns, such as Waterford, having 'Breteuil rights'. Ireland was ruled, in the absence of the king, by his Viceroy, who had been Lord Deputy during the 'Lordship of Ireland' but even under the new 'kingdom' was usually styled as Lord Deputy. The system now allowed for no holder of a Gaelic title to exist. These titles were not only abolished under statute law but by the *jus commune*, the unwritten law of English administered in the king's courts, based on a universal usage and embodied in commentaries and reported cases – common law. Only feudal titles, granted by the English Crown, had any legal existence in the new 'Kingdom of Ireland'.

The surrenders and the switch from one system to another were not peaceful processes. Many of the Irish nobility did not submit as meekly as the English administration had hoped for. The fierce opposition that was encountered caused the Tudors to abandon the original plan simply to Anglicise the population and, under Queen Mary, they started an experiment in Leinster, clearing the land of the natives and settling it with English colonists – a policy of 'ethnic cleansing'. This 'transplantation' policy, as it became known, was tried in Munster and in Ulster but it was to have its most marked effect on the Irish psyche during the Cromwellian administration of the mid-seventeenth century when the Irish population was ordered into a 'reserve' west of the River Shannon, into Co. Clare and the province of Connacht.

4

The Struggle for Survival

The struggle of the Irish against the Tudor conquests lay in the attachment of the aristocracy and the people to the Irish law, language and culture. This fierce adherence to their social system against the alien system which Henry VIII was now trying to impose on the country lasted for well over a century. The result of it was a brutal conquest by a foreign power which had the effect of changing the law, the social system and the status of the language. The changes were forced on the population of Ireland under duress by the use of *force majeure*.

From the perspective of Irish law, to what extent could the surrender of the Irish kings and aristocracy to the English Crown be considered a legal action? It has already been pointed out that under Brehon law, existing at the time of the conquest, an Irish king, and even a lesser chief, was not a creator of law nor was he above the law. Irish kings and chiefs were subject to the law and could not afford to ignore it.

The *Crith Gabhlach*, the best known of the law texts, has a clear instruction commencing:

> These are the qualifications of a just ruler with respect to his people, that he does not violate them by falsehood, nor force, nor superior strength; let him be a just, sound mediator between weak and strong. There are moreover three other things they demand from the King; let him be a man of full righteousness on every side, let him be a man who inquires after knowledge; let him be an abode of patience.

As has been explained, the kings and chiefs sat as judges in the law courts, but always sat with a Brehon and other learned people. The writer of one of the law texts on kings says: 'There are four rights which the king pledges his people to observe. The rights of *Fénechus* law first; it is the people that acclaim it.' The obedience of the king to the law was not meant as a slight to the king, explains the text, 'for the law, like the king, was ordained by the people'.

Any attempt to surrender his title on behalf of the kingdom and on behalf of his heirs and successors, and further, to surrender the rights of his people, was simply incompatible with Brehon law. A king could surrender his body, he could make a treaty within limitations, or, indeed, he could abdicate office for himself, and many Irish kings did abdicate when they felt they could no longer contribute to the welfare of their people by holding office. Ruaidri Ua Conchobhair, who abdicated his kingship in 1184 to enter the monastery of Cong, is one of the best examples of such an abdication. But no king or chief could abrogate the entire law and successional system. Any king or chief attempting to do so could be dismissed from his office, and his tanist – or, should the tanist support him, a new successor – could be appointed.

This is precisely what began to happen the moment the Irish kings began their surrender to Henry VIII and led to the bloody Tudor Wars of Conquest and the even more brutal conquests and devastations of the seventeenth century.

It is clear from Irish sources written at the start of the surrender policy that those members of the Gaelic aristocracy became the object of scorn and derision among the intellectual classes. One anonymous Irish text says:

Pride they [the Gaelic nobility] have bartered for a lowly mind, and bright perceptions for gloominess; this flaccid disposition of the erstwhile gallant host may in all earnest stand us in lieu of a sermon. They, the flowers of the freeborn clans of Tara's armies, have run out the term of their prosperity; envy has brought down her elbow on them, so that an eclipsing deluge has overwhelmed them. Their wonted good luck they have all forgotten, their battleground and their athletic feats; their ire, their turbulence, their aggressiveness; prowess of clean handed loyal warriors. No stripling now is seen to challenge combat, nor soldier's gear to hang by his pallet, nor sword to suck the hand's palm, while frost congeals the ringlet of the hair. No more the target is seen slung on the broad back, nor hilt girt to the side at coming of the moon, nor smooth soft skin coming into contact with chainmail; all this must once upon a time have been a dream. Their cheerfulness of spirit, their appetite for diversion and their propensity to give away, they have relinquished; likewise their charge in the fight, their industry in depredations – so that they being thus are not living men at all.[1]

This view was shared by the poet of The O'Carroll of Ely, who says not one of the Irish chiefs has life in him. His ten bitter verses name the leading Irish princes:

Fúbún fúibh, a shluagh Gaoidheal,
ní mhaireann aoinneach agaibh:
Goill ag comhroinn bhur gcríche
re sluagh síthe bhur samhail

Shame on you, oh men of the Gael,
not one of you has life in him;
The foreigner is sharing out your country among
themselves
and you are like a phantom host.

The O'Neills of Aileach and Navan
the King of Tara and Tailltean
in foolish submission
they have surrendered their Kingdom
for the earldom of Ulster.

O Nobles of the Island of ancient [King] Art
evil is your change of dignity.
O ill-guided cowardly host
henceforth say nothing but 'shame'!

Soon, incredulity at what certain of the kings and their nobles were doing turned to action. The action began in Ulster.

The king of Ulster, Conn Bacach O'Neill, had surrendered to Henry VIII at Greenwich on 1 October 1542, and accepted the English title Earl of Tyrone. His son Ferdorcha, now called 'Matthew' by the English, was told that he would inherit the earldom by the law of primogeniture and until that time would be styled Baron of Dungannon.

Shortly after his return to Ulster, Conn Bacach's *derbhfine* met and refused to regard Ferdorcha, Baron of Dungannon, as a legal successor and heir to Conn, nor, of course, could they support the surrender by Conn of his kingship. They simply disowned him. Conn Bacach was driven out and sought refuge among the English of the Pale, dying in exile there in 1559. The *derbhfine*, having rejected Ferdorcha because of his acceptance of an English title, elected as new king of Ulster Conn Bacach's youngest son Seán an Díomais, known to the English as Shane the Proud. He was duly installed as king at the ancient inauguration site of Tulach Óg. His cousin Turlough was named as tanist. Seán an Díomais was so secure in his position that in 1562 he paid a 'state visit' to Elizabeth

I's court where he took the opportunity to explain to her about the Brehon law of succession.[2] His visit is described in Holinshed's *Chronicles*:

> He pretended to be King of Ulster, even as he said his ancestors were, and affecting the manner of the 'Great Turk', was continually guarded with 600 armed men, as it were his Janissaries, about him, and had in readiness to bring into the field, 1000 horsemen and 4000 footmen.

The same rejection of the surrender of the title and abrogation of the law occurred even among the Gaelicised Norman-Irish Bourkes. MacWilliam Uachtar returned from England in 1543 with his title Earl of Clanricade. Suspiciously, within months, in 1544, the new Earl of Clanricade was dead and when his eldest son, Richard, attempted to proclaim himself head of the clan with the title of 2nd Earl, he was rejected by his *derbhfine* who elected a cousin, named Ulick. A dynastic struggle commenced and it was not until 1550/51, with the help of English troops, that Richard was placed in control of the MacWilliam Bourkes.

Even O'Brien was rejected in Thomond. That O'Brien knew well the consequences of his surrender is demonstrated in an interesting incident recorded beforehand. In February 1541 the Lord Deputy Andrew St Leger went to Limerick to meet Murrough O'Brien, the 57th King of Thomond, who had come to the throne in 1539, in order to open negotiations about the surrender of his title. The king asked for time to consult his *derbhfine* on the proposition. The English interpretation of this was given in a report stating that Murrough O'Brien demanded time to consult with his kinsfolk 'forasmuch as he was but one man, although he were captain of his nation'.[3]

Did Murrough O'Brien understand, and if he did, was he able to explain fully to his *derbhfine*, what was actually being asked? Did he really surrender his title of King to Henry VIII at Greenwich and become Earl of Thomond with the foreknowledge and approval of his *derbfhine*? It seems unlikely they realised all the consequences, but they were apparently happy to accept Murrough O'Brien returning to Thomond with an English title. They could have been led to believe that this title was in addition to his own for, during the rest of Murrough's life, there is no report of any disturbance.

When Murrough died in 1551 and was succeeded, as we saw in Chapter 3, by his nephew Donough, Baron of Ibrickan, there seemed to be no problem. The problem arose when Donough set about ensuring that his title as 2nd Earl of Thomond, and his role as head of the O'Briens, would pass to his eldest son under the new English system of primogeniture.

The *derbhfine* now saw the break with Irish law and elected Donal O'Brien of Dough, the brother of Murrough, as The O'Brien, King of Thomond. They rejected Donough, the 2nd Earl of Thomond. In 1553 Donal was inaugurated, according to custom, at Magh Adhair, where there stood a sacred tree under which The O'Brien had been invested for many centuries. He was supported by his half-brother Turlough. Faced with a general insurrection of the people of Thomond, the 2nd Earl took refuge in Clonroad Castle and sent messages to the English Lord Deputy for military help. Within five weeks he was dead, probably of a wound sustained in the attack on Clonroad Castle by his own people.

Donough's son Conor, who, under the English law, now became the 3rd Earl of Thomond, also sent appeals to the English for military aid. But this was not a good time for the English administration. Edward VI, who had succeeded his father in 1547, died on 6 July 1553, and there was an attempt to establish Jane Grey, daughter of the Duke of Suffolk, as queen in order to continue the Protestant Reformation in England. However, by 19 July 1553, Mary had become queen and started to return the country to Catholicism. The problems of the English Crown, and the fact that a condition of surrender of the Irish nobility was that they accept the reformed Anglican faith, caused the authorities in Ireland some confusion. The Earl of Thomond had recognised Henry as Head of the Church for himself and his heirs and successors. The situation was uncertain as to whether the English administration should send an army to support the 3rd Earl as a Protestant against Donal, calling himself King of Thomond, as a Catholic. Mary was asked for her express orders. She vacillated and it was not until March 1558, five years later, that she decided that English domination in Ireland was more important than religious questions. Her new Lord Deputy, Sir Thomas Radcliffe, Earl of Sussex, arrived with a powerful army at Limerick. Mary was dead by November 1558, and Elizabeth I resumed Protestantism as the national religion.

Donal, King of Thomond, was no match for the armies of Lord Sussex. Eventually he was forced to retreat and seek refuge with the king of Ulster. Conor O'Brien, 3rd Earl of Thomond, with the help of Lord Sussex, was placed in control of Thomond on the feudal terms agreed by his grandfather. According to Ivar O'Brien, 'He followed his father's example by forswearing the traditional title of "The O'Brien" and promising to be loyal to the English Crown.'[4] This ceremony took place in Limerick Cathedral on 10 July 1558 and 'was sworn upon the sacraments and on the relics of the Church with bell, book and candle . . .'

Yet this was not the end of the O'Brien dynastic struggle. After Lord Sussex's victorious English army had withdrawn from Thomond, Donal returned from Ulster and for some years a civil war continued in the kingdom. But with the 3rd Earl able to call on English troops, Donal stood no chance and eventually concluded a peace with Conor. In return for Donal's dropping his claims to the Gaelic title, Conor interestingly agreed to compensate him for his 'loss of rights'. Donal, of course, had no rights under English law but he certainly did under Brehon law. Was this a recognition of those rights by the 3rd Earl? Donal, in return, agreed to move into Ennistymon Castle and accept the 3rd Earl's position.

It was not the end of the dynastic conflict. Harassed by criticism and attacks from the O'Brien *derbfhine*, Conor finally rose up against the English but was defeated and fled to France in 1571. He sought pardon and died in 1581 having formally surrendered his estate as an act of contrition. His son Donough became the 4th Earl. But still the dynastic problems continued. That Donough was still regarded as a royal prince in the people's eyes is seen from a poem of Tadhg Mac Dairé Mac Bruaideadha (1570–1652), chief *ollamh* and poet to Donough. He wrote, addressing Donough, with what seems to be a warning to him not to betray the people of Thomond.

> *Teirce, daoirse, dith ana,*
> *Plágha, cogtha, conghala,*
> *Díombuaidh catha, gairbh-shíon, goid,*
> *Tre ain-bhfír flathafásaoid.*

Dearth, servitude, want of provisions, plagues, wars, conflicts, defeat in battle, rough weather, rapine, they arise through the falsity of a prince.

Tadhg was known for his biting verses. At the age of eighty-two, he was hurled over the cliffs to his death by English soldiers.

On 17 August 1585 the then Lord Deputy, Sir John Perrott, signed an agreement with Donough, the 4th Earl of Thomond, and Murrough, 3rd Baron Inchiquin, which agreed to divide the lands of Thomond on an English feudal model. Seventeen lesser chiefs of Thomond, four merchants with ostensibly English names, the Bishop and Dean of Killala and the Bishop Elect, Dean and Archdeacon of Kilfernora, signed their assent to this agreement. The principal clause was: 'They agree to abolish all captainships, tanistships and all elections and customary divisions of the land'.

In an effort to get everyone to agree, some chiefs were persuaded by being allowed to keep their Gaelic title for the term of their lives. For example, the agreement made by Seán MacNamara, otherwise The Mac-

Namara Fionn, allowed him to use his title for the rest of his life but stipulated that 'after the death of the said "Shane" all duties and customs as belonging to the name M'Nemarra Fynn, being but extorted, shall be extinguished'. The same condition was made for Donel Reagh MacNamara for 'after the death of the said Donnell the customs claimed as belonging to the name M'Nemarrae Reigh shall cease.'

The letters patent of 1587 are full of the names of chiefs whose titles had been abolished. A grant to William Bourke of Loughmask, Co. Mayo, says that no one can make a claim as 'MacWilliam Uachtar or tanist, which names are abolished'. This was the usual formula. A grant to Ross MacMahon stated that it 'shall not prejudice the rights of any of the Queen's subjects except any arising from the title of M'Mahowne or tanist which names are abolished'. Conal O'Molloy of King's County, former 'chief and captain of his nation', was given an estate to hold as a knight but could make no claims 'arising from the name O'Molloy and tanist which *titles* are abolished'.

The Ó Dochertaigh of Inis Eoghain, Seán, surrendered on 28 June 1587, and was knighted and allowed to hold certain lands but could no longer claim to be The Ó Dochertaigh. Some chiefs were allowed to receive fees from former clansmen but these were now called tenants. However 'these customs [are] not to be called by Irish names but to be known as the fees of the Chief Serjeant and Under Serjeant'. When Lucas Dillon was given the office of Seneschal of the barony of Kilkenny West, Co. Westmeath, it was expressly stated that 'the Irish customs taken under Irish names by the former captains [chiefs] [are] abolished.'

Even so, it was clear that many still rejected the English abolition of the titles and laws and that dynastic wars were breaking out where the *derbhfine* refused to acknowledge the authority of their chiefs and tanists to surrender.

On 20 March 1570/1 we find that 'Conley M'Goghegane [The MacGeoghegan] reputed Chief of the Name, had refused to surrender his name [title] of Magogegane or captain of that name . . . and the Queen desiring to change the name of captain to seneschal, a degree or name more usual in places of civil government' ordered that 'Conley' be removed. The title of 'seneschal of Kenalagh in Co. Meath' was then offered to the former chief's son, Ross MacGeoghegane. We can hazard a guess as to the manner in which Elizabeth's administration 'removed' The MacGeoghegan.

On 3 November 1570, 'Conwicke', The O'Farrell Buidhe of Clonconnogher, refused to surrender his title. The Lord Deputy merely ordered his 'removal' as chief. 'The Deputy, considering that the country is now shire ground, and no longer under Irish law, has resolved that the office of captain should be extinguished and that Her Majesty's laws, and the currency of her writs, shall take place as is convenient, but believes the services of some such office necessary, till the authority of a sheriff be better known'. The Lord Deputy then ordered that Tadhg Buidhe M'Hubbert O'Farrell should take the office of 'Chief Serjeant of Clonconnogher'.

We can only speculate as to what happened to these 'displaced' chiefs after their arrest by the English authorities.

Charles Blount, Lord Mountjoy (1555–1629), who became Lord Deputy in 1601, appeared somewhat bemused by the vehemence with which the Irish princely families rejected those relatives who surrendered their titles, by the way they clung to Brehon law, and by the complexity of the dynastic struggles which followed. He wrote to William Cecil, Lord Burghley, in 1603: 'Believe me out of my experience, the titles of our honours do rather weaken than strengthen them in this country.'

Quoting this letter, Constantia Maxwell sums up the situation thus:

The weakness of Henry's policy lay in the fact that by negotiating with the chieftains only, he neglected the mass of the clansmen. By tanistry, the Irish law of succession, a chieftain's authority descended not necessarily to his son, but to the strong man elected by the clan. Henry assumed that he was himself the absolute owner of all Irish lands, and acted accordingly, but the tribesmen naturally resented being deprived of their share of the tribe lands, and losing their power of election with regard to their chiefs. The English king, governed by feudal principles, confused the office of chieftain with the ownership of land, and made his bargain with individuals who were really subordinate to a system and could not bind their successors. There had always been domestic intrigues within the clans; these were now increased ten-fold by English policy. The Chiefs could not stand out against the public opinion of the clansmen, and as time went on they were literally unable to keep their agreements with the Crown. This blunder led to the breakdown of Henry VIII's policy under Elizabeth.

Indeed, within a few years, if not months in some cases, of submitting to the English administration, 'the Chiefs ... began to repent of their bargain'. Unrest and opposition were increasing. Edmund Tremayne, Clerk of the Privy Council, was sent to Ireland to make an assessment of the situation for Elizabeth I. In 1573 he reported that '[English] Law can take no place without the assistance of the sword'.[5] Tremayne's report, entitled 'Discourse whether it be better to govern Ireland after the Irish manner or reduce it to the English government', was, of course, an argument for direct rule from England. He says the role that the chiefs were now playing was intolerable and the *fons et origo malorum*.

St Leger maintained that the attitude of the Irish aristocracy to English law was:

> It is the death to all the lords and chieftains of both factions to have English government come among them, for they know that if the English government be established here, their Irish exactions is laid aground; the which to forgo, they had as lief die.[6]

The English Chief Justice of Connacht, Rokeby, writing to William Cecil in 1570, said: 'So beastly are this people, that it is not lenity that will win them . . . it must be by fire and sword, the rod of God's vengeance . . .'
Constantia Maxwell sums up:

> Gradually it was realised, however, that it was hopeless to graft feudal conceptions upon the clan system, and Elizabethan statesmen decided that war was the only satisfactory method by which peace might be obtained.

An interesting example of how the Irish kings and nobility began to oppose the 'surrender and regrant' policy took place in 1548 during the reign of Edward VI. The O'Moore of Leix and The O'Connor of Offaly had not submitted. Brían, The O'Moore, had been driven to declare that he would hear 'no more name of the King of England in Ireland than of the King of Spain'. The O'Moore and The O'Connor presented a considerable threat to the colonists in the Pale being adjacent to their now expanding territory, to the south-west. On a pretext of inviting the two chiefs to some festival, and relying on the Irish respect for the laws of hospitality to allay their fears, the newly appointed Lord Deputy, Edward Bellingham, seized them and dispatched them as prisoners to the Tower of London. Their clan lands were then declared confiscated.

From an English viewpoint this would have been good strategy had the chiefs operated under the same feudal laws as the English. However, the tanists of both chiefs pointed out that, according to Brehon law, the land did not belong to the chiefs but to the inhabitants and therefore the chiefs could not forfeit it. In the absence of the chiefs, the tanists controlled matters. Bellingham marched English troops into these territories and the people resisted. The war resulted in the near extermination of the clans and the residual population was driven from the land so that it could be settled by colonists.[7]

Yet the counties of Leix and Offaly were still not crushed ten years later. On 13 June 1558, a special commission was given to Sir Henry Radcliffe, the lieutenant of the newly named 'King and Queen's counties', to 'punish with fire and sword the Irish of the said counties otherwise called Leix and Offaly, Irre, Glinnahirry and Slemarge, Magowghegans, O'Moloyes, Ossories etc.' The clans who were to be particularly crushed were 'the O'Duns, O'Carrolls, Sinnots (alias the Foxes), O'Mollaghelins, MacOwghlans, O'Maddens, O'Kellies, O'Kennedies and O'Maughers [O'Moores]'.

Even then we find the remnants of the O'Moore clan led by Ruaidri Óg (Young Rory) and his son Eoghan (Owny) fighting in alliance with Fiach MacHugh of the O'Byrnes in 1572. Both Ruaidri Óg and Eoghan were killed at that time. Eoghan had instructed that if he were killed in battle, his head should be cut off and buried in a certain spot so that it should not fall into the hands of the English. Here we have an echo of the ancient Celtic belief that the soul dwelt in the head, which is why the ancient Celts venerated the head. They collected the heads of those they had admired and respected who had fallen in battle, even if they were their enemies, and took them to sacred spots, to sanctuaries, or consigned them as votive offerings to sacred rivers.

After the defeat at Kinsale and the arrival of James VI of Scotland on the throne of England as James I, it was reported that in the area there 'was not a Moore or a Connor to be heard of' and 'the Byrnes, the O'Tooles, the Kavanaghs, and all the rest continued good subjects'.

Perhaps one of the most heart-rending stories of the conquest came from the kingdom of Desmond. One of the Eóghanacht nobles, Ó Suile-abháin Beare, head of a cadet branch of Ó Súileabháin Mór of Kenmare, had fought at Kinsale. He was Donal Cam, known to the English as The O'Sullivan Beare (1560–1618). In the wake of the defeat, Donal Cam heard that Sir George Carew, appointed Lord President of Munster (later created Earl of Totnes), was about to attack the O'Sullivan heartland on the Beara peninsula. Donal Cam had several castles there including Dunboy Castle. After Kinsale, he gathered many survivors of the battle and set out for home. He was joined by Donal MacCarthy, illegitimate son of King Donal IX, recently dead, and therefore a claimant to the title MacCarthy Mór. Another chief who joined Donal Cam was The O'Connor Kerry.

O'Sullivan Beare and several of his men left Dunboy and went to Ardea Castle, on the other side of the peninsula, to meet a Spanish ship which was landing arms. Richard MacGeoghegan was appointed constable of the Dunboy in the chief's absence.

The Earl of Thomond, now fighting for the English, was asked to reconnoitre the Beara peninsula. He did so, ravaging and burning O'Sullivan Beare territory. On 1 June 1602, Thomond invested Dunboy and called on MacGeoghegan to surrender. He refused. A few days later Carew arrived and took command. He had brought up artillery and began to bombard the castle with its few hundred defenders. Watching the collapse of Dunboy's defences was Thomas Stafford, who wrote *Pacata Hibernia*. He described the massacre that took place. Once a breach had been made, Captain Doddington and Lieutenant Kirton led their men into the castle. Their orders appeared to be 'no quarter' and neither did they give any. Forty Irishmen, realising resistance was useless and unable to surrender, managed to break away from the fighting and threw themselves into the sea, hoping to swim away to safety. Carew commanded his boats to row after them and each one of them were killed, clubbed, stabbed or shot, while in the water. At the end of the fighting there were only seventy-five survivors crowded into a cellar of the castle, who offered to surrender. This was refused and, as dusk was falling, a guard was placed to prevent their escape. In the morning twenty-six men were allowed out. At first Carew ordered his cannons to fire into the cellar to bury the others under fallen masonry. Then he changed his mind and allowed the surrender. MacGeoghegan, mortally wounded, was stabbed to death. The survivors were then handed to the Earl of Thomond who, perhaps as a means of demonstrating his loyalty to his still suspicious English overlords, hanged fifty-eight of them in pairs in the English camp.

The massacre of Dunboy put cold determination into O'Sullivan Beare and he organised his forces into 'flying columns', not unlike Tom Barry's Cork No. 3 Brigade which was to fight in almost the same area during the War of Independence in 1919–21. O'Sullivan Beare held out for six months on the Beara. It was no mean feat. Munster was already a near desert. In 1583, after the earlier campaigns, the English had confiscated 574,628 acres, driven off the Irish and placed English settlers on the land. Ten further years of warfare had not improved the situation. O'Sullivan's people were suffering. The villages were burnt, the people were butchered. There were no supplies either of food or of armaments. Time was not on O'Sullivan Beare's side. News came that a considerable English force commanded by Sir Charles Wilmot (later Viscount Wilmot of Athlone) was marching against his territory. O'Sullivan Beare sent his young son to safety in Spain and with him went a twelve-year-old cousin, Philip O'Sullivan, who was to grow to manhood as a soldier and sailor and turn into a foremost Irish historian. His *Historia Catholicae Iverniae Compendium*, published in Lisbon in 1621, was a detailed history of the Elizabethan conquest told from an Irish viewpoint. He died in Spain *c.* 1660.

It was then that O'Sullivan Beare called upon the surviving members of his household and told them of the approach of the English army. They would be shown little mercy. Their only hope, he told them, was to march north, to seek refuge and protection with Brian O'Ruairc, Prince of Breifne, who was still holding out. It was a distance of two hundred miles through now hostile territory and at the height of winter. On 31 December 1602 he gathered a thousand of his people at Glengarriff on the north side of Bantry Bay. They were mostly old men, women and children, protected by four hundred soldiers of whom only thirteen had horses. Other groups, under other commanders, were to leave later. O'Sullivan Beare and his followers set out from Glengarriff through the winter mountains carrying all the food they had – enough for one day's rations each. The atrocious winter weather, the hardship of the march and attacks from English skirmishers resulted in terrible losses.

On 14 January 1603, the survivors arrived at the Leitrim Castle of O'Ruairc, Prince of Breifne. There were thirty-five, including sixteen soldiers. Among the surviving civilians were Dermot O'Sullivan and his wife, the father and mother of young Philip, who was then in safety in Spain. The O'Connor Kerry, and other leaders, bringing three hundred more survivors, arrived later. The O'Ruairc gave them what hospitality he could until a ship could be found to take the non-combatants as refugees to Spain. O'Sullivan Beare was anxious for revenge and decided to stay, joining Prince Brian Maguire of Fermanagh in fighting during what proved to be the final days of the war.

Donal Cam, The O'Sullivan Beare, was to die in exile in Spain in 1618. The Spanish king bestowed the title Conde de Berehaven on him and, like many other Irish nobles who had to flee into exile, he was warmly welcomed there. As late as 1792 the Spanish Council of State acknowledged that 'by the mere fact of settling in Spain, the Irish are accounted Spaniards and enjoy the same rights.'

Even after the defeat at Kinsale, the submission and eventual flight of the leading nobility, such as O'Neill, O'Donel and Maguire, there was still a stubborn refusal to abandon Irish law. Sir John Davies, writing to the Earl of Salisbury from Dublin on 8 November 1610, reported that he had accompanied the Lord Deputy and Commissioners to Co. Cavan to start the Plantation of Ulster. A total of 3,785,057 acres were about to be confiscated in Ulster and made ready to receive the new colonists. First the natives had to be removed. The leading Irish, who had survived the wars, were summoned to hear the proclamation which was to order them off their lands. Sir John Davies says:

When the proclamation was published touching their removal (which was done in the public session-house, the Lord Deputy and Commissioners being present), a lawyer of the Pale retained by them did endeavour to maintain that they had estates of inheritances in their possession which their Chief Lords could not forfeit . . .

Davies says that it had to be made clear 'whether the case be ruled by our law of England which is in force, or by their own Brehon Law, which is abolished and adjudged no law, but a lewd custom.'

. . . those lands in the county of Cavan, which as O'Reilly's country, are all holden of the King; and because the captainship or chiefry of O'Reilly is abolished by Act of Parliament by Statute second of Elizabeth, and also because two of the chief lords elected by the country have been lately slain in rebellion, which is an attainder in law, these lands are holden immediately of His Majesty.

'This estate of the chieftain or tanist hath been lately adjudged no estate in law . . .' he emphasises, and he goes on, showing his lack of understanding of Brehon law, to argue that even under Brehon law, James I had supreme rights over the people and the clan lands:

For he that was O'Reilly or chieftain of the country, had power to cut upon all the inhabitants, high or low, as pleased him; which argues they held their lands of the chief lord in the villeinage, and therefore they are properly called natives; for *nativus* in our old register of writs doth signify a villein . . . Thus, then, it appears that, as well by the Irish custom as the law of England, His Majesty may, at his pleasure, seize these lands and dispose thereof.

The term 'cutting' is an English form of the Norman *tallage* – probably deriving from *tal*, a yielding of cows – which was a tax on tenants towards public expenses. Sir John might have known his common law but his knowledge of the Brehon system of land tenure was abysmal.

Hogan, who is admittedly no admirer of Brehon law, sums up the situation:

This [Brehon] law of sovereignty, distinct from anything known to Roman or Feudal Europe, remained a living reality down to the end of the native order. As we have already remarked, the sixteenth century witnesses a revival of traditional sentiment and ideas in Ulster, and in general, under the pressure of Tudor England, Gaelic Ireland revealed itself to be traditionalists to the core. The Gaelic intellectuals, poets, historians, and jurists, equally with the ruling aristocracy, continued to live in the past, and to insist on development along lines entirely congenial to the native genius.

5

'Extinct For Ever'?

By the beginning of the reign of James I of England, according to the conquerors of Ireland and the law system they had imposed, all Gaelic titles had, in the words of the Act of 1587, been deemed to 'henceforth cease, end, determine and be utterly abolished and extinct for ever'. As a corollary to this, all Brehon law was abolished in the wake of the English victory over the Irish at Kinsale. But the enforcement of the new English system did not happen all at once and many parts of Ireland clung to their own law system during the following century. The difficulties of enforcing English law may be seen from the number of times that the English administration had to repeat their claim that Brehon law was abolished.

The King's Bench issued a decision in 1608, endorsing a judgement given earlier which had announced the abolition of Brehon law and the enforcement of English common law. This followed 'A Royal Proclamation' made to that effect in 1605 reiterating that Gaelic titles were to be surrendered as well as estates; regrants of the estates under English law would be accompanied, where warranted, by the bestowal of English titles. There is evidence that many Irish aristocrats came forward expecting to receive incontestable titles, but a grant of a title was made conditional on their giving up the clan relationship and chiefdom in favour of being a mere landlord in English feudal terms and many of their former clansmen becoming their tenants.

The proclamation in question had been issued in Ireland on behalf of James I by the Lord Deputy, Sir Arthur Chichester. One of its main aims was apparently to isolate the remaining chiefs from their people by prohibiting the people from obeying them. It declared that 'tenants or inhabitants ... are not to be reputed or called the natives or natural followers of any other lord or chieftain whatsoever, and that they and every of them ought to depend wholly and immediately upon His Majesty, who is both able and willing to protect them, and not upon any other inferior lord or lords . . .'

By way of further reinforcing the policy, the first 'Irish' parliament to meet in twenty-seven years assembled in 1613, and a bill was passed whereby the Irish were put under the jurisdiction of English law. Those members of the Irish aristocracy who had not formally surrendered or acknowledged the ending of the chiefdoms and clan systems were to be forcibly removed. In that single year, seven clans from Leix were forcibly removed to Co. Kerry and dispersed together with twenty-five petty chiefs, mostly from the O'Farrells of Co. Longford and the O'Byrnes of Wicklow. Their lands were then confiscated and given to colonists.

John P. Prendergast, an eminent lawyer and historian, sums up James I's continuation of the Tudor policies against the Irish aristocracy.[1]

The Irish gentlemen who did not forfeit their estates received proportions (intended to be three-fourths of their former lands, but often only one-half or one-third, as the English 'were their own carvers'), as immediate tenants of the king. Their lands were liable to forfeiture if the Chief took from any of his former clansmen any of his ancient customary exactions or victuals; if he went coshering on them as of old; if he used gavelkind, *or took the name of the great O, whether O'Neill, or O'Donnell, O'Carroll or O'Connor.*

Coshering, an Anglicised word deriving from the Irish *cos*, a foot, meant an act of wandering. In this instance it referred to a chief making a tour of his territory. Under Brehon law, hospitality had to be provided by those with whom he stayed. However, there seemed a change in meaning, probably due to the unsettled times when many members of the Gaelic aristocracy were 'on the run'. An Act for the Suppressing of Cosherers and Idle Wanderers describes cosherers thus:

Many young gentlemen of this kingdom that have little or nothing to live on of their own, and will not apply themselves to labour or other honest industrious courses to support themselves, but do live idly and inordinately, coshering upon the country and pressing themselves, their followers, their horses, and their grey-hounds upon the poor inhabitants sometimes exacting money . . .

The term gavelkind comes from the Irish *gabáil cenél* meaning 'maintaining the tribe'.

Prendergast continues:

On his death, his youthful heir was made ward to a Protestant, to be brought up in Trinity College, Dublin, from his twelfth to his eighteenth year in English habits and religion – often after his enforced conformity, all the more embittered, like Sir Phelim O'Neill, against English religion. The wandering *creaghts* were not to become his tenants at fixed money rents. He covenanted that they should build and dwell in villages and live on allotted portions of land 'to keep them as grievous as to be made bond slaves'. Unable to keep their cattle on the small portions of land assigned to them, instead of ranging at large, they sold away both corn and cattle. Unused to money rents, though of victuals they formerly made small account because of their plenty, they were unable to pay rents; and their lords finding it impossible to exact them fled to Spain. Similar Plantations followed in Leitrim, Longford, King's County and Wexford, except that in some (as in Leitrim) one-half of the lands of the Irish were seized.

The term *creaght* is an Anglicisation of the Irish *caoraidheacht*, meaning an act of wandering and later a foray or raiding party in search of cattle; it also meant a cattle herd and herdsman, like the cattle drovers of the American West in the nineteenth century, who herded their cattle in search of good pasture, living and sleeping as itinerants.

A penal code against the Catholic Irish had been emerging since the reign of Elizabeth I. Sons of Gaelic aristocrats and gentlemen were taken as 'wards of court' and sent to be educated in England, in the English language, attitudes and law as well as in the Protestant religion. The purpose was, of course, to eradicate Irish culture and the Catholic religion. However, in 1625 it was decreed that landowners of sizable estates could take an oath of civil allegiance as opposed to the oath of supremacy, which had previously recognised the English Crown as Head of the Church. At the same time the English Crown set up a commission to examine what were called 'defective titles' to estates. Landowners were only allowed to retain land if they could prove it had been held in their family by primogeniture for over sixty years, that is from the time of the original 'surrender and regrant' of 1541. This, of course, led to many confiscations of estates for such proof was almost impossible.

In 1634 a Statute of Wills and Uses confirmed that the Crown could intervene in the education of any Irish gentleman's 'heir apparent' and that they should be forcibly sent to be educated in the Protestant faith, English law and custom. Lord Deputy Thomas Wentworth, as early as 1635, was drawing up a new scheme to drive all 'chiefs' still clinging to the clan system out of Connacht and resettle the clan lands with new English colonists. This implies that some Connacht chiefs had survived the initial attempt to eradicate them and were cleaving to the native system.

In 1641 the Irish uprising began in the north and spread quickly throughout Ireland. One of the pertinent aspects of this uprising was that the main Irish forces were coming from the clan structures and these clans were still led by their chiefs. For example, in October 1641 the chiefs of the O'Rourkes in Leitrim, the O'Farrells in Longford, the O'Byrnes and O'Tooles of Wicklow and the Kavanaghs of Wexford, who one would have thought had disappeared before this time, were leading their peoples as their forefathers had done. The principal leader of the uprising was Sir Phelim O'Neill, later to be joined and superseded by his kinsman, Eoghan Ruadh O'Neill, the nephew of Aodh, The O'Neill Mór. Eoghan Ruadh, a general in Spanish service, was regarded by many Irish not only as a candidate for the throne of Ulster but as one who could reinstate the High Kingship. His initial victories ended with his premature death at Cloughoughter Castle, Co. Cavan.

There is a poignant illustration of the survival of the Brehon law of succession during the reign of Charles II. There were two rivals for the lands given to the head of the O'Rourke family, which in O'Rourke eyes meant that there were two rivals for the title Ó Ruairc of Breifne. Eoghan Óg, son of Eoghan Mór of Dromahair, was one claimant and the other was Aodh of Kilnagen, the tenant. Charles II had actually given the lands to Father Patrick Maginn, chaplain to his Queen. In 1662 Eoghan Óg petitioned Charles II, who sent an emissary, Captain Owen Lloyd, to Jamestown, Co. Leitrim to inquire into his claim – not, of course, into the chiefship as it did not exist in English eyes. When Father Patrick Maginn heard this, his 'honour of conscience urged him' to write to the *ollamhain* of Connacht to ask who was the rightful chief of the O'Rourkes and, thereby, who should have the land in question. The reply was signed by the *ollamhain* of Connacht – the Uí Mhaoil Chonaire, the Uí Dhuibhgeanain and the Uí Chuirnín. They were unanimous that Eoghan Óg, son of Eoghan Mór, was without question The Ó Ruairc of Breifne. Father Patrick cleared his conscience by authorising Eoghan Óg to collect a substantial sum of rent from Aodh as his tenant.

Through the seventeenth century, some Gaelic titles survived as well as the Brehon laws governing them. Some holders of titles did surrender when faced with no other choice; others, like Aodh (Hugh) O'Neill, 'Earl of Tyrone', resumed the style 'The O'Neill, Prince of Ulster' as soon as he sought political refuge abroad. He was buried under that title in Rome in 1616, where his tomb may still be seen in San Pietro in Montorio, in the Via Garibaldi. As a legal point, it could be argued that O'Neill never accepted that the surrender of his title while under duress was binding.

Two major and decisive blows were given to the remnants of the Gaelic aristocracy following the 1641 uprising. Oliver Cromwell's military campaigns of 1649–50 left an estimated one-third of the total Irish population dead from devastation or disease. Following this, the English administration began to enact policies that were designed to eradicate the Irish nation by ordering them, first, into a 'reservation' west of the River Shannon, into the province of Connacht and Co. Clare. The towns and rich lands in those areas were to be used as English military garrison lands. Any Irish person found on the east bank of the River Shannon after 1 May 1654 could be executed on the spot. Many were. Some 7,708,238 statute acres were confiscated. An estimated hundred thousand Irish men, women and children were seized from their villages between 1654 and 1660 and shipped off to the New World colonies, mainly Barbados, to serve as 'indentured labourers' who, because they were provided to the plantation owners free by the government, were usually treated in worse fashion than the African slaves, whom they had to buy. A further forty thousand, mostly the former members of the Irish army and many of the Gaelic aristocrats, fled to Europe where they were welcomed at the courts, and into the armies, of France, Spain and Austria.

The restoration of Charles II allowed for some alleviation to the situation although his administration's land settlement of 1662, with the court of claims of 1663, did little to put the Irish back in control of all the property they had held before the Cromwellian conquest. It was still, of course, against the law to use Gaelic titles although many members of the Gaelic aristocracy did re-emerge in this period and several sat in James II's Dublin parliament of 1689.

The Williamite conquest continued to crush the old system even further, if further it could be crushed. James II had been no friend to Ireland and was committed to maintaining English imperial rule. One of the essential planks of that rule was the land settlement, confiscations of rich farming land from the native Irish and its redistribution to the colonists. However, as James began to fight for his own power base and was driven out of England, he conceded certain rights to his 'Kingdom of Ireland'. His colonial Irish parliament repealed Poynings' Law and declared themselves independent from England. One has to remember that this parliament was predominantly an Anglo-Irish one with only a small section of the wealthier natives who could speak English being allowed to sit in it. Acts were passed which made all religions equal under the law. But the primary desire of the parliament was to repeal the Cromwellian land settlement. When this matter came up, James threatened to dissolve the parliament. But with his son-in-law, William, Prince of Orange, about to land in Ireland with an army, James gave his reluctant assent to the bill, which stated that the landowners of 1641 and their heirs could recover their confiscated property and declared the Cromwellian and later Acts of Settlement invalid.

The Irish gave their full support to James II. He was in alliance with Louis XIV of France, who was using James in his greater European plan. To counteract Louis's ambitions in Europe, a Grand Alliance had been set up at Augsburg in which William of Orange was a principal member. So also was Pope Innocent XI. It has become one of the later ironies of Irish history that the army of William of Orange, in their conquest of Ireland, was supported by Pope Innocent. There were Catholics in William's army just as there were Protestants in James II's army. Since the nineteenth century, Ulster Unionists have been fed the myth that William 'overthrew the pope and popery' at the battle of the Boyne in 1690.

The Boyne, in military terms, was not even a decisive battle. It was a year later, on 12 July 1691, that the defeat at Aughrim sealed the future of Ireland. Some seven thousand Irish and their allies were killed with four hundred officers, most of them the scions of the old Gaelic nobility and the Gaelicised old Anglo-Irish families. Colonel Charles O'Kelly, himself of an old chiefly family, observed that on that day the Irish lost 'the flower of their army and nation'.

The Irish fell back on Limerick and eventually negotiations opened. By 3 October a treaty was signed. A principal point of this treaty was that religious toleration was guaranteed. Those Irish who wanted to return home could do so unmolested and not all the Irish who had supported James II would have their estates confiscated. Those Irish soldiers who did not want to remain under the new regime would be allowed to leave for Europe. Some twelve thousand immediately did so and formed the famous Irish Brigade of the French army, created by Justin MacCarthy, Viscount Mountcashel, who was to be created Duc de Clancarthy and Baron Blarney, and whose heirs became the head of the MacCarthy dynasty in exile in France. Another Irish Brigade was formed in Spain in 1709.

Once the remnants of the Irish army were safely out of Ireland, the Williamite administration failed to ratify the Treaty of Limerick. Some 1.5 million statute acres were confiscated for a new colonisation scheme. The Act of James II's Dublin parliament which declared that all religions should be equal under the law was abolished. There would be no religious tolerance and only the established Church of England was recognised. A series of Penal Laws against Catholics and all Dissenting Protestant sects began to be enacted. Intermarriage between people of different religions was forbidden. Presbyterian ministers were liable to three months in jail for delivering a sermon, a fine of £100 for celebrating the Lord's Supper and so forth. If a couple had been found to have been married by a Presbyterian minister, they were dragged into an Anglican church and denounced as guilty of the sin of fornication.

All Irish Catholics were immediately banned from owning property above a few pounds sterling in value. They were forbidden from practising in any profession – they could not become doctors or lawyers, hold office in the army, navy, customs and excise or municipal employment. Presbyterian and other Dissenting Protestants were excluded in the same manner. In 1715 a further Act made it an offence for Presbyterian ministers even to teach children and this was punishable by three months' imprisonment. The 'religious liberty' won by William of Orange, which the Ulster Orange Order celebrate by their marches today, actually caused 250,000 Protestant Ulstermen to emigrate to the colonies of America between 1717 and 1776 alone in order to find religious freedom. There they became prominent in the American War of Independence and adherents of republicanism, which they transmitted to Ireland. In the republican uprising of 1798, in Co. Antrim alone some thirty-six Presbyterian ministers were named as local leaders of the United Irishmen movement, of whom five were executed by hanging, five were transported for life, ten received terms of imprisonment, nine were forcibly exiled, four escaped into voluntary exile and three were acquitted on guarantees of future good behaviour. The modern perspective dates from after 1834 when Ulster Presbyterians were allowed to join the élite Anglican Orange Order and soon took it over.

The betrayal by the Williamite administration of the provisions of the Treaty of Limerick, especially the breaking of the guarantee of religious freedom for all denominations, was a further scar on the Irish psyche. In 1745 when the Irish Brigade of the French army played a key role in the defeat of the English at Fontenoy, they charged the English lines with the battle-cry: 'Cuimnighidh ar Luimneach agus ar fhéile na Sasanaigh!' (Remember Limerick and the English treachery!)

So, in the eighteenth century, Ireland had sunk into the darkness of the Penal Laws under which some 85 per cent of the people of Ireland simply did not exist so far as civil rights were concerned. Only Anglicans were allowed full rights and could own land and pursue the professions.

Of the sixty kings and aristocrats listed by the English administration in 1534, a mere handful had survived the turmoil of continuing conquests and devastations. A few of these chiefly families went 'underground' in Ireland, while others, the most notable members of royal dynasties, had been forced into exile. With the start of the Penal Law period we can say that the conquests had finally brought about the general destruction of the Brehon law and Irish social system. The Irish language had been reduced to the language of the peasantry and working classes. A poignant example of the language shift is demonstrated in the *Reminiscences* of Michael Kelly, the Dublin-born singer and composer (1764–1826). Kelly, who became a friend of Mozart, sang the roles of Don Curzio and Don Basilio in the first performance of *The Marriage of Figaro*. He was singing before the Holy Roman Emperor, Franz I and after the performance he was presented to the emperor. The emperor, learning he was Irish, told him that there were a number of his compatriots at the court. He turned and introduced several titled Irishmen. Kelly does not identify them all but among them might have been Austria's Finance Minister, Count Joseph O'Donnell, and his son Field Marshal Maurice O'Donnell, married to Princess Christine of Belgium. They addressed Kelly in Irish. Kelly did not speak Irish, and the emperor remarked upon this fact with curiosity. Kelly, unthinkingly, told the emperor that 'only Irish peasants' spoke the language. The titled Irish exiles pretended not to hear him. In his *Reminiscences*, Kelly had the grace to reflect: 'I could have bitten out my tongue.'

The chiefly families in Europe, usually given recognition by the monarchs of those countries in which they settled, and bestowed with titles, often found it easier to maintain their genealogies and Gaelic titles than those left behind in Ireland.

An example of the continuance of active tanistry was a gathering of the *derbhfine* of The MacCarthy Mór held in Nantes in 1905. Pol, 7th Duc de Clancarty-Blarney, whose line had held the title MacCarthy Mór with opposition (*an fresabracht*), summoned the *derbfhine* of his house. They were the heads of the leading branches of the family. This was a 'kin-summoning' (*cenél thogairm*) which is well known in Brehon law by which the attending *derbhfine* confirms the tanist or heir to the title holder. The heads of the family were, in addition to the Duc de Clancarty-Blarney, Comte MacCarthy Reagh de Toulouse, Comte MacCarthy de la Marlière and Thomas Donal MacCarthy, Lord of Kerslawny. The Duc announced his abdication of the title The MacCarthy Mór and recognised the right of Thomas Donal MacCarthy, Lord of Kerslawny, to the title. He was duly invested as The MacCarthy Mór, Prince of Desmond, with the old Desmond royal regalia which had been rescued and taken into exile following the conquests. Some of this regalia – St Patrick's crown, King Cormac's ring, the *Généalogie*, portraits and many other items – is now in the personal possession of the current MacCarthy Mór, who has loaned the items to the Cashel Heritage Centre.

In Ireland it became the practice of many families, in order to keep some house or small estate within the family, to designate one of their number to 'convert' to the Anglican faith. Only an Anglican could own land. Through this means a family could keep security of tenure. Of course, not all families were so united; often a son, brother, uncle or cousin would convert and then denounce their family to get total possession of the property.

Some chiefly houses had, of course, converted wholeheartedly, the O'Briens, the O'Donovans and the O'Morchoes among them. Many merely followed the nomination scheme. Others existed as 'non-persons' under the Penal Laws, their identity known only to the local population. Now and again, they might emerge into record as when the English traveller, Arthur Young, made his tour of Ireland and discovered two noble families.

> At Clonells [Clonalis], near Castlerea, lives O'Connor, the direct descent of Roderick O'Connor, who was King of Connaught six or seven hundred years ago. The common people pay him the greatest respect and send him presents of cattle etc., upon various occasions. They consider him as the prince of a people involved in one common ruin.

After the relaxation of the Penal Laws, perhaps in the mistaken belief that it was only the Penal Laws which proscribed the use of Gaelic titles, The O'Conor Don began to use his title publicly and several O'Conor Dons stood successfully for parliament during the nineteenth century.

Arthur Young noted the survival of another Gaelic prince.

> Another great family in Connaught is MacDermot, who calls himself Prince of Coolavin. He lives at Coolavin in Sligo, and though he has not above one hundred pounds a year, will not admit his children to sit down in his presence.

The titles, therefore, were passed down in a surreptitious manner within the family during this period so that the state could not interfere. But, of course, these families were known and paid tacit deference by the local people who had been their former clansmen. So an 'underground aristocracy' was managing to survive in Ireland in addition to those exiled in Europe. Outwardly, such people were known simply as Connor or MacDermot, but it seemed that the old chiefs were still acknowledged when it was safe to do so.

The O'Connells, once hereditary Constables of Ballycarbery Castle, a principal residence of The MacCarthy Mór, Kings of Desmond, and afterwards petty chieftains settled at Derrynane, who, as Daniel Corkery pointed out, omitted the 'O' from their name unless in Europe, were still able to assert a chiefly authority in the area. Denis Gwynn gives an interesting example of this.[2] The family kept a crooked knife, said to be an old pruning knife, which was of no value, except that it had been handed down from one chieftain to another as a symbol of their authority. When Captain Whitwell Butler, a revenue collector of West Kerry, went to Derrynane to see Muiris-an-Cipín (Maurice 'Hunting Cap' O'Connell, 1727–1825) on business in 1782, he needed safe conduct to get out of the area. Captain Butler was hated for his exactions from the local people.

Muiris handed the knife to his nephew, an O'Sullivan of Couliagh, and told him to escort Captain Butler and his men out of the area. 'Angry faces met them as they walked out through the little village of Caherdaniel at the back of Derrynane, but young O'Sullivan let them see the crooked knife, and the crowd melted away.' As Daniel Corkery confirms: 'So long as any of the O'Connells, the chief's nephew, or his most abject menial, bearing the crooked knife, accompanied the Captain there was no fear of his being molested; and, as a matter of history, he was not set upon and beaten until he had himself persuaded the knife-bearer to leave him and return home.'

By the beginning of the eighteenth century, the aristocratic and intellectual classes of Ireland had been smashed, destroyed or driven into exile. The seventeenth century had seen the completion of what had been described so vividly by Fearflatha Ó Gnímh (c. 1540–1640), bard to The O'Neills of Clanaboy. He begins with a caution:

> *Nil eigeann eagla an ghallsmmaicht*
> *damh a hanstaid do do nochtadh:*
> *atá an chríoch réidhse rí Néill*
> *do chrú fíréin dá folcadh.*

> Fear of the foreign law does not permit me to tell
> [of Ireland's] sore plight; this smooth land of
> royal Niall is being washed with innocent blood.

Ó Gnímh goes on, however, to describe the chaos and loss.

> Ireland's learned are dead,
> Stuff of wise man and free poet,
> Successor to them isn't left
> Nor the stuff of an *ollamh*'s soul.

> At an end, all at one time,
> Ulster's schools, Leinster's learned,
> Of Munster poets not a tenth alive –
> That slaughter left no remnant.

The secular and ecclesiastical colleges of Ireland had been smashed and if any Catholic Irishman wanted to acquire an education he had to go to Europe or attend the 'hedge schools'. These schools were held in isolated spots where look-outs could be posted to alert the scholars of the approach of English soldiers. An itinerant schoolmaster, usually a man of sound and serious scholarship, would try to keep alive the fragments of an education in children – an education banned by the Penal Laws. In the shelter of hedges, in caves, and other remote locations, Irish poetry, Greek, Latin and advanced mathematics were taught. These schools continued until Catholic Emancipation in the nineteenth century.

Through the seventeenth and eighteenth centuries, books in the Irish language, grammars, dictionaries, tracts on history and philosophy, were printed in such places as Louvain, Antwerp, Paris, Rome and Lisbon and attempts were made to smuggle them back into the country. As a seventeenth-century poet, Aindrias Mac Marcais, wrote:

> *Gan gaire fa ghniomhradh leinbh*
>
> There is no laughter at children's doings,
> Music is prohibited, the Irish language is in chains.

Much knowledge was lost in this suppression, including a general knowledge of Brehon law. Without Brehons to advise them, it is no wonder that many of the 'underground' chiefly families began to forget the exact requirements of the old laws of succession. Not even Brehon law books were generally available to guide them. W.K. O'Sullivan explained:

> During the first part of the eighteenth century the possession of an Irish book made the owner a suspect person, and was often the cause of his ruin. In some parts of the country the tradition of the danger incurred by having Irish manuscripts lived down to within my own memory; and I have seen Irish manuscripts which had been buried until the writing had almost faded, and the margins rotted away, to avoid the danger their discovery would entail at the visit of the local yeomanry.[3]

But many Irish books and manuscripts did survive in spite of systematic burnings, burials and 'drownings'. Ironically, many law books lay forgotten in private collections owned by the Anglo-Irish families. Charles Graves (1812–1899), the grandfather of the famous poet Robert Graves, began a study of the Irish law system. He was a Dubliner, a graduate of Trinity College, Dublin, and a professor of mathematics who became Anglican Bishop of Limerick, Ardfert and Aghadoe. He was also an expert

on Ogham, the early Irish form of writing, and became President of the
Royal Irish Academy in 1860. In February 1852 Dr Graves petitioned
the English government to establish a commission to collect, edit and
translate the surviving Brehon law manuscripts in the cause of academic
knowledge. He was supported by James Henthorn Todd, founder of the
Irish Archaeological Society and Regius Professor of Hebrew at Trinity.
Surprisingly, but in a spirit of conciliation with the rising tide of the Irish
movement for self-government, a Royal Commission was appointed on
11 November 1852 to direct, superintend and carry into effect the tran-
scription, translation and publication of the law system as the *Ancient
Laws and Institutes of Ireland*. Six volumes were published between 1865
and 1901.

However, until then many chiefs in Ireland worked from only a faint
memory of the law which became tradition. Others merely accepted
English primogeniture.

As Ireland was allowed to pass into a more liberal age, with the Catholic
Emancipation Act of 1829 and other Reform Acts, and with a newly
enfranchised electorate moving towards demands for self-government,
those possessing the old Gaelic titles began to reassert them in public.
The O'Donoghue of the Glens (1831–91) became Member of Parliament
for Tipperary, 1857–65, and Tralee, 1865–85, and used his title in public
so that he was referred to by his title even in the English newspapers
and the *Hansard Parliamentary Report*. The O'Donovan and The O'Conor
Don also began to use their titles publicly.

Another O'Connor was using a Gaelic title even before that. This was
the colourful Roger O'Connor, from Connorville, Co. Cork (1762–
1834), who claimed to be The O'Connor Kerry. There has not been a
detailed examination of his genealogy but the claim might well have been
genuine. He was educated as an Anglican at Trinity College, Dublin,
and called to the English Bar in 1784. He joined the republican United
Irishmen and was arrested in 1797 but acquitted of sedition. Rearrested
in 1798, the year of the uprising, he was sent to Fort George in Scotland in
March 1799. In 1801 he was escorted to London but in 1803 was allowed
to return to Ireland. He rented Dangan Castle, Trim, which burnt down
soon after he had insured it for £5000. He eloped with a married lady
and, finally, in 1817, he was arrested for highway robbery, holding up
the Galway coach. His defence was that he had not wanted money but
meant simply to retrieve the love letters of his friend, Sir Francis Burdett.
He was acquitted by the jury, to the astonishment of the judge.

Even more curiously, his son, who likewise maintained his descent
'from the ancient kings of Ireland', born at Connorville, was Feargus
Edward O'Connor (1794–1855) who became the famous Chartist leader.

A graduate of Trinity College, Dublin, called to the Irish Bar, he became a Member of Parliament for Co. Cork (1832) seeking Repeal of the Union. He turned to radical agitation and settled in England, founded the weekly *The Northern Star* and helped to organise the People's Charter of the Working Men's Association. He became one of the best-known radical leaders of the nineteenth century, being elected as Member of Parliament for Nottingham.

Charles James Patrick Mahon (1800–91) claimed to be The O'Gorman Mahon. He was a barrister from Co. Clare and represented Ennis in Westminster from 1847 to 1852. A traveller and adventurer, an officer in the Tsar of Russia's bodyguard, a general in Uruguay, commander of a Chilean naval fleet against Spain and a colonel in the Brazilian army, his adventures became legend. He also fought in the Union army during the American Civil War and finally joined Napoleon III's chasseurs. A friend of Bismarck, he took up residence in Berlin. He was a noted duellist and survived thirteen encounters. He returned to Ireland in 1873 and won the Clare seat for the Westminster parliament in 1880, losing it in 1885. He then represented Carlow from 1887 to 1891.

But the emergence of those claiming Gaelic titles threw up several curious anomalies. We are told that George IV, visiting Ireland in 1821, was approached by a Colonel O'Hanlon who claimed to be The O'Hanlon and demanded the right to the office of hereditary royal standard bearer north of the Boyne.[4] It would be bizarre had George IV given any credence to this claim, based on the right of a Gaelic ancestor whose title had been abolished by English law, to carry an O'Neill royal banner.

Similarly curious was the appearance of The O'Conor Don bearing a flag dubbed 'the standard of Ireland' at the coronation of Edward VII at Westminster Abbey in 1902 and claiming to hold the right to carry it by a Gaelic title which had been abolished by English law in 1585. This was the Rt. Hon. Charles Owen O'Conor (1838–1906), who maintained he was a direct descendant of the 'last High King', Ruaidri Ua Conchobhair, and therefore 'senior chief of Ireland', claims which were total nonsense. Indeed, the carrying of this hastily devised 'standard', even though a fabrication, by O'Conor Don was seen as another sop by the English Crown to the rising tide of Irish political nationalism.

There also began to emerge a bizarre way of arbitrarily adopting Gaelic titles by deed poll. Reverend William Hanlon, the rector of Inishannon, Co. Cork, claimed to be The O'Hanlon, and so adopted it as a name by deed poll in 1907. Reverend Hanlon died in 1916, and his grave in Inishannon Old Cemetery bears the legend 'Commonly called "The O'Hanlon"'.

This example was followed by Pierce Charles Mahony (1850–1930) who became 'The O'Mahony' of Kerry by deed poll in 1912. Samuel Trant McCarthy, the High Sheriff and Deputy Lieutenant of Co. Kerry, a retired judge of the British Indian Imperial Civil Service, adopted the title MacCarthy Mór as his name by deed poll in 1921. His legal name therefore became 'Samuel Trant McCarthy MacCarthy Mór'. He justified his claim by primogeniture descent but this brought forth protests from other branches of the family. The genuine MacCarthy Mór, Thomas Donal MacCarthy, elected by the Brehon system in France in 1905, met Samuel Trant McCarthy and agreed not to take action against him on condition that he did not attempt to pass on his 'name' to a successor. This was done to protect the good name of the family. As he had no son and as it was a name adopted by deed poll only and not a genuine title, no further action was taken.

A small but growing band of those maintaining Gaelic titles were asking for some form of recognition from the English Crown. Among them was Reverend Thomas Arthur MacMorrough Murphy (1865–1921), rector of Kilkernan, Co. Dublin, and a graduate of Trinity College, Dublin. He had assumed the surname O'Morchoe by deed poll in 1895, and asserted his claim to be The O'Morchoe. In 1904 he published a booklet entitled *The Succession of the Chiefs of Ireland*.

The O'Morchoe, on a questionable basis, argued that Brehon law was merely inheritance by the eldest male heir. He says:

> Within the last two generations the representatives of the former Chiefs have reassumed the style and title of their ancestors, and courtesy recognition is accorded them, both officially and by the public. They are received at the Royal and Vice-Regal Courts by their titles, and are so described in official documents.

The O'Morchoe seems confused: at one point he says that the Gaelic titles are 'officially recognised' and that 'a certified copy of a pedigree in Ulster's Office has been issued which describes the pedigree as "establishing the right of — to be Chief of his Sept"' but on the other he is correctly stating that the English Crown does not determine the right to use the title.

> It would seem but justice that the Crown [of England] as the Fountain of Honour, and in accordance with the precedents to be now quoted, would grant a similar form of recognition in the case of the Irish Chiefs to that which is afforded to the native nobility of other countries that have come under the British Crown. To admit the titles at Court and not to determine the right to use them is unsatisfactory.

[83]

Of course, the issuing of a pedigree, certified or otherwise, by Ulster's office – the then heraldic office for all Ireland – expressing the establishment of a *right* to claim the chiefship was not a recognition of the title. There is a subtlety of language here.

The O'Morchoe gave some rather weak precedents on the use of foreign titles recognised by the English Crown. He misinterprets the law by thinking that the Act 11th of Elizabeth I merely 'reserved the rights of the Chiefs and recognised them by patents' (i.e. letters patent) whereas the Act made such titles 'utterly extinct'.

The O'Morchoe, disregarding the Irish law that no holder of a Gaelic title could surrender that title on behalf of his heirs and successors, believed that Henry VIII's Act had been willingly accepted by the Irish kings and aristocracy. 'The Act of His Majesty Henry VIII, previously referred to, merged all such independence, whether actual or implied, in such a title, in the Crown. All Ireland became a feud of the King, and then Chiefs held as feudal lords from the Crown.' That was the English intention but not, as we have demonstrated, the Irish reality.

The O'Morchoe's claim was:

> The evidence in support of a claim to represent a former recognised Chief must be a pedigree registered in Ulster's Office. Once the right to the use of the titles shall have been determined by the official act of the Crown, it becomes only a question of the proof of the claimant's pedigree that he is the lineal male representative of the last recognised Chief. To determine the right to the use of the titles rests with the Crown as the Fountain of Honour; and although the titles have been recognised by courtesy at the Royal and Viceregal Courts, yet the absence of any official act either to determine the right to their use or to accord them a definite precedence, as in the case of the Maltese Nobles, leaves the matter in an unsatisfactory state, which only the Crown can settle.

The English Crown was, in fact, irrelevant to the continued existence of Gaelic titles, and was to become even more so in the twentieth century as the Irish people began to reassert an independent state.

Perhaps one of the most famous characters in modern Irish history was a descendant of the Ó Rathaille chiefly line of Co. Kerry, Anglicised as O'Rahilly. This was the same clan as the poet Aodhagán Ó Rathaille who once wrote that his family had served the Eóghanacht kings before the Christian period. The O'Rahilly's family is sometimes mistaken as being of the Breifne O'Reillys. The family had ceased to use the 'O' during the years of suppression and lived as plain 'Reilly'. The 'O' was revived by Michael Joseph O'Rahilly (1875–1916). He was not consistent about its use until 1911 when he adopted the title The O'Rahilly. Richard Davis suggests that O'Rahilly's 'claim to his exalted title was dubious'.[5]

The O'Rahilly had joined Sinn Féin and was closely involved with the production of the journal *Sinn Féin*. From 6 May 1910 through to 1911, he was the anonymous author of a series called 'The Arms of the Clans'. Each article dealt with two clan names. That the author did not fully understand the nature of the subject is demonstrated by his assertion that the personal arms, crest and motto of the chief belonged to the clan itself and to any person bearing the name. This mistake occurs even today.

The O'Rahilly, while disagreeing with the timing of the 1916 uprising in Ireland, nevertheless fought in the insurrection and was killed at the GPO in Dublin, the insurgent headquarters during the fighting. There is still an O'Rahilly, Michael, although he is not inclined to use the title nor is he recognised by the Chief Herald of Ireland. His mother was Elgin Barry, a sister of Kevin Barry, executed by the British in 1920. Madam O'Rahilly had attempted to rescue her brother from Mountjoy Jail just before his execution but was unsuccessful. She married Richard ('Mac'), The O'Rahilly in 1935. The O'Rahilly was a barrister and he joined Nobel Laureate Seán MacBride (a former Chief of Staff of the IRA and son of the executed 1916 leader, Major John MacBride, and actress Maud Gonne) in forming Clann na Poblachta in 1946. The party joined a coalition Irish government in which MacBride was Foreign Minister from 1948 to 1951. The O'Rahilly became treasurer of the party. He later joined MacBride in forming the Irish section of Amnesty International. Madam O'Rahilly died in December 1997.

It is interesting that Arthur Griffith, founder of Sinn Féin, approved the idea of the resumption of Gaelic titles 'as part of the counter-movement aimed at de-Anglicisation'. However, it must be pointed out that Griffith was never at any time a republican. He had formed Sinn Féin in 1904 as a dual-monarchist party using the model of the Austro-Hungarian empire. It was mistakenly believed by the English government that Sinn Féin was the driving force behind the 1916 uprising. Sinn Féin, therefore, came to be perceived as a rallying symbol of the republic among the Irish. Republicans joined it and changed the idea of a dual monarchy to that of a republic in 1917. Griffith's subsequent role in the treaty negotiations accepting a Free State within the British Commonwealth begins to make more sense in the light of his ideas of dual-monarchism with England.

In December 1918 a general election was to change the face of Ireland. At the dissolution of the Westminster parliament the Irish Party, pledged to achieve 'Home Rule', held sixty-eight seats; ten were held by Independent Nationalists, seven by Sinn Féin and only eighteen by the Unionists. In the general election Sinn Féin, pledged to making a unilateral declaration of independence and asserting an Irish republic, won seventy-three seats out of the total 105. The Irish Party were reduced to six seats and the Unionists increased theirs to twenty-six, many of the extra seats being held on the split vote between Sinn Féin and the Irish Party. In accordance with their manifesto, the Sinn Féin Members of Parliament withdrew from Westminster and established an Irish parliament in Dublin, called the Dáil. They invited all Irish elected representatives to take seats in the new assembly. They then issued a Declaration of Independence on 21 January 1919.

The London government's reaction was to declare the Dáil an illegal assembly and arrest these democratically elected representatives. This led to the War of Independence. In spite of the continuance of this war and attempts by the English administration to destroy Sinn Féin's credibility with the electorate, the January 1920 municipal elections gave Sinn Féin control of seventy-two town and city councils, coalitions of Sinn Féin and the Irish Party taking joint control of a further twenty-six. Thus 98 out of 127 town and city councils recognised the Dáil as the legitimate government in Ireland.

Again, in June 1920 elections for county and rural district councils and boards of guardians saw Sinn Féin win control of twenty-eight out of the thirty-two county councils (giving republican control of five out of the nine Ulster counties); they also won 186 out of 206 rural district councils and 138 out of 154 boards of guardians.

Arbitrarily, the English government pushed through a Government of Ireland Act (1920) setting up 'Home Rule' parliaments in Dublin and Belfast, with the idea of partitioning Ulster. The problem in Ulster was that five out of the nine counties had voted overwhelmingly for the republic and only four counties were for the maintenance of union. Once more, arbitrarily, London declared a general election in May 1921 for the two parliaments, bringing in proportional representation in the hope of decreasing the support given to Sinn Féin. Even so Sinn Féin held 130 seats, the Irish Party winning six and the Unionists forty-four. Partition was thereby foisted on Ireland at gunpoint.

On 11 July 1921 in the wake of these elections negotiations between 'the Irish representatives' and the London government began. On 6 December 1921, under threat of the renewal of 'an immediate and terrible war', the Irish plenipotentiaries, without authority from the Dáil, signed the 'Articles of Agreement for a Treaty between Great Britain and Ireland'. It was placed before the Dáil as a *fait accompli*, making Ireland a Free State within the British Commonwealth but, under Clause 11, allowing the representatives of the Unionist Belfast parliament, already set up, one month from the passing of the ratification of the treaty to withdraw, if they so wished, from the Free State and rejoin the United Kingdom.

On 7 January 1922 the treaty was approved by the Dáil by sixty-four votes to fifty-seven. Some republican representatives, such as Laurence Ginnell, had been out of the country and not able to cast a vote. Of the Irish army commands, twelve were against the treaty and only seven in favour. The result was a slide into civil war which ended in 1923 after a bloody and bitter conflict.

In June 1922 a general election was held to decide the support for the treaty. Although the treaty spoke initially of a thirty-two county Free State, the territory under the control of the Belfast parliament did not take part so only 128 seats in the twenty-six counties were actually contested. Pro-treaty candidates won fifty-eight, Republicans thirty-six, Labour, Farmers and Independents thirty-four.

On 6 December 1922 the Free State came into being and on 7 December, only twenty-four hours later, the Belfast Unionist parliament petitioned King George V, under Article 11 of the treaty, to be allowed to withdraw from the Free State and rejoin the United Kingdom.

The Free State came into being inheriting the (English) statute and common law under which Ireland had been governed for three hundred years. Some voices had been raised earlier in support of reviving the spirit of Brehon law, if not its actual detail, as a means of creating an intrinsically Irish law system. The barrister Laurence Ginnell, an Irish Party Member of Parliament, and later a Sinn Féin deputy in the Dáil of 1919–21, favoured this idea. In practical terms it meant reintroducing the philosophical principles of the Brehon system.

Another legal mind who supported the idea was barrister and King's Counsel James Creed Meredith, who had been entrusted by the Irish government of 1919–21 with drafting the Constitution and Rules for the republic's law courts. Creed Meredith became President of the Irish Supreme Court. In one instance, while hearing a case, he pointed out that he considered English common law was retrograde in a matter of women's rights and applied Brehon law to give judgement in favour of the appeal of an unmarried mother for medical expenses. According to Dorothy Macardle, 'This created an interesting link with old Irish principles of justice and preserved continuity between the old Brehon Law of Ireland and the Republican courts.'[6]

However, when the Free State emerged, the inherited English law system was accepted and no further consideration was given to the matter. As the Free State moved, with the 1937 Constitution, into being a 'dictionary republic' and thence to a sovereign republic, by referendum, on 18 April 1949, the laws of the state remained unaltered. Under that law system all Gaelic titles were still 'utterly extinct'. This being so, a curious dissonance emerged between those holding Gaelic titles and the state bureaucracy.

6

'Courtesy Recognition': A Conflict of Perceptions

Following the change of status of Ireland in 1552, the English administration established an heraldic officer called the Ulster King of Arms. The first to hold this office was Bartholomew Butler, and his task was to record the titles granted or recognised by the English Crown in the new kingdom of Ireland. While it could, and did, eventually draw up genealogies for Gaelic aristocratic families, especially during the more liberal nineteenth century, it did not, nor could it in law, take cognisance of any Gaelic titles. Much depended on the individual character of the Ulster herald and how he interpreted his office. Sir Arthur Vicars, for example, was supposed to have accepted, on the genealogical certificate of O'Morchoe, that he had a *right* to claim a Gaelic title. Vicars also prepared a pedigree in 1905 for Thomas Donal XI MacCarthy Mór, Prince of Desmond, who had been recognised by his French kinsman as head of the Eóghanacht royal house of Munster.

After the Free State came into being, Ulster's office continued to operate from the Bedford Tower in Dublin Castle, fulfilling the same functions it had discharged since 1552. The Free State was, of course, part of the British Commonwealth and the head of state was still the English Crown as head of that Commonwealth. Therefore there was no inconsistency with the continued jurisdiction of the Crown's Irish herald over the whole of Ireland.

In 1940 Sir Neville Wilkinson, the Ulster King of Arms, died. Thomas Sadlier, the Deputy Ulster, continued to administer the office. De Valéra's new Constitution of 1937 had, however, removed the Crown as head of state, with its personal representative, the Governor-General, no longer a Viceroy. Under Articles 12/1 the office of President of Ireland (*Uachtarán na hÉireann*), 'who shall take precedence over all other persons

[89]

in the state', had been instituted. So far as the authority of the Ulster King of Arms is concerned, we enter a grey area. On 11 December 1936 de Valéra's External Relations Act was introduced, which delimited the functions of the Crown in the field of external relations of the Free State, but maintained the link with the British Commonwealth. This remained the position until the 1949 declaration of the republic and the repeal of the External Relations Act, at which point the Irish state was deemed to have left the Commonwealth. Did, technically, the Ulster King of Arms continue to have heraldic jurisdiction over all Ireland between 1937 and 1949 by virtue of the English Crown's position as head of the Commonwealth? It is a debatable point. Certainly, some heraldic experts have pointed out that as King George VI of England was crowned King of Ireland on 12 May 1937, and the 1937 Constitution was not enacted until 1 July 1939, coming into force from 29 December 1939, that Act could not retrospectively alter the legal authority of his herald.

Whatever the ambiguities, in 1943 the continuance of the office of the Ulster King of Arms in Dublin Castle came to the attention of Dr Richard Hayes, Director of the National Library of Ireland, and Dr Edgeworth Anthony Lysaght, who had adopted the name of Edward MacLysaght in 1920 and was on the staff of the National Library. MacLysaght was to create the new Genealogical Office. He later admitted that he was 'an amateur in genealogy and an ignoramus in heraldry'.[1]

He had been a republican in politics since his youth. When, in 1917, Lloyd George made an attempt to hustle Irish leaders into an agreement by summoning a gathering of representative Irishmen to find a basis for a settlement between Nationalists and Unionists, called the Irish Convention, MacLysaght was one of the 104 delegates who sat for the eight months. By 1943 he was very much a Fianna Fáil republican. He had been active in Sinn Féin and was imprisoned during the War of Independence by the British authorities. Because of his background he had ready access to leading members of the Fianna Fáil government party, which had broken away from Sinn Féin led by Eamon de Valéra in 1926. De Valéra was now Prime Minister. It is important to appreciate MacLysaght's background because it helps to understand his attitude which led to subsequent events. His personal contact with de Valéra resulted in the Irish government sanctioning the expropriation of the Heraldic Museum and offices of the Ulster King of Arms on 31 March 1943, and the confiscation of all manuscripts and properties connected with the office. Dr Edward MacLysaght was then appointed Chief Genealogical Officer with the remit of setting up a new office as a sub-section of the National Library of Ireland.

That this move was viewed with some concern by the English Crown's heraldic offices may be seen by the initial reluctance of the Garter King of Arms, Sir Algar Howard, to accept the validity of the new Irish office. Indeed, the office of the Ulster King of Arms was removed to the College of Arms in London, without its original records and properties, and a new Ulster King of Arms appointed. The office later combined into the Norroy and Ulster King of Arms and still exists. It continues to exercise its authority over Northern Ireland, as part of the United Kingdom territory.

There grew up a general but unsustainable myth that the Genealogical Office, and the subsequent appointment of a Chief Herald, in the person of Edward MacLysaght, was but a continuance of Ulster's office and the Ulster King of Arms. The Dublin office was, however, a new creation by the Irish state. Such a misunderstanding is perhaps explicable within the confusion caused by the creation of the new state of Ireland. A problem arises only where the Genealogical Office itself claims its authority from 1552. For example, on 25 August 1990 the Chief Herald, Donal Begley, was introduced as the 23rd 'Chief Herald' and it was stated that his office had been created in Tudor times. Neither the Chief Herald, nor Denis Lyons TD, the Minister of State for Culture and the Chief Herald's superior, attending these proceedings, felt obliged to correct this misstatement.

For those maintaining or seeking recognition for Gaelic titles, this background meant a problem was looming.

De Valéra had been aware of the survival of many of the Gaelic princely families. In preparing the 1937 Constitution he had even considered the idea of creating a 'Prince President' based on the model of Louis Philippe of France (later Napoleon III) who had abdicated to become president of the Second Republic. Emissaries had sounded out Lord Inchiquin (The O'Brien) as the direct descendant of the High King Brían Bóroimhe. Three Anglo-Irish peers were also mentioned: the 8th Viscount Powerscourt, who had been a senator in the Free State; the 8th Earl of Granard, a former Deputy Speaker of the United Kingdom House of Lords, who became a Free State senator from 1922 to 1934; and Eduard Carl Richard, 8th Count von Taafe of the Holy Roman Empire, who had returned to Ireland to live in Dublin and pursue the profession of a gemologist. The naming of these non-Gaelic peers in the matter of the presidency would indicate that de Valéra was not particularly concerned with securing a link to Gaelic Ireland. He was merely considering appointing someone from a distinguished Irish family.

In 1944 Edward MacLysaght started to consider the idea of giving 'recognition' to those with Gaelic titles. The problem, he felt, was how could these titles be recognised? That something had to be done by the new Genealogical Office was obvious. Several chiefs had been asserting their titles, listing themselves in *Thom's Directories* and in *Whitaker's*.

MacLysaght, admitting that he knew nothing of nobility law, was, however, aware that the new 1937 Constitution stated: 1. Titles of nobility shall not be conferred by the state, and 2. No titles of nobility or honour may be accepted by any citizen without the prior approval of the government.

He apparently did not realise that, if the Irish state wished to give 'courtesy recognition' to the Gaelic titles, they could simply do so under international usages then current. It was the 'Gaelic' aspect that seemed to confuse him. There was no problem about giving 'courtesy recognition' to those holding titles issued during the 'Kingdom of Ireland', 1541–1801, or its successor state, the 'United Kingdom of Great Britain and Ireland', 1801–1922. Courtesy was also paid to foreign titles, even titles of states that had ceased to exist, such as the Holy Roman Empire which Napoleon abolished in 1806. Similarly, the state did not question the right of George Noble Plunkett (1851–1948), created a Papal Count, to use his title. Why, then, was there such a problem with the Gaelic titles inherited from the old kingdoms of Ireland prior to the Tudor conquest of the country?

There can only be one answer and one which appears to be confirmed by MacLysaght's reported conversation on the matter with de Valéra. Knowledge of the subject had reached such an abysmally low level that these titles were not even considered to be titles of nobility. Three hundred years of historical propaganda had demeaned the role of the Gaelic aristocracy to the point where Charles O'Donnell, a Member of Parliament between 1906 and 1910, himself descended from the princes of Tirconnell, could say it was 'an ignorant practice' to talk of kings in Ireland. Aristocracy equalled English or Anglo-Irish aristocracy: this was all-pervasive in the Irish psyche. MacLysaght consulted de Valéra and the resultant decision, made without any reference to academic authorities, either historical or legal, remains the basis of the Genealogical Office's policy on the subject of Gaelic titles.

MacLysaght recalled:

When in 1943 the question of the recognition of Chiefs came up for consideration I – being then Chief Herald – consulted the Taoiseach, Mr de Valéra, and he agreed that the chieftainries were designations rather than titles and that consequently we (the Genealogical Office) should go ahead and, after thorough investigation, formally register any person claiming to be the Chief of his Name when the evidence was found acceptable.[2]

I am not alone in finding this passage incredible. The heraldic expert Gerard Crotty also finds it extraordinary, leaving aside the point that MacLysaght was not appointed as Chief Herald in 1943 but was then only the Genealogical Officer.[3] Crotty agrees that de Valéra and MacLysaght were avoiding confronting the reality that a Gaelic title was, in fact, a title. The attempt to find a word which would avoid this fact, and the choice of 'designation', seems less than worthy of de Valéra's reputed pedantry. Amusingly, it is merely a dictionary synonym for a title. A designation is 'a distinctive name; personal appellation, hereditary or not, denoting or implying office or nobility or distinction or merit'.

The implication of this sleight of hand is that MacLysaght must have thought that the Genealogical Office was empowered to create a 'designation' and that this was not the same thing as creating a 'title'. Yet we see an immediate contradiction in the very first list of chiefs whose 'designations' were recognised by MacLysaght. This was published in the official government publication *Éire Iris Oifigiúil* (22 December 1944). Among them is MacDermot, *Prince of Coolavin*. In recognising that Mac-Dermot was a *prince* of an Irish territory, even such a small one, the Genealogical Office, with government approval, was clearly recognising a *title* and not a 'designation' in their meaning of the word.

It is hard to accept the theory that de Valéra and MacLysaght believed that they were not recognising titles which already had an historical existence but were somehow bestowing these 'designations' guided by rules devised within the Genealogical Office. The attitude of some subsequent Chief Heralds is to hotly deny that they are making a 'creation' of any sort. Yet Donal Begley, at a public inauguration ceremony for The O'Long of Garranelong, in 1990, was quite clear what he was doing. He said: 'Accept this parchment designating you as O'Long of Garranelongy and Chief of the Name *by my office under the authority of the Government of Ireland.*' He was not thereby merely 'recognising' an already existing O'Long but creating one on the authority of the Irish government.

The action of the Chief Herald's office was not to acknowledge existing titles used in a previous Irish state but to arbitrate and designate who held the title on the basis of a primogeniture system derived from the very laws which abolished the titles and made them 'utterly extinct'. This caused immediate merriment in academic and legal circles. Edward MacLysaght admitted:

> Our action at the Genealogical Office in recognising Chiefs encountered some opposition from a few historians and Celtic scholars on the ground that to determine chieftainry by primogeniture was a departure

from the principles of the Gaelic Irish system. We argued ... that to reject primogeniture would result in taking no action at all in the matter ...

This was a curious justification for what was clearly a legally questionable and unconstitutional decision. It also demonstrated MacLysaght's lack of knowledge of the legal background to the granting of 'courtesy recognition' to titles of former states. These 'courtesy recognitions' began as an internal civil service office procedure. There was no Act of the Irish parliament nor ministerially approved written guidelines instructing the office on the methods of 'recognition'. What was happening, therefore, was that an office of the Irish government was taking upon itself the right to arbitrate retrospectively over the recognition of titles bestowed in a former state and altering the dynastic laws by which those titles were governed.

In 1998 an Italian court ruling concerning Gaelic titles, which we will deal with shortly, made the observation:

> Although it is true that the Chief Herald of Ireland has recognised several Gaelic titles ... the actual legality of such an act must in itself be highly questionable and has never been determined in any Irish court. A civil servant, irrespective of whatever titular office he may hold, is bound by the laws of his own state. As English common law has abolished Gaelic chiefly titles their very recognition by the Chief Herald of Ireland, even as a courtesy, must logically be questionable if not actually illegal under existing Irish law. Nor, as this court has previously ruled, could the mere fact that the Chief Herald grants such courtesy recognition to the bearers of Gaelic titles give him any lawful authority over them, whether to alter their original forms or nature, annul their laws of succession, or in any way to negate their hereditary rights vested therein.

This was the view of many people in the area of nobiliary studies at the time. Some holders of Gaelic titles refused to apply for 'courtesy recognition' by primogeniture when they had held their titles by tanistry. Thomas Donal, The MacCarthy Mór (1905–1947) and subsequently his son, also Thomas Donal, MacCarthy Mór (1947–1980) certainly did not recognise the validity of this 'recognition'. The current MacCarthy Mór was persuaded to apply at the direct request of the then Chief Herald, Gerard Slevin, in the early 1980s. MacCarthy Mór had succeeded when his father had formally abdicated by a document signed by the members of the *derbhfine* on 5 August 1980. He submitted himself for 'courtesy recognition' making clear that he held his title by tanistry and not primogeniture. In spite of the internal rules of the Chief Herald's office, his title was eventually given 'courtesy recognition' in 1992.

By 1944 Edward MacLysaght had decided to draw up what came to be known as *Clár na dTaoiseach*, the Register of Chiefs and Chieftains. The first announcement of the 'courtesy recognition' of chiefs was made in *Éire Iris Oifigiúil* on 22 December 1944:

For centuries and until immediately after the disbandment of the Gaelic system, the *derbhfine*, who could trace their ancestors for four generations, elected the successor of the chief.

Later, the chief was chosen from one of such a family according to seniority.

The Gaelic genealogists always accepted this latter tradition in addition to the practice of election.

With respect to the following, the Genealogical Office examined their pedigrees in accordance with primogeniture, from the last chief to be inaugurated or who had that particular distinction *de facto*, confirming his progeny. Their names are listed in this office as chiefs as well as by their family names, and their positions are acknowledged by 'courtesy recognition'. In addition to the list, the names of two chiefs are given who have a legal right to claim the title but the office has not made a confirmation of the lineage. In certain cases, not mentioned here, even though a claim of a chief is made from ancient chiefs we have no knowledge of it. In other cases even though we have knowledge of a chief, we have no claims or usage of the title at the Genealogy Office. If the list is added to from time to time, the chiefs' names will be announced in the *Iris Oifigiúil*.

The chiefs given 'courtesy recognition' were:

MacDiarmada (MacDermot, Prince of Coolavin)
MacGiolla Chuda (MacGillycuddy of the Reeks)
Ó Ceallacháin (O'Callaghan)
Ó Conchobhair Donn (O'Conor Don)
Ó Donnchadha an Ghleanna (O'Donoghue of the Glens)
Ó Donnabháin (O'Donovan)
Ó Murchadha (MacMorrough)
Ó Néill Clann Aodha Bhuidhe (O'Neill of Clanaboy)
Ó Sionnaigh (The Fox)
Ó Tuathal Fear Tire (O'Toole)

It was stated that The Ó Gráda (O'Grady) and Ó Ceallaghin (O'Kelly), 'while not representative of chieftainries in the strict sense, having long been styled under [these designations] and their pedigrees duly authenticated, are on record at the Genealogical Office.'

A slightly different English version of the announcement was given in *Thom's Directory* for 1945 and the names of O'Brien of Thomond, O'Donel of Tirconnell and O'Morchoe were then added. It was also announced that the title of MacDermot Roe was dormant. *Thom's* acknowledged that the titles had originated and passed down by Brehon law succession but went on:

> The descent of the following, by primogeniture from the last inaugurated or *de facto* chieftain, has been examined by the Genealogical Office, Dublin Castle. Subject to the possible survival in some cases of senior lines at present unidentified, they are recorded at the Genealogical Office as Chiefs of the Name and are recognised by courtesy. Certain Chiefs whose pedigrees have not been finally proved are included in this list on account of their prescriptive standing.

This was a reference to The O'Grady and O'Kelly whose names are referred to in the same manner as in the *Iris Oifigiúil*.

Immediately, another problem arose. When The O'Grady was finally fully recognised, he was designated 'The O'Grady of Kilballyowen', the territorial designation being an entirely new addition which no O'Grady had used in the past. The title had simply been 'The O'Grady'. Gerard Crotty observes: 'A number of other chiefs seem also to have acquired additional designations of this kind, through the courtesy of the Office'. MacLysaght does confess that he had reservations about the nature of the title The O'Grady for, as Gerard Crotty points out 'in creating a new designation, which after all is a title, he came perilously close to infringing Article 40 of the Constitution' which says the Irish state cannot confer titles.

The Genealogical Office decided that the Gaelic titles should be based on the Tudor English attempts to translate the Gaelic forms. 'Chief of the Name' was added. This also presented anomalies, such as the office recognising both The MacDermot, Prince of Coolavin, and The MacDermot Roe as 'Chiefs of the Name'. As Gerard Crotty pointed out in bemusement:

> Both of these belonged to the Moylurg house. Logic must surely demand that both cannot have been simultaneously Chief of the Name. While both may be described as chieftains, depending on how we

understand that term, only the Prince of Coolavin could have been chief of the whole sept: MacDermot Roe represented a minor though yet considerable branch and may best be referred to as a chieftain.

Another problem later arose over the question of heraldic territorial authority. It was argued that, having signed the Treaty of Rome which forbade member states from making territorial claims over other states, the Irish Republic should not be making claims over Northern Ireland. The Prime Minister, Bertie Ahern, was to explain that Articles 2 and 3 of the Constitution, in making such claims, were merely 'an expression of an aspiration'. In 1998 the matter was resolved when those articles were amended in accordance with an expression of the majority of Irish people's aspiration for reunification rather than stating a territorial claim. Yet the point that worried heraldic experts was that the Chief Herald's office, as a civil service department of the Irish state, was making territorial claims by exercising heraldic jurisdiction within Northern Ireland, which encroached on the judicial role of the Norroy and Ulster King of Arms. Similar concerns have been raised as to whether the office could arbitrate in the matter of titles held by citizens of other countries, such as Spain and Portugal and the United States. The United States declines to allow its citizens to bear any title.

Between 1944 and 1990 the Genealogical Office's list remained substantially unaltered although the Chief Herald, Gerard Slevin, gave 'courtesy recognition' to a new MacMorrough Kavanagh on 2 January 1959, after the Borris line had ended without male heirs in primogeniture terms. Curiously, the Genealogical Office advised no one of this recognition. The new chief's name was not inserted on the *Clár na dTaoiseach*. In fact, the Genealogical Office seemed to encourage, or at least made no attempts to deny, the idea that the line was dormant. In *Burke's Introduction to Irish Ancestry* (1976), Edward MacLysaght claimed the title had been dormant since 1958. This allowed two lobbies to emerge – one supporting the son of a daughter of the penultimate MacMorrough Kavanagh, who had died in 1953, and the other supporting an elected 'chief' of a Kavanagh clan society. In spite of the issue of the certificate of recognition in 1959, the family of the MacMorrough Kavanagh spent twenty years trying to persuade the Genealogical Office to issue correctives and place their name on the Register of Chiefs. It was only in 1998, forty years after that first 'courtesy recognition', that the office finally agreed.

In 1990 other 'courtesy recognitions' began to be made. One of the most astonishing recognitions of a 'Gaelic' title by the then Chief Herald, Donal Begley, was that of The Joyce of Joyce's Country. The name Joyce is from the Norman personal name Jois. They arrived in Connacht in the thirteenth century, became Gaelicised, intermarried and proliferated. They were considered 'degenerate English' and one of the 'Twelve Tribes of Galway'. Joyce's Country was to be found in the barony of Ross (Co. Galway). By no stretch of the imagination could a Joyce be regarded as possessed of an ancient Gaelic chiefly title.

Mr John Joyce was put in an invidious position by the Genealogical Office, in being introduced to the Irish President as a Gaelic chief, having his banner displayed along with those of other Gaelic chiefs in the Heraldic Museum, and having his name placed on the Register of Chiefs at the Genealogical Office. At a lecture given by Gerard Crotty to the Irish Congress of Genealogy in 1994, with Donal Begley in the chair, a questioner from the audience demanded to know how Mr Joyce could be recognised as a Gaelic chief. Mr Begley's ingenuous answer was, 'Because I recognised him as such.'

Adding to the embarrassing confusion of the Genealogical Office, the current Chief Herald, Brendan O'Donoghue, (in a letter to the author dated 15 April 1998 and also writing to the Standing Council of Irish Chiefs and Chieftains) stated: 'While John Joyce is accepted as head of the Joyce family, he has never been officially recognised as a Gaelic Chief of the Name.' Yet John Joyce was introduced in this manner to the Irish President while his brother Patrick was introduced by the Chief Herald as 'An Tanaiste', clearly identifying him as holding a Gaelic title.

When *Debrett's People of Today* appeared in 1992, it claimed that the Chief Herald's office had given recognition to a McDonnell of the Glens in Co. Antrim. It could be argued that Antrim, being in Northern Ireland, could only come under the Norroy and Ulster King of Arms – or even, as McDonnell of the Glens was only a cadet branch of a Scottish Gaelic clan which entered Ireland in the fifteenth century, that the correct heraldic authority would be the Lord Lyon King of Arms in Scotland. McDonnell of the Glens has never pursued an application for membership of the Standing Council of Irish Chiefs and Chieftains.

All these matters were leading to a discord between the Genealogical Office and the chiefs. The core of the problem appeared to be that, with one notable exception, none of the Chief Heralds appointed since 1943 has been qualified in heraldry, genealogy or international nobiliary law – let alone the Brehon law of dynastic succession. The problems became more marked as the holders of the Gaelic titles banded together and found a collective voice.

In June 1991 Maguire, Prince of Fermanagh, was visiting the Heraldic Museum in Dublin and saw the banners of those Gaelic title holders who had been given 'courtesy recognition'. He asked himself, 'Would it not be beneficial to our country if these Gaelic princes were to come together and form a Council?' He contacted his great-nephew, The MacCarthy Mór, who concurred. Then he wrote to each chief on the *Clár na dTaoiseach* proposing a meeting to discuss the formation of a Council.

Conor O'Brien, Prince of Thomond, replied: 'I strongly believe that we should have some say in the future of Ireland, not political but certainly cultural and economic, as we are, whether we like it or not, the representatives of the old Gaelic Order and represent a very large number of people worldwide.'

President Mary Robinson was also enthusiastic and invited the chiefs to a reception at *Aras an Uachtaráin*, the presidential residence, on the day of the inaugural meeting. The Maguire asked the Chief Herald, Donal Begley, to attend and Bord Fáilte (Irish Tourist Board) announced that they would sponsor an official lunch, while Jury's Hotel, in Dublin, offered the use of its services for the proposed council meetings in perpetuity.

On 5 October 1991, for the first time in centuries, several representatives of the Gaelic aristocracy of Ireland met together. Thirteen of those holding Gaelic titles attended with Admiral Pascual O'Dogherty representing The Ó Dochertaigh and his tanist together with John and Patrick Joyce. Also invited was Gerard Crotty, an expert on heraldic matters as well as a founder of the Heraldry Society of Ireland. He was elected Honorary Secretary to the Council, a position he held until 1995 when he became its Heraldic Adviser.

The first chairman was The Maguire, Prince of Fermanagh. Letters from the Prime Minister, Charles Haughey, and the Chief Herald greeted the establishment of the *Buanchomhairle Thaoisigh Éireann* (Standing Council of Irish Chiefs and Chieftains) as it was named. Letters of advice were offered by the Lord Lyon King of Arms, Sir Malcolm Innes, explaining how the Standing Council of Scottish Chiefs had been established.

During the debate on the draft constitution, the problem that has continued to bedevil the Irish Gaelic title holders emerged. MacCarthy Mór, who is accepted as the most academically qualified in this field among the current chiefs, having degrees in heraldry, genealogy and Irish history, pointed out that there were differences between the Irish and Scottish positions. The Lord Lyon was an officer of the Crown of Scotland, a Crown still in existence, and Scottish chiefs held their titles under that Crown. Irish chiefs, contrary to this, derived their titles from a state which had existed prior to 1541 when Henry had created his Kingdom of Ireland. Their titles were not a creation of this 'Crown of Ireland' nor were they a creation of the modern Irish state of which the Chief Herald was only a civil servant, unlike the Lord Lyon King of Arms. Any legal or judicial authority of the Chief Herald of Ireland did not apply to the Irish chiefs. Scottish chiefs were subject to the Lord Lyon King of Arms, representing his monarch. The Chief Herald's recourse to primogeniture ruling on their titles was arbitrary and without authority. It was a retrospective change of dynastic law by a successor state.

Gerard Crotty, at a meeting in July 1992, reiterated that no one could alter the mode of succession of the chiefs 'which by their nature emanated from Gaelic titles. In this connection the simple resort to primogeniture by the Office of Arms in 1943 had been most arbitrary.'

Eventually a constitution was drawn up giving the council the status of a company limited by guarantees. Its objects were:

a) to consider matters affecting Irish chiefs, chieftains and the clans they represent;
b) to submit its views and interests to government, to Departments of State, to local authorities, to press and public and to associations connected with clan and family in Ireland and overseas;
c) to educate the general public in matters connected with the rights, functions and historical position of Irish chiefs and chieftains;
d) to take such steps as may seem expedient to protect the titles, armorial bearings and other appurtenances of chiefs and chieftains from exploitation or misuse in trade or otherwise;
e) to promote and preserve the Gaelic heritage of Ireland;
f) any other objects related to the above objects.

The problem created by the Genealogical Office in 1943/44 could not simply be ignored. During a meeting in January 1993, The MacCarthy Mór again found himself pointing out that he could never accept that the Chief Herald had any judicial authority over holders of Gaelic titles. The Irish Peers Association, those holding Anglo-Irish titles, did not look to the Chief Herald as an authority on the descent of their titles, neither should holders of Gaelic titles. He believed that Council should move towards a position of taking responsibility for the recognition or non-recognition of those claiming to hold Gaelic titles under the dynastic laws which governed them. A committee to do this was eventually set up by the Council.

Unfortunately, the office of the Chief Herald simply refused to move from the procedure it had adopted based on English primogeniture law. When the Chief Herald sent a memo to the chiefs trying to exert his authority over the council, the council responded: 'The authority of the Chief Herald of Ireland, acting for and on behalf of the Irish State, is cognitive and not creative. The "act of recognition" is just that, recognition of an existing and inalienable right! Chiefs and Chieftains are not created by the Chief Herald but *recognised* by him.' While the council expressed its determination 'to give the Chief Herald every support in the proper discharge of his duties', several matters were felt to be an improper discharge of that duty.

The relationship continued to deteriorate. The National Cultural Institutions Act of 1997, which brought the Genealogical Office under the Board of the Library, even went so far as to make the remarkable claim that any coat of arms granted or confirmed by the office should be the copyright of the Board of the Library.

Another problem emerged affecting the public perception of the legitimacy of the Gaelic title holders with the formation of Clans of Ireland Ltd, which was established with offices in the Chief Herald's office. However, the current Chief Herald has asserted: 'As regards Clans of Ireland Ltd, I understand that this organisation was provided some years ago with limited office facilities at the premises occupied by the Genealogical Office in Kildare Street. The organisation no longer occupies this office accommodation. There is not, and has never been, any working or other relationship between Clans of Ireland Ltd and the Genealogical Office.' (Letter to the author, 6 March 1998.)

Clans of Ireland Ltd was formed as an independent company dedicated to assisting Irish clan societies and families to organise and hold gatherings. Government grants to help fund these clan gatherings were made available. Clans of Ireland Ltd wrote to the clan associations telling them that funds from Bord Fáilte could only be made payable to those which joined the organisation. This would appear to show that, whether or not the organisation was connected with the Genealogical Office in which it had offices, it was certainly supported by a government body.

The problem was that these clan societies, in electing their officers, were encouraged to elect a 'chief' or 'honorary chief'. This obviously led to a debasing, in the minds of the general public, of those who held a genuine Gaelic title. A 'chief' became merely someone elected at a public meeting of a clan association. The problem was explained to Clans of Ireland Ltd by both the council and individual chiefs and scholars. However, Clans of Ireland Ltd, controlled by a board of directors, have refused to acknowledge or advise its constituent clan associations that an office holder in a clan society taking on the title of 'chief' or even 'honorary chief' was insulting and denigrating to genuine Gaelic title holders. Furthermore, the title was the 'ideal property', in legal terms, of the genuine chief and his *derbhfine*. Should a clan association of, as an example, the O'Husseys meet and elect as their principal officer someone styling themselves 'Chief of the O'Husseys' when there existed a genuine chief of that name, then the elected officer could be sued in the courts to protect that 'ideal property'.

More irony followed in that Pádraig Flynn, Minister for Justice in Albert Reynolds' Fianna Fáil government in 1992, allowed himself to be elected as 'The O'Flynn' at one of the clan association rallies. One wonders how this Minister of Justice reconciled his action with the prohibition on the creation of titles?

As these problems continued, what had started out as scholastic disagreements began to take on personal aspects. As MacCarthy Mór was not only a published authority in the field but an outspoken one, he became the object of personal, as well as academic, criticism. Some voices even began to suggest that he did not have the right to use his titles.

Criticisms reached a point where MacCarthy Mór felt obliged to take out a civil action. A Professor Marco Horak had publicly repeated several assertions concerning the legal rights of MacCarthy Mór, which had emanated from sources in Ireland. As Professor Horak was a member of the Union of the Nobility of Italy, both plaintiff and defendant agreed to pursue the matter in the Italian courts. The controversy required the court to be uniquely qualified in the subjects of heraldry, genealogy and nobility law. Defendant and plaintiff agreed to a court of arbitration consisting of experts in the field and to accept its verdict as being without appeal.

The arbitration court met at Casale Monferrato. The President of the Court was Dr Roberto Messina, a holder of several nobiliary orders and author of numerous publications on heraldry, genealogy and nobiliary rights. He was assisted by two equally well-qualified judges, the Marchioness Professor Bianca Maria Rusconi and Professor Riccardo Pinotti. They began to examine the 3000 pages of documents placed in evidence before them on 2 December 1997 and eventually reached two verdicts, the first dated 27 February 1998 and the second 22 June 1998.

The judgements confirmed The MacCarthy Mór's right in international law to his title. The first declared that he bore the titles The MacCarthy Mór, Prince of Desmond, Lord of Kerslawny, Hereditary Head of the Niadh Nask, and that he legally bore the arms of the Eóghanacht royal house of Munster and had, as head of a sovereign house, the rights of *jus majestatis* and *jus honorum* which constituted the prerogative of *fons honorum*, according to the same rights that had been proved to have existed in the person of King Donal IX of Desmond.

The second verdict dealt more specifically with Dr Horak's claim that The MacCarthy Mór had no legal right to claim to be hereditary head of a nobiliary order, the Niadh Nask, whose history we shall deal with in Chapter 12. Dr Horak argued that MacCarthy Mór had no right to dispense nor bestow the order. The judges found against Dr Horak and said it had been proven that knighthood had existed as a rank in Gaelic Ireland before the advent of the Anglo-Normans in 1169 and that the Niadh Nask was a dynastic honour of non-chivalric knighthood which was recognised in international law. The judgement went on:

It must be accepted that the Chiefship of the Eóghanacht Royal House of Munster, with the title of The MacCarthy Mór, Prince of Desmond, with all the prerogatives therein lawfully vested, including the full possession of *Fons Honorum* with the absolute ownership of The Niadh Nask, or Military Order of the Golden Chain, has always descended, and continues to descend by the Laws of Tanistry as set forth in the Gaelic Law Codes known, collectively, as the *Fénechus* or *Senchus Mór*, because primogeniture was never adopted by the MacCarthy Mór Dynasty. Therefore it follows that the Republic of Ireland, accepting, in full, English common law as the basis of its Legal Code, has absolutely no jurisdiction in any matter determined by Brehon law, and, according to the accepted principles of International Law, any pretended right or juridical power asserted by it to resolve any schism arising in the Eóghanacht Royal House of MacCarthy Mór must be considered *Ultra Vires* particularly given the fact that the actual laws of succession are 'unknown to the Legal Code' of that State. Such an act of interference would be, from any perspective, unconstitutional, have nothing whatever to do with that State, and of no legal effect in International Law.

One would consider that this clear statement by the Italian courts, reflecting international law on the matter of Brehon dynastic succession of Gaelic titles, though specific to The MacCarthy Mór, would bring the controversy between the Gaelic title holders and the Chief Herald's office to a close. At the time of writing it has not. However, from January 1999, under the Treaty of Maastricht, the judgements became binding on all member states of the European Community.

The legal rulings led to a series of commentaries written by expert international legal opinion in support of the Italian judges' interpretations, including United States Federal Chief Judge, J. Michael Johnson, with Mitchell L. Lathrop and David V. Brooks. The Hon. Judge Johnson underlined the most important aspect applying to all Gaelic titles.

The court took cognizance of the fact that the Constitution of the Republic of Ireland forbids the bestowal of titles by the Government. It carefully distinguishes, however, this proscription from the transmission of existing titles by inheritance. It was specifically observed that the use of inherited titles has never been forbidden to either Irish citizens or visitors to the republic and, in fact, its constitution guarantees and protects the right of property, including that – such as hereditary titles – of an incorporeal nature. The court reasoned that it would be unconstitutional – essentially equivalent to the creation of a title – for the government of the Irish Republic to change the form of inherited titles by alteration of their historical nature, status, manner of succession, coat of arms, or their inherent quality. This view was recognised to be consistent with principles of International Law which deny any retrospective authority to successor states with regard to sovereign houses whose rule antedated their own.

Johnson re-emphasises this point:

> ... the court ... specially commented with regard to the relatively recent recognition of 'Chiefly Titles' by the Republic of Ireland, through the agency of the Chief Herald. Such 'recognition' of existing rights, it noted, confers no additional authority pursuant to International Law upon the Government of the Republic of Ireland. Hence, that Government possesses no legal authority to alter the status or the historic nature of the dynastic rights ...

David Brooks agrees:

> Whilst the Republic of Ireland may, as it has chosen to, recognise the existence of ... Gaelic titles ... by granting 'courtesy recognition' to the Chiefs thereof, it does not thereby acquire any right to alter the form, historical status or laws of descent of those Houses. This is an important point, since the law code of the Irish Republic is based upon English Common Law, which respects the principle of primogeniture, while it is evident that the Chiefship of a Gaelic House can only legally exist under the Brehon Laws and descend by tanistry.

Coincidentally, at about the same time a similar case regarding the dynastic law of a deposed royal house was being heard by the German Supreme Court. Their judgement took into account the same international law followed by the Italian judges, that a successor state could not interfere in dynastic law. The German Supreme Court, in December 1998, confirmed that dynastic laws of succession and inheritance of a noble house could not be changed. The case arose from an action of Prince Frederick William of Prussia, great-grandson of the last German

Kaiser. The prince's late father, then head of the former sovereign house of Hohenzollern of Prussia, Prince Louis Ferdinand, had disinherited his eldest son after he had contracted a morganatic marriage, in 1981, to Ehrengard von Reden. The Hohenzollern dynastic laws said that the head of the royal house of Prussia had to marry a daughter of a sovereign house. Miss von Reden did not have that qualification.

Prince Frederick William decided to pursue the matter in the German courts. Whereas two lower courts, basing their judgements on modern German law, found that Prince Frederick had every right to succeed his father like any other German citizen, the Supreme Court overturned those verdicts, pointing out that although the Hohenzollern dynasty had lost its throne in November 1918, when Kaiser Wilhelm II was forced to abdicate after Germany's defeat in World War I, the Hohenzollern dynastic laws of succession were still applicable to claims made concerning the titles and ranks within that house and the state could not retrospectively alter them. Prince Frederick William of Prussia had to give way to his nephew Prince George Frederick, who became the head of his house and pretender to the German throne.

The parallel was lost in certain quarters in Ireland.

The matter of the Brehon laws of succession was put to the current Norroy and Ulster King of Arms, Thomas Woodcock, who immediately supported the fact that only the Brehon law of dynastic succession was valid as a means of claiming a Gaelic title.

> One should not apply a common law inheritance system to a title which only existed under Irish Brehon law; if you argue that Irish Brehon law and the Gaelic titles could not be abolished by conquest, then the inheritance system under that law, i.e. the laws of tanistry, must be applied.

On 18 July 1998 the Standing Council of Chiefs and Chieftains, at their annual meeting, unanimously acknowledged that their titles stemmed from Brehon law; on 9 January 1999 they reaffirmed that fact, with the corollary that there was no legal power to retrospectively change those laws of succession. They agreed to continue to meet with the Chief Herald of Ireland in the hope of bringing the 'courtesy recognition' of the state into line with international law.

The current Chief Herald, Brendan O'Donoghue, has stated:

> When the practice of recognising Chiefs of the Name was introduced in 1944, it was made clear that recognition was based on descent by primogeniture from the last inaugurated or *de facto* chieftain. Subject

to the possible survival in some cases of senior lines then unidentified, the persons concerned were recorded at the Genealogical Office as Chiefs of the Name. There are no proposals to change the practice of the Genealogical Office in this regard.

However, he has admitted 'there is no basis for the practice in the Constitution or in statute law' and argues that 'the Genealogical Office does not grant titles' in spite of the peculiarities of the situation with regard to the Gaelic chiefly titles. 'Titles are not created and do not exist because of recognition: on the contrary recognition has been granted on the basis of evidence submitted by applicants as to their use of an existing courtesy title.' While this should be self-evident, one has to judge the statement in the context of the problems which have been created.

Disarmingly, however, the Chief Herald has made the statement, in a letter to the author of 15 April 1998: 'In so far as this Office is concerned, Chiefs of the Name are free to do what they wish in the matter of succession. Their actions are not matters to be either disputed or approved by the Genealogical Office.' This statement is hard to balance with the statement that the Genealogical Office will dispute chiefly titles handed down by tanistry – what is that but a disapproval of the dynastic laws of the chiefs? It also implies a contradiction that 'the Genealogical Office neither claims nor assumes legal authority over Gaelic titles, or any others'.

Anthony Carty, Eversheds Professor of International Law at the University of Derby, believes that a confusion has arisen in the attempts to restore Irish polity 'if not exactly as it had been, at least in a form, adapted to the present, which was, as far as possible, approximate to what had been lost.' Writing to the author on 21 July 1998, he considered that the dispute about Gaelic titles 'is a product of this confusion in the Irish imagination.' While on the one hand the civic tradition of Irish nationalism, proclaiming freedom and equality, and independence from the British state, would insist that titles of nobility could not be conferred by the state, the general rule need not exclude a constitutional amendment to admit the historical exception for the sake of ancient Gaelic titles. 'I think the appropriate solution would be to have the Irish Constitution amended to regularise the confirmation of the ancient Gaelic titles in accordance with the principles of the Brehon law. This would be consistent with the attempt to restore other aspects of Gaelic identity.'

Carty finds the 'conduct of the Chief Herald ... very unsatisfactory. I think the issues thereby raised are extremely important because they represent a fundamental confusion of legal identity of the Irish State and can only be deeply impoverishing to Irish culture. This is not an esoteric or somehow archaic matter. The enthusiasm for a common European Union identity in Ireland is not an adequate compensation, because the latter supposes, for other Europeans, that they still have to sort out the terms of their own national identity.'

The Gaelic princely families, having survived more than two thousand years in most cases and endured centuries of sustained assault to make them extinct, will doubtless continue to survive whatever the bureaucracy of the current state demands. Is there an irony in the fact that the founding fathers of the modern Irish state aspired, in the words of Pádraic Pearse, to an Ireland 'not free merely, but Gaelic as well' while the state is now trying to force the survivors of the Gaelic titled families to give up the old Gaelic laws of dynastic succession and follow English primogeniture? Carty seems correct in viewing it as a 'confusion in the Irish imagination'. As Gerard Crotty has written, the surviving Gaelic aristocratic families form one of the richest threads in the tapestry of Gaelic Ireland. It would be a myopic society indeed which would destroy such a profound cultural link with their past, a link stretching back to the primordial roots of their nation, by ignoring it or recreating it in a modern 'never-never land' setting.

PART TWO

The Families

7

The Kingdom of Munster (Desmond)

Munster is the most southerly and the south-westerly province of Ireland. Geographically, it is the largest of Ireland's four modern provinces and comprises the six counties of Cork, Kerry, Waterford, Tipperary, Limerick and Clare, a total of 9317 square miles. Before AD 1118 it was, therefore, the largest of the Irish kingdoms. The Irish name is Mumu, or in the popular genitive case Mumhain, to which the Norse added *stadr*, meaning a place, and thus the Anglicised form is Munster. Latin texts refer to it as Momonia.

Munster stands apart from the other provinces of Ireland in that in ancient mythology and legend it is considered the land of primordial beginnings. It appears as a place of origin; the place where most of the mythical invaders of Ireland landed. In Munster the occult powers were supreme for it was not only the place of origin but a place of ending, an alpha and omega of the Celtic world. Here, off the coast, was Tech Duinn, the gathering place of the dead souls where the god Donn would collect them and transport them to the Otherworld. It is not without significance that the ruling house of Munster was referred to in some texts as 'The House of Donn'. It is in Munster, in Kenmare Bay, that the sons of Míle Easpain landed. Here, Míle's son Amairgen, claimed as 'the first Druid' in Ireland, cried out his extraordinary incantations which could have come straight from the Hindu *Bhagavadgita*. Three miles from Tralee, in Co. Kerry, Scota, the wife of Míle Easpain, was killed by the Tuatha Dé Danaan and is said to be have been buried in Scota's Glen.

Indeed, it has been argued that it was in Munster that Irish literacy had its beginnings. Ogham, the earliest form of Irish writing, frequently referred to in Irish myth and sagas, is said to have been the gift of Ogma, god of eloquence and literature. The sagas refer to great libraries of Ogham books, written on bark and wands of hazel wood, in the manner of the first Chinese recorded books. The surviving Ogham inscriptions, however, are on stone. There are 369 such inscriptions, some found where Irish missionaries travelled but the bulk, of course, being in Ireland. Of these, the highest density is not only in Munster but in the extreme south-west. There are 121 surviving inscriptions in Co. Kerry alone.

The religious significance of Munster is seen in the story of its first Gaelic king Eibhear Fionn (Eber Finn). The sons of Golamh, or Míle Easpain, landed and fought their battles with the Tuatha Dé Danaan for the possession of Ireland; having achieved victory they agreed to divide the country between them. One son, Eremon, took the northern half of Ireland called Leth Cuinn. He became the progenitor of the Uí Néill. Another son, Eber Fionn, took the southern half of Ireland which was called Leth Mug Nuadat and he became progenitor of the Eóghanacht. Later Uí Néill scribes were wont to refer to the southern half as 'Leth Mug', missing off one important name, so that it could be translated as 'the slave's half'. This was part of the later propaganda war between northern and southern dynasties which denigrated the right of southern kings to the High Kingship. But the proper name was Leth Mug Nuadat, which is 'half of the slave of Nuada'. Nuada was a major god of the Celts. The word 'slave' in this context merely indicates that the early rulers of Munster thought of themselves as servants of the god in much the same way the early Christian Irish declaimed themselves as *giolla* (servant or follower) of St Patrick, St Brigit, etc., or *mael* (servant) of St Ruan, St Maedoc and so forth. It does not imply that they were literally slaves.

The size of ancient Munster and its power, not to mention its Indo-European origins, are indicated by the fact that the kingdom was divided into five 'provinces' ruled by a 'High King' who extended his rule over four lesser kings. It was the pattern that then emerged in Ireland generally.

The genealogies of the kings of Munster begin with one of the earliest *fursundud* or genealogical poems, dated by Kuno Meyer, who attributed it to Luccraid moccu Chíara, to the seventh century. Luccraid wrote it in praise of the ancestry of King Cathal Cú-cen-Máthair (d. AD 641). Most other genealogies survive from the twelfth century, tracing the descent of the kings from Eber Fionn who ruled, according to most chroniclers, in *Anno Mundi* (Year of the World) 2737. In Hebrew tradition, the year of creation corresponds to 3761 BC. However one places the dating of the Gaelic settlement in Ireland, the chronicles usually put it at the end of the second millennium. The date most often accepted is 1015 BC.

The early Christian scribes felt it incumbent on them to trace their kings back to Adam. Míle Easpain, a shared ancestor among all the Gaelic nobility, is claimed as the thirty-sixth generation in descent from Adam.

This genealogy, tacked on by Christian scribes to the traditions of oral genealogies, claims that Feinius Farsaidh, son of Baath son of Magog, at the time of the Tower of Babel, evolved the Gaelic language and people.

While O'Neill sources maintain that Eremon was the senior son of Míle, Eóghanacht sources claim it was Eber. A motto of the Ducs de Clancarthy in France proclaimed in Irish '*Sinasoir Clanna Milead*' (*sinnsear*, senior, eldest, a chief or head of a family). According to the early genealogies, the descendants of Eber Fionn shared with the descendants of Eremon the precedent of honour – the High Kingship. Between 691 BC and AD 146 some twenty-four Munster kings were also deemed as High Kings of Ireland. Only the Uí Néill and Eóghanachta lines succeeded to the High Kingship until the Christian era. Duach Donn Dalta Deagha appears in the early Christian period as the last Eóghanacht to hold the office, which he did for ten years.

From Eber Fionn, the Munster genealogies trace father to son down forty-eight generations to Eoghan Mór, from whom the Eóghanachta take their dynastic name. It is particularly significant to our discussion on the name of Eber Fionn's half of the country that Eoghan Mór was also known as Mug Nuadat. A text compiled in the thirteenth century, *Cath Maige Léna* (Battle of the Plain of Léna), gives a full account of the deeds of Eoghan. In this it is claimed that Eoghan, as a youth, helped the servant of a Munster fortress builder called Nuadhu Dearg in building a fort and thus earned his nickname this way. It is more likely that the name is linked with the pagan divinity whose epithet appears to mean 'cloud maker'.

Eoghan Mór is said to have reinforced the ancestral divisions of Ireland into two equal halves, setting the border between Átha Cliath Meadhraighe (Maaree, south-east of Galway) and Báile Átha Cliath (Dublin). He is recorded as dying in battle at Magh Léna (Moylena, just north of Tullamore, Co. Offaly) in AD 192. However, conservative scholarship accords Conall Corc, who died after AD 438, the role as the first proven historical king of Munster. He served with St Patrick on the nine-man commission to make the first known codification of the native Irish law system, and he established his capital on the Rock of Cashel, Co. Tipperary.

There were forty-nine Eóghanacht kings who reigned at Cashel between AD 438 and 963. This was the year when, after the death of Donnchadh II mac Cellacháin Chaisil, the Dál gCais of northern Munster usurped the throne by force. Mathgamain mac Cennétig, King of Thomond (Thuaidh Mumhan or North Munster) seized the Munster throne. But he was assassinated in 976 by Maelmuad mac Bríain, ruler of the Eóghanacht Rathlind, who assumed the throne until Brían Bóroimhe killed him in 978 and re-established the Dál gCais dynasty, expanding his power by military means to become High King. From then on there was a war between the Ua Bríain of Thomond and the Eóghanacht Chaisil until the Treaty of Glanmire in 1118 partitioned Munster into two kingdoms – Desmond and Thomond.

The leading branch of the Eóghanancht royal dynasty took the surname MacCarthy from Carrthach, King of the Eóghanacht Chaisil, who died in 1045. His son Muiredach became the first 'Mac Carrthach' (d. 1092) and hence MacCarthy in Anglicised form.

I

THE MACCARTHY MÓR,
Prince of Desmond, Lord of Kerslawny
(Mac Carthaigh Mór)

The current MacCarthy Mór, Prince of Desmond, is one of the most active and outspoken of the Irish princes, who runs his household in the same courtly manner as his ancestors. Having studied Irish genealogy and heraldry and obtained his degrees in these fields at an Irish university, he takes an active interest in such matters and has written and lectured extensively, serving on the International Commission for Orders of Chivalry and being honoured with numerous foreign knighthoods and orders. He represents the fifty-first generation in unbroken male line descent from King Eoghan Mór. No précis could hope to do justice to the long and fascinating history of his ancestry and the fortunes of his house.

When the Treaty of Glanmire established Desmond, the major part of Munster, as a separate kingdom from Thomond of the O'Briens, High Kingship politics played a great part. Tairrdelbach (Turlough) O'Conor of Connacht wished to claim the High Kingship for himself and his successors and that necessitated weakening the O'Briens, who had now provided three High Kings in the persons of Brían Bóroimhe (d. 1014), Tairrdelbach (d. 1086) and Muirchertach (d. 1119). When the High King Muirchertach O'Brien summoned Tairrdelbach Ua Conchobhair to help him crush the Eóghanachta in Desmond, Tairrdelbach and his men dutifully marched to join him.

Tadhg MacCarthy, the leading Eóghanacht prince, whose aim was to drive the usurping O'Briens from the Munster throne, with his army, had taken up positions at Glanmire in Cork. Muirchertach was confident of victory. *MacCarthaigh's Book* reports the event:

Turlough O'Conor, Murchad O'Mael Seachlainn and Aodh son of Donnchadh Ó Ruairc, came into the assembly of Tadhg son of Mac-Carthaigh, and made an enduring treaty with him and with Cormac (his brother) against Muirchertach, son of Toirdhealbach and Sliogh Briain (the Dál gCais). It was then that Muirchertach O'Briain was parted from the kingship of Munster and Ireland.[1]

In other words, Muirchertach's allies refused to wage war on the Eóghanachta and forced the High King to accept a treaty allowing the Eóghanachta to rule in South Munster (Desmond) while the O'Briens had to be content with North Munster (Thomond). A year later Muirchertach was dead and Tairrdelbach Ua Conchobhair was High King. No O'Brien took the High Kingship after that. The newly recognised MacCarthy kingdom of Desmond, according to *MacCarthaigh's Book*, was a continuing kingdom and its crown passed through the Eóghanacht dynasty. However, MacCarthy kings often claimed to be titular 'kings of the two Munsters' (both Desmond and Thomond).

Tadhg I MacCarthy Mór (1118–23), the grandson of Carrthach, was the first of the Eóghanacht line of MacCarthy kings to rule the new kingdom of Desmond following the Treaty of Glanmire, returning the MacCarthy dynasty to their ancient capital of Cashel for the first time in 150 years. Twenty-five MacCarthy kings ruled Desmond down to Donal IX MacCarthy Mór (1558–96), the last regnant king.

Many of the Eóghanacht kings were 'king-bishops', a Christian inheritance of the pagan sacral kingship of former times. One of the great literary kings of the Eóghanacht was Cormac II Mac Cuileannáin (836–908), who was king-bishop of Cashel. Born in Cashel, he succeeded to the kingship in 902 and married Gormflaith (c. 880–947) who was daughter of Flann Sionna, an Uí Néill High King of Ireland. Gormflaith was a poetess in her own right and herself the subject of a romantic cycle of tales and poems. *Triamhuin Ghormflaithe* (The Tragedy of Gormflaith) was considered one of the great medieval romances. She is not to be confused with another Gormflaith (c. 955–1042) who was queen of both Dublin and Munster.

Some of Cormac II's lyrics appear in the twelfth-century *Leabhar na Nuachonghbhála* (Book of Leinster), but his literary fame arises from his authorship of *Sanas Chormaic* (Cormac's Glossary), an early Irish lexicon. Cormac was also responsible for the compilation of the *Saltair* (The Psalter of Cashel) and for his involvement in the *Lebor na Cert* or *Leabhar na gCeart* (The Book of Rights), setting out the privileges, tributes and duties of Irish kings and nobles in mnemonic verse, and giving the genealogies of leading families. Having been revised two centuries later by the orders of Brían Bóroimhe, it was used as a standard for centuries.

The work also contains a very interesting story, *Senchas Fagbála Caisil andso sis agus Beandacht Ríg* (The Story of the Finding of Cashel). This is an account of how King Conal Corc came to choose Cashel as the seat of the Munster kingdom. This story also mentions how, sixty years after the event, when Nad Froich mac Cuirc was on the throne, St Patrick came to Cashel and, with a native Munster bishop, Ailbe, who established the abbey of Emly, they converted him and baptised him at Cashel. St Ailbe is the patron saint of Munster, and is regarded by scholars as having arrived in Ireland before Patrick to preach Christianity.

While Brían Bóroimhe justly receives credit for breaking the power of the Danes at Clontarf in 1014, little notice has been taken of Cellachán Mac Buadacháin (d. 954) who prevented Norse domination in Munster by a series of victories over the Danes. The Norse were isolated in their port city-states of Cork and Limerick and Waterford and made to pay tribute to the Munster kings. In the twelfth century, Cormac III, perhaps the best-known of the MacCarthy king-bishops at Cashel, commissioned the story of Cellachán to be set down in writing. *Caithreim Cheallacháin Chaisil* (The Battle Saga of Cellachán of Cashel) was written sometime between 1127 and 1138, and the earliest surviving manuscript is in the Royal Irish Academy. The current MacCarthy Mór has described it as a 'propaganda saga' written to cement Cormac's dynastic treaty with the Dál gCais.

Cormac III reigned in two periods, the first being 1123–27. It is implied in both the *Annals of Innisfallen* and *MacCarthaigh's Book* that Cormac attempted to reunite all Munster under Eóghanacht control. In 1125 he captured the Dál gCais capital of Limerick and thereafter is referred to as king of Munster. However, in 1127 he is reported as being 'deposed by the nobles of Munster'; perhaps the *derbhfine* did not want to enter into an all-out war with the Uá Bríain again. Cormac's younger brother Donnchadh II succeeded to the kingship while Cormac retired into a religious life at the abbey of Lismore.

Within months Donnchadh had proved himself an unworthy successor and he was sent into exile in Connacht while Cormac returned to reign until 1138. Now Cormac found that instead of fighting the Ua Bríain, the kings of Thomond were actually asking for an alliance against the power of the O'Conors of Connacht who were attempting to annex part of Thomond to their territory.

Cormac has a tenuous link with another great literary work. Christiaus, or more properly, Giolla Christa MacCarthy, a first cousin of Cormac, was Abbot of Ratisbon (Regensburg, the old capital of Bavaria). In 1149 an Irish monk from Munster, called Marcus, wrote in Latin a saga called

The Vision of Tnugdal, one of the great medieval tales of the Otherworld. Tnugdal is a Knight of Cashel, obviously a Niadh Nask, who, dining with some friends in Cork, falls into a deep sleep and we follow his journey to the Christianised Otherworld.

But perhaps Cormac is best known for the famous building on the Rock of Cashel, Cormac's Chapel. He ordered it begun in 1127 and it was consecrated in 1134. It appears to be the earliest Romanesque church in Ireland. Firmicius, the abbot of Regensburg, is recorded as sending four of his best craftsmen to help with the work. The monastery of St James at Regensburg was founded by Muiredach Mac Robartaigh (Marianus Scotus, d. 1088) and became a Benedictine abbey. It was regarded as an Eóghanacht foundation beyond the seas. The elaborately decorated sarcophagus inside Cormac's Chapel is popularly said to have been that of King Cormac himself. However, scholars believe that it was originally made for his brother King Tadhg. It was only returned to the chapel at the beginning of the nineteenth century. The copper crozier found inside, said to be proof of the interring of a king-bishop, is actually dated to a century after Cormac lived. This crozier, ornamented with Limoges enamel, now in the National Museum, Dublin, is similar to one in the Victoria and Albert Museum, London, and must have belonged to another bishop.

Cormac III was assassinated in 1138 by his erstwhile allies, the O'Briens. The *Annals of Innisfallen* state:

> Cormac, son of Muireadach MacCarthaigh, king of the two provinces of Munster [Desmond and Thomond], and defender of all Leth Mug, the most pious and valorous of men, the best for bestowing food and clothes [on the poor], was, after building the church of Cormac at Cashel and twelve churches at Lismore, treacherously killed by Diarmuid Súgach, son of Mathghamhain Ó Conchobhair Ciarraige [O'Connor Kerry] and Ó Tailcín, at the instigation of Toirdhealbhach son of Diarmaid Ó Bríain, in his own court at Magh Tamhnach.

That the royal court of Cashel was a highly civilised and literate one is, perhaps, stating the obvious. Apart from the works mentioned above, there is a fascinating 'Treatise on Music', written at Cashel in 1168. This was kept in the Cashel Diocesan Library. From the early medieval manuscripts it is clear that music played an important role in Irish courtly life.

On Cormac's death, his brother Donnchadh returned from exile and reigned until 1143. He attempted to punish the O'Briens for his brother's death but was himself taken prisoner by Toirdhealbhach and died in captivity.

King Dermod I (1144–85), the son of Cormac, has been placed second only to Dermot MacMorrough of Leinster in the demonology of Irish traitors. The reason for this is his submission to Henry II even before his kingdom was threatened. To put this in context he had emerged from years of continuous attacks on Desmond by the Dál gCais kings. The polity of Desmond was certainly not stable. A strong kingdom was only possible by political means and alliances. *MacCarthaigh's Book* reveals how Dermod I supported the O'Conors and MacMorrough against the O'Briens during this turbulent period. H.A. Jefferies observes: 'Dermod MacCarthy created one of the most powerful and united kingdoms of pre-Norman Ireland, and the endurance of Clan MacCarthaigh as a major political force in south Munster throughout the later middle ages was due in no small part to the work of this remarkable king.'[2]

King Dermod had heard reports of the landing of Norman knights and their men-at-arms during 1169, 1170 and again in October 1171, when the Angevin emperor, Henry II, himself came to Waterford. With the defeat of the High King's army, and the submission of other Irish kings and nobles, Dermod realised that the Normans were a foe that needed to be treated with consideration. Dermod certainly did not possess an army which could defend Munster when the High King's army had already been defeated. He went to see the Angevin emperor, who was then encamped at Waterford. According to the *Annals of Innisfallen*, '*ina theg an sin*', 'he went into Henry's house', which is interpreted as meaning that he submitted to Henry as his feudal lord. Hot on his heels came the Thomond king, Domhnall Mór O'Brien, who also submitted.

From Dermod's viewpoint, he saw a submission to Henry, acknowledging him as his 'overlord', as no different from a submission to Ruaidri Ua Conchobhair as High King. He saw it as another alliance to a powerful king against possible threats to his own kingdom. Now that the High King of Ireland had been rendered impotent by the Normans, he could not guarantee protection against the ambitions of the O'Briens.

The Normans were swift to repudiate the treaty. Dermod was murdered, according to the annals of the Regensburg monastery, on 6 November, by the Norman knight named Geoffrey de Cogan. Cogan was immediately slain by Domhnall Mór na Curra, who succeeded Dermod as Donal I of Desmond. The *Annals of Innisfallen* record Donal's obituary in 1206 thus:

Domhnaill, son of MacCarthaigh, High King of Munster, died in Corr Tige Meuc Urmainn this year on the Kalends of December [first of the month] . . . It was he, of all the contemporary Kings of Ireland, who was most feared by the foreigners. During the twenty years he held the kingship, he never submitted to the foreigner; and though an army of foreigners and Gaels often came against him, he gave them at all times no more than was their due, while at other times, he gave them nothing. And it was he who slew Geoffrey de Cogan, the most hated kerne that ever was in Ireland, and he flayed this Geoffrey. And it was he who inflicted the rout of Bern Meic Imuir, and who successfully attacked the castles of Lios Mór, Dun Cuireda, In Cora and Mag Ua Mairgili, and the castles of Uí Meic Caille. By him nine Justiciars were slain and twenty-one battles fought in Munster, and many other exploits were performed.

In the thirteenth century Norman knights were moving into Desmond and its kings were forced to protect themselves. In November 1259 the Norman Lord of Ireland, Henry III, granted all Desmond to John Fitz-Thomas as his fiefdom. John FitzThomas swiftly moved to take over this rich kingdom, and invited King Donal II (1247–52) to Airloch Castle on guarantees of personal safety to discuss matters. Once again, the sacred trust of hospitality was flouted. FitzThomas murdered the Desmond king and attempted to assert his authority throughout the kingdom.

Finghín V (1252–61) of Rinn Róin became king of Desmond and immediately took the field against FitzThomas and his Normans, destroying six Norman strongholds. FitzThomas called on William de Dene, the Norman Justiciar, for aid and a large Norman army marched into Desmond. On 24 July 1261 the army of the king of Desmond met that of King Henry III's personal representative in Ireland, the Lord Justiciar himself, with his armoured knights and men-at-arms. The battle site was at Callan near Kenmare. One wing of the king of Desmond's army was commanded by his own daughter, Étain. Never had the Normans suffered such a defeat. John FitzThomas and his son Maurice were killed with eight Norman barons, twenty-five knights and thousands of men-at-arms. Edmund Curtis comments:

> The important result of Callan was the check it gave to what seemed the inevitable triumph of Norman English speech, culture and law in the south-west corner, the conquest of which would have extinguished native Desmond. For centuries not a single English settler dare now set foot in the country of the MacCarthys . . .[3]

Technically, this is not entirely accurate. Milo de Courcy managed to ambush King Finghín near Kinsale in 1262 and kill him. Cormac,

Finghín's brother, now became Cormac V (1262) and was joined by the Princess Étain who seems a formidable military commander but, alas, we know little about her. Together they met the army of the new Lord Justiciar, Richard de la Rochelle, with his second-in-command, Walter de Burgo, on the slopes of Mangerton, Co. Kerry. The battle was another victory even though the king of Desmond fell in the thick of the fighting. His cousin, Donal Ruadh, became Donal III, reigning until 1302.

When Donal III was succeeded by his son, Donal Óg (1302–06), the *Annals of Connacht* record his passing in these terms: 'Domhnall Ruadha MacCarthaigh, King of Desmond, the most generous and valorous, the most terrible and triumphant of the Gaels of all Ireland in fights and forays, dies after a victory of repentance this year.' The term 'victory of repentance' meant he received the last rites of the Church.

By the late fourteenth century, the Norman barons were back in Desmond, carving out palatine estates, self-governing principalities. Among the first Norman settlers were the FitzGeralds, who were eventually to take the title Earls of Desmond, and the Butlers, who became Earls of Ormond – West Munster. However, this time, they sought liaisons and alliances with the Desmond kings. One of the most peaceful reigns in Desmond was that of Donal Óg (Donal V) (1359–90) of whom the *Annals of Innisfallen* record:

> there was none of his contemporaries, neither foreigner nor Gael, more comely, more humane, or more powerful than he, nor was there in his time one of greater generosity, prowess, kindliness or truthfulness. He died in his castle of Loch Léin and was buried in the same monastery as his father after a victory of penance and devotion. And no other calamity was so notable at that time.

His son Tadhg II na Mainstreach MacCarthy Mór (1390–1428) stands out as important as two of his three sons became the progenitors of important branches of the royal dynasty. His senior surviving son Domhnall continued the kingly line until Donal IX (d. 1596); his next son Cormac became Tiarna Chois Leamhna (Lord of Kerslawny) and tanist of Desmond. The *Annals of Loch Cé*, noticing his death in 1473, say: 'The son of MacCarthaigh Mór, Cormac, son of Tadhg, son of Domhnall Óg, Tanist of Des Mumha, died this year.' Tadhg's third son, Dermod, died without issue. It is from Cormac that the current MacCarthy Mór descends.

The last king of Desmond, the end of a line of twenty-four kings from Tadhg I (1118–23), was Donal IX (ante 1558–1596) of whom we have given some account in Chapter 3. In terms of territory, the kingdom had shrunk back into Cork and Kerry and Donal ruled this from his estate at Killarney. The Norman Earls of Desmond (FitzGeralds) and of Ormond (Butlers) had deprived him of much of the kingdom but the ordinary Irish people still looked upon Donal as their king, even though the Norman earls governed palatine estates.

Donal IX had several illegitimate children and, by his wife Honora, sister and daughter of FitzGerald Earls of Desmond, he had a daughter and a son. We have already examined how Donal IX, refusing to surrender his title and kingdom, was eventually kidnapped by Lord Roche and the Lord Deputy, Sir Henry Sidney, in 1565 and taken to Elizabeth I's court in England. Under duress he was made to acknowledge the English Crown and become Earl of Clancare (Clancarthy) and Baron of Valentia. But Donal was astute enough not to surrender his title as MacCarthy Mór which embodied his royal status. Once back safely in Desmond, he declared himself still king, sending ambassadors to the pope and the king of Spain, raising the standard of resistance.

From 1569 to 1572 he fought the attempt by Elizabeth to conquer Desmond. Elizabeth's generals eventually gained the upper hand and Donal's son, Tadhg, Lord of Valentia, was taken hostage in 1578 and held in Dublin Castle as a guarantee of Donal's good behaviour. Donal even wrote to Elizabeth I on 23 May 1583, seeking the boy's release; in the letter he also reveals that Elizabeth was holding his wife hostage in Cork. Elizabeth had Tadhg taken to England to be taught in English ways, language, law and customs. However, the boy was soon back in Dublin Castle and from there, with the help of William Barry, managed to escape to France. He died abroad in circumstances of mystery before 1 July 1588. The conclusion was that he probably died at the hands of the agents of William Cecil, Lord Burghley (1520–98), Elizabeth I's chief adviser and lord treasurer, who had organised a 'secret service' which assassinated several Irish aristocrats who fled to Europe. It has even been speculated that Florence MacCarthy, the son of MacCarthy Reagh, had a hand in the matter as he had much to gain by it.

Donal, who was still referred to as Earl of Clancare but consistently used his title of MacCarthy Mór, was now left without a legitimate son to name as his tanist. He had a daughter married to Florence MacCarthy. He also had an illegitimate son, Donal, who emerges as a considerable military commander. Even during the worst times, he continued to lead his men as guerrilla fighters in the Kerry mountains, and, with Eoghan MacRory O'More, was an architect of the Earl of Essex's famous defeat in March 1599 at Bearna na Cleitidhe (the Pass of Plumes) near Ballyk-nocken Castle, four miles south-east of Portlaoise.

Long before his death in 1596, however, faced with the terrible devastation of Munster by the Elizabethan conquests which had, to all intents and purposes, transformed the kingdom into a desert, not to mention his personal tragedies, King Donal had retreated into his castle at Killarney where he became more involved in religion and poetry. He was buried in Muckross Abbey where his tomb, bearing his arms, may still be seen in the chancel. Nearby are tombs of other Eóghanacht nobles – O'Donoghue of the Glens, MacGillycuddy of the Reeks and O'Sullivan Mór.

The war was carried on after his death, mainly by his illegitimate son Donal. But the succession of the title was disputed. Donal has been described, at his meeting with Aodh Ruadh O'Neill, as The MacCarthy Mór. He certainly had considerable support for that claim from the Desmond nobles. Reports that The O'Neill could create a MacCarthy Mór and did so, recognising at different times both Donal and Donal IX's son-in-law, Florence MacCarthy (popularly, but incorrectly, referred to as Florence MacCarthy Reagh of Carbery) are fanciful. The O'Neill had no legal right to interfere in such a matter. Although Donal fought at Kinsale, and joined O'Sullivan Beare in the aftermath of that defeat, a lifetime of fighting had exhausted him. He retired to his estates and dropped his claims to the title. His son, also illegitimate, did not pursue those claims either and his descendants are said to have left for America in the nineteenth century.

The other claimant who flirted with The O'Neill for recognition as The MacCarthy Mór, Donal IX's son-in-law, Florence (1562?-1640), was the eldest son of Donough MacCarthy Reagh, Lord of Carbery. He had married Ellen, only daughter, and only surviving legitimate child, of Donal IX. Florence showed some ambivalence in supporting his father-in-law against the Elizabethan conquest of Desmond. In 1589 he had been taken captive and imprisoned in the Tower of London. When he was liberated in 1591, he tried to negotiate with Elizabeth's ministers, suggesting that he would bring Desmond on to England's side if he were recognised as heir to his father-in-law's titles and estates. The title he was more concerned with was the one that Donal IX had rejected – that of Earl of Clancare.

When The MacCarthy Reagh died in 1594 it was his nephew, Donal na Pipi (d. 1612), who succeeded him under Irish law and not Florence. He was not, then, The MacCarthy Reagh as has been claimed in some accounts. Rejected by his own people as well as the English, Florence appealed to O'Neill, who had arrived in Munster with his army in 1600, to recognise him. O'Neill, as a political move, accepted him as MacCarthy Mór in place of Donal, even though he had no legal power to do so. Once Florence saw that the wind of change was now blowing in England's favour, he promptly surrendered to England, hoping to curry favour. However, he was committed to the Tower of London in 1601.

From then on he was virtually a prisoner. He had privileges in the Tower and wrote a history of Ireland in the early period dedicated to the Earl of Thomond as well as a treatise on antiquity and numerous letters. As for his claims, however, his cousin, Donal na Pipi, the legitimate MacCarthy Reagh, described him as 'a damned counterfeit Englishman, whose study and practice was to deceive and betray all the Irishmen in Ireland'. The burial register of St Martin in the Fields, London, marks Florence's passing on 18 December 1640.

His sons claimed to be The MacCarthy Mór after him. Charles was appointed governor of Carrickfergus Castle by James II. He surrendered it to the Duke of Schomberg, William of Orange's general. He was found hiding in the kitchen and, on being told, Schomberg remarked: 'If he had stayed with his men like a soldier, I would have sent for him, but if he would go and eat with servants in a kitchen, let him be doing.' Charles's son died in 1770 and a cousin of his, a major in Clare's Regiment of the Irish Brigade of France, tried to claim the title but died without issue. Thereafter no descendant of Florence made any attempt to seek the title.

The line that did claim the title with more success were the Lords of Muskerry. The Lordship of Muskerry had been bestowed by Cormac VI (1325–59) on his second son Diarmaid. Cormac MacTeige MacCarthy, who succeeded as 12th Lord of Muskerry in 1571, was, according to the MacCarthy *Généalogie*, granted '542 pardons issued to him from the Crown for such of his subjects as took part in the MacCarthy Mór and Desmond confederacy with Spain'. He had surrendered to Elizabeth on 9 May 1589, technically giving up his Gaelic title of Muskerry. Cormac Óg resumed the Gaelic title as 15th Lord of Muskerry in 1617. But with the new social order, he decided to make himself acceptable to the administration and, on 15 November 1628, the titles of Viscount Muskerry and Baron Blarney were bestowed on him by Charles I. He died in 1640.

It has been argued that under Irish law the Muskerry line retained the title of The MacCarthy Mór 'with opposition' until 1905. Viscount Muskerry's son, Donnchadh, who became the 2nd Viscount, fought in 1641–50 and fled to France, joining Charles II's court. He was created 1st Earl of Clancarthy in 1658. The line of his first son (d. 1665) ceased with the death of his infant grandson Charles James (1665–66). His second son Callaghan became 3rd Earl of Clancarthy (1666–76). Callaghan's son Donough, the 4th Earl, espoused James II's cause and welcomed James II in 1689 to his house. He was made a lord of the bedchamber and given command of a foot regiment. Defending Cork, he was taken prisoner by the Williamites in October 1690 and imprisoned in the Tower of London. He managed to escape in 1694 and made his way to St Germain, where James II had his court in exile. He was appointed commander of the royal horse guards. He was recaptured by Williamites in 1697 and sent to Newgate to be tried as a traitor. However, William granted him a pardon on condition that he went into permanent exile. He went first to Hamburg. The poet Aodhagán Ó Rathaille wrote:

> Darinis [Valentia] in the West – it has no lord of the noble race:
> Woe is me! in Hamburg is the lord of the gentle merry heroes:
> Aged, grey-browed eyes, bitterly weeping for each of these . . .

His line died with his son Robert, 5th Earl of Clancarthy, in 1769.

It must be pointed out that the current Earls of Clancarthy are only related to MacCarthys on the distaff side. This title was recreated in the United Kingdom peerage in 1803 for the family of Le Poer Trench, then holding the titles of Baron Kilconnel (1797) and Viscount Dunlo (1801). The family did claim a female MacCarthy descent which was why they chose the title. The 8th Earl (who died in 1995) was an enthusiastic supporter of the current MacCarthy Mór and served as his Referendary General of the dynastic order of the Niadh Nask between 1980–1995.

The line of the 1st Earl of Clancarthy, Donnchadh of Muskerry, had continued with Justin MacCarthy (c. 1642–94). His Irish name was Saorbhreathach but he has become better known under the Anglicised form of Justin. He had entered French service while his family were exiled during the Cromwellian period. In 1689 he took the side of James II and was at Cork to welcome James to Ireland. He was made master-general of artillery and also sat as a member for Cork in James II's 1689 parliament in Dublin. James II created him Viscount Mountcashel. During the decisive battle of Newtown Butler against the Williamite forces, Mountcashel saw the defeat of his troops and personally threw himself at the enemy hoping that death would exonerate his disgrace. The Williamites, recognising him, spared his life and took him captive.

He escaped from Enniskillen, where he had been held, reached Dublin and commanded a French regiment under the Duc de Lauzun. Lord Tirconnell, however, ordered him to France to negotiate reinforcements. After the initial Williamite victories, Mountcashel was instructed to take nearly 6000 Irish soldiers into exile. These formed the nucleus of the famous Irish Brigade of the French army which was to play the decisive role in the defeat of the English at Fontenoy in 1745. Mountcashel died at Barèges while taking the curative waters on 1 July 1694, 'of wounds' says the *Gazette de France*. He had received wounds in Ireland, at Moutine and in the Rhineland. He had wanted his body returned to Ireland for burial but this request was refused and he was buried at Barèges.

His will shows that he had been created Baron of Castle Inchy and Blarney, and Duke of Clancarthy by James II. These titles were confirmed by Louis XIV in whose service he had become a lieutenant-general. As he had no children, he had formally adopted his cousin, Florence Callaghan MacCarthy, son of Cormac MacCarthy, who, in turn, was son of Donal MacCarthy of Carrignavar, and bequeathed his titles and estates to him. 'I would counsel Florence to bear these titles with honour, and to endeavour by all means to reconquer what the English have taken from our family . . .'

The French king accepted Florence as 2nd Duc de Clancarthy and the line of Ducs de Clancarthy continued, recognised in the Jacobite peerage, in France until 1927 when Pol, the 7th Duc died. The line continued to assert the rights and prerogatives of The MacCarthy Mór as Prince of Desmond and the right to bestow the ancient dynastic order of the Eóghanacht royal house, the Niadh Nask or Order of the Golden Chain.

From the eighteenth century there were now three main branches of the royal line in France. The Ducs de Clancarthy, accepted as MacCarthy Mór, the Comtes MacCarthy Reagh de Toulouse, who had settled in Toulouse in 1776, and the Comtes MacCarthy de Marlière. It was Denis MacCarthy, who had been admitted to the ranks of French nobility in 1756 as *'seigneur de Beaju, Fondival et Marlière'*, having proved his noble lineage, who founded the MacCarthy businesses at Bordeaux. He opened a trading house and a vineyard at Château MacCarthy which still exists today producing, under that name, an excellent St Estèphe wine. The Hôtel de MacCarthy still exists in the Cour de Verdun in Bordeaux. The current owners of Château MacCarthy are the firm of Henri Duboscq & Fils.

By the early nineteenth century, the firm was one of the richest wine makers and exporters in France and was known as MacCarthy Frères in spite of one of the brothers, Daniel, a member of the Etats-Généraux (French parliament) during the time of the Revolution and imprisoned during 'The Terror' of 1793, having died from his experiences. The line continued from his brother John, who married Cécile O'Byrne of Château Houringue, to Comte Nicholas MacCarthy de la Marlière who died without issue in 1925.

These main branches of the MacCarthy family were in touch, not only among themselves, but with the family of the Tiarna Chois Leamhna (Lords of Kerslawny) whose line had descended from Cormac, son of King Tadhg na Mainistreach of Desmond (d. 1426). The Kerslawny branch had, in fact, been considered by most members of the family as the senior branch in terms of claimants under Brehon law. However, in the unsettled world following the conquest by England, there is no evidence that the Kerslawny family made any formal claim. They remained in Ireland through the worst excesses of the Penal Law period.

The matter of rightful descent of the title was discussed among the French branches and their relatives in Ireland. In 1765, Comte Justin MacCarthy Reagh de Toulouse (born in Co. Tipperary in 1744) commissioned Sir Isaac Heard, Norroy King of Arms, and Ralph Bigland, Clarenceux King of Arms, both later to occupy the position of Garter King of Arms, the highest office in the English College of Arms, to compile a genealogy and history of their house: the *Généalogie de la Royale et Serenissime Maison de MacCarthy*. The original two volumes were destroyed in the French Revolution but in 1775 a copy was made for another member of the family, and this has survived as the personal property of the current MacCarthy Mór, who has given it on loan to the Cashel Heritage Museum.

Daniel (Donal) MacCarthy of the Kerslawny branch was born in 1790 in Ireland and was sent to France at a young age where he was educated under the supervision of his cousin, Justin, Comte MacCarthy Reagh de Toulouse. He went to live at the Hôtel de MacCarthy in Toulouse, not to be confused with the Hôtel de MacCarthy in Bordeaux. This was the seat of the Comtes MacCarthy Reagh. In 1825 Daniel married Isabella Collins. His daughter Isabella married Daniel, Count of Clandermond (d. 1880) from whom the current Count of Clandermond descends. His son John (Eóghan), born in 1827, married Mary Corrigan in 1850. John was also educated in Toulouse. His son James, born in 1853, married Mary Early in 1876. His son Thomas Donal MacCarthy, Lord of Kerslawny, was born in 1880. As his father had died when Thomas Donal was only nine years old, Comte Nicholas MacCarthy Reagh de Toulouse brought him up as his ward. Nicholas, Comte MacCarthy Reagh of Toulouse died in 1906 without male issue.

The current MacCarthy Mór agrees that the Brehon law line of descent must be accorded to the Muskerry/Clancarthys. Under Brehon law, the line of descent of the title MacCarthy Mór, Prince of Desmond was:

Cormac Óg (Cormac VIII) 14th Lord of Muskerry (1596–1617)

Cormac Óg (Cormac IX) (junior) 15th Lord of Muskerry and 1st Viscount (1617–40)

Donnchadh (Donnchadh V), 2nd Viscount and 1st Earl of Clancarthy (1640–65), father of the 1st Duc de Clancarthy

Charles (Cormac X), 2nd Earl (1665–66)

Callaghan (Callaghan II), 3rd Earl (1666–76)

Donough (Donnchadh VI), 4th Earl (1676–1734)
Robert (Robert I), 5th Earl (1734–69)
Florence (Finchín VI), 4th Duc de Clancarthy (1769)
Florence (Finchín VII), 5th Duc de Clancarthy
Florence (Finchín VIII) 6th Duc de Clancarthy
Pol (Pol I), 7th Duc de Clancarthy (1903–27), abdicated his title of
    MacCarthy Mór, Prince of Desmond, at a *cenél thogairm* at Nantes
    in 1905.

At the start of the twentieth century two major events happened which
bore on the descent of the title.

On 1 July 1921 one Samuel Trant McCarthy of Srugrena Abbey
adopted, as his name by deed poll, the form Samuel Trant McCarthy
MacCarthy Mór. *Mr* MacCarthy Mór, as we should legally call him, was
High Sheriff and Deputy Lieutenant of Co. Kerry, a Justice of the Peace
and a retired judge of the Indian Imperial Civil Service. He had retired
to Ireland in 1905 and threw himself into researching his family history.
At eighty years of age, this eccentric gentleman, apparently unaware that
a genuine MacCarthy Mór existed, decided that he would adopt the title
as his name and claim the chiefship of the royal house by primogeniture.
His research was woefully inadequate and even at the time he announced
his claim, it was pointed out that if primogeniture was the basis of such
a claim, two other senior lines still existed. In his book *The MacCarthys
of Munster*, Samuel demonstrated that he was neither a trained historian
nor a genealogist, refusing to acknowledge the Brehon laws of succession.

All the editions of *Thom's Directory* between 1922 and 1927 listed his
name in the section 'Ancient Irish Chieftainries Claimed by Representatives'. This, of course, was an entirely unofficial list with the information
supplied by those listed. Mr Samuel Trant McCarthy MacCarthy Mór's
claim could not be sustained by Irish law nor even under English primogeniture.

Prior to Samuel Trant's spurious claims, in 1905, the heads of the
three main French MacCarthy families had held a meeting in Nantes to
finally resolve the matter of the title. As we saw in Chapter 5, the Duc
de Clancarty-Blarney, head of the House of Muskerry, formally abdicated
in favour of Thomas Donal, 15th Lord of Kerslawny, who, with the
approval of the heads of the other houses, became The MacCarthy Mór,
Prince of Desmond.

However, a problem arose when the eccentric old gentleman, Samuel
Trant, made a claim to be MacCarthy Mór. In 1923 Thomas Donal,
whose pedigree, like Samuel Trant's, had been undertaken by Sir Arthur
Vicars, the Ulster King of Arms, met Samuel Trant in Cork and the two

distant cousins agreed a plan to avoid a public scandal. In return for
Thomas Donal not making any public denouncement of Samuel Trant's
spurious claims until after Samuel's death (the old man was then eighty-
one years old), Samuel privately recognised the *pacte de famille* of 1905,
agreed to appoint no successor and allow that his deed poll surname
would die with him. Samuel died in 1927.

In 1947 Thomas Donal died and his son, also Thomas Donal (b. 1913),
was confirmed by the *derbhfine* of the family as the next MacCarthy Mór.
He was made a Knight Commander of the Military and Hospitaller Order
of St Lazarus of Jerusalem, by HRH Don Francisco de Borbon y de
Borbon, Duke of Seville. The duke (d. 1995) was a kinsman, being a
descendant of Countess Dona Margueritta MacCarthy y Shelly. MacCarthy Mór married the Hon. Harriet Maguire (d. 1985), eldest daughter
of The Maguire, Prince of Fermanagh (d. 1985), *de jure* Lord Enniskillen
in the Jacobite peerage. The family no longer had business links or were
domiciled in France and The MacCarthy Mór was then living in Co.
Antrim in the north of Ireland.

Thomas Donal (Donal XII) had five sons. In 1980 he decided to abdicate and a document was drawn up in which the *derbhfine* of the house,
in accordance with the Brehon dynastic law of succession, agreed that the
second son, Terence Francis, became the new MacCarthy Mór, Prince of
Desmond and 17th Lord of Kerslawny. Each member of the *derbhfine*
signed his name with his seal. The new MacCarthy Mór, born in 1957,
remains the current head of the royal house of Munster, and head of the
Niadh Nask. The MacCarthy Mór was educated privately and then took
his primary and master's degrees from Queen's University, Belfast. He
studied Irish history and genealogy and was appointed a Member of the
Advisory Board of the Heraldry Society of Ireland. He is one-time chairman and current president of the International Committee for Orders
of Chivalry and an honorary life member of several international heraldic
societies.

Until the 1980s the MacCarthy Mórs never sought the 'courtesy recognition' offered by the Genealogical Office in Dublin, although their pedigrees had been registered in various heraldic offices. However, Gerard
Slevin (d. 1998), perhaps the best of those who held the office of Chief
Herald of Ireland, suggested that this should be done as many other
members of ancient Gaelic noble houses were now seeking such recognition. It was made clear, and accepted at the time, that primogeniture
never played a role in MacCarthy dynastic succession and that the family
held to Brehon law in that respect. Not only did Gerard Slevin accept
this at the time but Edward MacLysaght also accepted Terence Francis
as The MacCarthy Mór before his death, knowing that his father and an

elder brother, with three sons of his own, were still living. Thus, both Chief Herald and former Chief Herald ignored their own primogeniture rulings and accepted the validity of Brehon law. However, the 'courtesy recognition' was not officially approved by the Genealogical Office until 28 January 1992, when a new Chief Herald, Donal Begley, and his assistant, Fergus Gillespie, issued the certified pedigree. The title has, of course, been recognised by other international heralds, such as the Castile and Leon King of Arms, while the right to use the prefix 'Royal Highness' has been acknowledged by the Italian courts. MacCarthy Mór refuses the use of such terms as not being part of the Gaelic Irish form of address.

The current MacCarthy Mór is a man of firm views but has a thorough knowledge of his subject. His views and his forthright manner of expressing them have, as has been mentioned, brought him enemies as well as friends. We saw in Chapter 6 how he was forced to take legal action in an international court, in which he has been successful.

He makes no secret of the fact that he would like to see his dynasty restored in Munster (not Ireland), pointing to a prophecy attributed to St Colmcille that a southern dynasty would restore native kingship in Ireland after a long absence. He agrees that, should such an event ever happen, the democratic spirit of the Brehon system would prevail rather than the feudal concepts associated with monarchy today. He has been criticised for expressing such ideas in a modern republic. But he has a puckish sense of humour which may not readily be understood by those who have too serious an opinion of themselves. When MacCarthy Mór heard that a bewildered tourist, visiting a museum, had been solemnly informed by a petty official that he was planning to 'overthrow' the Irish state, he confessed that he didn't know whether to be outraged or give way to laughter.

He has been one of the most active members of the Standing Council of Irish Chiefs and Chieftains since its inception. He is patron of the Royal Clan MacCarthy Society, the MacCarthy Clan Society and the Clan MacCarthy Society Inc. of North America. He is patron of the Royal Eóghanacht Society, devoted to historical research on the dynasty. As an heraldic expert and historian, he has written and edited numerous books on the subject as well as many articles, and has lectured widely. He is Honorary President of the Cashel Heritage and Development Trust, Patron of the Cashel Arts and Heritage Society and the Cashel Writers' Circle.

He has been bestowed with over a score of knighthoods, orders and honours from various foreign states and royal houses. In the United States, he has been made a substantive Colonel of the South Carolina State Guard and an Honorary Colonel in Alabama by both the State

Governors. The international honours received by him would fill a column of *Who's Who*.

Ireland, too, has honoured him in its way, not only by his being invited to the presidential reception, along with other members of the surviving Gaelic nobility, but by the many civic receptions which have been given for him.

A tireless worker to promote a knowledge of Gaelic Ireland and the Eóghanacht dynasty, MacCarthy Mór has given on permanent loan many of the treasures he inherited connected with his dynasty. These treasures are held in a trust for himself and his heirs during the tenure of their office as MacCarthy Mór. He has presided at various clan gatherings to help promote tourism to Eóghanacht Munster. One of the most successful Eóghanacht gatherings took place in 1996; this was a commemoration to mark the quatercentenary of the death of King Donal IX MacCarthy Mór in 1596. A plaque commemorating King Donal was unveiled in Cashel Cathedral. A replica of the ancient crown of Munster and Desmond was presented to MacCarthy Mór by The O'Donoghue of the Glens on behalf of all the surviving Eóghanachta chiefs. The events were preceded by a mayoral reception given for MacCarthy Mór in Clonmel where he is a frequent visitor.

In July 1996 MacCarthy Mór officially welcomed the President of Ireland, Mary Robinson, and her husband, to the capital of his ancestors. She opened the Cashel Heritage Centre, of which he was president. The Irish President, with Prime Minister John Bruton, the Bishop of Cashel, and ambassadors of the USA and India, then accompanied him to a concert at the Rock of Cashel, the seat of the Eóghanacht kings.

Through the Eóghanacht dynastic order of the Niadh Nask, MacCarthy Mór organises donations to various charities and worthy causes, including the restoration of Cashel Cathedral. The subject of the Niadh Nask and its history will be returned to in Chapter 12.

One might think that The MacCarthy Mór, one day welcoming members of the American MacCarthy clan associations to Cashel, or lecturing on Irish heraldic and historical matters, another day engaged in study for his own written works or running the affairs of his office, would lead such a full life that he would have no time for recreation. However, he is a keen painter, elected a member of the Royal Ulster Academy Association in 1991, and a music lover. He keeps his main residence in Morocco where he escapes to relax.

He is a member of the Eastern Orthodox Church. Asked whether he favoured the continuation of the clause in the Irish Constitution, even as amended, which gives a special position to the Catholic Church, his reply was unambiguous.

Most certainly not. In fact, nothing was more ironic than de Valéra's creation of what was, in effect, an 'Established Church of Rome' in his 1937 Constitution. Such a concept is at complete variance with any idea of liberal secularism, but then, of course, the 'long fellow' sought to establish a Catholic state rather than an independent Gaelic one. And, of course, anyone with a nodding acquaintance of Irish history could have told de Valéra that it was that particular Church which had done everything within its power to destroy Gaelic Ireland and the Celtic Church. It was a Roman Pontiff, Adrian IV, who 'granted' Ireland to Henry II and his heirs for a tax of a penny per household, and his successors kept that tyranny in place by excommunicating any and every Irish king who attempted to drive the English out. It was that same Church which, through its bishops and mitred abbots, sanctioned the first specifically anti-Gaelic laws, the Statutes of Kilkenny. Not only do I believe that the 'special relationship clause' should be rescinded but I hope that the See of Rome, having apologised to the members of the Jewish religion for its inactivity during the holocaust, and in Europe for the horrors of the Inquisition, will yet ask the pardon of the Irish people for its role in the eight centuries of tyranny and genocide Ireland endured through its actions.

In answer to the question whether he believed the holders of Gaelic titles could play a political role in the Irish state, he says:

Although the Irish Republic seems wedded to the idea of absolute equality and democracy, yet it is clearly attached to an 'hereditary element' in its legislature. One only has to look at the roll of TDs to see that the state accepts the principle. The Irish Republic is one of the few countries in the world which has that unique institution, an elective-hereditary lower house. I see no reason why the chairman of the Standing Council of Irish Chiefs and Chieftains should not sit, as an appointed senator in the Upper House, or that the chiefs of the four Royal Houses should not do so. The Senate is full of appointees. At least, if the chiefs sat *de jure sanguinis* they would not be beholden to a patron and thus absolutely independent. What is more they would represent millions of overseas Irishmen and women, presently left without a voice.

On the question of whether all the Irish chiefs should be allowed to hold Irish passports, MacCarthy Mór comes surprisingly close to agreeing with the view of the Irish government, which is discussed in the final chapter of this book.

To me this is a rather silly, if not racist idea. It is also grounded on an illogical premise that we are 'Irish' chiefs. We are in fact Gaelic chiefs and as such have nothing whatever to do with the modern Irish state. We are the remnants of a defunct culture and several kingdoms. I know that there are some overseas chiefs who feel that they should be granted Irish passports. But why? If you are one 128th part Irish by ancestry (and 127 parts Spanish) in what sense are you 'Irish'? It is surely racist to say that a tincture of Irishness in your blood cancels and annuls the predominant inheritance of the vast majority of one's ancestors. Within two generations some Irish chiefs will be one part Irish and 511 parts Spanish or Portuguese! But this dilution of 'blood' is of no importance in the context of Gaelic chiefship, for that is a position and right rooted in our native culture. In defending the laws of their ancestors, particularly with regard to succession, and promoting Gaelic culture, they make a reality of their titles. This equally applies to those of us who hold Irish passports. Gaelicness has nothing whatsoever to do with passports!

The MacCarthy Mór's cousin, the Count of Clandermond, administers both the Royal Eóghanacht Society and the Household departments. He is hereditary Chamberlain, or *Reachtaire*, of Desmond. The count is a descendant of Isabella MacCarthy, the daughter of MacCarthy Mór's great-great-great-grandfather. His title, which is feudal in origin, was created *c.* 1250 by King Donal II, confirmed in 1756 by Louis XV of France, and more recently by the Castile and Leon King of Arms.

The household has several other officers, including a Brehon, The McKerrell of Hillhouse, 15th Laird and Lord of Dromin, a Scottish chief who is a graduate from an Irish university. He has held the office of Brehon to The MacCarthy Mór since 1980 when he succeeded the then Maguire, Prince of Fermanagh, the elder brother of the current chief. There are also *ollamhain*, including an *ollamh* of music and an *ollamh* of history.

MacCarthy Mór is presently unmarried, and his tanist is his younger brother Eóghan, Lord of Valentia, a graduate of Trinity College, Dublin, who holds the Grand Cross of the Imperial Ethiopian Order of the Lion and is a Knight Commander of the Orders of Polonia Restitua and St Lazarus of Jerusalem.

What one witnesses with MacCarthy Mór and his household is, in fact, a Gaelic court still in existence in the modern world with its patronage, its support for good causes and its sponsorship of intellectual life, especially in the research and publication of information about the Gaelic world of Ireland.

II
THE O'CALLAGHAN
(Ó Ceallacháin)

Don Juan O'Callaghan Casas, The O'Callaghan, Lord of Clonmeen, Chief of the Name and Arms of O'Callaghan, lives in Barcelona, in Catalonia, Spain. A Niadh Nask and vice-president of the Royal Eóghanacht Society, he is head of a princely house which descends in unbroken male line from Morrough, second son of Ceallacháin Chaisil (Callaghan of Cashel), the 42nd Christian king of Munster, who died in 952. Morrough was thus the first O'Callaghan. His eldest brother, Donnchadh II, was king of Munster (d. 963).

The Eóghanacht king who gave his name to the O'Callaghan princely house was able to control the Norse attempts to dominate Munster in a series of famous victories which are recounted in the *Cathreim Cheallacháin Chaisil* (The Battle-career of Ceallacháin of Cashel), which was commissioned by Cormac III and which we have discussed earlier.

For some time following his death, the lines descending from Ceallacháin's two sons, Donnchadh II and Morrough, lapsed into a bitter and prolonged rivalry as to the succession of the throne of Munster. The conflict lasted for fifty years until in 1092 Callaghan O'Callaghan (d. 1115) slew his cousins, Muiredach MacCarthy, King of Cashel, and his tanist, Donough MacCarthy, Ríoghdamna (Prince) of Cashel. Eventually the two branches of the Eóghanacht dynasty realised that the only people to benefit in this internecine feud were the Dál gCais (O'Briens) who claimed the Munster throne. Both sides of the family came together under Cenede O'Callaghan, Chief of Pobul Í Callaghan, to support Tadhg I MacCarthy (d. 1124) against the O'Briens. This secured the restoration of the Eóghanacht to Cashel.

But, as a result of the partition between Thomond and Desmond in 1118, the O'Callaghans were driven from their ancestral lands, which lay in Thomond, by the O'Briens, and they resettled in Clonmeen as vassals of the MacCarthy kings of Desmond.

The O'Callaghans survived the destruction of Gaelic Desmond during the Tudor conquest. Donough O'Callaghan, Lord of Pobul Í Callaghan had, in 1543, decided to respond to the 'surrender and regrant' policy of Henry VIII of England. He was then resident at Dromaneen Castle, Co. Cork and had married a daughter of Edmund Fitzgibbon, the White Knight. However, the first record we have of the Lord of Pobul Í Callaghan having surrendered to the Tudors occurs in 1577, when Callaghan, son of Connor, was granted a pardon. He was drowned in the Blackwater in 1578. In 1578 we find that John Roche, the son of Lord Roche who had kidnapped King Donal IX and taken him to London in order to force him to surrender his kingdom, was given the wardship of Donough O'Callaghan and also the custody of his lands to hold during the boy's minority. Roche was to bring up the boy in obedience to the English Crown, law and language.

In 1609 the English administration held an inquisition to determine who owned Clonmeen. The court found in favour of Conogher O'Callaghan, Lord of Clonmeen, who had 'received the rod, the symbol of rule' from King Donal IX with 'a certain writing under the hand and seal of' the king dated 20 July 1590.

Donough O'Callaghan of Dromaneen and afterwards of Clonmeen and finally of Mountallen, Co. Clare, on his majority, was elected as The O'Callaghan. He supported the Irish uprising of 1641 and became a member of the Supreme Council of the Irish Confederate Parliament in Kilkenny. He was commissioned into the Irish army as a colonel and fought at the battle of Clonleigh on 2 August 1642. He and his brother, Callaghan, a former law student, were declared outlaws and had to flee to France. His estate was confiscated and given to Sir Peter Courthorp. Although Clonmeen came back into O'Callaghan hands at the restoration of Charles II, it was later burnt to the ground during the Williamite wars and the lands confiscated again.

A cadet branch of the family left in face of the Penal Laws and went to Europe in search of religious freedom. They found patronage among the European monarchs. Seán O'Callaghan became a captain in O'Brien's Regiment of the Irish Brigade of the French army. He died in 1712 having received the title of Baron in Baden-Würtemburg. His brother Conchobhar (Cornelius) settled in Spain and became an officer in the Ultonia (Ulster) Regiment of the Irish Brigade of the Spanish army.

The chiefly branch of the family continued to live in Ireland at Kilgorey until Eamonn (Edmund), acknowledged as The O'Callaghan, was killed in a duel at Spancil Hill horse fair, Co. Clare, in September 1791. As he had only daughters, the title went to his Spanish cousin, Don Ramon O'Callaghan (1765–1833). There was no authoritative arbiter to approve the matter as no *derbhfine* met. The Ulster King of Arms could not, of course, recognise a Gaelic nobiliary title. Therefore, the Lismehane branch of O'Callaghans and the O'Callaghans of Spain disputed the title between them.

When the Genealogical Office was established in 1943, they decided that Colonel George O'Callaghan Westropp would be recognised as The O'Callaghan. Leaving aside the question of how someone bearing the surname Westropp could be recognised as The O'Callaghan, *Chief of the Name*, Dr Edward MacLysaght soon realised that an error had been made and that the genuine heir to the title by both tanistry and primogeniture was Don Juan O'Callaghan. The Genealogical Office appeared in a quandary. The solution was announced in *Burke's Irish Family Records* (1976) which stated that Colonel Westropp 'was allowed by the Chief Herald to retain the title for his lifetime'. This, it was hoped, would avoid bringing the office into disrepute. However, the title The O'Callaghan rested clearly, and continues to do so, with the Spanish branch of the family.

The Chief Herald of Ireland finally recognised the right of Don Juan O'Callaghan (1903–79) to the title of The O'Callaghan. Don Juan was an advocate living in Tortosa. He was married to Enriquetta Casa of Tortosa. His son Don Juan O'Callaghan Casas (in Spain, the mother's surname is given last) was born in Tortosa on 3 October 1934.

Don Juan inherited the title on his father's death. He runs his own business as a consultant engineer, having taken his doctorate in electric engineering at Barcelona in 1960.

In accordance with tanistry custom the family has approved his second son as his tanist, another Don Juan, born in Tortosa, 14 June 1963. This Don Juan is also an engineer, holding doctorates from Barcelona and Wisconsin. He is currently a professor at Barcelona University. The O'Callaghan points out that he holds his title under the Brehon dynastic law of succession. He feels that the surviving Gaelic chiefs do have a role to play in the modern world in relationship with the Irish state in creating a better awareness of Ireland's Gaelic past.

The O'Callaghan is a regular visitor to Ireland and took his seat on the Standing Council of Irish Chiefs and Chieftains in 1994. While he is a Spanish citizen, he would, if allowed by law, like to hold an Irish passport by virtue of his lineage and title. He is liberal in religion and, while a Catholic, believes that 'any modern state must be secular and all the religious options must be accepted (except violent sects). Human rights must be fully guaranteed.'

III

THE O'CARROLL OF ELY
(Ó Cearbhaill Éile)

The house of O'Carroll of Ely descends from Ailill Olom, King of Munster in AD 300, through his son Cian, from whom descends Cearbhaill, the petty king of Éile, a territory consisting of north Co. Tipperary and north-western Co. Offaly in eastern Munster (Ormond). Cearbhaill was killed fighting the Danes during the battle of Clontarf in 1014. The current chief is thirty-four generations in direct line from King Cearbhaill and is the only United States citizen to sit on the Standing Council of Irish Chiefs and Chieftains.

Frederick James O'Carroll was born in Reddings, California on 2 January 1933, and was educated at Modesto College and the Ambassador College, Passenda, majoring in theology. In 1953 he enlisted in the US Navy where he was a cryptologist in naval intelligence. He served in Korea and left the navy in 1957 but was called up again in 1966–70 during the Vietnam War, dealing with intelligence and communications.

The petty kingdom of Ely was under the lordship of the MacCarthy kings of Cashel to whom the O'Carrolls paid tribute. Mánach, who succeeded Cearbhaill, was the first to take the surname of Ó Cearbhaill (O'Carroll). He was slain in 1022. As we saw in the Introduction, it was under the patronage of an O'Carroll king of Ely, Tadhg (Thaddeus) O'Carroll (d. 1152) that one of the great works of Irish art was produced: the Shrine of the Book of Dimma, now in Trinity College.

For many years after the Norman invasion, due to the geographical situation of their territory, the O'Carroll kingdom acted as a buffer zone against the Norman expansion. King Domhnall Fionn, defending his territory, was slain by them in 1205. The *Annals of the Four Masters* record that the English sustained a great defeat by O'Carroll in 1318. But the English also had their victories and, in 1407, Tadhg of Ely, regarded as one of the great benefactors to the Irish Church and clergy, was also slain. Other O'Carroll princes tried to make their kingdoms more secure by marriages into the families of the great Anglo-Norman lords, such as the Butlers who had settled in Urmumhu, eastern Munster, hence Anglicised as Ormond. Theobald FitzWalter had been created 'Chief Butler' of Ireland by Henry II in 1177, hence the surname Butler. They settled in eastern Munster and soon received the title Earls of Ormond.

O'Carroll women were very prominent. 'Mareague' O'Carroll (called Margaret), daughter of the Tadhg who had been a beneficiary to the church, summoned the learned people of all the Irish kingdoms to a meeting on the feastday of Da Sincchell, 26 March 1451, at Killeigh, Co. Offaly. The Chief Brehon of the kingdom, Gille-na-Naemh, recorded the names of the 2700 *ollamhain* present at the gathering.

Her daughter, Fionnguala, had become wife first of The O'Donel and then of Aodh Buidhe O'Neill. She was regarded as one of the most distinguished women of her time and in 1447 she entered the monastery of Killaghy where she died forty-six years later.

The O'Carrolls tended to use the title 'Prince of Ely' after the death of King Donnchadh in 1377. In 1532 the annals record the death of Prince Maelruna, whom the English regarded as having 'ever been one of the King's greatest enemies, and done most hurt to the King's subjects' (Carew MSS). The Irish view is different, of course. The *Annals of Loch Cé* record him as 'The noblest and most illustrious Gael in Leth Moga'. They continue:

> O'Carroll Maolroona, the most distinguished man of his tribe for renown, valour, prosperity, and excellence, to whom poets, travellers, ecclesiastics, and literary men were most thankful; and who gave most entertainment, and bestowed more presents than any other who lived of his lineage, died. He was the supporting mainstay of all persons; the rightful, victorious rudder of his race; the powerful young warrior in the march of tribes; the active triumphant champion of Munster; a precious stone, a carbuncle gem; the anvil of knowledge; and the golden pillar of Ely; and his son, Feranaim, was appointed his successor.

Curiously, Feranaim, or Fear gan Ainm, means Man Without a Name. There was a dynastic dispute within the O'Carroll *derbhfine* and Fear gan Ainm was challenged by the sons of Seán O'Carroll. Gerald FitzGerald, 8th Earl of Kildare, who was Fear gan Ainm's father-in-law, came to his aid in this internal O'Carroll dispute, and besieged the O'Carrolls in Birr Castle. It fell to him. Soon after that the Earl of Kildare was imprisoned in the Tower of London, suspected of plotting against the English king. In 1498 he was back as Lord Deputy, Henry VII of England having said: 'If all Ireland cannot rule this man, let him rule all Ireland.' In 1513 he died of wounds received fighting the O'Carrolls of Ely once again.

However, Fear gan Ainm continued as Prince of the O'Carrolls of Ely. On 12 June 1538 he concluded a treaty with Lord Leonard Grey, the Lord Deputy, that he would cease to be 'Prince' and thenceforth style himself as 'Captain of the Ely O'Carroll, and pay feudal tribute to the English kings'. The treaty outraged Fear gan Ainm's *derbhfine*. In 1541, he was assassinated in Clonisk Castle, near Shinrone. He was supposed to have been elderly and blind by this time and living as a recluse. If so, he would not have continued in office under Brehon law, for he would have been excluded by physical impediment as well as by reclusive habits. It is told that Fear gan Aimn's nephew, Tadhg, was able to gain entrance to the castle through his uncle's trust and then proceeded to slaughter the old man and twelve of his servants who tried to protect him.

Tadhg certainly succeeded his uncle. In May 1543 Henry VIII allowed Tadhg to be recognised as 'captain of his nation' but 'during good behaviour'. Tadhg did not behave as the English wanted, and in 1548 he led a rising in his territory. Sir James Ware curiously called him 'the one-eyed O'Carroll' – curiously, inasmuch as a physical impediment would have excluded him from office under the law. Tadhg initially managed to rout the English troops and drive them from Ely. Where the Tudors could not succeed in warfare, they resorted to diplomacy and guile. Inviting Prince Tadhg to come to Dublin to discuss ways of resolving the conflict, they simply seized him and imprisoned him in Dublin Castle. Having secured a promise of good behaviour under duress, they released him; in 1552, he was not only pardoned but made a knight and bestowed with the title Baron of Ely.

In 1554 Liam Odher O'Carroll, Tadhg's younger brother, supported by the *derbhfine* who, once again, objected to the surrender by their chief, challenged Tadhg. Liam Odher now found himself The O'Carroll. But he also found that the Tudor politicians were not so easily dealt with. He allowed himself to be knighted and then recognised by the English administration as 'captain of his nation'. It was, however, only a means of buying time. He finally rose up and fought an 'awful war' and met his death in 1558 at Kincor.

The English now used their 'influence' to ensure the new O'Carroll would be more sympathetic to their policies. Liam O'Carroll of Lemyvan-ane was installed as The O'Carroll of Ely. On 28 July 1578, he formally recited the surrender ritual, in which he agreed to give up the Irish language and laws, his titles and estates. In return, a portion of the estates were regranted on a feudal basis and he was made a knight. He accepted primogeniture, securing the succession of his properties to his four sons, John, Tadhg, Calloghe and Donoghe, to the exclusion of the rightful heir, his brother Donoghe Koghe O'Carroll, who had been named tanist by the *derbhfine*. He became 'Sir William' (Liam) in 1579, the year after his surrender of the title.

The opposition by the *derbhfine* to Sir William's English law successor resulted in a blood feud. The English administration supported the sons of Sir William, and several O'Carrolls of the *derbhfine*, such as the sons of Fear gan Ainm, putting forward their claims under Brehon law, were assassinated.

However, it proved impossible to impose English law on the O'Carrolls and when Cahir (Calvach), a son of Liam Odher, was appointed The O'Carroll in 1582, it was clear Brehon law still prevailed. He was initially courted by the Tudor administration and knighted by Sir John Perrott in 1584 in Dublin. He played a waiting game for several years until, with the defeat of the English at Yellow Ford, Cahir decided that the time had come to join his forces to those of the other Irish princes. Troops from O'Neill's army, under Eóghan MacRory O'Moore, had moved south and were joined by troops under the command of Donal MacCarthy, son of the late Donal IX. The O'Carroll took part with them in the famous victory over the Earl of Essex at the Pass of Plumes in 1599, where the O'Carroll battle-cry 'Seabhac a bu' (The Hawk to Victory!) is said to have panicked Essex's soldiers. Cahir returned to Lemyvanane after the battle. He had been host to a company of MacMahons from Oriel (Monaghan), some one hundred men, who had fought with him against Essex. Cahir now refused to pay them a promised sum for expenses. One thing led to another and hasty words were exchanged. The story is that Cahir, that night, led some of his men to where the Oriel warriors were sleeping and slaughtered all of them.

The following year when Aodh Ruadh O'Neill Mór was marching southward, the Ulster king took it on himself to punish Cahir for this crime. He devastated the countryside and left a garrison of his own men in it. He recognised the appointment of Mulroony O'Carroll as The O'Carroll. In July 1600 Cahir was assassinated by a group of O'Carrolls and O'Meaghers. The *Annals of the Four Masters* seem generous in recording Cahir as 'a strong arm against the English and Irish neighbours'.

Mulroony, the new chief, was knighted by Sir George Carew at Dublin Castle in 1603, on the day of the coronation of James I in London. Now the concept of the old Ely kingdom was completely gone. The O'Carrolls were soon to become merely Anglicised knights with large landholdings. Indeed, Thomas O'Carroll left the estates to settle in Dublin, becoming Lord Mayor of Dublin. He was knighted by Sir Arthur Chichester and given the Abbey of Baltinglass as his seat.

The family seemed to have adhered to the Stuart cause for a while, being compensated by Charles II for the losses of their estates during the Cromwellian confiscations. Eóghan O'Carroll represented Co. Offaly in James II's Dublin parliament of 1689.

The line of the princely house continued in a new guise, still producing strong leaders such as Antoine Fada (Long Anthony) who was one of Patrick Sarsfield's commanders in the Williamite wars. He was owner of

Emmell Castle. At his headquarters in Nenagh, hearing of the approach of the Williamite troops, he burnt the town and force-marched his troops to Barna. The Williamite soldiers were ambushed by him there and slain to a man. The battle became known as Bloody Togher.

It was Long Anthony's great-grandson, Richard O'Carroll, who lost the remaining lands secured by his family. He indulged in lavish hospitality and was generous to the point of foolishness.

There were many lines of descent of the O'Carroll princely family. One of the most fascinating was the branch founded by Charles O'Carroll who settled in Maryland in America in 1688. He was a direct descendant of King Tadhg who had endowed the Irish Church. He had managed to obtain a commission, from King James II, appointing him Attorney-General of Maryland. He married a daughter of Colonel Dernall, a kinsman of Lord Baltimore, who appointed him as 'agent and receiver general' of the colony. Charles' grandson, another Charles, of Carrolltown, signed the American Declaration of Independence. This Charles was born in Annapolis in 1737, educated by Jesuits, and studied law in Paris and London. He was thirty-six when he became active in politics and published a series of arguments against the administration, establishing himself as a leading member of the American independence movement. Early in 1776 he was sent by the American Congress, together with Benjamin Franklin and Samuel Chase, to the northern colonies (what is now Canada) to argue the case for independence. He was elected to Congress for Maryland soon afterwards and became one of the signatories of the Declaration of Independence.

He also worked on the Maryland State Constitution and served in the upper house of the state legislature. He worked in both the United States Senate and the Maryland Senate, retiring from public life in 1800. He died aged ninety-four in 1832 and was buried at Doughoregan Manor, near Elliott City. He was regarded as the richest man in the country. Charles left a line which provided a governor of Maryland in the person of John Lee Carroll.

William O'Carroll of Arabeg, Birr, was regarded as the senior representative in 1915 and the genealogy of the various lines of Arrabeg, Kilfada and Emmel, with certified copies of wills and deeds, was held by him. However the current chief traces his line from the Litterluna branch of Daniel O'Carroll, whose great-great-grandson, James Carroll, born c. 1815, emigrated with his son, also James, born 1840, to the United States in 1851. The latter had a son, Michael Frederick, who was born in 1864 and lived in New York where he died in 1938.

His son, the current O'Carroll's father, Winfrey Frederick O'Carroll, was born in 1909 and moved the family to Tehama, California. With the death of Winfrey Frederick in 1969, Frederick James claimed the succession to the title as The O'Carroll of Ely. He was finally given 'courtesy recognition' by the Chief Herald of Ireland on 22 January 1993.

After his career in the US Navy, The O'Carroll became an executive for the West Mark Tank Trailer Company. He retired in 1987 and became involved in the establishment of the Clan Cian Services, a company chartered in 1982, promoting the Clan O'Carroll. The O'Carroll also supports the Roscrae Heritage Society, in Roscrae, Co. Tipperary. Like other members of the surviving Gaelic nobility, he is anxious that Ireland's Gaelic identity should not be lost. He endorses the state's proclaimed policy to restore the Irish language and its constitutional place as the first official language of the state. He takes his role seriously:

> I feel the chiefs and chieftains should be allowed consideration for their titles within the future political scope of modern Ireland. Since 1982 I have been actively involved with representation, promotion of Irish culture, instructive at activities in regard to Irish heritage, primarily in the United States with visits to Ely O'Carroll territory.

O'Carroll says: 'I currently hold a US passport. If allowed, I would wish to hold an Irish passport. I consider my relationship to the Irish Republic as an Irish American seeking restoration of my family to the republic.'

The O'Carroll first married Agnes Heimstra, a descendant of the Butlers of Ormond. They were divorced, and he is currently married to Gracy Ann Block. His son, by his first marriage, is Frederick Arthur James O'Carroll, born 9 July 1968, and he is The O'Carroll's tanist. Frederick Arthur has two sons, Michael Frederick James (b.1991) and Seán Arthur James (b. 1993), and a daughter. The O'Carroll looks upon the promotion of his heritage very much as a family business. He personally took the attitude that his title should descend by primogeniture. He was one of only two chiefs out of the twenty who initially took this line. He explained: 'I feel Gaelic titles and the right of succession should remain meaningful today, even without the Brehon laws, in the modern Irish Republic. My title is acknowledged through a line of hereditary descent through the kings of Éile of the Litterluna branch of O'Carrolls originating with Brehon times.'

This is not an argument accepted by scholarship nor by his fellow chiefs; the reiteration by the Standing Council in January 1999 that Gaelic titles should be founded on the Brehon law of succession has not been challenged by O'Carroll.

IV
THE O'DONOGHUE OF THE GLENS,
Lord of Glenflesk
(Ó Donnchadha an Ghleanna)

The current O'Donoghue of the Glens is Geoffrey Vincent Paul O'Donoghue, born on 19 July 1937. Like other Munster princely families, the origin of the O'Donoghue line resides in the Eóghanacht royal house of Munster descending from Coirpre Luachra, one of the seven sons of King Conall Corc, whose descendants became known as the Eóghanacht Locha Léin – Lough Leane being the largest of the Killarney lakes in Co. Kerry. The family produced several kings of Munster, the last being Olchoba mac Cináeda (d. AD 851). The patronymic came from Donnchadh, who was head of the family in the twelfth century. The numerous islands in Loch Léin were the main strongholds of the Ua Donnchadha or O'Donoghues. Ross Castle, on the shores of the lake, was granted to them as their principal residence by the MacCarthy kings after the famous victory over the Anglo-Normans at Callan on 24 July 1261.

It was around this time that a legend sprang up around Donall, a grandson of Donnchadh, who was then The O'Donoghue Mór. There are two agnomens attached to his name. One is *na nGeimhleach* and it has been argued that this means 'of the fetters'. The alternative form *na gCaoil-each* means 'of the slender reeds'. No one really knows the correct form. The story, which is very traditionally Celtic, is that Donall fell into an enchanted sleep and rests in a hidden cavern beneath Loch Léin. Every May Day morning he may be seen at dawn riding his horse, shod with silver shoes, across the waters of the lake. He can appear at other times in order to protect the people against their oppressors.

The senior line of the O'Donoghues was that of The O'Donoghue Mór, which appears to have become extinguished during the Tudor conquests. Céitinn, in his *History*, mentions that The O'Donoghue Mór and the O'Sullivan Mór were the two princes who were allowed to perform the ceremony of inauguration for The MacCarthy Mór. Pardons had been granted to Rory O'Donoghue, given in the letters patent as 'alias The O'Donoghue More', and his son, another Rory, during the 1570s. In a grant of the former O'Donoghue estates at Ross to Nicholas Browne, which appears under a Lord Deputy's warrant of 7 March 1600, no mention is made of what had happened to The O'Donoghue Mór, just that the estates and lordship had been granted to him by King Donal IX MacCarthy Mór (referred to as 'earl of Clancar'). With Donal now being dead, the English Crown felt it could confirm the grant of the estates.

The O'Donoghue of the Glens, a cadet branch of this family holding the lordship of Glenflesk to the south-east of Killarney, also having received pardons at the end of the Tudor conquests, managed to survive the turmoil of the conquest and confiscations. It is a moot point whether The O'Donoghue of the Glens might be considered the heir to the title of The O'Donoghue Mór – not that there is any intention on the part of the family to make such a claim.

The history of the family is fascinating. The name Seafraidh (Geoffrey) has become a popular name among the holders of the chiefly title. Seafraidh, The O'Donoghue of the Glens died in May 1601, before the disastrous defeat at Kinsale. His brother Ruaidri (Roger or Rory) had been executed by the English in 1585. That the O'Donoghues still managed to retain their lands in Glenflesk (Gleann Fleisce, the Valley of the Hoop) in Kerry, might have been due to the natural fortifications of the Derryna-saggart Mountains.

Seafraidh's son, Tadhg, married the daughter of Donal MacCarthy Reagh. Their son Seafraidh was born in 1620, and succeeded his father to the title in the middle of the Cromwellian devastations in 1655. His father had been holding out against the Cromwellian General Ludlow in Killaha Castle. Whether Tadhg's death was from natural causes or the result of the siege is not clear. Certainly, General Ludlow reduced the castle that year. The new chief was already active in the war against the English. His brother Tadhg had married Griobha, daughter of Sir Phelim O'Neill, leader of the 1641 insurrection. Sir Phelim had been executed in Dublin two years before the new chief was elected.

Seafraidh Ó Donnchadha an Ghleanna appears as one of the most romantic chiefs of this time. He was not only a remarkable guerrilla leader but one of the most respected poets writing in the Irish language. He wrote in a courtly, traditional style which is known as the *dán díreach* metre, producing political poems, laments and elegies including a poem on a pet spaniel killed while in pursuit of a mouse. As a man of action, O'Donoghue of the Glens was able to make good use of the natural fortifications of Glenflesk. Glenflesk became a place of refuge for people from the conquered areas. As we have seen, in 1654 the Irish population had been ordered into a reservation consisting of Connacht and Co. Clare, Glenflesk lay outside this reserve but was still holding out, and it did so until the Stuart restoration in 1660. Although the castle and the estates of The O'Donoghue of the Glens had been confiscated on paper, no one had the courage to enter Glenflesk and enforce the confiscations. Most of the Irish landholders thought the Stuart restoration would mean a return of their confiscated lands. It did not. Seafraidh wrote a bitter poem:

's barra ar an gcleas . . .

This caps all their tricks, this statute from overseas
That lays the switch on the people of Eber Fionn.
A crooked deal has robbed us of our claim
And all our rights in Ireland are swept away.

The Gaels are stripped in Ireland at last
And now let the grave be dug of every man.
Or let them get their pass and cross the waves
And promise to stay gone to their dying day.

He ends, however, with a hopeful verse:

Although the English are stronger now than the Gaels
And though their fortunes are better than for some time here:
Relying on their titles, they will not yield a field.
On their backs God's anger will pour down in streams.[1]

Seafraidh died in 1678 before he could witness what further tricks and burdens Ireland was to suffer. He was buried in the chancel of Muckross Abbey and is also commemorated on a monument in Killarney, confusingly under another Irish version of the name Geoffrey – Goffraidh.

In spite of Seafraidh's anguish at the failure of the Stuarts to rectify the confiscations of Cromwell, his son Donal, the new chief, supported James II. Donal and his brother Florence joined with MacCarthy Mór, then recognised to be Lord Clancarthy of the Muskerry line. After the Treaty of Limerick, Donal remained in Ireland hoping that the English would keep to the treaty, and he even applied for a portion of his former Kerry estate in 1700.

His brother, Florence O'Donoghue, was not so trusting of English intentions and became one of those who, in the words of his father, received 'their pass and cross[ed] the waves' to become Chevalier Florence O'Donoghue, commander of the bodyguard to Queen Mary of Modena. Florence's second son Geoffrey O'Donoghue became an officer in the army of the French Republic. A descendant of this line achieved fame in the Irish Brigade of the Spanish army. He was Lieutenant-General Juan O'Donojú. Juan (1755–1821) was appointed Viceroy of Mexico in order to negotiate Spanish withdrawal. He devised the *Plan de Iguala* which gave Mexico its independence in 1821, thus taking his place in history as Spain's last Viceroy in Mexico.

The family of The O'Donoghue of the Glens managed to survive the Penal Law period and all attempts to eradicate them. They were one of those aristocratic families who 'went underground' during this period, known and respected by local people but, to the English administration, merely one more family bearing the name 'Donoghue'. They lived quietly under the Penal Laws, refusing to change their religion for political gain, until those pernicious laws were repealed in the nineteenth century. They then re-emerged to take an active part in public life.

Charles James, The O'Donoghue of the Glens (1806 – c.1833) died in Florence while on a trip to Italy. The family were then living at Summerhill, Killarney. His son Daniel O'Donoghue became The O'Donoghue of the Glens, and set out to place the family once more on the historical map of Ireland. His cousin had been a maternal aunt of the Irish republican revolutionary advocate and theoretician of the 1848 insurrection, the Young Ireland leader Thomas Davies. Educated at Stonyhurst, Daniel became a Whig Member of Parliament for Tipperary in 1857–65 and later for Tralee, 1865–85.

Daniel attracted a lot of publicity and he was not reticent about using his Gaelic title. Even *The Times* of London accepted its use and always referred to him as The O'Donoghue. While English law could not recognise those Gaelic chiefly titles abolished by statute and common law, *Thom's Directory* now published listings of those claiming such titles; The O'Donoghue was one of the first titles to be so listed during the Victorian period.

However, when *The Times* referred to The O'Donoghue, it was not without disdain and bitterness. A leader of 25 February 1862, stated:

> The O'Donoghue has been making one of those exhibitions which can only be made in just such a place as the British Parliament, and at just such a time as this middle of the nineteenth century. With the perfect certainty of no unpleasant consequences, he has been able to tamper with his allegiance to defy his Sovereign and finally to insult his opponent on the floor of the House of Commons. In the reign of Queen Elizabeth singular personages appeared in the streets of London under quaint Irish denominations, with bands of retainers in barbaric accoutrements. The Court connived at a breach of the law that would not have been tolerated in any rational Englishman, and which only amused the rabble, for there was no surer way to lay the ghost of Irish independence than to let it show itself in the streets at midday.

Apparently, The O'Donoghue of the Glens as a 'Home Rule' Member
of Parliament had addressed a meeting in Dublin's Rotunda. According
to *The Times*, he and his followers had 'denied the Queen's flag to be
the Irishman's flag, they denounced Englishmen as their natural foes,
they claimed sympathy with the Irishmen in the American Federal Army,
and they invited Irishmen to seize the opportunity of shaking off the
English yoke.' In the course of a debate in the House of Commons this
meeting was referred to, and the Chief Secretary for Ireland, Sir Robert
Peel, said that it consisted of 'manikin traitors' who sought to imitate
the 'cabbage garden' proceedings of 1848. This was a reference to the
fiasco of the Young Ireland uprising of July 1848, when some of the
leaders, including William Smith O'Brien, brother of Sir Lucius of Dromoland Castle, a direct descendant of the High King Brían Bóroimhe,
were surrounded by troops in Widow McCormack's farmhouse at Ballingarry and, after a skirmish, forced to surrender. It was later disparagingly called the skirmish in Widow McCormack's 'cabbage patch'.

The exact words of Sir Robert Peel's speech from the Parliamentary
Report were:

> A meeting was then held in the Rotunda, at which a few manikin
> traitors sought to imitate the cabbage garden heroes of 1848; but I
> am glad to say they met with no response. There was no one to follow.
> There was not a single man of respectability who answered the appeal.

Sir Robert Peel's reference to The O'Donoghue as one of the 'manikin
traitors' was considered by The O'Donoghue to be a personal insult. His
friend, the Member of Parliament for Limerick, Major G. Gavin, later
explained the subsequent actions to the Commons. 'I thought over those
expressions, and I arrived at the conclusion that they were words that no
gentleman should rest under. I had the honour of being in the army for
twenty-four years, and I am quite certain that no such language would
be tolerated in that honourable profession.'

Indeed, The O'Donoghue felt so strongly that he asked Gavin to 'act
as his friend', a euphemism in those days for a second in a duel, and
Gavin called on Sir Robert Peel to ask him to withdraw the words. Sir
Robert said that 'he would adhere to the words in their integrity'. Major
Gavin then asked him to refer him to a friend, conveying The O'Donoghue's challenge. Sir Robert told Gavin that he would need a letter
outlining the challenge. Gavin wrote a note:

> My dear Sir Robert – As the explanation given by you to me regarding
> the words you made use of towards The O'Donoghue last night in

the House is not satisfactory, and as the matter cannot possibly remain in its present position, I must request you at once to refer me to a friend.

Sir Robert told Major Gavin that he would refer the matter to his 'friend'.

The friend turned out to be Lord Palmerston, the Prime Minister. Palmerston brought the matter up in the House of Commons, accusing The O'Donoghue of a breach of privilege in challenging Sir Robert Peel. The Prime Minister had absolved Sir Robert from backing out of an 'affair of honour' by telling him that it was his duty to decline the challenge: 'It is our privilege to say whatever we think right in Parliament and it is a breach of the privileges of this House that what any Member says in this House should be questioned out of this House by any person whatsoever.' Instead of receiving an apology from Sir Robert Peel for his insulting remarks, The O'Donoghue was ordered by the Speaker to apologise to Sir Robert and the House. The O'Donoghue commenced his speech by saying that he deeply regretted if he had violated the privileges of the House. He was cut short by the Speaker when he referred to Sir Robert Peel's words and pointed out that they were personally insulting. Peel accepted the apology and assured the House that the matter would proceed no further. It did. Rather spitefully, Sir Robert removed The O'Donoghue from his position as a Justice of the Peace for Cos. Cork and Kerry.

The people of Tipperary demonstrated their support for The O'Donoghue by giving a sumptuous banquet in his honour in April 1862. With the ending of the Civil War in America and the demobilisation of tens of thousands of Irish veterans who had taken an Irish Republican Brotherhood oath, there now began a period of unrest in Ireland leading to the Suspension of Habeas Corpus in February 1866.

The Times began to describe The O'Donoghue as 'a defender of Fenianism' (the name derives from the Fianna, the élite bodyguard of the High Kings of Ireland). In a debate on the 'disturbances' in Ireland, on 9 February 1866, *The Times* reported:

The O'Donoghue . . . proceeded to point out the causes of this disaffection. The chief of these, he said, was the Act of Union, which had deprived the people of the right of self-government and prevented them from redressing the evils of which they complained. He denied that Fenianism had produced this disaffection; the Fenians, on the contrary, had found everything ready to their hands, and the foundation of Fenianism, with which he warned the House the majority of

[147]

peasantry deeply sympathised, was an impression that all the ills which afflicted the country were the result of English misrule.

Against the Fenian attempt to seize the munitions store at Chester Castle in February 1867 and then the insurrection, mainly confined to Dublin, Cork, Limerick, Tipperary and Clare, during March, *The Times* castigated the speeches of The O'Donoghue.

On 12 February 1867, *The Times* was able to report another speech by The O'Donoghue in which he boldly stated: 'English rule in Ireland was synonymous with oppression and tyranny'. The O'Donoghue's outspokenness in the cause of Irish independence caused Dr David Moriarty, the Catholic Bishop of Kerry, to publicly censure his conduct. The O'Donoghue replied in a letter in *The Times* telling the bishop that his admonition that Ireland must be subservient to the interests of England was not in accordance with the spirit of the Irish people.

With the defeat of the Fenian insurrection and a total clamp-down on republican activity, followed by the emergence of Isaac Butt's Irish Party to pursue domestic self-government in Westminster, The O'Donoghue, who was very much an individual, found several matters in the party policy to disagree with. *The Times* immediately started to lavish praise on him claiming that he had done a 'public service' by not joining the Irish Party.

In May 1874 The O'Donoghue wrote a letter explaining his apparent change of heart towards Irish self-government. 'I have not joined in the agitation for a separate legislature not, as you seem to think, because I am opposed to Irish rule in Ireland, but because I believe the Irish members can govern Ireland in the Imperial parliament.' In his view, a reform of Parliament with a stronger emphasis on Irish Members concluding domestic Irish business without the majority of English Members being allowed to vote on these matter was the answer. However, he soon realised that this 'ideal' would not be permitted by the majority English Members and when in 1879 Charles Stewart Parnell took over the Irish Party he became its active supporter.

The O'Donoghue was a man of extremes. At the same time as apparently supporting the Fenian cause he took a commission as a major in the Kerry Militia. He married the daughter and co-heiress of Sir John Ennis of Ballinahoun Court, Athlone, Westmeath, and that became his seat. But it seems he was a spendthrift, squandering his money. In 1870 he was in the Court of Bankruptcy and the hearing became a *cause célèbre*. His bankruptcy was annulled in 1871. In 1881 another bankruptcy hearing was begun and again the findings were annulled in 1882. This colourful O'Donoghue died in 1889.

The President of the Irish Republic receives some of the survivors of the old Gaelic aristocracy at Áras an Uachtaráin, the presidential residence in Dublin, in October, 1991. l. to r. back row: – John Joyce, head of the Joyce family; The O'Donovan; Patrick Joyce; O'Conor Don, Prince of Connacht; O'Ruairc of Breifne, MacGillycuddy of the Reeks; middle row: – Chevalier Gerard Crotty, The O'Morchoe; The O'Grady (d.1993); The O'Brien, Prince of Thomond; Mr Nicholas Robinson; The O'Neill, Prince of Clanaboy; front row: – MacCarthy Mór, Prince of Desmond; O'Donoghue of the Glens; Admiral Pascual O'Dogherty; Maguire, Prince of Fermanagh: Irish President, Mary Robinson; MacDermot, Prince of Coolavin; O'Long; Chief Herald Donal Begley and a representative of Bord Fáilte.

Three of the four heirs to the High Kingship wearing the
insignia of the Niadh Nask: MacCarthy Mór, Prince of Desmond;
O'Conor Don, Prince of Connacht and O'Brien, Prince of Thomond.

Donal IX MacCarthy Mór, King
of Desmond (d.1596). Dated 1568
the portrait shows the king
wearing the order of the Niadh
Nask, carrying the white wand of
office and his hand resting on the
crown of Munster. He wears St
Cormac's Ring (the coronation
ring of the Kings of Munster) on
his episcopal finger of his right
hand.

Display of heirlooms of the Royal House of MacCarthy Mór, on loan from the current MacCarthy Mór, to the Cashel Heritage Centre, Co. Tipperary.

Leopoldo O'Donnell, Duke of Tetuan, and heir to The O'Donel, Prince of Tirconnell, receives an honorary doctorate from the National University of Ireland in 1954. Eamon de Valéra, as Chancellor, then Prime Minister of the Irish Republic and eventually to become President, looks on.

Hugo O'Donnell, Duke of Estrada, heir to the Duke of Tetuan, being greeted by King Juan Carlos of Spain in 1997.

The MacCarthy Mór,
Prince of Desmond.

The MacMorrough Kavanagh,
Prince of Leinster.

The Countess of Clandermond with The O'Brien, Prince of Thomond, at Cashel Palace Hotel, 1996.

The Maguire, Prince of Fermanagh.

The O'Ruairc,
Prince of Breifne.

Desmond O'Conor, tanist
(heir-apparent) to O'Conor Don.

(Above) The O'Morchoe and his wife Margaret.

The O'Grady (d. 1998) at Cashel.

The O Dochartaigh of Inishowen at an inauguration ceremony.
He carries the sword of his ancestor Caothair, who was carrying it
when he was slain in ambush by English troops in 1608.

The O'Carroll of Ely.

The O'Donovan.

The O'Callaghan.

The Fox.

The MacCarthy Mór, Prince of Desmond, welcomes Irish President, Mary Robinson, and her husband, Nicholas, to his ancestral capital at Cashel in 1996.

The Standing Council of Irish Chiefs and Chieftains meeting at Cashel in 1994. Front row, left to right: – The O'Brien, Prince of Thomond; The O'Morchoe; The Maguire, Prince of Fermanagh; The MacCarthy Mór, Prince of Desmond; The O'Callaghan. Back row, left to right: – The O'Ruairc of Breifne; The O'Donoghue of the Glens; Chevalier Gerard Crotty (Heraldic Adviser to the Council), The O'Long of Garranelongy; The O'Grady (d. 1998) and The MacGillycuddy of the Reeks.

His eldest son Geoffrey Charles Patrick O'Donoghue succeeded to the title at the age of thirty. Like his father he was educated at Stonyhurst. Unlike his father, he preferred a quiet life. He married the daughter of a surgeon-general in the British army, Anne Charlton of Clonmacnoise House, Offaly. When he died in 1935 his son Geoffrey Charles Patrick Randal O'Donoghue succeeded as The O'Donoghue of the Glens.

Geoffrey had been born in 1895 and also went to Stonyhurst, which was becoming a family tradition. From school he went to Sandhurst and was commissioned, in January 1915, as a second lieutenant in the Connaught Rangers. By the end of 1915 he was a full lieutenant, serving in the 3rd Battalion, and was sent to France. He was wounded early in 1916 but, after a spell of convalescence, rejoined his unit. Today we know something about post-traumatic stress disorder. Those soldiers executed in 1914–18 by firing squad for 'cowardice' and recently accepted to have been cases of shell-shock, which was not then admitted as a physical trauma by the British army, have now been 'pardoned' and rehabilitated in the service records. Such a trauma is a possible explanation for the fact that Geoffrey seemed to go to pieces. His conduct led to a court martial on 2 March 1917, at Locre, resulting in his being cashiered.

Geoffrey, even before the verdict was confirmed, had enlisted as a private in the South Irish Horse, and some months later transferred to the Royal Dublin Fusiliers. He served until February 1919, officially being discharged in January 1920 with the rank of lance-corporal. The day after his discharge he re-enlisted as a private in the 1st Battalion of the Royal Dublin Fusiliers and was sent to India. One wonders if he was spurred on with the thought of redeeming himself for being cashiered.

Speaking on Radio Éireann some years before his death in 1974, The O'Donoghue told how he was stationed in Multan (Multoon) in the Punjab. It was here that he learned the news during June 1920 that soldiers from the 1st Battalion of his old regiment, the Connaught Rangers, hearing of the atrocities of the English 'Black and Tans' and 'Auxiliaries' in Ireland, had run up the Irish republican flag and refused to take orders from their officer. The incident happened at the battalion bases at Jullundur and at Solan. Only one soldier was eventually executed out of the sixty men who were sentenced to death and the others had their sentences commuted to penal servitude. The British army as well as the politicians had been keen to 'hush up' the mutiny and too many executions were liable to bring the matter to public attention. The consideration was not simply the effect such news would have in Ireland during the continuing conflict there, but also the reaction in India. This was only a year after General A.E. Dyer had ordered his troops to fire into a crowd of several thousands, including women and children, attending a peaceful protest meeting in Jallianwala Bagh, a square in the middle of the city of Amristsar. Casualties were 379 dead and over 1200 wounded. Subsequently, General Dyer had ordered public floggings and forced Indians to crawl on their hands and knees through certain streets in the city. The situation in India as well as Ireland under the '*pax Britannia*' was volatile.

The O'Donoghue, in his radio broadcast, recalled how he and three companions named Kirwan, Fitzpatrick and Murray had hoisted an Irish republican flag over their base in Multan on St Patrick's Day, 1921, to commemorate the event. There is no regimental record of any such incident in the official diaries of the Royal Dublin Fusiliers but, certainly, within seven months of his arriving in India, Fusilier O'Donoghue was discharged from the army, his 'services no longer required'. Returning to the newly established Irish Free State, Geoffrey became a captain in the Free State Army.

The current O'Donoghue of the Glens succeeded to the title at the age of thirty-six on the death of his father. Breaking with the previous tradition, he was educated at the Christian Brothers School in Enniscorthy, Co. Wexford, living for a while in Westmeath before making his home in Tullamore, Co. Offaly. He is a widower, his wife Frances, a schoolteacher, having been killed in a road accident in 1984, and has three sons and four daughters. He runs a small engineering business, having previously served as a non-commissioned officer in the Irish Army Air Corps. As an aviation engineer he later worked for the British Aircraft Corporation on the development of the VC10, TSR2 and Concorde.

The Irish *Who's Who* has called him 'a low profile chief'. He accepts that his title only has a real meaning if passed down through the Brehon laws of succession. Therefore it is not his eldest son Conor (born 1964) nor his second son Donagh (born 1970) who will succeed him as The O'Donoghue of the Glens, but his youngest son Geoffrey Paul (born 1971). He has already been appointed as tanist and heir to the title. Geoffrey Paul is a graduate of Trinity College, Dublin, and holds a degree in computer science.

While The O'Donoghue of the Glens is inclined to the belief that Gaelic titles might be seen as something of an anachronism in a democratic republic, he believes that they can only have validity if they are a link with Gaelic culture and law and not recreated in an English primogeniture system. He considers that only the Irish of the 'Diaspora' show any real interest in the old Gaelic nobility. 'Most Irish people in Ireland do not forget that many of the Gaelic nobility fled abroad leaving the ordinary Irish people to face the devastations and Penal Laws of the English conquest.' He feels that Irish people are generally unaware of the old Gaelic aristocracy and would not understand if they were now given any role in the modern Irish state. He thinks that perhaps subsequent generations of chiefs might overcome this lack of knowledge.

The O'Donoghue of the Glens is a mild-mannered man, passionately interested in studying Irish history in what time he can spare from running his business concerns. He is a vice-president of the Royal Eóghanacht Society and, like the majority of Eóghanacht chiefs, a holder of the Niadh Nask. His ambition is to ensure that there is an awareness among Irish people of the history of the Gaelic aristocracy. He also hopes that the Irish language will be preserved as 'it is an important link with the past and without it there can be no understanding of that past'. Although he is a Catholic, he does not believe in a special relationship between Church and state: 'The old Gaelic tradition was not religiously exclusive. It is time for Ireland to accept that it is a secular state.'

The accusation that the old Gaelic aristocracy were 'deserters' cannot be levelled against this chiefly line. There has always been an O'Donoghue of the Glens living, if not in Glenflesk itself, then close by in Co. Kerry, until modern times. Now the chief lives in Co. Offaly. The O'Donoghues have suffered equally with their people from the results of the conquests and played no small part in fighting those conquests. Additionally, they have played their part in the continuing struggle for independence. No consideration of the War of Independence (1919–21) can be made without reference to the historical studies of Florence O'Donoghue (1894–1967), from Rathmore, Kerry, who fought in Cork No. 1 Brigade of the Irish Volunteers as brigade adjutant and intelligence officer. He also served in the Defence Forces 1940–45. And no general review of Irish literature can ignore the diversity of the poems of their most romantic chief, Seafraidh Ó Donnchadha an Ghleanna. The history of the O'Donoghues of the Glens is truly reflective of the struggle for existence of Gaelic Ireland.

V
THE O'DONOVAN
of Clan Cathail
(Ó Donndhubháin)

The O'Donovan chiefs are of princely origin and the family stems from one of the royal septs of the Eóghanachta of Munster. The family take their name from Donnabháin, a son of Ceallacháin mac Buadacháin, King of Munster (d. AD 954). Donnabháin settled near Limerick where his father had defeated the Danes who had established their city state there. His name meant 'black' or 'swarthy-headed'. About 977 his son Crom Ua Dhonnabháin (O'Donovan), adopted the patronymic form, then becoming popular in Ireland. Castle Croim, on the bank of the Maigue, Co. Limerick, became a seat of their power.

They were eventually driven from their ancestral lands by the expanding power of the Dál gCais who were not only dominant in North Munster (Thomond) but were to wrest the throne of Munster from the Eóghanacht. The Uí Dhonnabháin and their followers moved south to settle in the area of Glandore Bay and Skibbereen, in south-west Cork, where the current chief still resides.

Crom's son Cathal O'Donovan, who became the head of his family, gave his name to the clan which became the Clan Cathail. The head of the O'Donovans was originally called the 'Lord of Clan Cathail' but the current O'Donovan points out that this title has not been used by his family for a considerable time. Another branch of the family became the Clan Loughlin. Both branches paid feudal dues and were installed by The MacCarthy Reagh, who in turn served their kinsmen, the MacCarthy kings of Munster.

Dermot O'Donovan of Castle Donovan, which is three miles north of Drimoleague, Co. Cork, received a pardon from Elizabeth I in May 1577 and surrendered his title and estates. The last acknowledged Lord of Clan Cathail to be installed under the Brehon system, receiving the white wand of office from The MacCarthy Reagh in 1591, was Donal O'Donovan of Castle Donovan. The English administration, in the person of the Lord Chancellor, Archbishop Adam Loftus, recognised him as 'captain of his nation', the euphemism for a senior Gaelic noble, on 12 February 1592. Dr John O'Donovan found an inauguration ode in Irish written by Maldoni O'Morrison which he translated in a personal letter to The O'Donovan dated 15 September 1841:

> Who is the prop of the name of the West
> Of the Princes of the Race of Fiaha?
> It behoveth one like me
> To point out the Chief of the Name,
> The one of Donal Fragon of Tonn Cleena
> Is the representative of the hereditary name . . .

Donal (called Daniel by the English) finally surrendered not only his title but the territorial estate in the reign of James I to Sir Nicholas Welsh, the English President of Munster, in 1601. In 1608 he is reported to have received a regrant of the entire estate, having agreed to convert

THE KINGDOM OF MUNSTER (DESMOND)

to the Anglican Protestant faith and become English in speech and culture and accept English law. He was, however, not rewarded with a title and is referred to as 'gentleman'. His Gaelic title had been abolished under law.

The Irish scholar, John O'Donovan, a member of a cadet branch of the family, wrote to The O'Donovan in 1841: 'I am satisfied that none of the name of O'Donovan ever had a [English] title; never! not even that of knight! . . . It does not appear that any of that family ever got a title under the Crown of England except Sir Owen who fought at Kinsale 1601–2.'

Donal's son Donal (also referred to as Daniel) was stripped of his estates during the Cromwellian devastations. His son, also Daniel, managed to have them restored by Charles II. An adherent of the Stuarts, Daniel served in James II's Dublin parliament of 1689 as Member for Baltimore. He became a colonel in the Jacobite army. Having commanded Charlesfort at Kinsale he was forced to surrender to the future Duke of Marlborough, John Churchill. He had the foresight to obtain honourable terms from Churchill who secured him in his estates in spite of the Williamite confiscations.

It was with another Daniel O'Donovan (whose will is dated 1770) that his direct line almost ceased. In his will, O'Donovan named as his heir Morgan Donovan, of the city of Cork, described as 'a kinsman'. This demonstrates that the Brehon concepts were not dead among the O'Donovans because Daniel had two living sons. So this kinsman Morgan, with family approval, was to inherit the residue of the estates in order 'to preserve them with the chiefship of the sept'. However, Morgan died before Daniel's own son Richard and so the inheritance went to him.

General Richard O'Donovan, born 1768, served in the 6th Dragoon Regiment of the British army in Flanders and Spain. He was married but without issue and his brother had died unmarried. Richard left the estate of Clan Cathail to his widow and his remaining property to his cousin, the son of the kinsman Morgan who had been named in his father's will. This son, Reverend Morgan O'Donovan, rector of Dundurrow, Co. Cork, (1769–1839) became The O'Donovan. He married Alicia, a daughter of William Jones, of the Bence-Jones family.

His son Morgan William O'Donovan (1796–1870) succeeded to the title followed by his brother Henry Winthrop O'Donovan (1812–90). Henry was High Sheriff of the county and married a daughter of Gerald de Courcy O'Grady who was The O'Grady at Kilballyowen. It was Henry who made a particular point of reviving the old Gaelic title. His son, Morgan William O'Donovan, became a colonel in the Royal Munster

Fusiliers and served in the South African War, commanding the regiment's 4th Battalion from 1903 to 1914. He also served as High Sheriff of Cork before he died in 1940.

His successor was Morgan John Winthrop O'Donovan, who followed his father into a military career serving in the Royal Irish Fusiliers during World War I, winning a Military Cross in 1917 and being mentioned in dispatches. As a brigadier he commanded the 1st Battalion of the regiment from 1937 to 1940 and retired to finish the war serving with the Red Cross. He died in 1969 to be succeeded by his son.

The current O'Donovan points out that among the famous members of the clan was Diarmuid (Jeremiah) O'Donovan Rossa (1831–1915), born in the family territory of Rosscabrery. His first language was Irish and he ran a small business in Skibbereen. He became a leading organiser of the Irish Republican Brotherhood in 1858. He became business manager of *The Irish People*, the journal of the movement, but was arrested in 1865 and sentenced to life imprisonment for treason. In 1869, while still in prison, he was elected by the people of Tipperary as their Member of Parliament. He was badly treated in English prisons and wrote a classic account of his ill-treatment, published in New York in 1874. He had been released due to the public outcry about this treatment in 1871 and exiled to America.

He continued to be active through his newspaper *United Irishmen*, urging the continued struggle for an independent republic in Ireland. He died in 1915 and his body was brought back to Ireland to be buried at Glasnevin in Dublin. Pádraic Pearse gave his famous graveside oration which wound up with the prophetic words:

> The Defenders of this Realm have worked well in secret and in the open. They think that they have pacified Ireland. They think that they have purchased half of us and intimidated the other half. They think that they have foreseen everything, think that they have provided against everything; but the fools, the fools, the fools! – they have left us our Fenian dead, and while Ireland holds these graves, Ireland unfree shall never be at peace.

Within the year the Easter uprising had taken place in Ireland.

Another member of the family was the antiquarian and scholar John O'Donovan (1809–61) whose works are legion, including pioneering translations and editions of many of the ancient manuscript books of medieval Ireland. His son Edmund O'Donovan (1844–83) became a famous war correspondent. In 1883 he went with the army of Hicks Pasha to the Sudan as a representative of the *Daily News*. On 1 November

General William Hicks' ten thousand troops were ambushed at El Obeid by the troops of the Mahdi. Three days later not a man had survived and O'Donovan was never heard of again.

The current holder of the title, Morgan Gerald Daniel O'Donovan, was born on 4 May 1931 in Pau, France, where his mother Cornelia, daughter of William Bagnell of the Royal College of Surgeons, Dublin, was also born and partially brought up. Daniel, as he is known, was educated at Stowe and at Trinity College, Cambridge, where he received his master's degree in 1954. He married Frances Jane, the only daughter of Field Marshal Sir Gerald Templer. His son and heir is Morgan Teige Gerald, born in 1961 and educated at Harrow. He is a barrister in London and is also married.

The family seat is still in the ancestral lands. The current O'Donovan settled his family in Skibbereen, Co. Cork, on the death of his mother in 1974. He had been managing director of an engineering business, but turned to farming and farmed his estate for ten years. Then he decided to rent the unusable acreage and improve two lodge houses and two more houses for tourist accommodation. He serves on the General Synod of the Church of Ireland, is a governor of Middleton College, Cork, and serves on the Standing Council of Irish Chiefs and Chieftains, being elected chairman in January 1998.

He accepts, but with qualification, that Brehon law succession is the only meaningful way to inherit a Gaelic title.

I claim that my being Chief of the Name is indisputable. My family being fortunate in that Dr John O'Donovan produced after lengthy research, and as a footnote to his great work in translating *The Annals of the Four Masters*, my family pedigree, the historical veracity of which has never been scholastically challenged or at any rate refuted. Possibly I beg the definition of 'meaningful' but since primogeniture has pragmatically been appealed to since the Brehon law of succession (i.e. by election, even though always within a confined definition of democracy) ceased to be adhered to for the reasons expounded by Edward MacLysaght and others, it must be regarded as valid. Probably I would be Chief of the Name had Brehon law been scrupulously followed, but I fear that it could only be a matter of conjecture, in my case and, I can't help thinking, in that of all chiefs and chieftains.

The O'Donovan holds both Irish and United Kingdom passports. He does not agree with some of his fellow chiefs that the holders of the ancient Gaelic titles could realistically have any other role in the modern Irish state than they do already. 'The Senate would be the only body which realistically might have representation but this country's constitutional views on titles make the possibility remote at this moment.'

He is interested in Irish history but in particular his own family, 'possibly of a greater interest to O'Donovans outside rather than inside Ireland'.

> It would be a tragedy were the [Irish] language and its literature to be lost, but I consider that preservation as the result of generous scholarships would be more effective than compulsory learning of the language by official decree, which probably kills a high proportion of potential enthusiasm as well as being manifestly wasteful of resources and talents.

Although a member of the Synod of the Church of Ireland, The O'Donovan does not wish to see the removal of the clause in the constitution which gives a special recognition to the Roman Church. He reasons:

> I might object to the constitutionally supported position of the Roman Catholic Church, particularly as the government of the country has on occasion unquestionably been influenced thereby. But Roman Catholicism, though like all religions in this age waning in its influence, is the church of the vast majority of Irishmen, and as a Christian I dislike the notion of a secular state. So my answer is a qualified 'yes' in support of the special position.

VI
THE O'LONG OF GARRANELONGY,
Lord of Canovee
(Ó Longaidh)

It is a common mistake today to regard anyone with the name Long in Ireland as being of English origin. The name belongs to a family who are one of the oldest branches of the Eóghanacht royal dynasty of Munster.

Oengus Mac Nad Fróich, the first Christian king of Munster (d. 490/ 492), had a brother named Cass. Cass was the great-great-great-great-grandfather of Prince Longadh, living c. 640, who was the patriarch of the Clan Longaidh, the O'Longs.

The present O'Long, Denis O'Long, was born in 1930; he is the thirty-sixth generation in unbroken male line descent from Longadh, and fortieth from Oengus who was said to have been baptised by St Patrick and St Ailbe on the Rock of Cashel. His early genealogical heritage survives in a poem attributed to the seventh century entitled *Duan Cathain*, preserved in *An Leabhar Muimhneach*. By the time of the Anglo-Norman invasion, the O'Longs were already well established in their present territory in Muskerry, Co. Cork – the lands of Canovee, Moviddy, Kilbonane, Kilmurry and Dunisky, straddling the River Lee.

From an early period the O'Longs were closely associated with the Catholic Church and references to them can be found in the *Calendar of Papal Letters* of 1484 and other papal documents. They paid feudal rents to the MacCarthy Lords of Muskerry amounting to some £4 10s annually. The O'Long chiefs, like all Gaelic chiefs of Munster, resisted the Elizabethan conquest; the then chief 'Donogh Rua O'Longe of Kanavoy' had to receive a pardon from Elizabeth I on 21 November 1576 for having fought for Donal IX MacCarthy Mór. His heir, Dermod, received a similar pardon on 17 February 1600. Numerous members of the family received pardons during the period 1602–3 in the wake of the Irish defeat at Kinsale. We have reference to a Dermot O'Long in 1602 fighting with Don Juan del Aguila, commanding the Spanish forces, at Kinsale. Dermot fled into exile in Spain. The title of The O'Long was then abolished and certainly the old Gaelic territorial lordship of Canovee was no longer admitted by the English administration. Presumably, although the records do not appear to show it, the O'Longs had made formal submission, surrendering the title and land in return for having a portion of the estate granted back under feudal conditions.

When Dermot O'Long of Canovee died on 2 March 1623, an inquisition found that he held lands in Canovee and several adjoining estates. It was ordered that, on the payment of £106, the O'Long heir could resume the ownership. The heir was John FitzDermot (the Fitz substituted for Mac) O'Long, born *c*.1598. He was twenty-five and married. The O'Longs were ordered to render military service to the English Crown as part of the rents due on their lands.

For a short period, the O'Longs enjoyed comparatively settled conditions. In 1636 John Long, for the administration required the dropping of the Gaelic 'O' and 'Mac', a son of Thomas Long, who had been educated at the University of Paris, was given permission to build the manor of Mount Long in a thousand acres of land near Oysterhaven. In 1641 this John Long of 'Rynynyan', a cousin of the claimant to the title of O'Long, became High Sheriff of Co. Cork and with the rising of 1641 he formed the 'rebel camp' at Belgooly near Mount Long. In 1642 this was attacked by the English and dispersed. Mount Long was abandoned. John Long was taken prisoner and, in 1652, John Cooke was sent by Parliament to preside at his trial in Cork. Cooke had been the solicitor for Parliament at the trial of Charles I. Long could expect no mercy nor was he given any. Cooke himself, as a regicide, was to be executed in London, at Charing Cross, in 1660. The ruins of Mount Long still stand and are now the property of the Irish state.

John Long was not the only member of the family to fight during the wars from 1641 and pay the supreme penalty. The O'Long himself fought alongside Donnchadh an Chúil, Viscount Muskerry, head of the MacCarthys of Muskerry, against the English Parliamentary forces. For this, following Cromwell's victory, the O'Long estates were confiscated. He died in 1653.

At the time of the restoration, Donough MacCarthy, the new Earl of Clancarthy, was able to use his influence to get Charles II to restore all the Muskerry lands under his lordship, and the estate of Canovee returned to the O'Longs in the person of another John O'Long. He held the ancestral home bearing the name Garranelongy (Grove of the Longs) which had been renamed by the English settlers as Bellmount.

Darby O'Long, the successor to the chiefship, was appointed a judge of the law courts in 1687. He held the office of Recorder of the City of Cork and sat in James II's Dublin parliament of 1689 representing Old Leighlin, Co. Carlow. In the same parliament, other distant kinsmen Dermot and John Long represented Middleton. For his support of James II, Darby O'Long was outlawed in 1691.

By some means, he seems to have reconciled himself with the new Williamite administration and returned to his estate. The confiscations and devastations and Penal Laws of William's conquest passed Darby O'Long by for a few years. Then, in 1711, the estates of Canovee were passed into the ownership of Joseph Damer. Perhaps Darby O'Long's experience in law helped him for he was able to retrieve the ownership.

When the Anglican Bishop Dive Downes of Cloynes later made a tour of his diocese, he noted in his journal that the church at Canovee was in ruins. 'Counsellor Long's lands bound upon it – the Earl of Clancarthy had, and Counsellor Long has, an estate in the parish. No other proprietors.' The O'Longs had saved their ancestral home at Garranelongy.

Darby's son, Darby II, who died in 1786 and is buried at Kilmurray, succeeded to the estates. When the Gaelic gentry began to be reduced by the oppressive Penal Laws and the heirs to many of the chiefly houses drifted into exile in Europe, the O'Longs remained in Canovee and Garranelongy, enduring and surviving quietly. Their only genuflection to the new order was the Anglicisation of their name and the excising of the 'O'. However, maintaining their Catholic faith, they were excluded from office and bounded by disabilities: because no Catholic could own lands under the Penal Laws, a member of the family had to convert to the Anglican faith in order to maintain them. The Longs were still acknowledged as members of the Gaelic nobility of Muskerry.

In 1706, Ellinor, the daughter of Darby I O'Long, married Daniel FitzGerald, son of John, the 13th Knight of Kerry and his wife, the daughter of Viscount Clare. Their son Maurice became an officer in the regiment of Lord Clare in the Irish Brigade of the French army. Their eldest son married Mary Butler, eldest daughter of Theobald, 7th Lord Cahir of Cahir Castle. In 1789, James, The O'Long, married Johanna Sweeney, one of the Mac Suibhnes who had been lords of Mashanaglass.

With the easing of the Penal Laws and the admission of Catholics into the professions, life changed for the O'Longs. Like other Irish Catholics they were now free to follow what careers they chose. They could also reassert the 'O' in their name. Denis O'Long (b. 1886) was educated at the Christian Brothers College in Cork and qualified as a surgeon at the Royal College of Surgeons in Dublin. He succeeded his father William in 1908 as The O'Long and married Elizabeth, daughter of John F. Corkeran, a Justice of the Peace, of Blarney, Co.Cork.

His son is Denis Clement Long, the current chief, born in 1930. Like his father, he was educated at the Christian Brothers College in Cork. In 1971 he married Lester Jean O'Rorke Clarke, and has two sons. His tanist is James Stephen Long, born on 21 May 1973, who followed the tradition of an education at the Christian Brothers College in Cork and later took an honours degree at University College, Cork. He is now a director of his father's company D.C. Long Ltd.

The O'Long has been chairman of the Blarney Pigs Company since 1972. He became managing director of D.C. Long Ltd in that year also. His hobbies are hunting with the Muskerry Foxhounds and sailing with the Royal Cork Yacht Club and, of course, the study of Irish history. He has written and lectured about his own family history. He has been Patron of the Kilmurry History Society, Honorary Secretary of the Canovee Historical and Archaeological Society and a council member of the Cork Historical and Archaeological Society. He is also a vice-president of the Royal Eóghanacht Society. He holds the Niadh Nask.

When the Chief Herald of Ireland, Donal Begley, granted 'courtesy recognition' to his title, endorsing his pedigree, in 1989, The O'Long organised an O'Long clan rally, held on 25 August 1990 and officially opened by the Irish Minister of State for Culture (now the Ministry for Heritage) Denis Lyons TD. The Chief Herald was there to present the documentation along with Gene FitzGerald, Member of the European

Parliament, and a collection of dignitaries including The O'Conor Don, The O'Brien (Lord Inchiquin) and The O'Grady.

The O'Long considers that the Irish chiefs ought to have representation in the Irish Senate and other Irish institutions by virtue of their titles. He is a strong supporter of Gaelic culture and of the attempts to preserve the Irish language in Irish life.

He is a Catholic and agrees with the Irish Constitution recognising the special position, within the state, of the Holy Catholic and Apostolic and Roman Church as a guardian of the Faith.

Although The O'Long recognises that his title must, in reality, only have meaning if held under the Brehon law of succession and feels that he does hold his title with the approval of his *derbhfine*, he adds the *caveat*: 'I still must have regard to and respect for the laws of the land as a citizen of the Republic of Ireland, which must have a part in the equation too.'

VII

THE MACGILLYCUDDY OF THE REEKS,
Lord of Doonebo
(Mac Giolla Mochuda)

The house and title of MacGillycuddy, Lord of Doonebo – for the appendage 'of the Reeks' was a nineteenth-century one – is a comparatively new arrival by Irish standards. The MacGillycuddys originated as a distinct line in the sixteenth century, having previously been a cadet branch of the house of The O'Sullivan Mór. In turn, the O'Sullivans were a branch of the Eóghanacht royal dynasty of Munster. Súileabháin (the Hawk-eyed), who flourished in AD 950, traced his ancestry back to Eoghan Mór (d. AD 192). Buadhach, Súileabháin's successor, was the first to use the patronymic Ó Súileabháin and the senior prince of this house became, in Anglicised terms, O'Sullivan Mór, whose stronghold was in Kenmare Bay in Kerry. A second branch occupied the Beara peninsula, straddling Kerry and Cork, and took the title O'Sullivan Beare.

The territory of MacGillycuddy was on the Iveragh peninsula, more popularly known these days as the Ring of Kerry. Ireland's spectacular mountain range, containing the country's highest mountain, Carrantuohill (3414 ft), is called MacGillycuddy's Reeks. It is here that 'The Reeks', a mansion at Beaufort, still stands, home of the MacGillycuddy of the Reeks family until it was sold in 1985.

A popular first name among the O'Sullivans from the thirteenth century was Giolla Mochuda, Servant of Mochuda, the pet form of St Carthach of Lismore. In 1563 Conchobhar (Conor) Giolla Mochuda Ó Súileabháin slew his kinsman Donal, The O'Sullivan Beare. The fact is mentioned in the *Annals of the Four Masters*. It was from this time that his line became known as Mac Giolla Mochuda.

The MacGillycuddys had already been given a territorial lordship by the MacCarthy kings of Desmond and were lords of Doonebo. Sir Warham St Leger, reporting to the Privy Council of Elizabeth I, said:

> The eighth [lordship] is the country of MacGillicuddy. It containeth 46 ploughlands. He [Donal IX MacCarthy Mór] claimeth there rising out, the giving of the rod, the finding of 30 gallowglasses, and the value of £30 a year in spending.

In other words, the MacGillycuddys were not allowed to take office unless they were handed the white wand or rod of office by The MacCarthy Mór. They also had to provide him with military service, which included thirty gallowglasses – mercenaries originally from Scotland.

There is little known of the details of the early MacGillycuddys. One was described by the poet, Aonghus Fionn Ó Dálaigh, *c.* 1599, as hating mankind 'as a daisy hates the night'. Domhnall Geraltach MacGillycuddy was slain during the Tudor conquest in 1595. Some of his estates were confiscated and granted to Edmund Barrett. John MacGillycuddy was pardoned in 1600 but in 1615 other sections of the MacGillycuddy lands were confiscated and granted to Sir Charles Wilmot and Walter Crosbie.

Donough MacGillycuddy of Carnbeg Castle supported the Irish uprising in 1641 and the establishment of the Irish Confederate government in Kilkenny which returned the estates. Came the Cromwellian conquest and the MacGillycuddys suffered confiscation again. On the restoration of Charles II, in 1661, Donough MacCarthy, the new Earl of Clancarthy, certified the good service of The MacGillycuddy against the Parliamentary forces and Charles II confirmed the restoration of the estates. Donough thereby became Sheriff of Co. Kerry and obtained a grant of arms from the Ulster King of Arms.

With the conflict between James II and William of Orange, the MacGillycuddys thought it prudent to have members of the family supporting both sides. The lessons of the previous wars had been taken to heart. Donough's son Conor (Cornelius) MacGillycuddy secured a commission in Lord Slane's Regiment of the Jacobite army. Another member of the family fought in Limerick during the siege in 1691. Yet another MacGillycuddy was Governor of Cork and had to surrender it to John

Churchill, the future Duke of Marlborough. But Donough, The MacGillycuddy, was to take the oath of allegiance to William and Mary in November 1694. Denys MacGillycuddy, his great-nephew, had taken a commission in William's service and his immediate family served William of Orange in various military capacities.

It would appear that the family now fully accepted the Tudor conditions of surrender, embracing the Anglican faith and English law and language, and were thus able to retain ownership, influence and power over part of their former estates in Kerry long after the collapse of the Gaelic aristocracy.

They continued to aspire to high office in Co. Kerry. Richard, b. 1750, not only became High Sheriff but in 1793 was deputy governor of the county. As it became fashionable to reassert the old Gaelic titles in public, The MacGillycuddy also reassumed his title. It was only in the nineteenth century that 'of the Reeks' was added. The *Kerry Evening Post*, in June 1866, reported the death of Richard MacGillycuddy (b. 1790) in these terms:

Richard M'Gillycuddy, called, as chief of his sept 'The M'Gillycuddy of the Reeks', died on the 6th instant, at his temporary residence, 6 Upper Pembroke Street, Dublin, after a protracted illness. He was the eldest son of Francis M'Gillycuddy Esq by his wife Catherine, widow of Darby M'Gill Esq, and third daughter of Denis Mahony Esq of Dromore Castle, and was nephew of The M'Gillycuddy, his predecessor. He was born January 1, 1790, and inherited November 19, 1826, the chieftainship and the considerable property and much influence possessed by the family in Kerry of which county he was a magistrate and Deputy Lieutenant. He was High Sheriff of Kerry in 1823.

The obituary continues in glowing terms, evidence of the acceptance by the newspaper and its readers of the Gaelic title. Referring to the ending of the Gaelic order, the report adds: 'Since that period down to now the M'Gillycuddys have, by high alliances, constant loyalty, and honourable conduct, maintained a prominent position among the leading gentry of Ireland.'

The same newspaper, ten years later, was able to report the return of the MacGillycuddys to their estate after an absence:

Madam M'Gillycuddy (after an absence of two years in England) and The M'Gillycuddy, her son, arrived on Monday evening last at the family mansion as permanent residents. The tenants and people of the neighbourhood generally made it the occasion of rejoicings and festivity. A large bonfire blazed in front of the principal entrance as well as several on the surrounding mountains round which the people assembled, amused themselves and vindicated the national character for hilarity by dancing to the enlivening strains of the bagpipes. Triumphal arches spanned the approaches to the house with 'Welcome' '*Cead míle fáilte*' and other suitable devices in flowers and evergreen.

The *Kerry Evening Post* ended its enthusiastic report with the comment: 'It would be well if all the landed proprietors of Ireland deserved and returned the invariable kind and cordial feelings that have always existed between the tenants and this ancient family.'

The family estate was still 15,518 acres of Kerry land by the end of the nineteenth century.

Perhaps the most influential of the MacGillycuddys was Ross Kinloch MacGillycuddy, born in 1882 and educated in Edinburgh. He pursued a military career in the British army, joining the Dragoon Guards. By the end of World War I he was a colonel of the Royal Irish Dragoon Guards holding the Distinguished Service Order and Légion d'Honneur. He had served with Lawrence of Arabia and is credited with designing the tripod fixing of the Lewis machine gun. In June 1921 he retired to an Ireland full of optimism: talks were taking place which it was hoped would finally bring Irish independence after the hundreds of years of conflict. Yet within six months the country was teetering on the brink of civil war as an unfavourable settlement was forced on it.

Ross MacGillycuddy's father Donough, The MacGillycuddy who had arrived at 'The Reeks' as a young boy with his mother, as reported by the *Kerry Evening Post*, had died at the estate. Now Ross, as the new MacGillycuddy, arrived with his wife and family to take charge of the family property.

The Irish Civil War seemed to pass the family by, even though Kerry was to suffer greatly from the fighting between Free Staters and republican forces and witnessed some of the most appalling atrocities of this war. Ross concentrated on getting the estates in order, building up a herd of pedigree Kerry cattle. His wife Helen engrossed herself in the garden. A new wing was added to the house and more furnishings were bought.

With the end of the Civil War and the emergence of the Irish Free State, Ross entered local politics and was elected to Kerry County Council. He then stood as an elected member for the Irish Senate in 1928, being nominated by Lord Landsdowne, but was defeated. That same year came another opportunity to stand for the Senate and this time he was elected, supporting Cumann na nGaedheal, the Free State party which had won the Civil War. In 1933 this party became Fine Gael.

The Senate at this time was dominated by anti-republicans, mainly representatives of the old Ascendancy families. Ross was to write:

> When de Valéra came into power, the opposition (Cumann na nGaedheal) still had a majority in the Senate and used their power on several occasions to hold up legislation. This led to the temporary abolition of the Senate, but not long after a new Senate was set up by decree to be elected by the Dáil and County Councils ... My years in the Senate left very definite impressions on my mind. Those who control modern Ireland, whatever party they belong to, are bitterly jealous of those who came before them and are glad to be rid of them. This attitude will take many years to change and meanwhile the standards of the new order are going from bad to worse.

He remained a Senator until 1943. In 1939, with the outbreak of World War II and Ireland's policy of neutrality, which he believed was a political mistake of first importance, he had no hesitation in volunteering for active service in the British army, although he was fifty-seven. He rejoined an Irish regiment but had to retire in 1942. Curiously, although serving in the armed forces of a country which had become belligerent in the war while his own country remained neutral, MacGillycuddy felt that he should not resign from the Senate and continued to sit during the period of his active service and for a year thereafter. This is something no seriously neutral country could have tolerated but as Enno Stephan has demonstrated, Ireland was neutral in name only and served the allied cause better in its neutral capacity than as an official belligerent.[1]

According to records, some 183,000 Irish citizens with addresses in the Free State served in the British forces. Due to neutrality, many recruits were deemed 'British' on the muster rolls and a figure of 250,000 Irish citizens is more likely – excluding Northern Ireland. An Irish Brigade, consisting of three battalions, of the volunteers from 'neutral' Ireland was formed. It was designated the 38th but its Irishness was never stressed. Similarly, because large numbers of Irish pilots were serving in the Royal Air Force, Winston Churchill wanted to form a 'Shamrock Wing'; this unit was not formed and, like the Irish Brigade, no publicity was given to it because it was deemed a breach of neutrality under international law. It was perhaps ironic, though, that the Commander-in-Chief of Fighter Command, RAF, immediately after the war was a much-decorated Galway man named Basil Embry. Citizens of the 'neutral' Irish Free State serving in the British forces alone – for many more Irish men and women were to be found in the forces of the United States, as well as Canada, Australia and other Commonwealth countries – won 780 decorations for valour, including eight Victoria Crosses. This was almost as many as the Canadian forces, with three times as many service personnel.

The strange position of MacGillycuddy as Senator of a neutral country while an officer in the army of a belligerent state has therefore to be seen in the context of how Ireland saw its 'neutrality'. The popular joke goes that when being informed the country was neutral in 1939, an Irishman in the street replied: 'Good. Who are we neutral against?' Evidence shows that Senator MacGillycuddy was in regular contact with Lord Rigby (John Mahaffy) informing him of matters within the Irish Senate with respect to the policy of Irish neutrality.[2]

He finally retired from public life and devoted himself to his estate in Kerry. He was deerstalking in Muckross Forest, near Killarney, in 1949 when he suffered a severe heart attack. This confined him in his room until his death in April 1950.

It was Ross who started the tradition of having his sons educated at Eton. His son John Patrick, who was a major in the Northamptonshire Yeomanry during World War II, wounded twice and mentioned in dispatches, succeeded his father. He made little impression as MacGillycuddy and died in 1959.

The current MacGillycuddy of the Reeks is Richard Denis Wyer, born on 4 October 1948. He was educated at Eton and then at Aix-en-Provence University. He is married to Virginia Astor, daughter of the Hon. Hugh Astor. They have two daughters, Tara (born 1985) and Sorcha (born 1990). After living in France for twelve years, where he was an executive in a real estate business, and during which time the Co. Kerry estates were sold off, MacGillycuddy returned to Ireland and now lives in Westmeath.

His tanist is Donough MacGillycuddy, his first cousin, who currently lives in Northamptonshire in England. MacGillycuddy takes his role as a member of the Gaelic aristocracy and holder of an ancient title seriously. He is an active member of the Council of Chiefs, a Niadh Nask and vice-president of the Royal Eóghanacht Society. He has presided over MacGillycuddy clan gatherings; the clan society is run by distant cousins Rosemary and Nicholas MacGillycuddy who live in Baltimore. Rosemary has written *A Short History of the Clan MacGillycuddy*. Her husband is a descendant of John 'Jackgillycuddy' of Flesk Castle who was High Sheriff of Kerry in 1894 and whose sister Agnes married Dr George Stoker, a younger brother of the famous Dublin writer, Bram Stoker, best known for his classic Gothic novel *Dracula* (1897).

Another branch of the family who settled abroad produced Cornelius McGillycuddy, born in East Brookfield, Massachusetts in 1862. He informally shortened his name to 'Connie Mack' and became a famous baseball player, manager and club owner for whom the Connie Mack Stadium, formerly Shibe Park, Philadelphia was named. He died in 1956 not long after his sons forced him to sell his club for $3.5 million. His grandson, also Cornelius McGillycuddy, was Connie Mack III, who became a Republican US Senator in 1989 for Florida. A Catholic, he was one of the Republican Senators who took a prominent role in the impeachment proceedings of President Clinton early in 1999 which ended with Clinton's exoneration.

The present MacGillycuddy, who is a member of the Church of Ireland, would prefer that the state was a secular one in terms of its constitution but, he admits, 'in practical terms it has never had any effect on my life'. MacGillycuddy and his wife Virginia are interested in Irish history and culture and support the attempts to preserve the Irish language. Furthermore, MacGillycuddy believes that the old Gaelic titled nobility, the chiefs, should have some representation in the Irish Senate. He even looks forward to the day that one of the Gaelic chiefs might be elected as President of Ireland.

8

The Kingdom of Munster (Thomond)

Thomond (Thuaidh Mumhain) or North Munster no longer exists as a geographic territory – only as an historical memory. As a separate kingdom it came into being in 1118 at the partition of Munster by the Treaty of Glanmire. Historically it consisted of modern Co. Clare, with portions of Co. Limerick and some bordering areas of Co. Tipperary. When the O'Brien royal house were no longer able to claim the High Kingship, after 1119, the O'Conor kingdom of Connacht, then frequently in the ascendant, claimed overlordship of the tiny kingdom. As a kingdom it vanished in the sixteenth century after King Murrough O'Brien surrendered it to Henry VIII. It became an English earldom between 1543 and 1741, and during the seventeenth century shiring of Ireland, its territory was reduced to Co. Clare. The actual estate of the earldom was also reduced in size. It was then a marquessate from 1800, which became extinct in 1855 with the death of Admiral James O'Brien, 3rd Marquess Thomond. The O'Briens are unique among the old Gaelic aristocrats in having survived the conquests with their ancestral estate still in their ownership, and having a continuous history as kings, earls, marquesses and baronets while retaining their subsidiary title as Barons of Inchiquin, the name coming from the place Inse Cúinne (Water or Island Nook) in Co. Clare. Yet, in spite of these English titles, the head of the family can still boast the Gaelic title The O'Brien, Prince of Thomond.

I

THE O'BRIEN,
Prince of Thomond
(18th Baron Inchiquin in the Peerage
of Ireland and 10th Baronet)
(Ó Bríain)

The O'Briens, the royal house of Thomond, claim to be descended from
Cormac Cas, a brother of King Eoghan Mór (d. AD 192), the progenitor
of the Eóghanacht. According to scholars, such claims are spurious and
the genealogies were forged when the Dál gCais, the people of Cas, tried
to justify their usurpation of the Munster throne and then the High
Kingship. Francis J. Byrne comments:

> Perhaps the most blatant example is the fiction that the Dál Cais,
> rulers of a petty state in east Clare, were a collateral branch of the
> Eóghanacht, entitled from remote antiquity to share in the over-
> kingship of Munster. So deeply rooted were the claims of aristocratic
> descent that the spectacular rise to power of Brían Bóruma, and the
> consolidation of that power by the O'Briens, were not sufficient to
> promote the Dál Cais in the political hierarchy without the spurious
> lustre of ancestral prestige.

It is accepted that the warlike Dál gCais with their ruling house were
originally the Déisi Becc who had settled in east Clare in the fifth century.
According to Byrne:

> A branch of the latter, the Déisi Becc, are said to have conquered
> Thomond (North Munster) from Connacht in the fifth century, and
> by the tenth century their ruling dynasty, the Dál Cais, were able to
> seize the kingdom of Munster almost painlessly from the enfeebled
> grasp of the Eóghanachta: they justified their success on the patently
> false grounds that they were not Déisi at all but of common descent
> with the Eóghanachta with whom they had anciently enjoyed alterna-
> tive rights of kingship.

The Eóghanacht kingdom had been weakened by its wars against the
Danish incursions, in which, if we are to believe the twelfth-century
Caithbreim Cheallacháin Chaisil, the Dál gCais had formed alliances against
the Cashel kings. The Dál gCais had built up their forces and on the

death of Donnchadh II mac Ceallacháin Caisil in 963 they were able to challenge the Eóghanacht.

The first notable Dál gCais ruler recorded in the annals was Lorcan, *c.* 920. Cennétigh, presumably his son, is mentioned as 'Rí Tuathmuman' (North Munster) in 951 and he was slain by King Ceallacháin in his wars against the Danish threat. It is Mathgamain mac Cennétigh who led the attack on Cashel and seized the throne. It was a tenuous occupation and in 976 he met his own death at the hands of Maelmuad, a prince of the Eóghanacht Raithlinn, according to the *Annals of Innisfallen*. The throne returned to the Eóghanacht for two more years.

Mathgamain's brother led a fresh assault on Cashel and slew King Maelmuad at the battle of Belach Lechta in 978. The brother's name was Brían mac Cennétigh and he would become known as Brían Bóroimhe – the *bóroimhe* being a tax in cows which the kings of Leinster agreed was payable to the High King and which Brían was able to extract.

Brían mac Cennétigh became the catalyst for the ambitions of the Dál gCais for he not only seized the kingdom of Munster but went on to seize the High Kingship with the aim of converting what had originally been a precedence of honour between the Uí Néill and Eóghanacht, an office which the Uí Néill had been more interested in maintaining during the centuries immediately prior to the appearance of Brían. The Uí Néill seemed concerned in creating a real central power-base. Then the Dál gCais arrived in power with a fine disregard for the laws of regnal succession and a reliance on the power of their swords. As Brian Ó Cuív wrote: 'the accession of Brian Bóroimhe to the High Kingship marked a break with the past. It paved the way for a strong central monarchy . . .' It was no wonder that the Dál gCais chose to name their dynasty after, perhaps, their greatest king.

Brían was an aggressive ruler and soon his armies were ravaging Connacht, Meath and Breifne. He was by no means recognised as legitimate High King; indeed, the Eóghanacht had not even acknowledged his claim to Munster's throne and were still waging war. The Uí Néill High King, Mael Sechnaill, met Brían in 998 at the Abbey of Clonfert and, for the sake of peace, agreed to recognise him as king of the southern half of Ireland, if Brían would accept him as king of the northern half. At this time the Leinster king, Donnchadh Mac Domhnaill Cláin (984–1003), allied himself with the Norse-Irish city kingdoms and denied Brían's authority in that kingdom. Brían inflicted a crushing defeat on them in Co. Wicklow and occupied the Danish kingdom of Dublin. He married Gormfliath, mother of Sitirc, king of Dublin.

Brían was now strong enough to be able to break his agreement with Mael Sechnaill and assert his claim to the High Kingship. Mael Sechnaill, failing to secure support from the northern Uí Néill, surrendered the High Kingship to him. Brían was now High King but with opposition from the outraged more ancient royal dynasties.

In 1005 Brían marched to Armagh 'with the royalty of Ireland', say the *Annals of Ulster*, and left twenty ounces of gold 'on the altar of St Patrick'. By this action he was clearly acknowledging Armagh as the foremost ecclesiastical seat in Ireland, a position which its bishops had long demanded.

In 1006 Brían, conducting a campaign against the Uí Néill of the north, had obtained some submissions and recognition of his kingship. However, opposition continued, for seizing the kingship without the backing of the law was not acceptable to the kings of Ireland. Brían's *ollamhain* therefore began to devise the genealogy making them Eóghanacht princes, in order to justify the seizure of power.

Brían tried to exert a strong central authority over Ireland and once more the Leinster kingdom rose up, this time in alliance with the Uí Néill of the north. The Leinster king Mael Morda mac Murchada (1003–14) also sought alliances with the Danes, not only those of the Irish city kingdoms but from the Isle of Man and the Western Islands, the Orkneys and even as far as Norway itself. The Norse had their own agenda to dominate Ireland rather than merely help the Irish kings curb the power of Brían. The Uí Néill now stood aloof; although not supporting Brían, they had no liking for the idea of such a strong Norse army being invited into Ireland.

On 23 April 1014, Good Friday, Brían Bóroime defeated the king of Leinster with his Danish and Norse allies at Clontarf. While Brían was slain beside his tent by a retreating Norse warrior, his army was victorious. His body was taken and buried at Armagh by the clergy who had seen in him a king who had recognised their claims to the primacy and who was bringing about a centralised Irish kingdom.

Brían's death brought about a weakening of the Dál gCais who now became the O'Briens. Brían's son Donnchadh (d. 1064) had become king of Thomond but continued to claim the kingship of Munster with opposition from the Eóghanacht. Donnchadh had made a foray into the territory controlled by the Eóghanacht princes in 1013 and had managed to take captive Domhnall of Dubhdabhoreann, the progenitor of the O'Donoghues. He tried to follow his father's example and began to raid Meath and Leinster but he lost his right hand in a single combat in 1019 and was also wounded in the head. He suffered several defeats and even made war on his own kinsman, Maelruanaidh, whom he killed. When he invaded Leinster again he found himself ranged against Dermot Mac Maelnamboo of the Uí Cheinnselaig, who routed him in a battle in the

Glen of Arklow. In 1064 he was finally deposed by his dissatisfied *derbhfine* and went off on a pilgrimage to Rome. He died in Rome in the monastery of St Stephen.

He was succeeded by Murchadh who reigned for four years before being defeated by his kinsman Tairrdelbach in 1064. The next O'Brien king was more in the mould of Brían Bóroimhe. Tairrdelbach, often given as Toirdhealbhach and Anglicised as Turlough (1009–86), had the same desire to be a strong central monarch. He began to assert his claim to be king of all Munster with strong opposition from the Eóghanacht. Like his grandfather, Brían, he was determined to seize power by force. He fought with the Connachtmen and even against his own kinsman, Murchadh an Sceith Ghirr (short shield), in a battle in which four hundred men and fifteen Dál gCais nobles are recorded as being slain.

He was only a year into his claim to be king of Munster when he led his warriors into Leinster, which had an alliance with the Dési Mumhain, settled around Waterford, to whom the Déisi Becc, the original Dál gCais, were said to be related. In 1072 Tairrdelbach claimed the High Kingship by force. He sacked the Abbey of Clonmacnoise, and marched against the northern kingdoms of the Uí Néill who were able to repulse him. In 1077 he devastated Leinster once again. He plundered at will, taking hostages and booty.

It seems that after the looting of the Abbey of Clonmacnoise, Tairrdelbach became ill, a fact which the Christian scribes made capital out of. He died on 14 July 1086 at Ceancoradh (Kincorra) in his Co. Clare homeland.

His son Muirchertach was to become the third and last O'Brien to claim the High Kingship. Muirchertach managed to defeat Donnchadh mac Domnaill Remair, the king of Leinster, in 1087, near Howth, Co. Dublin, but in the following year he was himself defeated and forced back into Thomond. He made several forays against Meath and Connacht and plundered the Abbey of Clonmacnoise, obviously emulating his father. His raids caused even the Archbishop of Armagh to interpose. Every year witnessed O'Brien raiding and in one year he is said to have made a circuit of Ireland in six weeks with his army.

During this period, the violence of the Dál gCais king of Thomond shook the political status quo to its core, not just in Munster but throughout Ireland. In 1113 he was badly defeated in the north and fell ill. In 1118 he was back campaigning again and found that his hold over Munster was now precarious. He was facing the army of the Eóghanacht prince, Tadhg MacCarthy, at Glanmire in Co. Cork. Muirchertach had demanded, as High King, support from the other kings to crush the 'troublesome' Eóghanacht. The kings of Ireland finally saw their opportunity to place the O'Briens in a position whereby their power base was weakened and they would not be able to continue to threaten the peace of the kingdoms.

The *Book of MacCarthaigh* reports that Tairrdelbach Ó Conchobhair, King of Connacht, Murchadh Ó Mael Seachlainn, of the Uí Néill, and Aodh, son of King Donnchadh Ó Ruairc of Breifne, who had arrived with their armies as allies of O'Brien, now pressured Muirchertach to make a treaty with the Eóghanacht. 'It was then that Muirchertach O'Brien was parted from the kingship of Munster and Ireland.'

The Treaty of Glanmire formally partitioned Munster into north and south, Thomond and Desmond. Desmond retained the bulk of Munster with their capital at Cashel, restoring the dynasty with Tadhg I. Muirchertach O'Brien died the following year, probably of pulmonary consumption, and was buried in Killaloe. He had been deposed twice from his kingships but his sword had restored him. He had not been so lucky the third time.

The position of High King was now filled by Domhnall Ua Lochlainn, a branch of Uí Néill of Cenél Eóghain. He was displaced by Tairrdelbach Ua Conchobhair of Connacht who turned from the role of kingmaker at Glanmire into claimant for the High Kingship with alacrity.

The O'Briens had returned to kingship of Thomond but not without protest. They did not remain passive for long and after the arrival of the Normans Donnchadh Cairprech (d. 1247) helped the newcomers to raid Connacht. However, in 1235 the Normans turned on Thomond itself and Donnchadh found himself having to defend it from his erstwhile allies. He founded the Franciscan monastery at Ennis, Co. Clare, and is said to have been a patron of literature supporting poets like Muiredeach Ó Dálaigh, a member of one of the great literary families in Munster who also had branches in Meath.

His son Conchobhair na Sindaine (1247–68) had some successes in turning back Norman attempts to take over Thomond and was one of the princes who decided to support Brían O'Neill's bid to become High King and unite the country against the Anglo-Normans. He is recorded as having sent a hundred horses to O'Neill as a gift. After the death of his son Tadhg in 1248 Conchobhair seldom appeared in public and never attended any official feasts. His people became bitter at his lack of concern for their welfare and showed their displeasure by refusing to pay the royal rents and dues. Conchobhair resorted to his ancestors' method of dealing with matters. He raised an army and began to raid the countryside and even raided into Eóganacht territory in Desmond.

In 1267, Conchobhair Carrack Lochlainn met O'Brien's army at Bela-clugga, Co. Clare, defeated and slew him. Conchobhair was buried in the monastery of East Burren which is now the Abbey of Corcomroe. His tomb and full-length effigy wearing a crown are still there.

Brían Ruadh (1268–76) was his third son. It is reported that when his title was proclaimed not one of the assembled chiefs in his *derbhfine* voiced any opposition. Their attitudes soon changed. Brían Ruadh began to campaign against the Normans in 1270 and captured Clare Castle. By 1275, however, his military campaigning was proving to be as unpopular as that of his father. His kinsman, Sioda MacNeill MacConamara who had supported him in the first place, now rose against him, declaring that Tairrdelbach Mac Tadhg, the nephew of Brían Ruadh, should be king.

The conflict came to a major battle at Moygressan in which Tairrdelbach's ally, the Norman baron Richard de Clare, was defeated. De Clare, however, managed to capture King Brían Ruadh and promptly hanged the unfortunate king of Thomond. Tairrdelbach O'Brien (1277–1306) is remembered in *Caithreim Thoirdhealbhaigh*, a work that was composed during his lifetime and which was discovered in the nineteenth century by the scholar, Standish Hayes O'Grady. Tairrdelbach was buried in Ennis Friary which became the burial place of succeeding kings of Thomond until Conor O Brien was buried there in 1581.

In 1318, at the battle of Dysert O'Dea, the Normans, under Richard de Clare, were driven from Thomond. But within fifty years the Fitz-Geralds were moving northwards and encroaching on O'Brien territory in east Limerick. Brian Sreamhach, King of Thomond (1369–1400), decided to attempt to check the FitzGeralds. In July 1370 he inflicted a crushing defeat on them at Monasteranenagh, two miles east of Croom, where, in the twelfth century, King Tairrdelbach O'Brien had ordered the building of a monastery (Mainistir an Aonaigh, Monastery of the Fair) in thanks for his defeat over the Norsemen in 1148. It was a significant site. His descendant, King Brian Sreamhach, even captured the 3rd Earl of Desmond, Gearóid Iarla FitzGerald (*c.* 1335–95), famous for his poetic compositions in Irish. O'Brien brought the earl to Ennis Clonroad and during his imprisonment there, he wrote several poems.

> The harp of O'Brien at whose playing I drink beer
> The sound of the bell of Ennis to the west
> The wail of the rock as it juts into the sea water
> These are my three constant melodies.

William of Windsor was dispatched from London to curb King Brian Sreamhach's successes over the Anglo-Normans.

The Thomond kingdom survived, sometimes under pressure not only from the Anglo-Normans but from the kings of Connacht who maintained that they had a right to overlordship over it. By 1528, the end of the kingdom of Thomond was approaching. Conchobhair mac Toirdhealbhaigh Duinn succeeded his father that year. His brother Donogh was nominated his tanist. Donogh died in 1531 and a third brother, Murrough, became heir-elect. Conchobhair (or, in English form, Conor) had become king at a very critical period not only for Thomond but for all Ireland. Two Anglo-Norman families, the FitzGeralds and the Butlers, were vying for power. Conor was married to a daughter of James FitzGerald (Earl of Kildare) and therefore took the side of Kildare. Conor's son Donough, however, had taken the side of the Butlers (Earls of Ormond) having married a daughter of the Earl of Ossory, one of that family. Donough was wounded in a battle but the FitzGeralds were eventually defeated. Son now turned against father. In 1536 Lord Leonard Grey, the new Lord Deputy, advanced into Thomond with the guidance of Donough. For six months his father, King Conor, held out. At his court, as a refugee, was Gerald FitzGerald the 11th Earl of Kildare. As it appeared that the Lord Deputy would finally defeat Conor's forces, he fled Thomond's protection and went to France. In 1537 King Conor surrendered to Lord Grey and a treaty was made between them at Limerick.

Conor died c. 1539 to be succeeded by his brother Murrough. It is wrongly claimed that Conor was the last independent king of Thomond.

On succession to the kingship, Murrough sought to join O'Neill and O'Donel in the north in a confederacy against the English. With the arrival of Anthony St Leger as new Lord Deputy, however, negotiations were opened between them and Murrough was identified as 'the Achilles heel' of Ireland. In February 1541 the Lord Deputy met Murrough at Limerick. He was told the conditions for surrendering his kingship in return for an earldom. Murrough asked for time to consult his *derbhfine* for, he pointed out, under law he could not make such a decision by himself. By the summer he had accepted the terms offered. He sent his representatives to attend the Dublin parliament called in June 1541 by Henry VIII. Leading them was his nephew, Donough O'Brien, the son of the late King Conor, who had been elected as tanist. It was at this parliament that Henry VIII's emissaries officially announced that the King of England would no longer be Lord of Ireland but King of Ireland instead. The Lord Deputy's report makes no mention of the attendance of any other major Irish king such as MacCarthy, O'Neill or MacMorrough Kavanagh. However, O'Brien's acceptance of the 'new deal' was the probable reason why his former ally, Conn Bacach O'Neill, made his extra-ordinary early submission.

There was a problem, however, in reconciling the new primogeniture law of England with Irish law and succession by tanistry. As we saw in Chapter 3, the English, ever good on political compromise, allowed the O'Brien king to be created Earl of Thomond and Baron Inchiquin for his lifetime, with the title Earl of Thomond descending not to his son, who would simply become the 2nd Baron Inchiquin, but to his elected tanist, his nephew Donough who, meanwhile, would be known as Baron Ibrickan. After that genuflection to the Gaelic system, the title Earl of Thomond would descend through Donough's line by primogeniture.

King Murrough arrived in England in June 1543 with the Norman-Irish MacWilliam Uachtar Bourke, who became the first Earl of Clanri-cade. Murrough went to Greenwich Palace, where he personally surrendered to Henry VIII. He died in 1551 and was succeeded as Earl of Thomond by Donough who immediately began to prepare the path for the succession of his son Conor by primogeniture. Ivar O'Brien says that Henry had granted personal arms to the Earl of Thomond which have become the arms of the head of the O'Brien family down to this day.[1] There is no reference to this in the letters patent nor in the office of the Ulster King of Arms. One would also doubt that the motto *Lamh Laidir an Uachtar* (The Strong Hand Uppermost) was approved when the policy was to eradicate the language. Another motto still used today by the baron is *Vigeur de Dessus*, an inaccurate translation actually meaning 'Strength from Above'. Indeed, the tomb of Domhnall Mór Ua Bríain (d. 1194) in Limerick Cathedral displays a different coat of arms featuring a lion. There is no sign of the embowed arm holding a sword which was an Eóghanacht crest until that time.

The outrage felt among the O'Briens, and the people of Thomond, at the disregard of Brehon law quickly erupted into warfare. In April 1553 the 2nd Earl of Thomond died while besieged in one of his castles, probably from a wound, when the *derbhfine* chose his brother Donell as King of Thomond. The 3rd Earl of Thomond was Donough's son Conor, nicknamed *Groibleach* (Long-Nailed), but he too was denied the Gaelic title.

His uncle Donell was formerly inaugurated as The O'Brien, King of Thomond, under Irish law and supported by most of the country. His nephew, Conor, was forced to surrender his central, principal residence at Ennis Clonroad, and he retired into Connacht for safety.

King Donell was now *de facto* king of Thomond as well as *de jure* king by Irish law. Yet, curiously, he petitioned the Lord Deputy St Leger for recognition as Chief of the O'Briens, which, as such titles had been abolished, St Leger neither would nor could grant. In 1558 Queen Mary, for reasons we have discussed in a previous chapter, ordered her troops to reinstate the ousted 3rd Earl of Thomond and an army commanded by the Earl of Sussex arrived at Limerick. King Donell as well as his brother Teige (d. 1582) and their cousin Donough, of Lemanagh and Dromoland, were proclaimed traitors. King Donell sought refuge with The Maguire, Prince of Fermanagh, while Teige and Donough found sanctuary with The FitzGerald, Earl of Desmond.

With Conor, 3rd Earl of Thomond, back in his Ennis stronghold, Lord Sussex's army withdrew. In 1559 Teige and Donough also returned and once again raised their supporters for Donell, inflicting a severe defeat on the army of Conor and his ally Lord Clanricade. The English had to come to the rescue again and the Lord Justice, FitzWilliam, intervened and managed to capture Teige who was imprisoned in Dublin Castle. Early in 1562, Teige escaped and rejoined Donell, who had now raised a formidable army in Thomond. It was clear that Conor O'Brien, the 3rd Earl, was not popular nor did his people recognise the legitimacy of his claims to rule over them by the English laws. He was even forced to borrow artillery from the English.

It took some years of conflict before a war-weary Donell offered in April 1565 to surrender his claims on condition that he receive the lordship of Corcomroe. He had been exhausted by the continued conflict but his offer of negotiation was ignored. Conor saw victory approaching. The new Lord Deputy, Sir Henry Sidney, arrived in Limerick in April 1567 and made a brief report to the Privy Council on the Earl of Thomond's 'insufficiency to govern'. Donell, at last, surrendered his claims on the kingdom and was allowed to retire to his castle, accepting a knighthood, and died in 1579.

Rejected by his own people and despised by the English, the 3rd Earl had joined James FitzMaurice FitzGerald, the Earl of Desmond in his wars against the Elizabethan conquest of Munster. Forced to surrender by the Earl of Ormond, he fled to the French court. He appeared to the English to be more trouble in France than he was worth and the English ambassador at the French court, Sir Henry Norris, later Baron Norris of Rycote, reported that he was intriguing with the French. Negotiations were, therefore, opened with him and he was persuaded to return to Thomond where he made public confession of his treason to England in return for being formally pardoned by the Lord Deputy. He surrendered all his lands to Queen Elizabeth. After showing his good behaviour, he had a portion of his lands restored in 1573.

Conor was dogged by disaffection among his people and continuing dynastic disputes in Thomond, which was now designated the new county of 'Clare'. He even asked Sir William Drury to place the territory under martial law. He died in January 1581.

His eldest son Donough succeed him as 4th Earl of Thomond while his third son Daniel was created first Viscount Clare.

Donough (d. 1624) is called the 'Great' Earl of Thomond. He was brought up at Elizabeth's court as a hostage for his family's good behaviour and as a way of turning him into an Englishman. He had succeeded as Baron Ibrickan and was still at Elizabeth's court when his father died. He returned to Ireland in 1582 and was assiduous in support of the Lord Deputy and the English administration. He tried to ensure that Co. Clare, which was going to be placed under the administration of Connacht, remained as Thomond. He not only attended the Dublin parliament of 1589 but, during the Elizabeth wars, commanded troops against the Irish. After campaigning for some years, he returned to England and remained there for a while.

The Irish victory at Yellow Ford was followed by the O'Briens and Thomond immediately attempting to reassert their own independence from the English administration. Teige O'Brien, brother of the 'Great' Earl of Thomond, who had not been Anglicised, entered an alliance with Aodh Ruadh O'Neill, who was to be the last regnant king of Ulster. In 1599, Aodh Ruadh O'Donell (1571–1602), O'Neill's principal commander, fresh from the victory of Yellow Ford, arrived in Thomond with his troops. Teige's youngest brother, Donal (Daniel), who supported the English, was made prisoner. Teige was killed when his own brother, the Anglicised 'Great' Earl, pursued his forces in 1599. The 'Great' Earl had returned from England with fresh English troops, invaded Clare and laid siege to the Irish strongholds. He hanged captured Irish soldiers and civilians on trees at Dunbeg after they had surrendered. During 1599 he accompanied the Earl of Essex in his attempt to invade Desmond and suffered defeat with him at the Pass of Plumes. Lord Thomond was appointed governor of Co. Clare in August that year and a member of the Privy Council the following month.

Lord Thomond remained a staunch supporter of the English administration. In 1600 he was wounded when he, Sir George Carew and Lord Ormond had to cut their way out of an ambush. During the remaining years of the war he fought against The O'Donel and The O'Neill. He appears to have been fond of hanging and ordered sixteen men hanged at Limerick in one assize. He went to England but returned in 1601 to bring reinforcements to Kinsale. He was also at Dunboy, the castle of The O'Sullivan Beare, when its garrison surrendered and he immediately hanged fifty-eight survivors of the siege.

Elizabeth was so grateful for his services that she ordered that his name should always be placed next to those of the Lord Deputy and Chief Justice in Commissions of Oyer and Terminer and Gaol Delivery. On 6 May 1605 he became President of Munster and a leading advocate of the Protestant party. He died on 5 September 1624, and was buried in Limerick Cathedral.

Approved of by the English as 'the most influential and vigorous of Irish loyalists', he was seen by his own people as nothing less than a traitor or, at best, not even Irish, having been raised at the English court as an Englishman. He had two sons, Henry, the 5th Earl, who died without issue in 1639, and Barnabas, the 6th Earl.

Before following the fortunes of Barnabas, reference should be made to the line of Daniel (1577?-1663). He had been left to defend his brother the 'Great' Earl's estates while he was in England. Daniel had been attacked in his Castle of Ibrickan when his brother Teige had joined the Irish army of O'Donel, and taken him prisoner. On his release he accompanied Lord Thomond to Elizabeth's court. In 1604 he was knighted for his services to England.

Afterwards, Daniel decided to switch his religion from Protestant back to Catholic. He attended the Dublin parliament of 1613 but his actions caused him to be summoned to England to account for his conduct. In 1641 he joined the Irish insurrection and became a member of the Confederation parliament at Kilkenny. He vigorously supported it and was elected to its Supreme Council. During the Cromwellian period he had to flee to France but on the restoration he returned to his estate and in 1663 was created Viscount Clare. His grandson Daniel, the 3rd Viscount, was Lord Lieutenant of Clare under James II, and raised a regiment of dragoons and two regiments of infantry to fight against William of Orange.

He died in 1690. The Clares went into exile in France following the Williamite conquest. Clare's Dragoons were to go into Irish folklore. The famous victory of France over England at Fontenoy in 1745 was due to the conduct of the Irish Brigade of the French army, whose six regiments were commanded by Charles O'Brien, 6th Viscount Clare and 9th Earl of Thomond.

Barnabas, 6th Earl of Thomond, proved another firm adherent of English government in Ireland. He succeeded in 1639. He was Lord Lieutenant of Clare but when the insurrection of 1641 broke out he tried to remain neutral. However, in 1644 he opened negotiations with the English Parliament allowing a Parliamentary force to take over Bunratty Castle. He went to live in England where he abruptly changed politics to the Royalist cause. He joined Charles I at Oxford and was created

Marquis of Billing (Northamptonshire). He died in 1657 and was succeeded by his son Henry.

The line of the Earls of Thomond passed down to Henry, the 8th Earl
(1688–1741) who was also created Viscount Tadcaster in the English
peerage. When he died the Earldom of Thomond was claimed by the
Jacobite Viscounts Clare. Charles, the 6th Viscount Clare (1699–1761)
claimed entitlement to be 9th Earl of Thomond and his son Charles, the
7th Viscount, claimed to be 10th Earl of Thomond in the Jacobite peerage. However, in England, Percy Wyndham (*c.* 1713–74), the nephew
of the 8th Earl and son of Sir William Wyndham Bart., took the
additional name of O'Brien and was created Earl of Thomond in 1756.
He died unmarried and the title again became extinct.

As a curiosity, that was not the end of the story for in 1936 a descendant
of the Wyndham family, calling himself Raymond Moulton-O'Brien,
managed to obtain a judgement decree from a court in Juarez, Mexico,
stating that he was Earl of Thomond. The German government ratified
the decree in December that year and then Luxemburg and France followed in 1937. Moulton-O'Brien applied to the Genealogical Office in
Dublin for a recognition as 'The O'Brien'. In 1944 he concocted an
elaborate charade to obtain evidence for his claim by trying to get the
Registrar of the High Court to register a claim for damages against a
non-existent person on the grounds that this person had claimed that he
was not The O'Brien.

In spite of the fact that Donough O'Brien, the 16th Baron Inchiquin,
had already been given 'courtesy recognition' as the rightful O'Brien,
Moulton-O'Brien obtained an official Vatican document in 1948 which
conferred blessings on his son as 'the Catholic heir to the Principality of
Thomond in the person of His Highness Prince Turlough the Strong,
a seaghan, Baron of Ibrickan'. Moulton-O'Brien even managed to get a
transfer of lands to his son registered with the Registry of Deeds signing
himself as 'Colonel His Highness Raymond Moulton Seán, by the Sovereign authority of the Roman Pontiff, Prince O'Brien of Thomond, The
O'Brien, Prince of the Dalcassians of Thomond, Earl and Count of
Thomond, Baron of Ibrickan, of Castle Clare, Co. Clare.'

Moulton-O'Brien set up his own 'Most Honourable Dalcassian Order
of the Princely House of Thomond', maintained his own 'embassy' in
Dublin and was, surprisingly, listed in *Thom's Directory* for 1950. His
entry was deleted in subsequent editions although he registered the birth
of his daughter as 'Her Highness Princess Grania Bebhin'. Refused recognition by the Genealogical Office, as well as the College of Arms in
London and Lord Lyon King of Arms in Scotland, Moulton-O'Brien
conducted a campaign against 'The Arch Communists of The Kremlin

and their dupes at the Genealogical office, Dublin Castle' who he claimed were plotting against him. He died in Dublin in 1977, but was buried in Birmingham, England.

In 1741, with the death of the 8th Earl of Thomond, the chiefship was deemed to have passed to the next senior line, that of King Murrough's son who had taken the title of 2nd Baron Inchiquin. This title had been passed down to Murrough, the 6th Baron (1614–74).

Murrough is one of the 'bogeymen' of Irish history; he is known as Murchadh na dTóitheán or 'Murrough of the Burnings'. Like the Thomonds, he was ardently supportive of the English in Ireland and his grandfather had been killed at the Erne fighting for Queen Elizabeth. He was brought up as a ward of William St Leger, as an Englishman, but in 1636 he was in the service of Spain fighting in Italy. He returned to Ireland in 1639, and was made Vice-President of Munster, sitting in the Earl of Strafford's Dublin parliament. He even approved of Strafford's scheme to colonise Co. Clare with English settlers, removing the local population.

When the insurrection broke out on 23 October 1641, Baron Inchiquin devoted his energies to fighting the Irish. Like his cousin the Earl of Thomond, who had fought for Elizabeth, Murrough was a brutal soldier. All Irish prisoners taken at Carrick-on-Suir were executed. Inchiquin now became Governor of Munster and fought several engagements. He devastated the counties of Cork and Waterford, looting and executing those he deemed guilty of 'rebellion'. When Ormond concluded a peace deal with the Irish Confederation on 15 September 1643, Inchiquin signed his approval but obviously unwillingly.

He took his regiments to England and went to Oxford to join the king. It seems that during this time King Charles gave him a warrant creating him 1st Earl of Inchiquin. He did not use the title and indeed was discontented. In July 1644 he urged the king to make peace with Parliament so that troops could be released to fight in Ireland. He was so vehement that he began to be thought of as a supporter of Parliament. It was also a fact that the English Parliament made him President of Munster. In August, he ordered the expulsion of all Catholics from the towns of Cork, Youghal and Kinsale, allowing them to take only what they stood up in.

Inchiquin's devastations in Munster are still a byword among Irish people. He gave no quarter to any Irish and destroyed abbeys and monasteries, such as the Franciscan friary of Adare, in Co. Limerick. In 1647 he attacked the ancient royal capital of Cashel. He slaughtered everyone, including thirty priests and friars. According to an eyewitness, Inchiquin put on the archi-episcopal mitre during these proceedings to mock those about to be slaughtered. A few months later he changed sides again from Parliament to Royalist.

When Cromwell landed in Ireland on 18 August 1649, Inchiquin chose to remain committed to the Royalist cause. In 1650, he fled to Brittany and joined the court of Charles II. In May 1654 he was confirmed in the earldom. Incredibly in view of his past actions, he became a convert to Catholicism. He was made Governor of Catalonia in French service. He went to England in 1663 after the restoration and became Vice-President of Munster. He was restored to all his honours and given an estate of 10,000 acres with £8000 compensation for his losses. He ended his days at Rostellan, Cork Harbour, where he died on 9 September 1674.

Murrough's son William, the 2nd Earl, had also gone into exile, serving Charles II, and was later Vice-Admiral of Tangier and then Governor of Jamaica. His grandson, the 4th Earl Inchiquin, became the head of the O'Brien family in 1741. His son, another Murrough, became the 5th Earl Inchiquin and 1st Marquis of Thomond. The line ended with James (d. 1855) who was 3rd Marquis and 12th Baron Inchiquin.

Once more the chiefship of the O'Briens moved to another branch of the family. The next senior surviving line was that of the youngest son of King Murrough, the 1st Earl of Thomond – Donough of Lemanagh and Dromoland, who had supported the challenge under Brehon law to the succession of Conor as 3rd Earl. While members of the line were bestowed with knighthoods, it was only with Donough (d. 1717) that the line were created baronets. The chiefship of the O'Briens passed to Sir Lucius, the 5th Baronet (d. 1872) who became the 13th Baron Inchiquin.

Their residence was Dromoland Castle. 'Dromoland' is said to denote a ridge of honeysuckle. The castle was originally built in the late fifteenth or early sixteenth century and King Murrough had left it to his son Donough who was hanged by the English in 1582 having been active in trying to retrieve the Thomond kingship for his cousin. This allowed Sir George Cusack, the sheriff, to attempt appropriating the castle for himself. However, the O'Briens returned. There was a legal battle between the Earls of Thomond and the O'Briens of Dromoland for the ownership of the castle. In 1642 Colonel Conor O'Brien of Lemanagh managed to expel the adherents of Lord Thomond from the castle.

Conor was killed in a skirmish with the Cromwellian General Ludlow's troops in 1651. His widow was one of the famous women of Irish history, Máire Rua O'Brien (1615–86).

Máire Rua was probably born in her parents' home of Bunratty Castle, Co. Clare, the daughter of Torlach MacMahon and Máire, the daughter of the 3rd Earl of Thomond. She was wealthy in her own right being the widow of Daniel Neylon of Neylon Castle, Dysert O'Dea. Her second marriage to Conor O'Brien of Lemanagh produced eight children. Máire was thirty-six when Conor O'Brien was killed fighting the Cromwellians.

In 1653 the Cromwellian administration announced the confiscation of all property but Máire Rua, it seems, contracted marriage to a Cromwellian officer named John Cooper. Cooper, therefore, became the 'legal' owner, in English terms, of the property and soon after the marriage he conveniently died. Folklore has it that Máire Rua killed him once he had served his purpose to safeguard the property. Indeed, murder charges were brought against her. She finally received a royal pardon in 1644. She had reared her son Donough, by Conor O'Brien, as a Protestant and he moved into Dromoland becoming the 'richest commoner in Ireland'.

Sir Donough became the 1st Baronet of the line and entertained the Duke of Berwick, James II's illegitimate son, who commanded the Jacobite troops at Limerick in November 1690.

The family of Lemanagh and Dromoland was more radical and sympathetically Irish than the other branches. In fact, the brother of Sir Lucius, who inherited the title of Baron Inchiquin, and the chiefship as O'Brien, was one of the leading figures of the Irish republican uprising of 1848. William Smith O'Brien (the Smith taken from his mother Charlotte Smith) was born at Dromoland in 1803, the son of Sir Edward, the 4th Baronet. Educated at Harrow and Cambridge University, he became a Conservative Member of Parliament for Ennis in 1825 and then for Co. Limerick in 1835. But his views were changing as he saw the suffering of the Irish people and he sought first the re-establishment of a parliament in Dublin, the Repeal of the Union as it was called, before becoming convinced that the answer lay in a sovereign republic. He became a leading member of the Young Ireland movement.

In March 1848, after four years of an artificially created famine, in which Ireland lost, in real terms, two-and-a-half million of her population, he urged the formation of an Irish National Guard with the example of the Paris Revolution in mind. With other Young Ireland leaders he sought to make preparations for an armed uprising. In July 1848 a 'War Directory' consisting of O'Brien, the lawyer John Blake Dillon, lawyer and politician Thomas Francis Meagher and Thomas D'Arcy McGee, was elected. While on an excursion to organise the movement, O'Brien and his companions were cornered by police and soldiers in Ballingarry, Co. Tipperary. The skirmish ended any hopes of an uprising. O'Brien escaped but was later arrested at Thurles. He was tried at Clonmel and found guilty of high treason. The death sentence was commuted to life transportation to Australia.

His health broken, he eventually received a pardon in 1854 on condition that he should not set foot in Ireland nor, indeed, any part of the

United Kingdom. He settled in Brussels and eventually his pardon was made unconditional. He died at Bangor in Wales in 1864, and his body was returned to Ireland. His coffin was escorted by the radical students of Trinity College across Dublin and put on a train for his ancestral home in Dromoland.

After Irish independence, Sir Lucius, 15th Baron Inchiquin, and his family continued to live quietly at Dromoland Castle. His son the 16th Baron took his duties as The O'Brien seriously and organised a major O'Brien clan gathering on St Patrick's Day, 1936. In 1937 the government of Eamon de Valéra was passing a new state constitution, using the abdication of Edward VIII in 1936 to distance themselves from the English Crown as head of state. Between 1922 and 1937 Ireland had had three Governors-General, who had replaced the office of Lord Lieutenant or Viceroy. De Valéra decided to abolish the Governor-Generalship and replace it with a President of Ireland as titular head of state.

It was the year that the Gaelic Monarchist Party were supporting O'Conor Don as a potential 'King of Ireland'. The *Cork Examiner* announced that Lord Inchiquin was a more suitable choice for President.

If heredity counted, he would be first favourite, for he is in the direct line descent from Brian Boru who, whatever his faults, was the strongest ruler Ireland ever had. If he had survived Clontarf he might have established the O'Brien dynasty so firmly that the present Earl [*sic*] would be King of All Ireland and there would be no Irish problem to be solved – unless in the meantime the O'Neills had asserted the independence of Ulster, as they probably would try to do; which brings us back to the fact that there was an Ulster problem nine hundred years ago as well as today.

According to the daughter of the 16th Lord Inchiquin, Grania R. O'Brien Weir,

Donough had been approached about accepting the Presidency of Ireland on 13th December, 1937 when Captain Charles Spring Rice, 'representing certain influential people in Ireland' came to ask if he would accept it, if it were to be offered to him. He was asked to go to Dublin for discussions. Donough's reply was in the negative.[2]

There was little doubt who Charles Spring Rice was representing. This was the family name of the old Jacobite Barons Monteagle of Brandon who owned estates in Co. Kerry and in Foyles, Co. Limerick. Charles succeeded as the 5th Baron Monteagle in 1937. His notable cousin, daughter of the 2nd Baron, was the Hon. Mary Ellen Spring Rice, an enthusiastic member of the Gaelic League, an Irish speaker and committed nationalist. She took part with Erskine Childers in the gun-running operation for the Irish Volunteers in 1914, when the *Asgard*, Childers' yacht, landed guns near Howth. Captions to the famous picture of Mrs Erskine Childers handling the guns aboard *Asgard* do not state that her female companion is Mary Ellen Spring Rice. Two other yachts were engaged in bringing arms to the Volunteers, one skippered by Spring Rice's cousin, Conor O'Brien. Ellen was also active in the Society of United Irishwomen and during the War of Independence she served as a nurse for the Volunteers. She died aged only forty-four, and was given a full republican burial at Loghill, Foynes. Her family had close connections with de Valéra and the leading members of the Fianna Fáil government.

During Sir Donough's last years lack of finances caused a depletion of the estate. Dromoland Castle was sold off in 1962 to be turned into a luxury hotel by Bernard McDonough. The sale caused the break-up of the historic collection of portraits and works of art, including a painting of King Murrough surrendering to Henry VIII at Greenwich and a portrait of the famous Máire Rua. The Dromoland estate around the castle remained within the family control. Sir Donough died in 1968.

When Sir Donough's brother Sir Phaedruig O'Brien, then 17th Lord Inchiquin, died on 20 May 1982, the titles and estates were inherited by his nephew. Conor Myles John O'Brien was born in Surrey, England, on 17 July 1943, the son of the youngest son of the 15th Baron Inchiquin, the Hon. Fionn O'Brien. He was educated at Eton and served in the British army in the 14/20th King's Hussars in the Middle East, Far East and Europe from 1963 to 1975, retiring with the rank of captain. He then ran his own trading company in Hong Kong and Singapore.

On becoming the 18th Baron Inchiquin and 10th Baronet, O'Brien, as he is simply referred to in Ireland, moved to the ancestral estate in Co. Clare. He lives in Thomond House on the Dromoland estate and has since turned the estate into a major sporting and leisure centre. Married to Helen O'Farrell of Co. Longford in 1988, he has two daughters, the Hon. Slaney O'Brien (b. 1989) and the Hon.Lucia O'Brien (b. 1991). The O'Brien and his wife run Thomond House as a de luxe guesthouse.

Conor O'Brien is a member of the Standing Council of Irish Chiefs and Chieftains, of which he was elected vice-chairman in January 1998. He is another holder of an ancient Gaelic title who believes there is a place for him in modern Irish life:

With the tremendous interest in roots and clans, the Irish chiefs have a major role that they can play in the Gaelic and cultural heritage of Ireland and in helping the state authorities in the promotion of tourism through the medium of the clan associations and clan gatherings as well as ensuring that the country recognises the importance of the link between the old Gaelic culture and our modern-day republican culture.

However, he does not feel that holders of Gaelic titles should have a permanent representation in the Irish Senate unless it has been achieved by due democratic process.

He was responsible for the formation of the O'Brien Clan Association and the first clan gathering since 1936 was held in Co. Clare in 1992. A special commemorative book, *The Royal O'Briens*, was issued to mark the occasion. He is actively working on the formation of the O'Brien Clan Foundation as a worldwide organisation and launched this in the USA in 1998. He has scheduled other major clan gatherings for the O'Briens including one in 2002, a Dál gCais Festival at Killaloe, Co. Clare, which will commemorate the thousandth anniversary of the accession of Brían Bóroimhe to the High Kingship. O'Brien is an adviser on a prospective film production about the life of Brían Bóroimhe based on the best-selling novel *The Lion of Ireland* by Morgan Llywelyn.

He believes he is an ambassador for Gaelic Ireland in all senses. He supports the attempts to preserve the Irish language. Like his republican forebear, William Smith O'Brien, he is a member of the Church of Ireland; his branch of the family have been so since Máire Rua brought her son Donough up in that faith in order to protect the family estates. He does not agree that any religion should have a special relationship with the state:

The Church has had too much control since the formation of the state, which in many ways has held back progress and helped with the demise of the Protestant faith particularly in the rural areas. It is not good to have the monopoly of one Church. I believe that we should become a secular state.

II
THE O'GRADY
(Ó Grádaigh)

The O'Grady chiefly line are a branch of the Dál gCais of Thomond and generally regarded as a cadet branch of the O'Briens. They were princes of the Cenél Dunghaile whose territory was in Co. Clare. One of their main centres was a fortress on Inis Cealtra (the Island of Burials, now referred to as Holy Island) in Lough Derg. The island has five churches and the remains of a monastery founded by St Cainín in the seventh century. O'Grady sites occur all around Lough Derg and Lough Grady, one of the smaller lakes nearby.

The family traces its roots to Donal O'Grady who was killed in battle in 1309. In the same year his son Aodh acquired the lands of Kilballyowen in Co. Limerick through marriage to the daughter of the neighbouring chief of Anlan Cliath. Kilballyowen remained in the possession of the family until 1994 when the estate was broken up. There is, however, still a family connection there.

There seem few members of note in the family in its early period except 'Johannes' who became Archbishop of Tuam (1364–71).

During the frenetic Tudor period Donough O'Grady, known to the English as 'Dionysius' and referred to as 'captain of his nation', followed the example of the king of Thomond. In 1543 he surrendered his title and lands to Henry VIII. He was then accorded the rank of an English knight and allowed his lands at Kilballyowen back on feudal tenure. Since then the main branch of the family has tended to support the English administration in Ireland. In 1582 Donough's son Seán went further by taking the name John Brady as a means of integrating with the English. His brother Hugh Brady was to become the first Protestant Bishop of Meath. He was also the progenitor of the Bradys of Raheen, Co. Clare. However, the chiefly line seems to have quickly resumed the more phonetical Anglicised form of O'Grady.

In 1633 Darby O'Grady married the daughter of Sir Thomas Standish of Lancaster; thus the name Standish has appeared often in the names of the O'Grady family. In fact, a grandson of a John O'Grady of Kilballyowen, recorded as marrying in 1698, was Standish O'Grady (1766–1840) who was raised to the English peerage as Viscount Guillamore of Cahir and Baron O'Grady of Rockbarton in 1831. He won notoriety as the Attorney-General who prosecuted the Irish revolutionary leader Robert Emmet in 1803. He was succeeded by his brother, whose son

Standish James O'Grady (1846–1928) became one of the great Irish historians and novelists. Standish James studied at Trinity College, Dublin and was called to the Bar, but his interest in Irish history was aroused by O'Curry's *Manners and Customs of the Ancient Irish*. O'Grady was assured by a professor at Trinity College that the native Irish 'had no history' and that the High King Brían Bóroimhe was a mythological character.

His most famous work was *The History of Ireland: Heroic Period* (1878–80). His writings awakened his contemporaries to a creative sense of Ireland's epic past and he has often been called the 'Father of the Irish Literary Revival'. O'Grady's influence is acknowledged by W.B. Yeats and AE (George Russell) as well as Katharine Tynan and Aubrey de Vere. He is, however, often confused with his cousin Standish Hayes O'Grady (1832–1915) who was the son of Admiral Hayes O'Grady. Standish Hayes became a leading Irish language scholar who compiled a *Catalogue of Irish Manuscripts in the British Museum*; his collection of tales from early Irish manuscripts, *Silva Gadelica* (1892), was an important contribution to understanding early literary endeavour in ancient Ireland.

In 1751 John O'Grady married the Hon. Mary Elizabeth de Courcy, eldest daughter and co-heiress of the 14th Baron Kinsale. The de Courcy family were among the first Normans to settle in Ireland during the twelfth century. John de Courcy led the first Norman expedition into Ulster, and even claimed the title 'Princeps Ulidiae' having defeated the Uí Néill king. Therefore de Courcy also appears as a name among the members of the O'Grady family.

Generations of O'Grady chiefs seem to have led uneventful and quiet lives according to *Burke's Irish Family Records*. They emerged into the unfavourable light of history during the Land War, a struggle to break the insidious system of absentee English landlordism, the still feudal relationship of landlord to tenant, which had been the cause of many terrible famines in Ireland. Famine was a common feature of Irish life in the eighteenth and nineteenth centuries. In a famine in 1740 it was estimated that 400,000 people died while famines in 1757, 1765 and 1770 increased the desperation of the people. There were further famines in 1800, 1807, 1817, 1821/22, 1830/34, 1836, 1839, 1845/49, 1878/81 and during the 1890s.

With the fall in world prices for produce and large-scale agricultural improvements in the USA, Irish farming was hit. Between 1875 and 1879 prices for produce fell by 75 per cent yet landowners still expected their tenants to continue to pay rents in accordance with previous production figures. When they could not, they were evicted, often left to starve by the side of the road. Between 1878 and 1886 some 130,000 families were turned out of their homes. Ireland, at this point, was owned by 20,000 landlords of whom just 750 owned half of the acreage in the entire country. The Land League initially sought fair rents and a fixity of tenure but, in the face of the intransigence of the landlords, the League began to develop a philosophy of overthrowing the great feudal estates. During this time the O'Grady property in Limerick was the site of grim scenes.

In 1887, Thomas de Courcy O'Grady (1844–98), who freely used his title The O'Grady, announced that he would be evicting any of his tenants who obeyed the Land League's call not to pay the rents demanded by landlords if they were unreasonable. O'Grady's tenants believed that they were. Some days later, seventy men of the 2nd Battalion, Leinster Regiment, with 130 men of the Royal Irish Constabulary, commanded by Inspector Moriarty, marched from Kilballyowen, the residence of The O'Grady, where they had been encamped, and began to evict those tenants who would not, or could not, pay. The first tenant to be evicted was John Carroll, near Herbertstown. Within days some forty tenants on the O'Grady estate were evicted in spite of demonstrations. Many protesters were arrested including three women.

By March of the following year the action of the tenants, organised by the Land League, was beginning to hit the landlords in their pockets. A new tactic had been devised by the Land League. Captain Charles Cunningham Boycott (1823–97) was land agent for Lord Erne's estate at Lough Mask, Co. Mayo. His name was given to the new tactic. Instead of being subject to physical attack, as they had been in the eighteenth century, the landlords and their agents were boycotted, their crops left to rot or harvested at great expense by labourers brought in under military protection.

The O'Grady now offered to sell the holdings to his tenants, but at a price none could afford. Later that year O'Grady took the confiscated cattle from his evicted tenants' farms and shipped them to Liverpool for sale. He was immediately denounced and, through Land League pressure, was unable to find a buyer. His cattle were boycotted.

A.G. O'Donnell, the High Sheriff of the county, was obviously a supporter of the Land League and is reported as stating: 'It was simply disgraceful to the city of Limerick that any man in it should be found mean enough to give assistance to The O'Grady against his oppressed tenantry.'

The conflict between O'Grady and his tenants continued and was reported in *The Times* on 11 February 1889. In 1886 Thomas Wallace Russell (1841–1920), the 1st Earl Russell, had defeated William O'Brien (1841–1920) of the Land League as Member of Parliament for South

Tyrone, standing as a Unionist. He wrote an extraordinarily long letter to *The Times* of two-and-a-half columns in support of The O'Grady. Referring to John Dillon MP and William Smith MP, leaders of the Land League and the League's activities against The O'Grady, he said: 'The O'Grady is as Irish as either of these gentlemen and certainly more Irish than Mr Parnell. He is one of the old stock; and is the 17th in direct succession to the family estate during the past 400 years.'

He could not, of course, make the same claim against O'Brien. Referring to the Land League, Russell said: 'If there be a place in all Ireland where this wicked combination should be fought with outright, where the most hearty and loyal support ought to be given to the landlord, Kilballyowen is the place and The O'Grady is the landlord.'

The O'Grady, however, was to see the passing of the Land Purchase Acts and other measures which prohibited arbitrary eviction and the unilateral raising of rents, and established peasant ownership by state laws. With the passing of the Wyndham Act of 1903, the end of the feudal system of landholding in Ireland was assured. In thirty-six years some thirteen million acres, divided into 400,000 smallholdings, were purchased by the tenant farmers.

Thomas's brother William de Rienzi O'Grady (1852–1932) succeeded him in 1898 as The O'Grady, followed in 1932 by a cousin, Gerald Vigors de Courcy O'Grady (1912–93), who had joined the British army, serving as aide-de-camp to the commander-in-chief in India 1939–40. He won the Military Cross in 1945 and left the service with the rank of lieutenant-colonel, having commanded the Oxfordshire Yeomanry and been an instructor at Sandhurst.

He turned to the management of his estate, becoming the president of the Irish Grassland Association. He was an outspoken man and vehemently criticised the fact that the Genealogical Office had added 'of Kilballyowen' to his title. He had said: 'I am *The* O'Grady, where I live is irrelevant to my title.' He was enthusiastic when the Standing Council of Chiefs was established. He died on 7 January 1993, and his widow, Madam Mollie O'Grady of Maryland, USA, still lives on the estate.

His successor Brian de Courcy O'Grady was born in 1943, went to his father's old school of Wellington and studied at the Northampton College of Agriculture. However, he went into the insurance business and made his home in Sussex. He took an interest in his heritage and participated in the activities of the Standing Council. He spoke several times with the author but it soon became evident that he was fighting cancer and he died on 7 May 1998.

He was succeeded by his son Henry Thomas Standish O'Grady, born on 17 April 1974. He was educated at Harrow. At Bristol University he took a master's degree in engineering and French; he then did a second master's degree in Oxford and in Paris in European business management. He now lives in Paris and works for a French management consultancy firm.

He is not married, and his tanist is his cousin, Donagh Philip Standish O'Grady, born in Kuala Lumpur in 1960, the son of Colonel Philip O'Grady of Askeaton, Co. Limerick. Donagh, too, went to Wellington College, and to Oxford and Brisbane Universities. He farms in Limerick.

The O'Grady is taking his title seriously. 'I am honoured to have a seat on the Standing Council of Irish Chiefs but, given my lack of experience of its workings, I feel it would be inappropriate at present for me to comment on either its role, or the role of the O'Grady family.'

An O'Grady Project has been set up by the East Clare Heritage Centre to refurbish the O'Grady Castle at Tuamgraney as an O'Grady Centre. The castle actually belongs to William MacLysaght, the son of the late Edward MacLysaght, the first Chief Herald of Ireland. It is hoped to incorporate a museum and the cost, in 1998, was estimated at IR£300,000. This is envisaged as an important centre which will be a focus for all members of the O'Grady and Brady clan as well as the chiefly family.

9

The Kingdom of Connacht

Connacht, sometimes given as Connaught, is a western province of Ireland having, for the greater part, the River Shannon as its eastern boundary. It now includes the counties of Galway, Mayo, Sligo, Leitrim and Roscommon and consists of some 6610 square miles. The Irish name Connachta is said to have derived from the name of Connmac, one of the sons of the fabulous Queen Medb whose royal residence was at Cruachain, now Croghan, Co. Roscommon. She features prominently in the saga *Táin Bó Cuailnge* (The Cattle Raid of Cooley). This epic was certainly already known and popular in the late sixth century when Seanchán Tórpeist, a Munster poet who became Chief Bard of Ireland, was said to have saved the manuscript from destruction by having the only known copy returned from Brittany. The earliest complete version survives in the twelfth-century *Leabhar na hUidre* (Book of the Dun Cow). R.A.S. Macalister described the *Táin* as 'a literature which comes down to us right from the heart of the La Tène period' (*c.* 500–100 BC).

A Gaelic dynasty certainly arose at an early period with its capital at Cruachain. Connacht was initially associated with the land of the Fir Bolg of Irish myth, who are often claimed as a pre-Gaelic people. After the defeat of the Fir Bolg at the first battle of Magh Tuiredh (Moytura), Connacht was given as part of a peace settlement to Sreng, a Fir Bolg who had cut off the arm of Nuada, the leader of the Tuatha Dé Danaan, the gods and goddesses of the Gaels.

The ruling dynasty of Connacht trace their line back to Brión, a brother of Niall of the Nine Hostages, and therefore the royal dynasty of Connacht became known as the Uí Briúin, descendants of Brión. More particularly they descend from the line of the Uí Bríon Aí. Most of their pedigrees start with Eochaidh Moydedon (AD 358–66), a king of

Connacht who claimed the High Kingship and is said to have reigned thirteen years and died peacefully at Tara.

The dynasty then took, as their patronymic, the name Ó Conchobhair from Conchobair (Anglicised as Conor) who died in 973. He was the son of Tadhg of the Three Towers (d. 956) who was said to be eighteenth in descent from Duach Galach, the first Christian king of Connacht (d. 438), who was converted by St Patrick. The first to use the O'Conor patronymic was Cathal, who reigned for thirty years, acknowledged Brían Bóroimhe as High King, and finally abdicated in favour of his son Tadhg to became a monk for his remaining years. Tadhg 'of the White Steed' reigned until 1030.

Tairrdelbach Ua Conchobhair, who came to the throne of Connacht in 1106, finally made the O'Conor dynasty a power in all Ireland. His father Ruaidri na Saidhe Buidhe had been blinded by an O'Flaherty in 1092 and had to abdicate. He ended his days in a monastery in 1118. His son Domnall was deposed from the kingship in 1106 and also died in 1118. And it was in 1118 that Domnall's brother Tairrdelbach found himself in the role of king-maker, forcing the O'Brien High King to accept the treaty which partitioned Munster.

This Tairrdelbach became supreme in Connacht. He is regarded not so much as a warrior but as a statesman, although he fought and won a famous battle at Moin-mór, near Emly, in Tipperary, in 1151, where he shattered the forces of Tairrdelbach O'Brien, King of Thomond (d. 1167). The O'Briens having shown how the High Kingship could be simply taken by the sword, Tairrdelbach Ua Conchobhair seized the office on the death of the Uí Néill king, Domnall Ua Lochlainn, in 1121. Like the O'Briens, the O'Conor High King became a centralising monarch, best remembered for building stone bridges, improving the road network, building castles and organising a strong naval force, based in the mouth of the Shannon. His greatest naval victory was against the fleet of the kingdom of the Isle of Man and the Isles in 1154. He also maintained a mint producing silver coins and was especially remembered as the king who commissioned the magnificent Cross of Cong, about 1123, which was said to have enshrined a relic of the True Cross that had been sent from Rome in 1112. The famous High Cross of Tuam was also erected during his reign. Even the usually independent Norse city states, such as Dublin, acknowledged his suzerain rule.

He died in 1156 and was buried in the church of St Ciaran at Clonmacnoise. For all his achievements, Tairrdelbach's period as High King was opposed by many of the other Irish kings; the kingdoms of Desmond, Thomond and Leinster, as well as the Uí Néill kingdoms, were ranged against him. But his policy was to divide and rule and, where he could not do so, to bring the weight of superior force to bear. As he grew older, however, the Uí Néill began to gain the upper hand and Muirchertach Ua Lochlainn emerged as the 'front runner' for the High Kingship. He forced Tairrdelbach's dutiful sub-king, Tiernán Ó Ruairc, the king of Breifne, to submit to him in 1150 and support his claim. In fact, from this time, Muirchertach was referred to as High King and was able to consolidate that position by weakening the kingdom of Midhe (Meath) which had, through its king Murrough Ó Maoil Sechlainn, been an ally of the O'Conor king. The kingdom was divided into three, a third allowed to O'Conor, a third to Ó Ruairc and a third to The O'Carroll of Oriel, while Maoil Sechlainn was sent into exile.

Muirchertach controlled the High Kingship for the next ten years.

Tairrdelbach's son Ruaidri Ua Conchobhair had become king of Connacht on the death of his father in 1156 by the simple process of blinding the eldest of his three brothers, who was thought to be the most accomplished and qualified for the kingship. He immediately challenged Muirchertach Ua Lochlainn for the High Kingship. In 1159, Muirchertach defeated his armies in a battle at Ardee and, after two years of prevaricating, Ruaidri formally acknowledged Muirchertach as High King.

Yet, with the inevitability of a Greek tragedy, other forces were gathering. The personalities, politics and intrigue are brilliantly portrayed in Nicholas Furlong's study *Dermot, King of Leinster and the Foreigners* which tells of the events which led Muirchertach, the High King, to commit 'high crimes and misdemeanours'. Growing paranoid about the security of his support from the Uí Néill princes, he demanded the son of each prince as a hostage and then put them to death in the spring of 1166. This was considered so extraordinary and heinous a crime that Muirchertach was denounced by the Church, regarded by the Brehons of Ireland as unfit to be High King any longer, and finally, isolated and alone, hunted from bog to bog like a beast and run to ground in the Fews of Armagh called Leitir Luin. The *Annals of Ulster* are triumphant:

> A great marvel and wonderful deed was then done; to wit, the King of Ireland to fall without battle, without contest, after his dishonouring the successor of Patrick, the staff of Jesus and the successor of Colmcille, and the Gospel of St Martin and many clergy besides.

Muirchertach's one remaining ally, Dermot MacMorrough, the king of Leinster, chased from his kingdom, set out to get mercenary assistance from the Angevin emperor, Henry II, setting in train a series of events which still reverberate in Ireland today.

Ruaidri Ua Conchobhair, with his close ally, Tiernan Ó Ruairc, now made straight for Dublin, to fill the power vacuum. He was inaugurated as High King 'as honourable as any king of the Gael was ever inaugurated', say the *Annals of the Four Masters*. In spite of the kingdom of Desmond remaining aloof, the Uí Néill being in utter disarray and the king of Leinster having left the country, Ruaidri's reign started auspiciously. In 1168 Ruaidri seemed popular and his great festival at Taillteann symbolised the new unity of Ireland. But in 1169 King Dermot returned with the first of the Norman adventurers, the mercenary knights of Richard de Clare, Earl of Pembroke. The next year more followed with the earl himself, and soon the Angevin emperor came to claim lordship over all Ireland.

Ruaidri fought from 1169 to 1175, in spite of truces and submissions, by which time his exhausted army had taken up positions on the western shore of Lough Derg. Ruaidri knew he could not sustain the war any longer. He opened negotiations with Mylor FitzHenry and envoys were sent to Henry II at Windsor. These were Ruaidri's chancellor, Archbishop Lawrence O'Toole of Dublin, Bishop Cadhla Ó Dubhthaigh of Tuam and 'Cantordis', Abbot of Clonfert. They agreed to sign what became known as the Treaty of Windsor, in October 1175. This recognised Henry as Lord Paramount of all Ireland. Ruaidri was to hold his kingdom of Connacht as a vassal king to the Angevin emperor.

There are some points that many forget about this act. Ruaidri agreed to the treaty not as High King, which office he had automatically lost under Brehon law once he had admitted defeat. Even when he had held the office, it had been held with 'opposition' from the Uí Néill of the north, the king of Leinster, the king of Desmond and the king of Thomond. He agreed the treaty only as king of Connacht, and therefore the treaty was not binding on any other Irish king. Also, under Brehon law, his own people of Connacht were not bound by the surrender and, indeed, there was much dissension in the kingdom. His own sons rebelled and drove him into Munster. Henry II had demanded hostages for Ruaidri's good behaviour, including one of Ruaidri's own sons. These were sent to the Angevin court in France in 1180. Ruaidri now tried to strengthen his bond with the Norman conquerors by marrying his daughter to Henry II's Viceroy, Sir Hugh de Lacy. In 1186, Ruaidri was forced to abdicate as king of Connacht and did so in favour of his son Conor Moin. Ruaidri then entered the monastery of Cong where he died in 1198. Some thirty years after his death, his remains were transferred for burial to Clonmacnoise being placed alongside his father, Tairrdelbach.

Ruaidri is misremembered in history as the last High King of Ireland. He was not even the last native High King for an Uí Néill aspired to that position, albeit with opposition. This was Brían O'Neill whose brief term of office between 1258 and 1260 ended when he was slain by the English. And, of course, the last *de facto* High King was the Norman Scot, Edward Bruce, brother of King Robert I of Scotland, who was invited by certain of the Irish princes, including Fedlimid mac Aeda of Connacht, to take that position. However, it is true that the concept of the office of High King had diminished; with the settlement of the Norman lords, paying tribute to the Angevin empire, the centralising impetus of the High Kingship ceased and power devolved back to the constituent kingdoms.

There was a period of instability in Connacht following Ruaidri's abdication and his son and his half-brother took the crown in swift succession. Yet in the three years that Conor Moin was king he did manage to inflict one major defeat on the Normans, who were commanded by the Viceroy, John de Courcy. Conor Moin was able to throw off Norman supremacy until 1189 when he was assassinated.

In 1201 Ruaidri's half-brother, Conor's uncle, Cathal Crobhderg (Cathal of the Wine Red Hand) was inaugurated as king at the traditional site of Carnfree. His reign lasted twenty-three years and he did much to stabilise the kingdom, marrying Mór, daughter of the king of Thomond. He endowed the building of twelve abbeys in his kingdom, including the famous Abbey of Ballintober, which illustrates the change of architecture from Irish Romanesque to Gothic. He also built the Abbey of Knockmoy. Cathal met King John of England, whose misrule had reduced most of the Continental Angevin empire and brought the centre of the Norman kings from France to England. He acknowledged John as his suzerain lord.

On the death of Cathal in 1224 his son Aodh (Hugh) became king though not without opposition from the surviving sons of Ruaidri. In 1228 Aodh was killed by a Norman knight in a fit of jealousy.

In 1235, while Fedlimid mac Cathail Chrobhdeirg, brother of Aodh, was king, Maurice FitzGerald, the Justiciar (or Viceroy), crossed the Shannon with an army of Norman knights and men-at-arms and laid waste the kingdom, allowing the Normans to seize part of it for their own estates and thus breaking the treaty with Ruaidri and his successors. However, many of these Norman adventurers settled down and intermarried so that families such as the Joyces, the de Burgos and the de Lacys, within a few generations, had become more Irish than the Irish, adopting the language, laws and customs of the indigenous people.

As previously mentioned, among the Irish kings who invited Edward Bruce to come to Ireland as High King was King Fedlimid mac Aeda of Connacht. It is interesting that the request of the Irish princes had gone to Robert Bruce. The Scottish king's reply is still on record and demonstrates the Gaelic kinship felt between the two countries:

Whereas we and you and our people and your people, free since ancient times, share the same national ancestry and are urged to come together more eagerly and joyfully in friendship by a common language and by common custom, we have sent over to you our beloved kinsmen, the bearers of this letter, to negotiate with you in our name about permanently strengthening and maintaining inviolate that special friendship between us and you, so that with God's will your nation may be able to recover her ancient liberty.

Edward Bruce was crowned on May Day, 1316. Fedlimid mac Aeda fought at the battle of Athenry on 10 August, 1316. He was facing the armies of Richard de Burgo and Richard de Bermingham. The battle was a great defeat for the Irish and fifty-six leading members of the Gaelic aristocracy were killed, including King Fedlimid. He was succeeded by his brother Tairrdelbach, who had married the daughter of The O'Donel, Prince of Tirconnell. The famous 'Remonstrance of the Irish Princes to Pope John XXII' was drawn up in 1317 under the instigation of Domnall O'Neill, King of Ulster (1283–86 and 1295–1325) in which the princes listed their grievances. On 14 October 1318 King Edward Bruce was killed at the battle of Faughart.

Fedlimid became the ancestor of a branch of the family which took the title Ó Conchobhair Ruadh (O'Conor Roe) while his brother Tairrdelbach became the ancestor of the Ó Conchobhair Donn (O'Conor Don). At that time there was also a third distinct branch of the O'Conor royal dynasty in Connacht, the Uí Conchobhair Sligigh, or O'Conor Sligo. This branch had descended from Brían Luigheach, one of the sons of the High King Tairrdelbach Ua Conchobhair. After the abdication of his brother Ruaidri in 1186, Brían had retired from Connacht politics to concentrate on maintaining his castle and estates and raising his cattle. His family were lords of Carbury and Sligo; later the head of the house bore the title O'Conor Sligo. They intermarried with many of the great Norman families who had settled in their area, showing an unusual disposition to be of service to the Anglo-Normans. Cathal Óg allowed them a strategic foothold in Sligo. O'Conor Sligo was one of the first to surrender his Gaelic title to Henry VIII.

Donal O'Conor, The O'Conor Sligo, also surrendered to Elizabeth I of England through the auspices of her Lord Deputy Sir Henry Sidney in 1565, travelling to Hampton Court to pledge his allegiance in person. The account of his visit says that he came

... and there, in his Irish tongue, by an interpreter, declared that the chief cause of his coming was to see and speak to the powerful and illustrious Princess whom he recognises to be his Sovereign Lady, acknowledging that both he and his ancestors had long lived in an uncivil, rude and barbarous fashion, destitute of the true knowledge of God, and ignorant of their duty to the Imperial Crown of England.

He made a solemn promise that he would raise his clan against any of his own countrymen fighting the English. For this Elizabeth was pleased to give him a knighthood. The Tudors recognised his authority from Ballyshannon to Sligo and from Sligo to the Curlew Mountains. Sir Donal O'Conor died in 1588 still a firm ally of the English. Donough his nephew succeeded him but not without great opposition from Sir Richard Bingham, the Elizabethan commander who was made 'President of Connacht' and who saw Sligo as 'the key of the door of Connacht' by which he could invade and conquer the kingdom. Bingham did not trust Donough and felt he needed total control of Sligo to achieve his purpose.

However, Donough continued his father's policy as a staunch ally of England and devoted himself with the greatest zeal to promote the English interest throughout his country. At the outbreak of the renewed war led by Aodh Ruadh O'Neill as king of Ulster, O'Neill's general Aodh Ruadh O'Donel, Prince of Tirconnell, was besieging O'Conor Sligo's castle at Colloney. Now, with an eye for the main chance, and with the defeat of the English army at the Yellow Pass through the Curlews (not to be confused with Yellow Ford) which had been Donough's hope for relief, O'Conor Sligo decided to join the Irish side. Aodh Ruadh O'Donel was always mistrustful of this alliance and in 1601 finally accused him of being a spy for the English authorities, which undoubtedly was true. Donough O'Conor Sligo was, therefore, imprisoned on an island on Lough Esk for two years until the Treaty of Mellifont of 1603 ended the war.

Sir Donough O'Conor re-emerged as a firm ally of England once again and married Lady Eleanor Butler, Countess of Desmond, receiving a knighthood in 1604. He died in 1609 and was succeeded by his half-brother. The son of this half-brother was Charles O'Conor, created a baronet in 1622.

Twenty years after this, three brothers of Tadhg, the new O'Conor Sligo, broke away from his English allies and led the Sligo men in the insurrection of 1641. With the early successes of the Irish forces, Tadhg decided to join his brothers and was given command of the garrison and town of Sligo. In 1645, however, Sir Robert Stewart forced him to surrender. Tadhg O'Conor Sligo was executed in Boyle in 1652. His estates were confiscated and divided.

Tadhg's grandson Martin claimed the estates during the restoration and supported James II but, with the Williamite conquest, the O'Conor Sligos lost any hope of recovering anything. Martin's son fled to Europe and subsequently became a general in the Austrian service. He died in Brussels in 1756 regarded by historians as 'the last O'Conor Sligo'.

The first O'Conor Roe was Tairrdelbach Ruadh, king of Connacht from 1384 to 1425/6, also referred to in the annals as Ó Conchobhair Ruadh, O'Conor Roe (*ruadh* – red or foxy-haired). He was the grandson of King Fedlimid mac Aeda, who fell fighting for Edward Bruce in 1316. His cousin Tairrdelbach Óg, grandson of Fedlimid's brother who was king of Connacht three times from 1317 to 1345, became known as Tairrdelbach Óg Donn from about 1392. It has been argued whether Tairrdelbach was nicknamed *donn* meaning brown-haired to differentiate him from his red-haired cousin, or whether the name had another significance. It has been suggested by John O'Donovan that the word *don* could have implied a rightful king, for a similar ancient word did mean 'kingly' or 'princely'. The personal arms of The O'Conor Don bear the symbol of the mystic oak tree associated with royalty in the ancient Celtic world and the motto *O Dhia! Gach Cú Cabhrach*, Oh God, every hero's protection.

The two related houses of O'Conor Roe and O'Conor Don could not agree on succession and the kingdom of Connacht was divided between them. The division was not without opposition. Tairrdelbach Óg O'Conor Don was killed in 1406 by Cathal Dubh, son of O'Conor Roe. When Tairrdelbach O'Conor Roe died in 1426, there seems to have been a reunification; The O'Conor Roe was styled as King of Connacht and not 'half-king' as previous O'Conor Roes and O'Conor Dons had been. However, a few years later the internal warfare erupted again and The O'Conor Roe and The O'Conor Don went their separate ways, once more dividing the kingdom in two.

In 1585 Tadhg Óg O'Conor Roe subscribed to the Composition of Connacht abolishing all Gaelic titles in the former kingdom. His seat was at Bealnamulta (Bealonemilly). He had previously surrendered his Gaelic title and lands in 1568 and been recognised as 'captain of the country of Clountie'. In 1617 Balinfad, Co. Roscommon, was, according to the records, held by Cathal O'Conor Roe as his family's chief seat. During the seventeenth century the family were forced into exile and a Roger O'Conor, who was governor of Civita Vecchia, Italy, *c.* 1734, is regarded as the last O'Conor Roe.

I
THE O'CONOR DON,
Prince of Connacht
(Ó Conchobhair Donn)

Tairrdelbach Óg, the first O'Conor Don, submitted to Richard II at Waterford on 29 April 1395. Tairrdelbach claimed total sovereignty over Connacht as did his cousin. The annalists reconciled the counter-claims between the cousins by calling them both 'half-kings'. This submission to Richard II angered some sections of his people and he was inveigled into the house of a Burke kinsman and attacked. He was killed by Cathal Dubh, son of O'Conor Roe, on 9 December 1406. The O'Conor Don line maintained their 'half-kingship', until the time of Cairbre mac Eóghain Chaoich (1475–1546). According to Piers O'Conor Nash:

> ... in 1543 the O'Connors like the O'Neills and O'Brians nominally surrendered their titles and agreed to adopt English customs and laws and to obey the precepts of the English Crown, promises they had no intention of keeping but preserving their hereditary lands.[1]

Cairbre's son Aodh mac Eóghain Chaoich succeeded but was deposed after four years in 1550 and his brother Diarmuid, who married Dorothy, the daughter of Tadhg Buidhe O'Conor Roe (1519–34), succeeded as 'half-king' in 1550. When he died in 1585 it could be said that he was the last O'Conor king of Connacht for, notwithstanding his father's nominal surrender, he was the last to exercise jurisdiction, with opposition from his brother-in-law, Tadhg Óg mac Taidhg Buidhe, O'Conor Roe, over Connacht. In 1570 Sir Edward Fytton had been made 'President of Connaught' to oversee the English administration of the newly surrendered country. The state papers record that he took troops through Connaught burning churches and expelling the religious. In 1571 he demanded a meeting with King Diarmuid and gave him safe passage to come to his headquarters. As usual, safe passage did not mean much to the Tudor administrators and Diarmuid was made captive to be used as a hostage for his people's good behaviour.

Diarmuid's son, Aodh, together with the son of Diarmuid's brother-in-law, O'Conor Roe, led a daring rescue bid which succeeded in releasing the king from Fytton's castle. On 14 February 1571, Fytton wrote to Lord Cecil: 'O'Conor Don, the ancient King of Connaught, lying pledge for his whole sept, escaped very presumptuously by night.' Fytton immediately marched on Diarmuid's main castle and captured it.

Diarmuid, with other Connacht nobles such as MacDermot of Moylurg, organised an army and recruited 1200 Scots gallowglasses or mercenaries. Diarmuid was indicted for high treason when he attacked the English garrison at Athlone, the seat of the English administration in the region, and destroyed it. The Connacht king continued a war which lasted until 1576.

Even as late as 1582, Diarmuid's son Aodh was still conducting a guerrilla warfare against the English with the aid of the Ó Ruairc, Prince of Breifne. King Diarmuid had become feeble as the war and his age took their toll. The new Lord Deputy, Sir John Perrott, appointed a governor of Connacht in the person of Sir Richard Bingham. The Irish sources abound in reports of Bingham's cruelty and injustice, both towards his own men and towards the Irish. Perrott himself was little better. The Lord Deputy organised a parliament in Dublin and according to the *Annals of Loch Cé* invited several leading Irish nobles to attend it. He then promptly hanged those he deemed the most troublesome.

In September 1585 King Diarmuid died. The annals accord him thirty-five years of sovereignty. He was buried in Roscommon. That year, of course, was the year of the Composition of Connacht which finally abolished all Gaelic titles in Connacht.

Aodh, now The O'Conor Don, surrendered to Lord Deputy Perrott and this coincided with the removal of Sir Richard Bingham, whose massacres, hangings and confiscations in Connacht were eventually seen to be non-productive. Bingham was sent to Flanders. The English administration began to look forward to the fruits of their conquest.

After a period of quiet unease, Aodh Ruadh O'Neill, King of Ulster, rose up. The victory of the Irish at Beal an Átha Buidhe (Yellow Ford) annihilated the English army commanded by Marshal Sir Henry Bagenal. The news from the north brought Aodh O'Conor Don back into the conflict, in support of O'Neill. There was even mention of O'Neill becoming the new High King once the English were totally defeated. In 1599 the Earl of Essex arrived with a new English army. For no apparent reason, Aodh O'Conor Don abruptly decided to throw in his lot with Essex for which the grateful earl bestowed a knighthood on him. Essex was later to answer charges about his indiscriminate bestowal of knighthoods on all and sundry.

Sir Aodh O'Conor Don joined forces with the army of Sir Conyers Clifford, the new Governor of Connacht, and was at the battle of the Curlews. When O'Donel, Prince of Tirconnell won this battle, O'Conor Don fled but was soon made a captive of the Irish forces. When the Earl of Essex entered negotiations with Aodh Ruadh O'Neill, it would appear that part of the agreement was O'Conor Don's release.

With the end of the war and the flight of many of the leading heads of the Gaelic aristocratic families in 1608, a parliament was summoned in Dublin in 1613. O'Conor Don was returned to this parliament as 'first knight of shire' for Roscommon. He married the daughter of Brian Ó Ruairc, Prince of Breifne, and died in 1627. Sir Aodh had received a regrant of some of his estates in 1617 from James I. These were centred at Ballintober Castle which became a refuge for persecuted Catholic clergy. O'Conor Don seized the chance to take a civil oath, allowed by James, rather than an Oath of Supremacy, which would have caused him to have to convert to the Protestant Church of England.

When he died he left four sons; it was the third son, Cathal Óg, who inherited the estate and assumed the title O'Conor Don. Cathal (Charles) (1584–1655) married Mary, daughter of Tadhg na Loing (Theobald of the Ships) whose mother was the celebrated Gráinne (Grace) O'Malley (1530–1603) nicknamed Gráinne Mhaoil (Grainuaile) because she wore her hair close-cropped like a boy. She was an O'Flaherty noblewoman who had fought the English both on sea and on land and even went to negotiate with Elizabeth I at Greenwich on equal terms. There is a famous painting of the two women in conversation. Elizabeth was said to have had an Irish phrase book printed for the occasion so that she could speak a few words to Gráinne in her own language. Certainly such a phrase book in Irish, Latin and English does survive. It was compiled for Elizabeth by Christopher Nugent, 9th Baron Delvin.

Records indicate that Cathal, who became O'Conor Don in 1632, continued to regard himself as 'King of Connacht', issued proclamations from Ballintober and raised a regular army.

Charles O'Conor Don joined the insurrection of 1641 and died in 1655 having witnessed the Cromwellian conquest and confiscations. Out of the 6000 acres of his estate his widow was allowed to keep 700. His son Aodh or Hugh (1617–69) had been appointed colonel in the Irish army and was captured in 1642 in the attack on Castlecoote. He was released after seven months and rejoined the Irish forces. In 1652 he was forced to surrender to Cromwell's forces. He was declared an outlaw when he managed to flee to France, where he joined the Duke of Gloucester's regiment in Charles II's army. On the restoration, Hugh, now O'Conor Don, appealed for the restoration of his father's estate. Decisions were delayed until his death in 1669.

His son, also Hugh O'Conor, succeeded him and in 1676 he finally regained some 1100 acres of the original 6000. He died unmarried in 1686 and the estate went to his uncle Charles with the remainder to his cousins, the O'Conors of Castlerea and Belanagare, Co. Roscommon. Charles gave his land at Ballintober to Colonel Burke in payment for a debt. He died without issue in 1699.

Andrew O'Conor, a grandson of Charles, became the next O'Conor Don. His father had fled into exile after the Cromwellian conquest and remained in Spain until the restoration. Andrew's mother, however, had managed to retain some 440 acres of profitable land and some unprofitable bogland with a house at Clonalis. Clonalis House is still O'Conor property. Andrew died in 1718 to be succeeded by Daniel (1718–69). He was succeeded by a son Dominick (1769–95) who died without issue. His brother Alexander (1795–1820) then succeeded but also died without issue.

The line passed to the O'Conors of Belanagare who descended from a son of Cathal Óg's third son, Sir Hugh (d. 1632). Owen (1632–92), Cathal's first son, was declared an outlaw and fled to France. He became a major in the same regiment as his cousin, the Duke of Gloucester's regiment. During the Williamite conquest he was captured and died a prisoner in Chester Castle in 1692. The line of Belanagare descends from his brother who was convicted of treason and died in 1696. His son Donough Lia (1674–1750) and Donough's sons converted to the Anglican religion, and thus managed to restore some 800 acres of the ancestral estates. However, while theoretically Anglican to maintain ownership, they also secretly adhered to the Catholic Church.

Charles O'Conor of Belanagare (1710–90), a son of Donough Lia, became a famous historian whose principal work was *The Dissertations on Irish History* (1753). His grandson was Dr Charles O'Conor, a Catholic priest and ecclesiastical scholar who wrote *Rerum Hibernicarum Scriptores*. He appeared to suffer from dementia in later life and returned to Belanagare in 1827, where he died in 1828.

Other members of the family were more political. Charles of Mount Allen (1736–1808) was the grandson of Charles the historian of Belanagare. He became much involved in politics and was a close friend of John Keogh, a leading spirit of the Catholic Committee to get the repressive Penal Laws repealed. He became one of the first people in Connacht to join the United Irishmen in November 1791.

He was elected to the Catholic Convention in Dublin with Myles Keogh for Leitrim. The MacDermot, Prince of Coolavin, represented Sligo while Owen O'Conor represented Roscommon. Charles's son Thomas (1770–1855) also joined the United Irishmen. The Rt. Hon. Charles Owen O'Conor Don, in his book *The O'Conors of Connaught*, tried to water down his ancestors' commitment to the republican movement by curiously claiming, 'Whilst Charles O'Conor and his friends thus joined heartily with the founders of the Society of United Irishmen, they never contemplated going outside the constitution or having recourse to means inconsistent with their loyalty to the [English] Crown.'

In the wake of the failure of the 1798 uprising, Charles O'Conor and his son Thomas fled to the United States. Charles's other son, Denis, was already settled there. Tom became a journalist and during the '1812 War' with England he edited the weekly newspaper *The War* and then the *Military Monitor*. He also edited *The Shamrock* and *The Globe*. His major work was *A History of the War* (of 1812–15).

Thomas's son Charles (1804–84), born in New York, became a Democrat lawyer and at the end of the American Civil War was senior defence counsel for Jefferson Davis, former President of the Confederate States. In 1872 he was the Democratic candidate for the Presidency of the USA but lost out to U.S. Grant, attributing his failure to his Irish Catholic background. In his house on Nantucket Island, he collected a library of 18,000 volumes and was vice-president of the New York Historical Society.

Owen O'Conor of Belanagare (1763–1831) became head of the family in 1820 on the death of his cousin Alexander O'Conor Don. Owen became a tireless worker for Catholic emancipation and a close friend and associate of Daniel O'Connell, 'The Liberator'. Before that he had joined the Irish Volunteers and been a delegate to the 1793 Catholic National Convention. Wolfe Tone wrote approvingly of his 'political fiery ardour' in his diary. He seems to have been on intimate terms with Tone, Keogh, Byrne and other republican leaders but left the United Irish movement in 1795. He joined Daniel O'Connell's party to pursue Catholic emancipation by parliamentary methods. He was on its control committee from 1811. He was elected to serve as a delegate from the Catholics of Ireland to England. Following the repeal of the last of the Penal Laws in 1829, when Catholics could at last take public office, he was elected to Parliament for Co. Roscommon. It is worth commenting that Sir Hugh O'Conor Don had represented Co. Roscommon in the Dublin parliament of 1613.

Denis O'Conor (1794–1847) succeeded his father in 1831 as O'Conor Don and also as Member of Parliament for Co. Roscommon. He became Lord of the Treasury. With the restrictions on Catholics now gone his second son not only became High Sheriff for Roscommon but Member of Parliament for Sligo (1868–83).

His eldest son, who inherited the title, was Charles Owen O'Conor (1838–1906) and perhaps the best known of those bearing the title O'Conor Don. He was the author of *The O'Conors of Connacht*. He had been educated at Downside by Benedictines and studied at London

University, becoming a doctor of law. He was elected Liberal Member of Parliament for Roscommon in 1860 and held the seat for the next twenty years until defeated by an Irish Party candidate from the Parnellite wing.

In Parliament he became a leading spokesman of Catholic opinion; he urged reform of land tenure in Ireland and also supported 'home rule'. He was interested in education, penal reform and reform of work practices in factories and workshops, serving on royal commissions in those areas. He was supportive of the Irish language and president of the Society for the Preservation of the Irish Language, being instrumental in procuring the introduction of the Irish language into the curriculum of the Intermediate School Board. He was a friend of Douglas Hyde, founder of Conradh na Gaeilge (the Gaelic League) in 1893 who became President of Ireland from 1937 to 1947. The O'Conor Don was also president of the Royal Society of Antiquaries of Ireland and of the Royal Irish Academy.

Unfortunately, in spite of his activities for self-government and the restoration of the Irish language to its rightful place in Irish society, The O'Conor Don is still remembered in Ireland for his appearance at the coronation of Edward VII when he carried 'the standard of Ireland'. As we saw in Chapter 5, it was thought that O'Conor Don was claiming to speak for all the Irish nobility in recognising Edward VII as lawful monarch of Ireland and not ruler merely by right of conquest. The fact that the artificial standard was carried by someone whose title had been 'utterly abolished and made extinct for ever' by the same English monarchy left a nasty taste in many Irish mouths.

At a time when the struggle for Irish independence was growing, his ill-advised action was compounded when his son, Denis Charles Joseph O'Conor, appeared as The O'Conor Don in the coronation procession of George V in 1912 bearing another 'standard of Ireland', which is still displayed in the hall at Clonalis House. Denis, who died in 1917, was a Privy Councillor and served as both Lieutenant and High Sheriff of Roscommon. He died unmarried and was succeeded by his brother Owen Phelim O'Conor (1870–1943).

In the 1930s a Monarchist Party emerged in Ireland and in 1937 a report appeared in the newspapers with a portrait of Owen Phelim under the headline 'May Become King of Ireland'. The report announced that he was 'the direct descendant of Roderic O'Conor, last monarch of Ireland [sic], who may be invited to become King of Ireland by the Monarchist Party, if and when they come into power.' Unfortunately, no other trace of this party has come to light. Owen Phelim had no male issue and therefore his cousin, Father Charles Denis O'Conor SJ, became The O'Conor Don between 1943 and 1981. His sister Gertrude Mary married

Group Captain Rupert Nash of the Royal Air Force and their son Piers O'Conor Nash is the current owner of Clonalis House which houses the O'Conor archives, library and memorabilia.

In 1981 the title was inherited by Denis Armar O'Conor, born in 1912 and educated at Downside, where most of the family have received their schooling. He was a grand-nephew of Charles Owen O'Conor Don. He went to Sandhurst in 1931 and was commissioned into the Lincolnshire Regiment. He served with the British army in India and China in World War II. Retiring with the rank of major in 1945, he returned to live in Ireland and became a company director. His residence is in Dun Laoghaire.

He remains the current holder of the title O'Conor Don, Prince of Connacht, and the recipient of various decorations from foreign governments. He became president of the Dun Laoghaire Historical Society, and is a former Master of the Delgany Beagles, having bred beagle hounds. He was active in the early years of the Standing Council of Irish Chiefs and Chieftains.

During his active years, Denis Armar tried to bring the title of O'Conor Don into a higher profile. Realising that the Eóghanacht Niadh Nask had survived as a dynastic order, even during the years of exile in France, he was advised that the royal house of Connacht ought to have some similar order but attempts to create one were ill advised, as will be examined in Chapter 12.

The O'Conor Don is now elderly and in ill health; affairs pertaining to his title are handled by his tanist, Desmond O'Conor. Desmond was born on 22 September 1938. He was a corporate finance director of Dresden Kleinwort Benson, with special responsibility for Latin America and Iberia, and is a fluent speaker of Spanish and Portuguese. He has lived in Guatemala, Honduras, Peru and Brazil, and was chairman and vice-chairman of his company's subsidiaries in Latin America and Spain. He retired in September 1998.

Although he holds Irish citizenship, he lives in Sussex and is married to Virginia Williams, daughter of Sir Michael Williams KCMG, and has three children, including a son, Philip Hugh, born on 17 February 1967.

Speaking as the heir apparent to the title, he has decided views on his role.

It would, in a republic, in my view, be unconstitutional for any Irish chief or chieftain to hold any unelected political position unless he were elected like any other Irish citizen. In theory, I suppose, there could be a nomination to the Senate but this would probably also need a constitutional change. I definitely do not think that chiefs or chieftains should have *by right* any such position. In my view they would have to earn it and most likely then only by election.

Every holder of the title should in my view do what he can for Ireland but inevitably (and it was my father's case) this is likely to be confined to supporting, wherever and whenever, Irish culture. If he also happens to be a businessman, then support and help, particularly to help create employment, seems to me to be a good use of one's legacy. One may also add to this, the promotion of tourism.

I, and my father, support completely the importance of encouraging and sustaining the use of the Irish language. My ancestors have a distinguished history in this regard particularly Charles O'Conor of Bellanagare and Charles Owen O'Conor Don who was the first vice-president for the [Society for the] Preservation of the Irish Language and largely responsible for the Irish language being included in the school curriculum.

Until the time of his retirement, Desmond kept a low profile in chiefly affairs, although he is a committee member of the Irish Genealogical Society. His half-brother, Dr Kieran O'Conor, is an archaeologist who is knowledgeable on O'Conor history and currently works in the field of medieval rural settlement in Ireland. Kieran lives in Roscommon.

II
THE O'KELLY
of Gallagh and Tycooly
(8th Count O'Kelly of the Holy Roman Empire)
(Ó Cellaigh)

The pedigree of The O'Kelly is traced back to Maine Mór of Connacht, who is recorded in AD 457 as a prince or petty king of a territory known as Uí Maine, often given as Hy Maine, stretching from South Roscommon into East Galway. His descendants, as princes, were hereditary marshals to the kings of Connacht. The surname is taken from Cellagh, 'Bright-Headed', who is listed as the twelfth prince of Hy Maine and whose son Tadhg Mór was killed in the battle of Clontarf in 1014.

It is a tradition that the crest on their coat of arms – 'on a ducal crest – coronet or an enfield passant vert' – dates from the time of Tadhg Mór because, so the story goes, this fabulous animal arose from the sea to protect the body of the O'Kelly prince from the Danish warriors until it could be recovered by his comrades and removed from the field of battle.

The O'Kellys became one of the most prolific clans in Ireland, spreading at one time into eight different branches, but the senior branch was that of Gallagh or Uí Maine. They produced an Archbishop of Tuam who compiled the historic *Book of the O'Kellys*.

The O'Kelly princes made good political marriages over the years, marrying into the O'Brien kings of Thomond and the O'Conor kings of Connacht and the kings of Moylurg and princes of Coolavin. Donough, the son of Mealachlan Ó Ceallagh and Finola, daughter of King Tairrdel-bach O'Conor, king of Connaught, is given as twenty-fourth O'Kelly prince of Hy Maine in most genealogies.

The O'Kelly princes had a reputation for hospitality and in 1351 Uilliam Buidhe (William Boy), who built the castles of Callow and Gaile, invited all the bards of Ireland to a Christmas feast. His Chief Bard was Seán Mór Ó Dugabhán (d.c. 1375) whose long genealogical poem *Ríoga síl Eibhir* (The Kings of the Race of Eibhear) has recently been reprinted with a commentary by The MacCarthy Mór.

The O'Kellys initially fought against the Elizabethan conquest but Conor O'Kelly, known as Conor na Garroghe O'Kelly of Gallagh, was forced to surrender and seek pardon. On 10 September 1578 he was granted the castle of Gallagh with ten 'quarters' of land called 'Twonepallice' in Galway, to hold for ever by the service of a twentieth part of a knight's fee. In November 1581 he also surrendered his Gaelic title, and in return, not being considered a significant aristocrat, was granted the office of 'seneschal of the barony of Kylconnel'. He was to hold this 'during pleasure as fully as Mellaghlen m'Eabbe O'Kelly held it'. A few weeks later 'William m'Mellaughlen m'Enabbe O'Kelly' was recognised 'to be tanist or second person of the Kellies country beyond the river Suck in the province of Connaught'. The letters patent show that the princes had now become merely seneschals in the new English order of aristocracy.

They made more political marriages with the Anglo-Norman Burke family, the Earls of Clanricade. However, William O'Kelly, The O'Kelly, fought during 1641–49, was exiled in Spain and returned at the restoration. He then became a colonel in James II's army in Ireland while his kinsman Charles O'Kelly (1621–95) sat in James II's Dublin parliament of 1689. In spite of Charles's advanced age, he commanded his regiment under Patrick Sarsfield, the Earl of Lucan, until the surrender in 1691. He was imprisoned on Inisbofin. He was finally allowed to retire to a small estate at Aughrane where he wrote an account of the Williamite war from the Jacobite viewpoint. As Ireland was under Williamite occupation, he wrote it in Latin using ciphers as an account of the conquest of 'Cyprus': *Macariae Excidium; or the Destruction of Cyprus containing the last War and Conquest of that Kingdom.* He also wrote his personal memoirs but the manuscript has been lost.

William O'Kelly, The O'Kelly, fared little better after the great defeat of Aughrim in 1691. He was driven out of Gallagh Castle by the Williamites and found a refuge in Tycooly. It was his second son, Festus, who succeeded him to the Gaelic title and, by Imperial Letters Patent of 25 November 1767, Emperor Joseph III created him Reichsgraf (Count) of the Holy Roman Empire with remainder to all descendants male and female in the male line, the females to bear the title until their marriage. The honour was granted because of the services to the Holy Roman Empire by Festus' son, Dillon. Dillon John O'Kelly was not only a distinguished soldier in the Imperial army but also Imperial Chamberlain and Minister Plenipotentiary of the Empress Maria-Theresa in 1755. His brother Connor succeeded to both Gaelic and Austrian titles. The Holy Roman Empire came to an end in 1806 following the triumph of Napoleon Bonaparte. No attempt was made to resurrect it and Emperor Francis II called himself by the new title Emperor of Austria.

Many of the family had been killed during the Williamite conquest while others went into exile in Austria, Spain, Germany and the Low Countries. John James O'Kelly-Farrell was created a count by Louis XV in 1756. The family still live in France. Marshal William O'Kelly was created a count of the Holy Roman Empire in 1767. Dionisio O'Kelly became a knight of Santiago in Spain in 1772, while Lorenzo O'Kelly de Galway became a count in Belgium.

In more liberal times in the nineteenth century Cornelius Joseph O'Kelly of Gallagh Castle, the 5th Count, became High Sheriff of Galway and a Justice of the Peace. He had been educated at Trinity College, Dublin.

Among the distinguished members of the family was James J. O'Kelly (1845–1916) who joined the Irish Republican Brotherhood in 1860 while, at the same time, joining the French Foreign Legion to gain military experience. He fought in Mexico when Napoleon III of France made his ill-starred attempt to set up a Hapsburg prince as emperor of Mexico in 1864. O'Kelly was a member of the Irish Republican Brotherhood's Supreme Council. He later became an Irish Party Member of Parliament for North Roscommon and was imprisoned for his Land League activities. He supported John Redmond as leader of the Irish Party after the death of Parnell in 1891.

Equally prominent was Count Gerald Edward O'Kelly de Gallagh

(1890–1968) born in Portumna, Co. Galway, and educated at Clongowes Wood College and University College, Dublin. After the general election of 1918, which swept Sinn Féin into power, and the Irish Declaration of Independence in January 1919, Count Gerald was sent by the *de facto* Irish government, after the United Kingdom government had declared it to be an illegal assembly, to present the Irish case to the League of Nations. He then became the Irish emissary to Belgium. He served abroad in diplomatic positions during the War of Independence (1919–21).

After the Civil War and the establishment of the Free State, his talents were ignored because of his republican sympathies but when de Valéra came to power in 1927 he was appointed ambassador to France. During World War II he acted as special Counsellor to the Irish mission to France and managed to negotiate the release of many Irish citizens interned by the German occupation forces. In 1948 he was made chargé d'affaires in Lisbon, where he died in 1968 while still serving in this capacity.

The current O'Kelly, and 8th Count, was born on 17 July 1921. He was educated at Stonyhurst and Trinity College, Dublin, taking degrees in engineering. He served in the British army during World War II as a captain in the Royal Engineers. Returning to Ireland after the war he had a career as an executive with the Bord na Mona. This state company was formed in 1946 to develop the country's energy resources. The O'Kelly lives in Dalkey near Dublin. He has one son and three daughters. His heir is Robert O'Kelly, who can, according to the Imperial Letters Patent, also use the style Count Robert O'Kelly while his father is alive. He lives in Co. Kildare.

As regards his Gaelic title, The O'Kelly takes a rather different view to most of his fellow chiefs. He accepts that English law has abolished and made extinct his title, and that the Irish Republic has inherited English law, but still believes that the Irish state can give 'courtesy recognition' to his Gaelic title under the English laws of inheritance.

> In 1585 it was agreed that the chieftainship of the county called O'Kelly's country or Hy-Many (Uí Maine), all elections and Irish divisions of land be utterly abolished and extinct for ever. These and other items brought an end to the Gaelic Order that had existed for centuries in Hy-Many.
>
> The lands of Hy-Many, already much reduced by the inroad of Norman families, were allocated to various branches of the O'Kelly clan on the special condition that they bind themselves and their heirs, that they shall henceforth behave themselves like subjects, bringing up their children in the English fashion and in the use of the English tongue, hence my title The O'Kelly is a courtesy title.

The O'Kelly certainly does not believe that the surviving holders of the Gaelic titles should have any position in public life because of their titles. 'Ireland is a democracy and those in public life are elected by public ballot.'

He is a Catholic and agrees in principle with Ireland giving a special place to the Catholic Church within the state; 'however, all faiths should be catered for satisfactorily. I support ecumenism and would like to see a Catholic Church or Cathedral with chapels covering the recognised faiths or religions of those believing in one God.'

His personal aim is to promote the O'Kellys and Kellys both at home and abroad. There is an O'Kelly Clan Association (Muintir Uí Cheallaigh) of which he is patron. Her Serene Highness, the late Princess Grace of Monaco supported the association. The association is run by Seán Ó Ceallaigh, who owns a firm of Dublin solicitors. It produces a regular newsletter and holds clan gatherings.

The O'Kelly is supportive of Irish cultural endeavours which he sees as the main function of bearing a Gaelic title. 'I favour bilingualism. However, being now part of Europe perhaps English is more useful together with other European languages. But in no way should the Irish language be lost.'

Perhaps the most famous member of the O'Kelly clan was Seán T. O'Kelly (1883–1966) the first President of the Irish Republic (1949–59). He fought in the GPO in 1916, was elected as Sinn Féin Member of Parliament in 1918 but became Speaker in the breakaway Irish parliament, the Dáil, in 1919. He acted as a delegate to the Paris Peace Conference. He rejected the Anglo-Irish Treaty and was sent as an envoy to the US during the Civil War. He later had a distinguished career in the Fianna Fáil governments between 1932 and 1945 when he became President. He died in 1966.

Another member of the clan is Lieutenant-Colonel the Baron O'Kelly de Conejera, who is heir to a Polish title, vice-president of the International Commission on Orders of Chivalry, and vice-chancellor of the Niadh Nask.

III

THE MACDERMOT,
Prince of Coolavin
(Mac Diarmada)

The princely house of MacDermot of Coolavin is unusual in that, even during the worst excesses of the Penal Laws, the princes remained suffering with the people of their former kingdom and, in spite of the penury to which they were reduced, the people around Loch Gara still acknowledged them as princes. The English traveller Arthur Young, in his *A Tour in Ireland* (1776–79) notes:

> Another great family in Connaught is MacDermot, who calls himself Prince of Coolavin. He lives at Coolavin in Sligo, and though he has not above one hundred pounds a year, will not admit his children to sit down in his presence.

The family traced their original descent from Brión, brother of Niall of the Nine Hostages. From Brión came the Uí Briúin who divided into three main branches: the Uí Breifne, ancestors of the Ó Ruairc, the Uí Briúin Seola, ancestors of the Ó Flaithbheartaigh (O'Flahertys), and the Uí Briúin Aí, ancestors of the O'Conors and the MacDermots.

The MacDermots trace their line especially from Muiredach Mullethan, King of Connacht AD 697–702. The successors of King Tadhg of Three Towers, King of Connacht 925–56, were King Conchobhair (966–73) and Conchobhair's brother, Maelruanaidh Mór, who became king of a substantial division of Connacht encompassing Sligo, Roscommon and parts of Mayo. The ancient name for the kingdom was Magh Luirg (Moylurg), the Plain of the Tracks of The Dagda, the Good God of the Tuatha Dé Danaan. The Moylurg sub-kings, of course, acknowledged that they were a division of the authority of Connacht.

The principal seat of the kings of Moylurg was the Rock of Loch Cé (Loch Key). The *Annals of Loch Cé* record a curious event as occurring in 1184. On the Friday after Shrovetide the palace of King Conor MacDermot was struck by lightning. The *Annals of Ulster* and the *Annals of the Four Masters* give the date as 1187 and as Conor did not succeed as king until 1186 we can accept the latter date as correct. We are told that Conor's wife and his granddaughter and fifteen of the nobility, along with six or seven score of their retainers, were killed; it seems that panic set in for the annals say, 'every one of them who was not burned was suffocated in this tumultuous consternation in the entrance of the place'. King Conor and a few others managed to escape. Conor reigned until 1197.

Conor's son, Tomaltach na Cairge (of the Rock), succeeded his father. He is credited with building the first stone castle on the Rock of Loch Cé, and his first wife died in the lightning strike. It became known as MacDermot's Castle.

The Norman invasion did not impinge on the political situation in Connacht immediately. The Connacht king Ruaidri Ua Conchobhair had lost the High Kingship but retained power over Connacht. His daughter married King Cathal MacDermot of Moylurg (1207–15). It was only in 1235, during the reign of King Cormac MacDermot (1218–44), that Richard de Burgo with five hundred mounted Norman knights and men-at-arms set out to conquer the kingdom of Connacht and its sub-kingdoms.

The last military engagement of the campaign was when the army came to Port na Cairge on Loch Cé, which was the MacDermot capital. A fleet of ships with galleries and perriers, or catapults, came into the loch and the catapults were used to fling boulders at the king's palace. The palace was set on fire and the Irish came out to surrender. King Cormac asked for terms and Justiciar Maurice FitzGerald, who had joined de Burgo, demanded recognition and payment of feudal dues to Henry III as Lord of Ireland.

However, under successive kings, Moylurg never lost the opportunity to assert its independence and the sporadic campaigns by the Normans and, later, the English failed to bring it to absolute obedience.

The Moylurg kingdom continued into Tudor times. Ruaidri MacDermot became king in 1538 but, in a situation not unusual under Brehon law, he shared the kingdom with his kinsman Aodh MacDermot, Abbot of Boyle. The abbey was a short distance from Loch Cé on the Boyle River. When the abbot died in 1549 Ruaidri was the sole king. He is renowned for his largesse and the invitation he gave to the leading scholars of Ireland to attend his court during Christmas 1540. He and his wife, Sadhbh, distributed gifts to the poets and professors at the Rock of Loch Cé. His wife died there on Holy Thursday, 1542 and is buried at Athenry.

In 1543, when Lord Deputy St Leger called the Gaelic nobles to attend a council in Dublin, to sort out their submission to Henry VIII, newly proclaimed King of Ireland, we find King Ruaidri in attendance. He took the opportunity to purchase the confiscated churchlands of Clonshanville and Kilnamanagh from the Anglican archbishop and gave them back to the people. One might presume that, merely by his attendance, Ruaidri surrendered his title 'king' and agreed to the other terms but this does not appear so. In 1549 Ruaidri summoned another great Christmas gathering of scholars to his court and again distributed gifts and patronage. Certainly, much of his reign was then spent in conducting a defensive warfare to keep his kingdom secure from English incursions. He died on Maundy Thursday, 1568, and his obituary in the *Annals of Loch Cé* described him as the last king of Moylurg. He was eighty years old.

However, he was succeeded by Tairrdelbach (Turlough) MacDermot (1568–76) who was inaugurated king with due process under Brehon law, with the consent of Church, laity and *ollamhain*. Tairrdelbach was the son of Eoghan MacDermot, Ruaidri's brother, who had been king in 1533/4. Ruaidri's third son, Brian, married to Medbh, daughter of the O'Conor Sligo, was angry that the *derbhfine* had not elected him to the kingship and he began courting the English as the Tudor wars of conquest clearly swung in favour of them. Brian did not immediately succeed in his ambition of becoming king of Moylurg for the successor of Tairrdelbach was Tadhg (1576–85).

With the Composition of Connacht we find that Brian was deemed by the English to be 'captain of his nation'. Brian and The O'Conor Sligo, his brother-in-law, had already submitted to the English and been rewarded with knighthoods. In 1577 they had joined Colonel Sir Nicholas Malby, deemed even by English writers as a 'tough and formidable man' and now appointed 'military governor of Connacht'. He assembled an army on the borders of Sligo and Donegal to fight the O'Donel, Prince of Tirconnell. In 1578 Brian was at a great council in Dublin. Brian surrendered the Moylurg kingship, which he was not qualified in law to do, Tadhg still being king. Brian was then appointed by the English on 6 June 1578 to 'the office of seneschal of the barony of Moylurg in the province of Connacht'.

Thus the kingdom had been eliminated in English eyes. Brian died on 31 October, 1592. He left nine sons but his *derbhfine* still cleaved to Brehon law and he was succeeded by his cousin Conor Óg MacDermot. After the devastating English defeat at Yellow Ford, an Irish renaissance was taking place. In August 1599, O'Donel, Prince of Tirconnell was besieging England's ally, Sir Donough O'Conor Sligo at Collooney Castle. Sir Conyers Clifford had marched from Roscommon town with an army in an attempt to rescue his ally. They came to the Yellow Pass through the Curlew Mountains, on the western side of Moylurg. O'Donel's men ambushed them. Spearheading the attack were Conor Óg MacDermot and Brian Óg Ó Ruairc of Breifne. The English commander, Sir Conyers Clifford, was among those killed in the attack. The English, in retreat, refused to send anyone to recover his body which the

Irish were willing to return. Sir Conyers was buried on Trinity Island on Loch Cé by courtesy of the MacDermots. Conor Óg commanded a contingent from Moylurg to Kinsale. He died in 1603 after the defeat of the Irish forces.

Brian MacDermot, the son of the Brian 'named as seneschal of the barony of Moylurg', had been brought up as a ward of court to be an Englishman. He died in 1636 and his son Charles was styled 'Cathal Ruadh Chief and Prince of Moylurg'. Following the Irish uprising of 1641, when O'Conor Don had raised a Connacht army, MacDermot took troops from Moylurg to join it. However, they were routed by English forces at Ballintober in 1642. Cathal Ruadh's son Eoghan was one of the Irish company who captured Sligo Castle. He was married to Sineád Plunkett. Cathal Ruadh's estates were confiscated during the Cromwellian administration. He was allowed to remove to an estate called Coolavin, by the shores of Loch Gara in the western part of the former kingdom. The name is Anglicised from *Cuil o'bhFinn*, the Corner of the Fionns, so called, because it had been inhabited by a clan called the O'Finns. At the restoration, Cathal Ruadh was restored to his lands but after the Williamite conquest the family was forced back to Coolavin.

Cathal Ruadh's son Terence sat in James II's Dublin parliament in 1689 and other members of the family held seats in it. They also held several commissions in the Jacobite army including command of a regiment raised by them and called MacDermot's Regiment. Its commander was Colonel Brian MacDermot. Hugh MacDermot was now called the Prince of Coolavin, a title which arose by the popular choice of the people, remembering that the family had once been kings of Moylurg. He garrisoned Sligo at his own expense in support of the Jacobites. He was captured at the battle of Aughrim 'of the Slaughter' in 1691 and died in 1707.

The MacDermots refused to leave Ireland as some of the other Irish nobility were doing and submitted themselves to William of Orange. Perhaps they, as others, believed that the conditions of the Treaty of Limerick, which had guaranteed civil and religious liberties, would be maintained. When the provisions of the treaty began to be broken by William, in 1699, no fewer than ten leading members of the MacDermot family were indicted and outlawed for high treason. For some reason Hugh of Coolavin was not among them.

The family settled quietly at Coolavin. As Sir Charles MacDermot wrote: 'When I was young, the family tradition was that our ancestors were penniless princes who sat by the shores of Loch Gara reading the Latin classics. There is some truth in this.' In writing about the adoption of the title 'Prince of Coolavin', Sir Charles admits it arose by popular usage and was not the original Gaelic title.

> In the Composition of Connacht of 1585 . . . the Irish chieftains agreed to renounce their Irish titles . . . When the MacDermots were compelled to leave their estates in Moylurg and find a new home in the barony of Coolavin, they could not thereby be divested of their royal antecedents. They continued to regard themselves as princes and, which is more important, to be called princes by the people among whom they lived. This local custom, which continues into the present day, can be regarded as a survival of the respect held in ancient times for persons who were, by heredity, '*Rígdamna*'.

Indeed, when the Genealogical Office in Dublin gave 'courtesy recognition' to the Gaelic title 'MacDermot' it also, in the official government publication, recognised the title 'Prince of Coolavin'.

Some members of the princely family did go to Europe to seek education and professional status away from the constraints of the Penal Laws, but always returned home to Coolavin. Roger MacDermot was an officer in the Hibernia Regiment of the Irish Brigade of the Spanish army, receiving his full commission in 1753. He often returned home on leave to Coolavin. Others went to India. However, wherever the members of the family went, the member designated 'Chief and Prince' remained domiciled at Coolavin. As knowledge of Brehon succession faded, the title was handed down by primogeniture.

Among the more fascinating of these princes of Coolavin was Hugh MacDermot, who pursued medical studies in Paris and Edinburgh. He returned to Ireland in 1782 having qualified as a doctor at the age of twenty-six. He was a cultured and learned young man given to voluminous correspondence. He also wrote a play entitled *Litigation* which was turned down by the Drury Lane Theatre in London although a copy still survives at Coolavin. When his father, Myles, Prince of Coolavin, died in January 1793, Hugh succeeded to the title. However, he always preferred to call himself 'Dr Hugh' rather than MacDermot or Prince of Coolavin. In July 1793 he married his cousin Elizabeth, the daughter of Denis O'Conor of Belanagare.

Like the O'Conors, Hugh joined the United Irishmen. He managed to avoid the attention of the authorities during the insurrection and so, unlike his O'Conor in-laws, was not forced to flee to America. In fact, so 'respectable' did the former United Irishman become that he was appointed Deputy Governor of Co. Sligo in 1830, and one of his sons, Henry, became a District Inspector in the Royal Irish Constabulary. The

Irish Constabulary was formed in 1836 and the 'Royal' was prefixed in 1867.

Henry's son, Henry Roderick MacDermot (1849–1915) also became a County Inspector of the Royal Irish Constabulary. With one of those ironic twists of Irish history, County Inspector Henry's eldest son Rory (1893–1942) was a member of the garrison in Dublin's GPO during the 1916 uprising. He survived the War of Independence but took the pro-Treaty side during the Civil War to became a captain in the Irish Free State army.

'Dr Hugh's' grandson had no reticence about using the title when he became The MacDermot. In fact, he was styled the Rt. Hon. Hugh Hyacinth O'Rorke MacDermot, Prince of Coolavin, a Privy Councillor (1892), Queen's Counsel, and Solicitor-General for Ireland in 1886 and Attorney-General in 1892. He was born in July 1834, educated at the Catholic University (now University College, Dublin), and died in 1904.

His youngest son was Frank MacDermot, born 1886, educated at Downside and Oxford. Frank became a barrister, went into the British army during the 1914–18 war and then worked in a merchant bank in New York. Returning to Ireland in the late 1920s, he was elected to the Dáil for Roscommon in 1932 as an Independent. He joined James Dillon in forming the National Centre Party which won eleven seats in the following year. Right-wing in politics, the party grew close to Cumann na nGaedheal and the Blueshirts (Irish Fascist movement) whose philosophy was based on the papal encyclical *Quadragesimo Anno* and Mussolini's theory of the corporate state. Frank MacDermot brought about a merger of these parties into Fine Gael in September 1933, becoming their vice-president. However, when Fine Gael supported Mussolini and his invasion of Abyssinia (now Ethiopia) in 1935, Frank MacDermot resigned from both the party and his seat. He became a Senator on the nomination of Eamon de Valéra and served until 1942 when he returned to journalism. He wrote a lengthy and heavily critical biography of the Irish republican leader of 1798, Theobald Wolfe Tone, published in 1939.

The eldest son of the Rt. Hon. Hugh succeeded to the title and also went into law. He was born in 1862, and became a barrister and Justice of the Peace. He died in 1947. His eldest son Hugh had been killed in Gallipoli in 1915, and so his second son Charles John succeeded. Charles was born in 1899, educated at Stonyhurst and Trinity College, Dublin. During World War II he had been assistant manager of a rubber plantation in Malaya and was an officer in the local defence corps. He became a prisoner of the Japanese from 1942 to 1945.

When he died without issue, his brother Sir Dermot Francis MacDermot KCMG, CMG, CBE, born in 1906, educated at Stonyhurst and Trinity College, Dublin, became Prince of Coolavin. He was in the British Diplomatic Service from 1929 to 1965, having been Minister to Rumania 1954–56, Ambassador to Indonesia 1956–59 and to Thailand 1961–64. Sir Dermot MacDermot spent many years researching his family history; when he died in 1996 he left a manuscript which was published by the current chief's brother, Conor.

The current MacDermot, Prince of Coolavin, Niall Anthony MacDermot, was born in Yokohama in 1935, in the British Consulate where his father was on a posting. He was educated in St Gerard's, Bray, and at Downside. He served in the Royal Air Force, retiring with the rank of Squadron Leader. He is now chief executive of Coolavin Systems Ltd (Co. Kildare), his own computer software company. Married to Janet Frost, he has a very active tanist in his son Rory, born on 29 July 1960. Rory and his sister Siobhán run the MacDermot Clan Association, of which The MacDermot is patron. It has its own journal and is on the Internet. A clan rally is held every three years.

The MacDermot accepts that his title has been handed down by eldest son inheritance since the seventeenth century but, like the other chiefs on the Standing Council, admits it has its basis in Brehon law and that there is no legal authority to change that succession. However, he states:

> Under the old law, and within the strictly defined rules of eligibility, a chief occupied his position by consent and not by right of descent. Recognition by an official of the state, however grand his title may be, does not therefore establish the *bona fides* of the chief of an Irish Gaelic clan. If one is to apply the spirit of the Brehon law, one would need to be able to show three things; acceptance of the chief as such by the population of the old territory, reasonably continuous occupation of the land and a general recognition within the family of one's pre-eminent position. It is worth noting that The MacDermot has lived in Moylurg continuously for the past thousand years and that my princely title is still recognised by the people in and around Boyle, the centre of the old kingdom.

He does not see any official role for holders of old Gaelic titles in the modern Irish state by simple virtue of their titles.

> If one of us were to become influential politically, it would be by virtue of his own personal capabilities not his title . . . As MacDermot, Prince of Coolavin, I feel that I have a considerable responsibility, shared by my immediate family, for preserving our own ancient Gaelic heritage

and, where possible, to promulgate and publish relevant information to all and sundry but most particularly to MacDermot descendants wherever they may be.

He believes that the government should have no hand in trying to preserve the Irish language. 'If the poor thing were left alone, it might yet revive itself. Even people in the various Irish-speaking parts of the west are pessimistic about its eventual survival.'

The MacDermots are mostly Catholic, although the current Madam MacDermot is a member of the Church of Ireland.

Many of us feel quite strongly that Ireland needs to free herself from the oppressive domination of our people by the Roman Catholic hierarchy. The country is fundamentally very strongly Christian and, God willing, it will remain so but we need to espouse ecumenism more whole-heartedly and put a bit of charity into our dealings with other parts of Christ's flock.

The MacDermot is an active member of the Standing Council of Irish Chiefs and Chieftains and a Niadh Nask.

IV
THE Ó RUAIRC,
Prince of Breifne
(Ó Ruairc)

Geoffrey Philip Colomb O'Rorke, The Ó Ruairc, Prince of Breifne, is the thirty-second in male line descent from Tigernán, King of Breifne (d. AD 888) and is recognised as head of the ancient princely house of Uí Briúin Breifne. The Uí Briúin are descended from Brión, brother of Niall of the Nine Hostages and father of Daui Tenga Umi (d. AD 502), the first Uí Briúin king of Connacht being the common ancestor of the Uí Briúin Breifne (Ó Ruairc) and the Uí Briúin Aí (O'Conors of Connacht and MacDermots of Moylurg).

At its greatest extent, during the twelfth century, the kingdom of Breifne stretched from the coast on the Leitrim-Donegal border, south-eastward to the abbey of Mellifont and nearly reached Tara in Westmeath. This was when the High King, Muirchertach Mac Lochlainn

(d. 1166) forced the division of the kingdom of Midhe (Meath) into three and gave one-third to Breifne.

Ruairc, the son of Tigernán, was king of Breifne and died in 893. The first Ó Ruairc was his grandson 'Sean' Fergal Ua Ruairc (Old Ferghal), King of Connacht. He was killed in 966/7. It is claimed that the name Ruairc is a derivation of the name Ruaidri. 'Sean' Fergal, in fact, was the first of the Uí Briúin Breifne to be elected king of Connacht after generations of Uí Briúin Aí held the kingship. There was a conflicting claim by the two Uí Briúin houses which resulted in many bloody clashes. Domhnal Ó Ruairc (d. 1102) was the last king of Breifne to also be king of Connacht. The annals claim that he was a man of peace but this did not stop him being killed by his own people.

His successor, as king of Breifne, was Aodh Ó Ruairc who was given the unusual nickname of 'Gilla Sronmael' (Flat-Nosed Man). He was one of the kings who refused to accept the authority of Muirchertach Ó Brían as High King. Muirchertach twice invaded his territory, in 1109 and 1111. In 1118, however, Aodh Ó Ruairc, pretending to be the High King's ally, joined his army in Munster, by which The O'Brien hoped to eliminate the Eóghanacht threat to his power base. Aodh Ó Ruairc then joined Tairrdelbach Ua Conchobhair in withdrawing support and forcing him to agree to the Treaty of Glanmire.

According to the annals, however, this Aodh Ó Ruairc was a plunderer of monasteries and churches and even killed the Abbot of Kells in one attack. That could not be tolerated and in 1122 Aodh himself met his death at the hands of the king of Midhe (Meath), Murchadh Ó Maoil Seachlainn (sometimes given as Ó Maelachlann) with the support of the ecclesiastics. Murchadh Ó Maoil Seachlainnn supported Aodh's cousin, Tigernán, in his claim for the kingship of Breifne. Tigernán had married his daughter Dervorgill (1108–93) who has been called 'the cause of the Norman invasion of Ireland'.

Dervorgill – or, to give her her correct Irish name, Der bForgaill meaning 'Daughter of Forgall', Forgall being an ancient Irish god – was one of the most fascinating people in Irish history at a time when one of the most important events was about to happen. In 1152 Dermot MacMorrough of Uí Cheinnselaig, the king of Leinster, who was then aged sixty-one arrived in Breifne, and Dervorgill, aged forty-three, eloped with him. To add insult to injury, she took her belongings and her cattle herds.

Tairrdelbach Ua Conchobhair, kinsman to Ó Ruairc, had become High King. He lost no time in taking an army into Leinster and attacking King Dermot's fortress at Ferns, burning it and taking Dervorgill back to her husband. Fines and compensation were demanded from King Dermot.

In 1157 King Tigernán Ó Ruairc and Dervorgill are recorded as attending the consecration of the church at Mellifont Abbey, the first Cistercian abbey in Ireland. The Archbishop of Armagh, seventeen bishops, the Papal Legate and the High King as well as King Donnchadh Ó Cearbhaill of the Uí Néill petty kingdom of Oriel also attended. Dervorgill presented a spectacular chalice to the Mellifont. In the very year that her former lover, King Dermot, was inviting Norman mercenaries into Ireland to help him secure Leinster against Ruaidri Ó Conchobhair, she endowed the building of the nuns' church at Clonmacnoise in Co. Offaly. Clonmacnoise was one of the great monastic settlements, founded by St Ciaráin in 545 on the east shore of the Shannon. It was a focus of early Irish Christian art and literature. The *Leabhar na hUidre*, or Book of the Dun Cow, was compiled there about 1100, and seven High Kings were buried there. It was not abandoned until its sack by English troops in 1552. The priceless *Leabhar na hUidre* later disappeared after being stolen by Cromwellian troops. It was found in the hands of a Dublin bookseller, George Smith, in 1837.

Dervorgill went on a pilgrimage to Mellifont and decided to end her days there. She died in 1193. Her husband, King Tigernán, had been killed in 1172, fighting against the Normans. He was slain by one of Henry's commanders, Hugo de Lacy. Aodh, grandson of Tigernán and Dervorgill, became king of Breifne, recognising Conchobhair Maenmaige (d. 1189), King of Connacht, as his overlord.

The kingship of Breifne then passed by Brehon law to the descendants of Tigernán's brother Cathal. During the next 150 years, which saw the rise to a more powerful position of The Ó Raighilligh (O'Reilly) of East Breifne, there seem no rulers worthy of comment. The chronicles record that in 1213 Ualgharg Ó Ruairc, King of Breifne, died while on a pilgrimage to the River Jordan. Unfortunately they do not elaborate further.

By the early fourteenth century the Connacht O'Conor kings still claimed lordship over Breifne. But Breifne was fast becoming a chaotic border country in which various Norman and Gaelic factions were fighting for control. The annals are full of raids and battles and a new power arose; the Norman de Burgos (Burkes) who were busy carving out their own kingdom. In 1316, Fedlimid O'Conor became undisputed king of Connacht, being acknowledged by the Ó Ruaircs of Breifne, albeit with some reluctance. Fedlimid, however, at the age of twenty-three, was slain at Athenry. Ualgharg Ó Ruairc quickly formed an alliance with Maelruanaidh MacDermot, King of Moylurg, and married his daughter Derbhail. Later, Ualgharg married the daughter of The O'Brien, King of Thomond as a means of consolidating the balance of power in the area.

In the crucial Tudor period, Brian Ballach Mór became king of Breifne. He was inaugurated in 1536, according to the *Annals of Loch Cé*, and died in 1562. He built Leitrim Castle in 1540 and formed various alliances to keep English incursions in check. He is generally regarded as the last regnant king of Breifne although the *Annals of the Four Masters* clearly record that his son Aodh Gallda was inaugurated as king. Two years later, in 1564, Aodh Gallda 'was maliciously and malignantly slain by his own people in Leitrim . . .'

There was some dispute about succession until Brian na Murtha (of the Defence), knighted by the English in return for surrendering his Gaelic title and lands, became 'Lord of Breifne'. Brian was not a good English subject however. Sir Nicholas Malby, the English Governor of Connacht, wrote to Elizabeth's Secretary of State, Sir Francis Walsingham, that 'O'Rourke thinks himself too great a man to be a subject – O'Rourke is the proudest Irishman of them all.'

In 1584, Ó Ruairc (O'Rourke and O'Rorke now became Anglicised forms of the name) was forced to hand over his fifteen-year-old son Brian Óg as a hostage for his good behaviour. Brian was sent to New College, Oxford, to be brought up as an Englishman. His father, however, was keeping the English on tenterhooks as to whether he was on their side or still forming alliances with the other Irish princes. Four years later Ó Ruairc made clear his intentions.

In 1588, Sir Richard Bingham, the notorious Governor of Connacht, wrote to the Lord Deputy: 'Sir Brian O'Rourke hath written to the Spaniards in the north to join him.' This was in the wake of the destruction of the Spanish Armada, a fleet of sixty-five heavily armed galleons, twenty-five store ships and thirty smaller vessels, which carried an invasion force to England. Buffeted by high winds, harried by experienced English seamen, the fleet was dispersed and, in an attempt to return to Spain, sought a route north around Scotland and Ireland. Several ships were wrecked along the Irish coast and Bingham reported that no fewer than twelve were wrecked on the shores of Connacht: 'The men of these ships all perished, save 1100 or more who were put to the sword, amongst whom were officers and gentlemen of quality to the number of fifty and whose names have been set down in a list. The gentlemen were spared until the Lord Deputy sent me specific directions to see them executed – reserving alone de Cordova and his nephew.' Bingham clearly blames the Lord Deputy, Sir William FitzWilliam, for the massacre of the Spanish shipwreck survivors on the shores. 'I spared them . . .' he writes, 'but the Lord Deputy FitzWilliam came to Connacht and ordered all killed except de Cordova and his nephew who were at Athlone.'

Later propaganda by the English administration tried to put the blame on the 'barbaric Irish' for the slaughter, doubtless in the hope of driving a wedge between the natural alliance of Spain and Ireland. Some five thousand Spaniards were massacred, being clubbed, shot, stabbed and hanged once they had managed to reach the shore. Contrary to the propaganda put out by Elizabeth's officials for Spanish consumption, many Irish nobles placed their lives in jeopardy by aiding the Spaniards, offering them food and shelter and securing them passage back to Spain. Foremost of these was Brian Ó Ruairc of Breifne. We have the testimony of Captain Francisco Cuellar of the *San Juan de Sicilia* wrecked off the coast of Sligo. He survived the wreck and while trying to find shelter came across two fellow survivors, one badly wounded. They had just escaped from where English soldiers had killed hundreds of their companions. The three of them hid and, after the English soldiers passed on, they counted four hundred bodies, including several senior officers.

Cuellar encountered an Irishman who managed to communicate with him in Latin and directed him to Ó Ruairc's stronghold. Cuellar calls Ó Ruairc 'Lord de Ruerge'. Ó Ruairc provided clothes, food and shelter and Cuellar was asked for an account of his adventures. 'Had it not been for these people not one of us would now be alive,' wrote Cuellar. Ó Ruairc passed Cuellar and the survivors on to a chieftain called Mac Fhlannchaidh (MacClancy), 'always a great enemy of the Queen and never loved anything that was hers, nor would he obey her, and therefore the English Governor of this part of the island wanted very much to take him prisoner.' Governor Bingham eventually achieved his ambition. He caught MacClancy in an ambush and, with MacClancy's arm broken in the skirmish, the Irish noble was brought to Sligo and beheaded. Bingham reported: 'He was a most barbarous creature; his country extended from Grange to Ballyshannon: he was O'Rourke's right hand; he had fourteen Spaniards with him, some of whom were taken alive.'

Fortunately Captain Cuellar had already passed through MacClancy's hands and reached Spain in safety to write the truth of what had happened.

In 1589, The Ó Ruairc's son Brian Óg had escaped from England and was back in Breifne. His English indoctrination had been in vain. He joined his father in raids on the English and their allies. In 1590 his father decided to go to James VI of Scotland to seek aid for the Irish cause. It was a mistake. King James, whether blackmailed by Elizabeth or not, handed Brian Ó Ruairc to her officials. There is a mysterious comment in a letter from James VI to Elizabeth: 'Remember what you promised by your letter of thanks for the delivery of O'Rourke.'[1] Had Elizabeth promised that in exchange for Ó Ruairc she would raise no objection to James being appointed her successor to the English throne?

By May 1591 Ó Ruairc was imprisoned in the Tower of London, and in November he was executed at Tyburn. The *Annals of the Four Masters* record in that year:

> The death of this Brian was one of the mournful stories of the Irish, for there had not been for a long time any one of his tribe who excelled him in bounty, in hospitality, in giving rewards for panegyric poems, in sumptuousness, in numerous troops, in comeliness, in firmness, in maintaining the field of battle to defend his patrimony against foreign adventurers; for all which he was celebrated until his death on this occasion.

Brian Óg, who was now called Brían na Samhthach (of the Battle Axes), was forced to seek shelter with The Maguire, Prince of Fermanagh, while the English were devastating Breifne in search of him. He took a prominent and active part in the full-scale wars that followed, acknowledging the leadership of Aodh Ruadh O'Neill, King of Ulster. After the Irish defeat of Kinsale, he returned to Breifne to find his half-brother Tadhg had secured the title as 'Lord of Breifne'. He wrote to James I asking him to reinstate him in his father's title and inheritance. It was not surprising that James refused. The English had seized all of Breifne. Brian wandered Ireland and finally settled in Galway, where another half-brother, Andrew, was a merchant. Brian Óg died in 1604, aged thirty-five, in the Franciscan abbey of Rosserrilly, Co. Galway.

Tadhg (Teige) Ó Ruairc, as head of the Breifne Ó Ruairc, was knighted by the English but they did not trust him. He died in mysterious circumstances in 1605 aged only twenty-eight. His son Brian, aged only six, was immediately taken to the Tower of London as a 'ward of court'. Sir Oliver St John reported to the Earl of Salisbury in 1611: 'The inhabitants of O'Rourke's country, the heir of which is His Majesty's ward, a country very wild and apt to stir, take pleasure to declare themselves in troublesome and disorderly times.' Young Brian was sent under strict supervision to Dublin, where he studied at Trinity College; in 1617 he was sent to Oxford and thence to the Middle Temple Inns of Court. In 1619, he was confined again and ended his days in 1641 as a prisoner in the Tower of London, aged forty-two. His petitions for his freedom over the years make heart-rending reading. The last was dated 8 January 1641, and he died a week later. The burial register of the Tower of London records: 'Brian O'Rorke, Irish prisoner, buried the 16th day of January, 1641.'

His younger brother Aodh had managed to escape to join the service of Spain. The territory of the Breifne Ó Ruairc was confiscated and divided into the shire or county of Leitrim, to prepare the way for the new colonisation.

Although the title of The Ó Ruairc had now been abolished under English law, Ó Ruaircs still survived. Owen Mór, son of Tigernán Bán, tanist of Breifne and brother to Brían na Murtha, was given a commission as colonel in the Irish army in the uprising of 1641. His son, Owen Óg, was a captain. They managed to survive the wars and the Cromwellian conquest, and were exonerated after the restoration of Charles II.

Owen Óg's son Donagh had a son Seán, who had a son Tadhg (Teige), a parish priest of Killanumery near Dromahair, who was lodging with his cousin at Rathbaun, Killanumery. The cousin was Elinor, daughter of Farrell O'Rorke of Carrowcrin. She was also the widow of John Gallagher by whom she had three children. The Gallaghers belonged to the established Church. In 1770 Father Teige caused a great scandal not only by converting from Catholicism but by then marrying Elinor Gallagher. The couple moved to Galway where Teige used the Anglicised form of his name, the Reverend Thaddeus O'Rorke. He had not only converted but taken Anglican holy orders to become curate of Ballinlough and Kiltullag from 1785 to 1798 and then curate of Cong, Co. Mayo, until he died in 1799. Two of his sons became clergymen in the Church of Ireland.

From then on, the Ó Ruairc chiefly line have been Anglican, or Church of Ireland as it is now. It is from this line that the current Ó Ruairc, Prince of Breifne descends.

There were other cadet lines of the family who threw up remarkable branches. O'Rourkes served the Austrian empire. An Eoghan O'Rourke became the Austrian ambassador to St James's Court. A John O'Rourke, who also styled himself 'Prince of Breffy', served the Russian Tsar and the French kings and was made Count O'Rourke.

Perhaps the most famous O'Rourke of the princely house is the one whose portrait hangs in the Heroes' Gallery of the Hermitage, in St Petersburg, in Russia. This is General Count Joseph Kornilievitch O'Rourke of Breifne. He was one of the 'Russian' generals who defeated Napoleon in his invasion of Russia in 1812. At the age of forty-eight he was, in fact, General-in-Chief of the Russian army and married to a Polish lady. Settled in Poland, his descendants fled the German invasion in 1939 and went to England. Other members of the family moved on to Canada.

The current Ó Ruairc, Prince of Breifne, was the first of his immediate family to be born in England, on 20 January 1943. He was educated privately and is a member of the International Stock Exchange. In 1981 he married Penelope Barclay, the sister of Peter Barclay of Towie Barclay, chief of the Scottish Clan Barclay. Although based in London he maintains his Irish passport and is a frequent visitor to his relatives in Ireland. He is a Niadh Nask.

The Ó Ruairc points out that since the execution of his ancestor, Brían Ó Ruairc, and the imprisonment of Brían's sons by the English monarchs at the beginning of the seventeenth century, no one in his family, of the legitimate princely line, had ever publicly claimed the Gaelic title. He recalls that members of his family had long maintained they had a legitimate claim to it, including his father who had never officially pursued it. During the 1980s, Ó Ruairc presented his lineage to the Genealogical Office in Ireland, having, with family (*derbhfine*) approval, made public his claim to the title. The claim was given official 'courtesy recognition' by the Chief Herald of Ireland in 1991. Ó Ruairc argues:

> The essence of a Gaelic title must depend on the Brehon law of succession. However, in practice, most of the current recognised chiefs hold their titles *de facto* by primogeniture.
>
> My claim to the title of Ó Ruairc was recognised by the Chief Herald some ten years ago on the basis of the genealogical evidence that I provided. Up to that point there had been no recognised Ó Ruairc since the mid-seventeenth century.
>
> I should prefer to pass on my title under Brehon law concepts. I have no son and the primogeniture heir is my nephew. However, under Brehon law tanistry, I would name my first cousin as a more suitable chief.

He agrees with other members of the Standing Council that his title stems from Brehon law and there is no legal authority to change that form of succession.

He foresees the representatives of the old Gaelic aristocracy as having a more prominent part in Irish state affairs.

> Our Council has, thus far, eschewed any political role, though I could see a case for the chiefs of, say, the five major Gaelic kingdoms having a permanent representation in the Irish Senate and, possibly, influence with the Office of Public Works. In the non-political field I think one major role should be to foster much more awareness of our Gaelic history and culture.

In this respect he wants to see the Irish language preserved and encouraged.

10

The Kingdom of Ulster

Ulster is a province of Ireland which occupies the northern part of the island. As a province it consists of the nine counties of Donegal (the most northerly county in Ireland), Derry, Antrim, Fermanagh, Tyrone, Cavan, Monaghan, Armagh and Down, covering 6486 square miles. On 7 December 1922 the Unionists, who constituted an electoral majority in only four of the Ulster counties, petitioned King George V of England to allow a territory consisting of six of these counties – Armagh, Antrim, Fermanagh, Derry, Down and Tyrone, constituting only 52.3 per cent of the total Ulster territory – to withdraw from the Irish Free State, which came into existence on 6 December, and remain within the United Kingdom as 'Northern Ireland'. The arbitrary border was imposed by force to include the two counties (Fermanagh and Tyrone) that had republican majorities. The name 'Ulster' is now often erroneously given only to these six counties.

The territory at the start of the Christian period was ruled by the Uí Néill which, as with the Eóghanachta of Munster, was not a patronymic but a dynastic appellation applied to several families sharing a common remote ancestry. This fact is often confused as the senior royal house of the Uí Néill became known as the O'Neills. The dynasty is, with the Eóghanachta, one of the two oldest and most powerful in Ireland. The Uí Néill trace their kingship descent in unbroken line, if we are to believe the ancient genealogies, back to Eremon, son of Milé Easpain, who arrived with his brothers and followers in Ireland at the end of the second millennium BC.

The early Christian scribes in Ireland, like the scribes serving other European dynasties at the time, embellished the genealogies of the Uí Néill so that the line of Eremon could be traced further back, father to son, via the biblical characters of Baath, son of Magog, son of Japeth, son of Noah and through nine more generations back to Seth the son of Adam. While it was necessary, in Christian times, to trace such an ancestry for a king, the Celtic peoples would have done so in pre-Christian times as well, but their genealogies linked back to Celtic gods and goddesses. Feinius Farsaidh, given as son of Baath, is the first to appear in the genealogies with a Celtic name and according to the *Lebor Gabhála* (Book of Invasions) was present at the Tower of Babel during the separation of the languages of the world. He alone retained a knowledge of them all. His son Niul went to Egypt and married the pharaoh's daughter, and their son Gaedheal Glas fashioned the Irish language out of the seventy-two languages in existence. Feinius appears to be the same word as Féni, a name for Ireland's earliest Celtic inhabitants – hence Brehon law is technically the 'Law of the Fénechus'.

It is thirty-seven generations from Adam and twenty-three from Feinius Farsaidh that we encounter Eremon and his brother Eber Fionn, the sons of Míle Easpain. Having conquered Ireland, the brothers, as we saw in Chapter 7, divided Ireland into two sections. This has been variously dated at 1498 BC (*Annals of the Four Masters*) and 1029 BC (*Annals of Clonmacnoise*). The border between the two sections was a continuous line of low gravel hills stretching from Dublin to Co. Galway and called Eiscir Riada.

The quarrel between Eremon and Eber, about who had the right to rule all Ireland, continued through their descendants. Eremon and Eber, so legend had it, had originally made a wager on which of them would reach Ireland first. Realising that Eber was about to reach the shore before him, Eremon is said to have cut off his hand and thrown it on to the shore, claiming to have won the bet. Thereafter the O'Neill kings adopted the symbol of the Red Hand. But a hand reaching forth is a symbol of kingship and the severed hand is a fanciful tale. By one of those ironies which fill Irish history, the Red Hand is now the symbol of the Ulster Unionists who deny the Gaelic heritage.

It is an interesting fact that apart from the Eóghanacht descendants of Eber, and the Dál gCais, the other royal dynasties in Ireland are all branches of the line stemming from Eremon.

Fifty-three generations down the line from Eremon, the northern Uí Néill High King was Niall Naoighiallach, known as Niall of the Nine Hostages, from whom the Uí Néill dynasty take their name.

By this time Ulster – Uladh is the Irish name to which the Norse *stadr* (or *ster*) meaning 'a place' was added – had become divided into three major kingdoms. That of Uladh, or Ulidia, was confined to Antrim and Down. Oirghialla, or Oriel, was south of this and Tir Eoghain (Tyrone) covered the north-west and must not be confused with the modern county name. Tir Conaill was a sub-kingdom of Tir Eoghain in the extreme north-west.

The exact dates of the reign of Niall Naoighiallach, historical king of Tara and progenitor of the Uí Néill, are, like most things, the subject of debate. An examination of chronologies tends to the conclusion that he died *c.* AD 405. The name Niall is thought to come from *nél*, a cloud, indicating an affinity with some sky god. Naoighiallach indicates 'having nine hostages' and symbolises his power and success as a ruler.

Niall was the son of Eochadh Muighmheadhon, whose seat of power was in Connacht. Niall's brother Bríon was the progenitor of the Uí Briúin kings of Connacht. The role of Niall in the political history of early Ireland is crucial but the literature devoted to his life is interwoven, in traditional Celtic style, with much fantasy and religious symbolism.

We do know that he was given to conducting military expeditions outside Ireland. He is said to have gone to Gaul and also to Italy and to have conducted sea raids around the coast of Britain. Although annalists accord him the High Kingship of Ireland, Dáithí Ó hÓgain has pointed out that 'it is unlikely that Niall's power extended far into the south of the country, but this did not prevent the medieval writers from describing how he gained the overlordship of Munster also by a speedy invasion of that province.' Niall's *ollamh* and chief bard was Torna Eisgeas, who appears in three of his poems as an ambassador or mediator between Niall and the Munster king.

Niall's death was the stuff of sagas. We read in one account that when visiting Alba (Scotland) he was shot with an arrow by Eochu, son of the Leinster king Énna Cennsalach, whose kingdom Niall had ravaged. A variant account has this happening in the Alps. As both 'Alba' (Scotland) and 'Alps' derive from the same Celtic word for 'high country' confusion is understandable. A third tradition has become even more popular – that he was slain by Eochu in a sea battle in what is now the English Channel (*muir Iocht*). Sources agree that the body was returned to Ireland and that he was buried at Ochann (Faughan's Hill), near Navan, Co. Meath. On hearing the news, Torna, the bard, is reported to have fallen dead from grief.

By the time of his death, Niall's brothers and his sons had established their dynasties in various kingdoms even as far south as Leinster. Long before Niall's period, a kingdom called Midhe (Meath) had been established as 'the middle kingdom'. It must not be confused with modern Meath and Westmeath for it also incorporated tracts of Cos. Offaly, Longford, Louth and Dublin. The chronicles claim that this was the seat of the High Kings and that it had been created by Tuathal Techtmar (the Legitimate) in the second century BC as the estate of the High King so that he would not be prejudiced towards his native province when ruling. By the Christian period the Uí Néill were also in control of the High Kingship of Midhe, or Tara.

Archaeology and mythology identify an eighteen-acre hill-fort site at Navan, Co. Armagh, as Emain Macha, the court of the Ulster kings, made famous by the stories of Conchobhair Mac Nessa and the Red Branch knights in the Ulster Cycle. These are also the tales featuring the Ulster hero Cúchullainn which scholars have described as belonging to an age several centuries before Christ. We know that the epic *Táin* is referred to in written form from the seventh century while other tales were being transcribed in the eighth century. However, these tales, being written by Christian scribes, underwent a certain bowdlerisation to eradicate the more outrageous affronts to the new faith.

Among those who ruled at Emain Macha was Macha Mong Ruadh, Macha of the Red Tresses (d. *c.* 377 BC) who is said to have established the first hospital in Ireland, called Bróin Bherg (House of Sorrow). By comparison, the Hindu *Annals of Charake* tell us that the Indian emperor Asoka (*c.* 273–32 BC) established the first hospitals in India while it was not until the time of St Fabiola (d. *c.* 399) that the first hospital in Rome was set up.

Whether myth or not, we know that the Brehon laws included strict rules on the running of hospitals and the provision of medical care. The laws also governed the qualifications of doctors, prohibiting unqualified doctors from practising.

When the Normans arrived in 1169, the Uí Néill kingdoms soon felt the effects. The Norman knight John de Courcy moved northwards and established himself as 'Conquestor Ultoniae'. He established an earldom of Ulster, with its territory partly in north Co. Down and partly in south Co. Antrim. With the Irish renaissance at the end of the thirteenth century, however, the O'Neills could still claim to be kings of an Ulster which we can recognise as, more or less, the modern province.

I
THE O'NEILL MÓR,
Prince of Tyrone
(Marques de la Granja y del Norte,
Conde de Benagiar in the Spanish peerage)
(Ó Néill Mór, Thír Eóghain)
and
THE O'NEILL,
Prince of Clanaboy
(Ó Néill, Chlann Aedha Buidhe)

It was during the fourteenth century that the O'Neill royal house separated into two distinct branches – the O'Neill Mór of Tyrone and the O'Neill of Clanaboy. Their common ancestor was Aodh Macaemh Toinsleag (the Lazy-Arsed Youth), who was the Uí Néill king of Cenél Eoghain, or Tir Eóghan (Tyrone) the major part of what is now called Ulster. He had avenged his father who had been murdered during the excesses of the High King Muirchertach Mac Lochlainn (d. 1166). By 1176 he had become supreme ruler of the Cenél Eoghain through the north of the country; a Norman French poem records that he and three thousand of his warriors came to the aid of the High King Ruaidri Ua Conchobhair against Henry II. Aodh was killed in battle against the Normans in 1177.

He left four sons. The eldest was Aodh Meth, 'the Fat', who became king (1196–1230). His brother Niall Ruadh is recorded as 'King of Uladh', succeeding Aodh Meth but reigning for only one month. He was the progenitor of the line of O'Neill Mór of Tyrone. However, he was immediately succeeded by a son of Aodh Meth, his nephew, called Domhnall Óg, who ruled between 1231 and 1234. His son Aodh Buidhe (1260–83) was the last to whom the then archaic title of King of Aileach was given. It was from this Aodh Buidhe that the name Clann Aedha Buidhe (the people of Aodh the Yellow) or Clanaboy takes its name.

The kingship descended as usual in Brehon law with the candidates chosen from both branches of the family. However, most kings of Ulster came from the line of the O'Neill Mór while the O'Neill of Clanaboy line produced only two more kings.

Niall Ruadh's son Brian O'Neill, King of Ulster 1241–60, also became the last native High King of Ireland (1258–60). His supremacy in the north was unchallenged. He joined an Irish confederacy to drive the Anglo-Normans out of Ireland in 1256. A meeting of the Irish kings and princes, with the notable exception of the Eóghanachta of Munster, but including The O'Brien of Thomond, Ua Maoil Seachlainn of Meath, The O'Conor of Connacht and lesser members of the nobility, acknowledged Brian as High King in 1258.

In 1260, at Catha an Duin, the battle of Downpatrick, Brian was defeated and killed by the Anglo-Normans. His head was sent to London to be exhibited. 'The Lament of King Brian O'Neill' was composed just before his own death by Ulster's chief bard Giolla Brighde 'Albanach' Mac Conmidhe (c. 1180–1260). He bore the nickname 'Albanach' (Scotsman) not because he was one but because he went there to recover the famous harp of Donough Cairbreach O'Brien, King of Thomond. He went to Palestine during 1218–21, probably as a pilgrim, and returned with poems about the hardship of his journey. The kings of Thomond, Connacht and Ulster patronised him and his work has been studied and discussed by several scholars during this century.

Brian's son Domhnall became king of Ulster in 1283 but was deposed in 1286 by the Normans. Restored by the Irish in 1295, he continued to reign until 1325. He decided, in the interests of Irish independence, to renounce the claims to the High Kingship based on his father's short rule, and invited Edward Bruce, brother of King Robert of Scotland, to come to Ireland to be High King. Supported by other Irish kings, Edward was duly crowned, but the resultant military campaign ended in his defeat and death along with that of many of the Irish nobility. Domhnall survived and his name heads the 'Remonstrance to Pope John XXII' signed by the Irish princes in 1317.

The Clanaboy line was able to claim the kingship after the death of King Domhnall in 1325. Henry, as Prince of Clanaboy, had not supported his kinsman in acknowledging Edward Bruce as High King. He and his father were, in fact, allied to the Norman 'Earl of Ulster' against Brian and his son Domhnall and had used the time to expand and consolidate their own power base east of the River Bann and south of Lough Neagh, establishing a kingdom which was fairly independent of their O'Neill kinsmen. Assisted by the Justiciar, Sir Ralph D'Ufford, Henry was able to prevent the succession of Domhnall's son Aodh and establish himself as king of Ulster. However, in 1344 he was deposed by Aodh, and he died in 1347.

Aodh Ramhar ('The Stout') ruled as king of Ulster until his death in 1364. His seals bear the inscription 'ODONIS O NEIL REGIS HYBERNICORUM ULTONIE' and the famous Red Hand emblem of his dynasty.

The O'Neill Mór line then held the kingship of Ulster with only one interruption and that was the grandson of King Eóghan (1432–55), Art (1509–14). His father Aodh (d. 1475) was named the tanist of Cenél

Eoghain who had, in 1435, extended his rule over the Fews (*fea*, a wood) in Armagh, an area 'full of woods and impassable fens, a long ridge of mountainous waste'. Art was an ally of his cousin King Conn Mór O'Neill against the English in 1487, and succeeded him as king of Ulster.

Art's son Fedlimid Ruadh became known as Lord of the Fews. When the line of the last king of Ulster, Aodh Ruadh (Red Hugh), known to the English as the 2nd Earl of Tyrone, died out on the Continent, the descendants of the line of the Lord of the Fews became represented by Don Arturo O'Neill, first Marques del Norte (1736–1814).

Conn Mór O'Neill, King of Ulster 1483–93, was noted as founding a Franciscan friary near Dungannon in 1489. His second wife was the daughter of the Lord Deputy of Ireland, Thomas FitzGerald, 7th Earl of Kildare. His son Art Óg became king of Ulster in 1514.

He was succeeded in 1519 by his brother Conn Bacach ('The Lame'). Conn Bacach is often wrongly regarded as the last king of Ulster. Certainly, in 1542, he submitted to Henry VIII and surrendered his kingship, for which he was rewarded with an English title, the Earl of Tyrone. His eldest son Ferdorcha, whose name was promptly converted to Matthew in English records, became 1st Baron of Dungannon. Within weeks of Conn Bacach returning to his Ulster kingdom, his *derbhfine* were in revolt at this betrayal. As an anonymous poet wrote:

> The O'Neills of Aileach and Navan,
> The King of Tara and Tailltean,
> In foolish submission,
> Have surrendered their kingdoms for the Earldom of Ulster!

Conn Bacach immediately wrote to Henry VIII seeking help to put down his own people but was driven into exile in the Pale as a refugee. He died there shortly afterwards in 1559. Conn Bacach's youngest son, Seán an Díomais (Shane the Proud) was inaugurated as The O'Neill Mór and King of Ulster in his father's place. Ferdorcha, the 1st Baron of Dungannon, was not even considered. Ferdorcha did not accept the decision lightly and rebelled against his brother. He was finally killed in 1558, the year before his father died. He had two sons, Brian the 2nd Baron of Dungannon, killed in the continuing dynastic quarrel, and the famous Aodh Ruadh.

For the next few years, the new king, Shane the Proud, having rejected the earldom and restored the kingdom, was at war with the English administration, and the Lord Deputy, the Earl of Sussex. During Elizabeth's reign a tenuous peace was agreed. Shane the Proud went to London to discuss the situation with Elizabeth I, and tried to explain to her the successional laws of Ireland. He married Catherine, daughter of The McDonnell of the Glens, chief of a cadet branch of the Scottish Mac-Donalds who had settled in the Glens of Antrim in the fourteenth and fifteenth centuries. They had two sons. His second marriage was to Catherine, daughter of Lachlan MacLean of Duart, Chief of Clan Gillean, who could speak five languages. He had two more sons. Shane, in maintaining control over his kingdom, defeated the army of The McDonnell of the Glens, capturing him and his brother, Somhairle Buidhe (Sorley Boy) MacDonnell, Lord of the Route in Antrim. He was invited to a conference by The McDonnell of the Glens on 2 June 1567, and assassinated.

Tairrdelbach Luimneach O'Neill, the grandson of Art Óg, was now installed at Tulach Óg as The O'Neill Mór, King of Ulster. Walter, the Earl of Essex, not to be confused with his more flamboyant son, Robert, who became one of Elizabeth I's favourites, was sent to bring Tairrdelbach to submission. He found him an astute general and politician. After a battle in June 1575, it was the Earl of Essex who had to come to terms with King Tairrdelbach. The Ulster king was left in peace to consolidate his kingdom. Lord Essex, Earl Marshal of Ireland, died of dysentery in Dublin in 1576.

Shane the Proud's eldest son, Seán Óg, was killed in 1592. A son, Henry, was imprisoned in Dublin Castle with his half-brother Art. They escaped in 1592 with Aodh Ruadh O'Donel, Prince of Tirconnell. Art O'Neill died of exposure in the Wicklow mountains.

Ferdorcha's only legitimate surviving son was Aodh Ruadh and he was inaugurated on the royal stone at Tulach Óg. Aodh Ruadh, born in Dungannon in 1550, had, at the age of nine, been taken to England as ward to the former Lord Deputy, Sir Henry Sidney, and raised in Ludlow, Penshurst and London to be an Englishman and an Anglican. 'Red Hugh', as 3rd Baron of Dungannon and 2nd Earl of Tyrone, returned to Ireland in 1568 and proved loyal to his English foster parents. He commanded a troop of Elizabeth's horse against Donal IX, the MacCarthy king of Desmond, during the war there. He even hanged Aodh Geimleach, the surviving son of Shane the Proud, in 1590.

He married several times. The most tempestuous marriage was to Mabel, the daughter of Sir Henry Bagenal, commander of the English army in Ireland. Mabel left him after a few months, making public complaint against him, and Aodh Ruadh began to retract his allegiance to England. Whether there was any significance in the stormy ending of his marriage is a conjecture which may be left to novelists. In 1593 Aodh Ruadh became the 'darling of Ulster' and the old king, Tairrdelbach, even abdicated in his favour. Aodh Ruadh was still regarded as Earl of Tyrone by the English. His installation at Tulach Óg, with due ceremony, made him The O'Neill Mór, King of Ulster. For this, in June 1595, he was proclaimed a traitor by the English colonial administration. In Irish records he is recorded as 'the last and one of the greatest of Gaelic kings'.

His defeat of Sir John Norris's army at the battle of Clontibert in the year of his inauguration began a warfare that did not end until the defeat of the Irish at Kinsale. With the defeat of Marshal Sir Henry Bagenal's army at Yellow Ford near Armagh in August 1598, Aodh Ruadh began to be regarded as virtually High King. In panic, in 1599, Elizabeth I sent her favourite, Robert, Earl of Essex, with an army of twenty thousand fresh troops to Ireland. She gave him unlimited power to deal with the situation. The first set-back Essex received was his defeat at the Pass of Plumes, near Portlaoise, by forces led by Donal MacCarthy, son of Donal IX of Desmond, and Eoghan MacRory Moore, when he attempted to invade Desmond. He then turned north. In September, Aodh Ruadh offered him a parley. Essex and Aodh Ruadh met in the middle of a river near Dundalk and agreed a cessation of hostilities until 1 May 1600.

When Essex returned to England, Elizabeth was so enraged at his actions that it led to his disgrace and execution. Charles Blount, Lord Mountjoy, was sent to Ireland to reconquer it. Mountjoy was a past master at *divide et impera* and he managed to split some of the Irish forces. O'Neill and his right-hand man, O'Donel, Prince of Tirconnell, were lured into Desmond, the kingdom being in a state of confusion following the death of Donal IX. Spanish allies, four thousand men commanded by Don Juan del Aguila, had landed. But, on 24 December 1601, at Kinsale, the Irish forces were defeated.

O'Neill retreated to Ulster, harried by English forces. In March 1603, at the very time Elizabeth I was on her death-bed, O'Neill decided that he had no alternative but to submit to Mountjoy. Hearing that the English planned to assassinate him and other leading Irish aristocrats, he fled into exile. This has been called the 'Flight of the Earls', for the Prince of Tirconnell went with him. Aodh Ruadh, as the last king of Ulster, died in Rome on 20 July 1616.

Aodh Ruadh's son Conn had died from wounds in 1601. Conn's son, Ferdorcha, accompanied his grandfather into exile. Aodh Ruadh's next son Hugh, 4th Baron of Dungannon, died unmarried in Rome in 1609 and his third son, Henry, 3rd Conde de Tyrone, died childless in 1610. His fourth son John, 4th Conde de Tyrone, was killed near Barcelona in 1641, leaving a son Hugo, known as Eugenio, styled Prince of Ulster and 5th Conde de Tyrone, but he died childless. Aodh Ruadh's fifth son, Conn na Creige, died in the Tower of London in 1622. His sixth son, Brian O'Neill, was murdered in Brussels by an English secret agent in 1617 aged thirteen. Aodh Ruadh had eight daughters.

Ferdorcha, the son of Conn Bacach, had left an illegitimate son Ferdorcha, Art 'Mac Baron', d. 1618. His line produced the famous Eoghan Ruadh O'Neill who became Lord General of the Irish army in 1642, defeating the army of General Munro at Benburb in 1649. His son, Henry Ruadh, was beheaded by the Cromwellians. His grandson was styled as 7th Conde de Tyrone, Knight of Calatrava, Colonel of an Irish regiment in Spanish service. The last Conde de Tyrone was Eoghan (Eugenio), 9th Conde, and Colonel of the Tyrone Regiment of the Spanish army. He died sometime after 1689, and from then on another O'Neill branch in France assumed the title. The last of the French family styling themselves Comte de Tyrone was Augustus Eugene Valentine O'Neille of Martinique. When he died towards the end of the nineteenth century, he left three daughters. One of them, still styling herself Viscomtesse de Tyrone, died in France in 1932. However, the daughters, in a dubious family pact which we will discuss shortly, agreed that Jorge, The O'Neill of Clanaboy was the senior male heir.

According to the genealogist, the late Sir Iain Moncrieff of that Ilk, the Albany Herald, with the extinction of Aodh Ruadh's line at the end of the seventeenth century, the title of The O'Neill Mór was vested in the next senior branch, that of the line of the Lords of the Fews. But we do not know what happened to Aodh Ruadh's grandson, Ferdorcha, who had accompanied his grandfather into exile. Was he, in fact, the progenitor of the French O'Neill line of the 'Comtes de Tyrone'? The O'Neill of Clanaboy believes not. And, before examining the line of the Lords of the Fews, we should consider two members of the family who have earned their own place in Irish history. Sir Feidlimid (Phelim) Ruadh O'Neill (1604?–53) the leader of the 1641 uprising, and Eoghan Ruadh O'Neill (1590–1649) who commanded the Irish armies between 1642 and 1649.

Sir Phelim O'Neill was descended from Seán, son of Conn Mór, King of Ulster (1483–93) by his second wife. Seán became tanist of The O'Neill Mór, but died in 1517. Phelim was the eldest son of Turlough O'Neill (d. 1608). He had been cheated out of his estates by Sir Arthur Chichester. He studied law at Lincoln's Inn in London and was elected to the Dublin parliament in 1641. It is claimed that he had been inaugurated at Tulach Óg as O'Neill Mór, Prince of Ulster, although the ancient Uí Néill inauguration stone had been smashed to pieces by Lord Mountjoy.

He organised and led the Irish uprising of 1641, which started on 22 October. As Lord General of the Irish army, Sir Phelim captured Charlemont Castle, a place of considerable strategic importance, commanding the Blackwater on the great northern road. When his kinsman Eoghan Ruadh (Red Owen) arrived in Ireland in 1642, Sir Phelim immediately went to Lough Swilly to meet him and escort him by way of Ballyshannon to Charlemont. He at once yielded the command of the Irish forces to him. This is curious for Phelim was a legitimate son, heir of Ulster kings, whereas Eoghan Ruadh was the son of the illegitimate son of Ferdorcha, son of the deposed King Conn Bacach. Could Phelim, if he had been legitimately endorsed as O'Neill Mór, Prince of Ulster, simply abdicate his rank as well as his command to his distant cousin? Under Brehon law, and even by primogeniture, Eoghan could not have claimed the Gaelic title.

Eoghan Ruadh had entered Spanish service in 1610 and had a distinguished military career. With the uprising in 1641, he sailed for Ireland and landed at the end of July 1642. His most famous victory was the defeat, on 5 June 1646, of the Scottish general, Robert Munro, at Benburb on the Blackwater.

Whereas Eoghan Ruadh sought a free independent Ireland, Phelim gradually drew to the side of those fighting the Cromwellians for the Stuart king. There was a confusion of interests and when Eoghan Ruadh died in November 1649, Phelim was bitter not to be returned as his successor in command of the army. With the victory of the Cromwellian forces he went into hiding on an island in Co. Tyrone. On 23 August 1652 a reward of £300 was offered for his apprehension. He was betrayed by a kinsman, Philip Roe MacHugh O'Neill, taken to Dublin and brought to trial on 5 March. Several times he was offered a pardon if he would admit that Charles I had given him a commission to start the uprising. He refused. On 10 March 1653 he was executed as a traitor in Dublin.

Eoghan Ruadh's nephew, Hugh O'Neill (fl.1642–60), had been born in the Spanish Netherlands and appointed a major-general in the Irish army. In February 1650 he was appointed Governor of Clonmel with 1200 troops. He faced an overwhelming force commanded by Oliver Cromwell. Cromwell opened the attack on the town on 27 April having besieged it since February. Never had Cromwell met with greater resistance and, although he breached the wall, the attackers, when they poured through, were caught in a trap by O'Neill's men and pushed out again. Cromwell is reported to have lost two thousand of his 'Ironsides'. It is claimed that Seathrún Céitinn (Geoffrey Keating, c. 1570–1650), the Tipperary-born historian and doctor of theology, was killed in the attack on Clonmel. His *magnum opus* was *Foras Feasa ar Éireann* (History of Ireland) which he began while hiding in a cave in the Glen of Aherlow during a previous penal period.

When it was obvious Clonmel would fall, O'Neill and his surviving soldiers slipped away in the dead of night with instructions for the mayor to agree terms with Cromwell. Cromwell was outraged when he realised that he had been outwitted and counted Clonmel one of his worst military disasters. However, he kept his treaty with the city. O'Neill arrived in Limerick and was given command of the city against General Ireton's siege of it. His luck did not hold and he was forced to surrender the city; he was taken captive in October 1659 and eventually sent to the Tower of London. As O'Neill had been born under Spanish jurisdiction, the Spanish ambassador, Alonso de Cardenas, applied for his release as a Spanish subject. He ended his days in Spain sometime after 1660. In October of that year he had sought to claim from Charles II the title Earl of Tyrone, which had been held by his kinsman, John O'Neill, who died in 1641. But Hugh O'Neill, like his uncle Eoghan Ruadh, was a descendant of an illegitimate son of the Baron of Dungannon.

Sir Iain Moncrieff believed that the title of O'Neill Mór now resided in the descendants of Feidlimid, Lord of the Fews. In this line, Tairrdelbach (Turlough), Lord of the Fews, was transplanted to Mayo during the Cromwellian confiscations and died in 1676. His son Conn, also transplanted, had a daughter who married distant cousin Henry O'Neill, brother to 'French John' O'Neill, who had managed to retain ownership of Shane's Castle in Antrim. Conn's son Henry served in the Jacobite army in 1689–91 and his grandson, Henry Ruadh, studied law in France during the Penal Years. He had issue with Isabel, daughter of Don Tadhg O'Sullivan, Conde de Berehaven, Knight of Santiago.

Henry Ruadh's son Don Arturo (1736–1814) became the first Marques del Norte. He had served in South America and the West Indies, was Governor of Pensacola, 1781, Captain-General of Yucatan, Governor of Merida, and a member of the Spanish Supreme War Council in 1803. As a general he played a prominent part in the Peninsular War against Napoleon's forces. His nephew, Don Tulio, who succeeded him, was a Lieutenant-General of Cavalry and won many decorations for his gallantry in the Peninsular War at the sieges of Salamanca, Pamplona and Bayonne. The king of Spain presented him with a ceremonial sword of honour. He married the Marquesa de la Granja.

Their son, Don Juan Antonio Luis O'Neill, inherited his mother's family titles in 1857, becoming 8th Marques de la Granja and Conde de Benagiar. The direct line of the Spanish O'Neills continued to the current Marques, Don Carlos O'Neill y Lastrillo, Marques de la Granja y del Norte y de Villaverde da San Isidro, Conde de Benagiar, O'Neill Mór, Licenciado, Maestrante de la Réal de Silla. He is married to Doña María de Orutea y Gatan de Ayala and they have six children. His heir is Don Carlos O'Neill y Orutea, born in San Sebastian in 1970. The family live on their estate in Seville. Don Carlos is the 12th Marques de la Granja and the 5th Marques del Norte.

Although he is a member of the Niadh Nask and states his title The O'Neill Mór in the Spanish nobility guide, he will not comment on whether he wishes to continue to pursue recognition of the Gaelic title from the Chief Herald of Ireland. There is a Royal O'Neill Clan Society to which he has given some patronage. The society is run by Don and Kathleen O'Neill from Belfast and in 1998 held its seventh international rally. The Marques has made no official application to join the Standing Council at the time of writing.

There is another O'Neill clan society, supported by The O'Neill of Clanaboy, whose chairman, by one of those curious ironies of history, is Raymond Arthur Clanaboy O'Neill, 4th Baron O'Neill of Shane's Castle in Antrim. The irony here is that Lord O'Neill's ancestor, the 1st Baron O'Neill, was actually a Chichester, descended from Sir Arthur Chichester, architect of the Ulster Plantation, who was instrumental in driving the O'Neills from their ancestral kingdom. Arthur Chichester was Lord Deputy of Ireland (1604–14). Cyril Falls wrote: 'While to uninstructed Irish Nationalists Cromwell is the English villain of Irish history, the better read reserve that place to Chichester.'[1]

Arthur Chichester, more than any other administrator, was the instrument of the suppression of the Brehon laws and Irish social system and the destruction of Gaelic aristocracy. How, then, can a descendant be called an O'Neill and be chairman of an O'Neill clan society?

Brian O'Neill, Prince of Clanaboy had surrendered to Sir Henry Sidney and exchanged his title for a knighthood. He had even welcomed the Earl of Essex (Walter Devereux) to Ulster with three days of feasting in Belfast. In payment, the English slaughtered two hundred of his people, including women and children, and carried off Clanaboy and his wife in chains. In 1575 he was hanged, drawn and quartered. His son Seán was set up as 'seneschal of Clanaboy' by Marshal Sir Henry Bagenal, desperate for allies in his fight against O'Neill Mór. Seán was unable to hold his own kinsmen in obedience and retreated into the north by Kellswater. His alliance was worthless for, after the English were victorious, Sir Arthur Chichester confiscated 600,000 acres of Clanaboy lands while Seán was allowed to keep only the ancestral seat of Edenduffcarrick Castle which became known as Shane's Castle in Co. Antrim.

His son Henry O'Neill of Shane's Castle had been created a baronet by Charles II in 1666 and retained some of his personal estate. He married the sister of Lord Deputy Richard Talbot, Earl of Tirconnell. His son Sir Niall (1658–90) fought for James II at the Boyne, defending the crossing at Rosnaree with his dragoons. He died of his wounds. His brother Sir Daniel did not suffer any act of attainder and kept Shane's Castle. He died in 1700. His son, Charles, had a son John O'Neill

(1740–98), born at Shane's Castle. Matriculating from Christ Church, Oxford, this John O'Neill was elected to the Irish parliament three times for Randalstown.

In 1793 he was raised to the Irish peerage as Baron O'Neill and then became Viscount O'Neill. He was also governor of Antrim. During the 1798 republican uprising, O'Neill was mortally wounded while leading the 'loyalists' against the insurgents. He was succeeded by his son Charles Henry St John O'Neill (1779–1841) who became the first Earl O'Neill for his support for the union of the parliament of Ireland with that of the United Kingdom of Great Britain in 1801. O'Neill became Lord Lieutenant of Antrim and Grand Master of the Orange Order. When he died unmarried the earldom became extinct and the viscountship devolved on his younger brother, John Bruce Richard O'Neill, 3rd Viscount (1780–1855). He died of gout and influenza at Shane's Castle. He had no sons and his daughter Mary had married the Reverend William Chichester, a descendant of Sir Arthur Chichester.

On 18 April 1868 William Chichester, who had now inherited Shane's Castle through his wife Mary, was created a baron. He decided to change his name to O'Neill and so became Baron O'Neill of Shane's Castle. It is to this O'Neill family that Terence Marne O'Neill, who was Prime Minister of Northern Ireland 1963–69, afterwards Lord O'Neill of the Maine, belonged. Also, from the same family, came James Chichester-Clark who succeeded his cousin as Prime Minister of Northern Ireland, 1969–71, and became Baron Moyola.

The current Lord O'Neill of Shane's Castle is Raymond Arthur Clanaboy O'Neill, 4th Baron, who inherited the title in 1944 at the age of eleven when his father was killed serving in the British army in Italy. The link, therefore, to the O'Neill royal house of Ulster by this family through one distaff connection, descended from the Clanaboy line in the nineteenth century, is very tenuous indeed.

The last of the Clanaboy line to be king of Ulster was Henry (1325–44) and his sons took the title Princeps Cloinne Aodha Buidhe (Prince of Clanaboy). Under Brehon law they did not succeed to the kingship nor become O'Neill Mór, which implied chiefship of Cenél Eoghain after that date, a point disputed by the current O'Neill of Clanaboy. Indeed, there were dynastic struggles within Clanaboy itself with Aodh claiming chieftainship from his cousin Murtough in 1548 and hiring seven thousand Scottish mercenaries to back his claim. Although the English backed Aodh, Murtough (Muirchertach Doibhlenach, 1548–52) was the last prince of Clanaboy who was properly inaugurated according to the Irish laws.

His grandson Conn Buidhe initially received a grant of several thousand acres of the land seized from Aodh Ruadh, after he had fled in 1608. But this was confiscated when he took part in the plot to rescue Aodh Ruadh's son, Conn, from Charlemont Castle. He died in 1630. During that time Sir Arthur Chichester tried to set up his own candidate to be 'captain of Clanaboy'. This was Conn of Castlereagh whom Chichester actually 'installed' in 1601. Conn was alcoholic and a spendthrift who was quickly tricked out of his estates by colonial adventurers such as James Hamilton (who became 1st Viscount Clandeboye) and Hugh Montgomery (1st Viscount Montgomery of Great Ardes). He died in 1619. Chichester commented cynically that if the Irish had hanged his Clanaboy candidate the world would not miss him.

Conn's sons were of a different hue. Domhnall became a major-general in the army of Charles I, fought at Marston Moor and Naseby and escaped from the Tower of London disguised as a woman. On the restoration he was Postmaster-General. The second son, another Conn, was a colonel in the Irish army in 1641; he was captured and murdered by a Protestant minister who had promised him quarter at Clones in 1643.

However, the genuine line of the princes of Clanaboy continued with Feidhlimidh Dubh (Black Phelim) who took part in the Irish uprising in 1641 and distinguished himself under the command of his kinsman, Eoghan Ruadh O'Neill. His grandson was fighting for James II; he took part in the siege of Derry, and fought at the Boyne, at Aughrim and then in defence of Limerick. He sailed with his regiment into French service and was killed on 11 September 1709 while fighting with the Irish Brigade against the English at Malplaquet.

His son, however, was living in Dublin and married Cecilia, a daughter of Captain Felix O'Hanlon, who had descended from a sister of Aodh Ruadh O'Neill. Their son, Seán (Joâo), settled in Portugal in 1740 and bought an estate on the Tagus, opposite Lisbon. His son Charles (Carlos) was educated at St Omer in France and became a Knight of the Order of Christ and a friend of the Portuguese royal house. He entertained King John VI of Portugal who visited him at his château at Setubal. He died in 1835.

His son José Maria O'Neill (b. 1788) was Consul-General of Denmark at Lisbon and entertained Queen Maria II and King Ferdinand at his house at Setubal. His eldest son José-Carlos (1816–89) played host to King Pedro V and King Luis I at the O'Neill estate called Quintas das Machadas near Setubal. His youngest son became Visconde de Santa Monica, Grand Officer of the Royal Household of Portugal and Minister of Justice (1821–89). The second son Jorge Torlades O'Neill, a friend, incidentally, of Hans Christian Andersen, received many Portuguese orders and also Danish and Brazilian orders.

His eldest son Jorge began to reassert his Gaelic title as 'The O'Neill, hereditary Prince of Ulster and of Tyrone and Clanaboy'. Jorge (1848–1925) was a Peer of Portugal, Knight of Malta, Knight of the Grand Cross of the Papal Order of St Gregory the Great, Grand Cross of Isabella the Catholic of Spain, officer of the Legion of Honour of France, Grand Officer of the Royal Household to the King of Portugal.

Although a French branch of the O'Neill family assumed the title 'Conde de Tyrone', and claimed descent from Sir Phelim Roe O'Neill, the pedigree of this branch has never, so far as is known, been proved. As we have seen, at the death of Augustus Eugene Valentine O'Neille, 'Comte de Tyrone', a Martinique politician who was succeeded by three daughters, Jorge O'Neill of the Clanaboy branch in Portugal organised a meeting in Paris before an attorney. It was not however attended by the Spanish branches of the family, the Marques de la Granja y del Norte, nor by a branch settled in Majorca who had descended from Turlough, The O'Neill Mór (1567–93). A family pact was signed in 1901 by which the daughters recognised that the O'Neills of Clanaboy were the senior branch and entitled to the style of Count of Tyrone. Despite the many rights enjoyed by females under Brehon law, disposing of Gaelic chiefly titles was not one of them, nor could the daughters of the late Comte dispose of what was essentially an English title stemming from the 'Earl of Tyrone' abolished by James I fully three centuries earlier.

The pact carried the implication that the head of the Clanaboy family was also to be recognised as head of the Cenél Eoghain, therefore as O'Neill Mór. With the line of the Marques de la Granja in Spain apparently, according to Sir Iain Moncrieff, having a more direct descent from the line of the O'Neill Mór, such a claim was arguable. In 1989, François Henri O'Neill of France, claiming to be an heir male of the French 'Comte de Tyrone', argued his primogeniture right to be senior, although primogeniture is not valid in Gaelic titles. François believed that the daughters of the last French 'Comte' had signed away their birthright without knowing the implications and declared his intention to pursue his claim.

The current O'Neill of Clanaboy, Dom Hugo, has firm views on the matter and on the claim of the Marques de la Granja y del Norte to be O'Neill Mór:

I do not believe that to be O'Neill Mór is necessarily synonymous to being the head of the Cenél Eoghain ... Mac Uí Néill Buidhe chiefs were never subjects of O'Neill Mór and, as heirs of Aedh Bhuidhe, they always considered themselves to be the rightful heads of the Cenél Eoghain. This was the attitude of my forefathers and mine is not different. I also believe that judging by the way tanistry was applied in our sept there cannot be any qualified candidate to the title O'Néill Mór.

Dom Hugo believes he will be proved correct once the *Leabhar Cloinne Aodha Bhuidhe* (The Book of Clanaboy) is examined by scholars, translated and contextualised. 'I am sure it will bring new light and will help to understand better the role of the two branches of the Cenél Eoghain in the fourteenth and fifteenth centuries.' He continues:

> At the risk of being judged a vain fool who dares challenge the views of the most reputed scholars in Irish history and succession laws, I support the view that in the case of the Cenél Eoghain, the tanist was, as a rule, the eldest surviving son of a former chief and elected from the four generations of the *derbhfine* . . .

When Dom Jorge submitted his genealogy to the Ulster King of Arms and the Somerset Herald, they issued certificates confirming that he was 'a lineal descendant and representative of the Royal House of O'Neill, Monarchs of Ireland, Kings of Ulster and Princes of Tyrone and Clanaboy'. The genealogy and the arms and motto, '*Lamh Dearg Éireann*' (Red Hand of Ireland) were registered as being those of O'Neill of Clanaboy.

It must be said that scholarship does not agree with the Portuguese O'Neills that the Clanaboy line are the senior claimants in the royal house of Ulster family. Nor would scholars endorse the claim that the line of The O'Neill Mór usurped the Ulster throne from the descendants of Henry (d. 1344). They argue that the reverse was the case. Yet the argument will doubtless continue. It is one that has its roots in the fourteenth century, with generations of tradition and doctrine on both sides.

After 1901, the king of Portugal offered to make Dom Jorge a Portuguese count bearing the title Count of Tyrone but he declined this. He was formally addressed, however, as The Most Serene Prince and Count of Tyrone and Clanaboy by both Pope Leo XIII and Pius X as well as being enrolled as such by the Registrar of Portuguese Nobility. By this Dom Jorge was accepted as a former sovereign prince. The current O'Neill, Prince of Clanaboy, Dom Hugo, is happy being addressed simply by his Gaelic title.

Dom Jorge contributed significant financial support to the cause of Irish independence, sending money to help arm the Irish Volunteers in 1914. He became a close friend of Sir Roger Casement, who wrote him a letter thanking him for that support, now in the National Library in Dublin. He also sent money to help Casement establish an Irish language medium school at Tawin near Galway.

Jorge's eldest son was Hugo Joseph Jorge Ever (1874–1940) who entered the Portuguese Royal Navy. His wife Julia could trace her descent back to Charlemagne. Hugo Joseph ensured that he employed an Irish governess for his children. His son Jorge (b. 1908) was given 'courtesy recognition' as O'Neill of Clanaboy by the Chief Herald of Ireland. He presided at the first international gathering of the Clan O'Neill at Shane's Castle, Co. Antrim, in June, 1982. A ceremony of inauguration was performed at the castle.

It was during this week that the current MacCarthy Mór, Prince of Desmond, hosted a dinner in Dom Jorge's honour at the residence of The McKerrell of Hillhouse. Several other O'Neills attended as well as Sir Iain Moncrieff, O'Conor Don, The McKerrell and O'Kelly de Conejera. O'Neill of Clanaboy was invested with the Niadh Nask. At the same time O'Neill, O'Conor Don and MacCarthy Mór discussed the idea of bringing all the Gaelic title holders together in a council. At that time the idea went no further.

The current holder of the title, Dom Hugo, also a Niadh Nask, attended the 1982 gathering and succeeded as O'Neill of Clanaboy in 1992. He was born in Lisbon on 7 March 1939. He took his degree in Lisbon and in 1962 married Rosa Maria Empis, a descendant of the 5th Marques de Valenca, premier marques of Portugal. From 1958 to 1986 he was chief executive of an industrial conglomerate and now runs his own company as a financial and corporate consultant. His eldest son, his tanist, Dom Jorge Maria Empis O'Neill, born 6 August 1970, is a junior consultant in the office.

Dom Hugo's interpretation of the native Irish law system is:

The maintenance of the Brehon law of succession, and of the values and lifestyle of Gaelic leaders, compelled Ireland to remain throughout the eleventh to the sixteenth centuries a conglomerate of small ultra-conservative tribal nations, unable to face the clash of the Anglo-Norman invasion and succumbing in the end when challenged by Tudor imperial England.

Having made the *caveat*, Dom Hugo firmly believes that his Gaelic title has always descended by Brehon law. 'It is obvious my forefathers never accepted the English domination of Ulster and the enforcement of English law,' he points out.

My branch of the family has never surrendered to English rule . . .

If, from a political viewpoint, I think that Gaelic values were bad for Ireland, I cannot be more proud to descend from a long line of great men who were prepared to pay, and most times paid, with their lives, to challenge and be challenged, who generously dedicated themselves to provide glory and well-being to their people, who had to be without blemish and fit for war, who were great lovers and masters of cunning, who were artists and protectors of art.

Dom Hugo is a man of strong opinions.

I think that it is most unfair that the dispossessed Irish aristocrats (who up to the end of Gaeldom in the sixteenth century were Ireland itself) forced to leave the country after the Treaty of Limerick, have to remain exiled from their country now that it has been freed from English domination. They should be asked to hold an Irish passport and I have pointed that out to the former President of Ireland (a famous constitutionalist) during her state visit to Portugal. [Mrs Mary Robinson.]

It must be said that in my case the territory which formed our *tuatha* is not part of the Irish Republic.

Dom Hugo even prepared a recommendation to Senator George Mitchell, chairman of the Ulster Peace Talks, suggesting that a referendum be held as to the view on the maintenance of an independent Ulster run by a constitutional monarchy under the return of an O'Neill dynasty.

This makes sense from an historical and also from a political point of view as Ulster was always an independent nation and politically an independent Ulster would help to save the face of the two contending communities in their search for a lasting peace. It is however certain that such a suggestion will never be accepted as it goes against the interests of all those who are party to the talks.

In that respect, Dom Hugo was perfectly right and events have now passed on. However, he suggested in his envisaged rebirth of a kingdom of Ulster, a two-chambered parliament with the Ulster Gaelic nobility sitting with those Anglo-Irish peers who would be prepared to sever their ties to the Crown of England and accept the restoration of the Gaelic O'Neill monarchy. Obviously, if O'Neill of Clanaboy was proposing himself as head of the royal house of O'Neill, such a suggestion, had it been seriously considered, might have soon floundered on the issue of dynastic rights.

Dom Hugo thinks that all Gaelic aristocrats who live in the Republic should be allowed to sit in the Irish Senate.

He describes his own role, as the holder of a Gaelic title, as follows:

> Apart from a political role and from a participation, in association with his peers, in the promotion of Gaelic heritage, the role of a modern chief is to be the effective head of his sept or his clan.
>
> As a consequence of the Irish Diaspora clans have most of their members dispersed around the world. Present-day data processing and telecommunication resources enable one to communicate easily and cheaply with millions of others wherever they are. It becomes therefore possible for an Irish chief to 'go global' and bring virtually together his clan members around the world, for instance using the Internet World Wide Web . . .

Dom Hugo is a firm believer in this technology.

> What I propose to do as O'Neill was put forward in the speech delivered at the ceremony of my presentation to the Clan held in June of 1992 at the Grian an Aileach, the prehistoric fortress conquered by the founder of the Cenél Eoghain, Eoghan son of Niall . . .
>
> . . . Let us therefore try to revive the O'Neill Clan by making it instrumental in reconciling O'Neills with their true heritage, in soothing the hardship of O'Neills in friendship and in fostering those blessed with natural abilities to ease their way in today's competitive world, in short, helping each one of us to enjoy our lives better than if left just to ourselves . . .

In practical terms, 'The Irish language should be preserved as a patrimony of the ancient Irish culture. Yet it is my firm belief that the reconciliation of the Irish of today with their true historical heritage is more important for the consolidation of an Irish national identity than the learning of the Irish language.' He continues:

> Most of the cultured Irish persons I have met don't know the history of their country or have just a very romantic view about some of its episodes. Irish history can and needs to be made intelligible to the Irish of Ireland and to the Irish of the rest of the world, but the Irish language will just be spoken by the very few that use it as a mother language or by a handful of academics who take pleasure in

communicating that way. Language is above all a communication tool and English became the international language adopted everywhere in the world, hence losing its former significance as a symbol of British imperialism. I see the mastering of the English language by the Irish (who provided the best modern writers, poets and playwrights in English literature) as a very important asset that helped Ireland become one of today's European business leaders and centres of artistic creation. I think therefore that although Irish should be preserved and revived, English should remain Ireland's basic language.

Dom Hugo believes that the best role he can play with regard to cultural endeavours is to support the serious research of Irish history and his idea is that a more uniform view of the history of the Irish kingdoms could be presented. He has been in touch with certain Irish academics to assist in an English translation of the *Leabhar Cloinne Aodha Bhiodhe*.

II
THE O'DOGHERTY OF INISHOWEN
(Ó Dochartaigh, Inis Eóghain)

Dr Ramon Salvador O'Dogherty, born in Cadiz, Spain, in 1919, holds the title of The O'Dogherty of Inishowen. Inishowen is the most northerly of the peninsulas of Ireland, in Co. Donegal. He is forty-fourth heir male from Niall of the Nine Hostages, King of Ulster and Tara. He is a firm believer in working for his family motto *Ar nDuthchas*, Our Inheritance.

According to the medieval genealogies, the O'Dohertys descend from the royal house of the Uí Néill through Conall Gulban, son of Niall of the Nine Hostages. The variants of the name, through Anglicised spellings, include O'Doughtery, Doherty, Docherty, Dockerty, Daughterty, Dorrity and several others. This patronymic comes from Dochtarach which has been interpreted as either 'disobliging' or, more likely, from Uí Doire Teagh, Lord of the Oak Houses.

The first reference to an Ó Dochartaigh occurs for the year 1171, in the *Annals of the Four Masters*, when an Ó Dochartaigh's death is mentioned. It is uncertain when they became Lords of Inishowen but in 1413 it is noticed that 'Conor O'Dogherty, chief of Ard Miodhair, and Lord of Inishowen, a man of unbounded generosity and general hospitality to the poor and needy, died.'

There are few recorded cases of conflict between the Ó Dochartaigh family over succession compared to the feuds among the O'Neills and O'Conors.

It seems that Seán Mór Ó Dochartaigh was among the first, with his king, Conn Bacach O'Neill, to surrender his title to Henry VIII for which he was given an English knighthood in 1541. The family joined the Irish wars against Elizabeth but Seán Óg, the son of Seán Mór, surrendered and received a knighthood in 1585. That year the *Annals of the Four Masters* noted that all the princes of Ulster were ordered to attend a parliament in Dublin under the English administration. Among those who attended was Seán Óg (d. 1601). He was later imprisoned by the Lord Deputy, Sir William FitzWilliam, for giving food and shelter to the survivors of the Spanish Armada ships wrecked on the northern coast of Ireland. He was forced to purchase his freedom after two years of captivity.

In 1600 Sir John Chamberlain, commanding a force of English troops from Derry, entered Inishowen determined to bring the people of the peninsula into submission. Ó Dochartaigh and his troops ambushed Chamberlain's men and defeated them. Seán Óg died the following year.

His successor was Caothaoir Ruadh, styled 'Sir Cahir' by the English (1587–1608). He was said to be extremely tall and handsome. Caothaoir Ruadh initially made friends with the English. When still only a teenager, he was knighted by Lord Deputy Mountjoy as a tribute to his courage in battle. He also visited the English court in London. On his return to Ireland he was made admiral of Derry city.

Caothaoir Ruadh's uncle, Felim, was Lord of Culmore Castle, on the Isle of Doagh at the mouth of Trawbreaga Bay by Lough Foyle. The castle had been captured by Sir Henry Docwra and English troops in May 1600. Docwra was to become Lord Docwra of Culmore. He became Governor of Derry and he strengthened the castle as a means of controlling the people of Inishowen. It seemed that Caothaoir Ruadh now realised where his allegiances should lie.

At the time of the flight of the Ulster nobles in 1608, Caothaoir Ruadh became the last Irish noble in the north holding out against the English conquest. In May 1608 he began his resistance by attacking the English garrison at Culmore and recapturing the castle. He then marched on Derry. In the attack, the city's Governor, Sir George Paulett, was killed. The city was taken and looted. Caothaoir Ruadh attacked other English fortifications in Derry, Donegal and Tyrone. The English Lord Deputy, Sir Arthur Chichester, offered a reward of five hundred marks for his head.

An army of four thousand, commanded by Marshal Wingfield and Sir Oliver Lambert, marched into Donegal in an attempt to trap Caothaoir

Ruadh and his men. But he evaded the English forces for some months before Wingfield laid siege to Burt Castle, the main residence of Caothaoir Ruadh, near Lough Swilly. Outnumbered and with provisions low, the garrison negotiated a surrender. Wingfield promised that their lives would be spared. However, after they had surrendered, he had them all put to the sword.

This outrage put a new spirit of determination into the Donegal men. But on 18 July Caothaoir Ruadh's forces were encamped at a place called Doon Rock, near Kilmacrenan, the place where the princes of Tyrconell were traditionally inaugurated. The English made a surprise attack. One of their number, recognising Caoathoir Ruadh by his stature and plumed helmet, took aim with a musket and shot him dead. His body was sent to Dublin where it was publicly exhibited. The head was severed and put on a spike at Newgate. His sword and its sheath were taken as trophies and have managed to survive to this day. They are now on public display in the O'Dogherty Castle Museum, Derry. Many of Caothaoir's subchiefs and followers were put to death after they had surrendered. Sir Arthur Chichester himself seized the chief's expensive estates and cleared the lands of some six thousand people who were sent off to Livonia, pressed into service as soldiers. A 'bestselling book' in England at the time was entitled *Overthrow of an Irish rebel in a late battle: or The death of Sir Cahir O'Dogherty* (1608).

The family of Caothaoir Ruadh retain a document written in Irish by Seán, brother of Caothaoir, who says:

After the loss of the unfortunate battle in which my brother Caothaoir fell no tongue could express the misfortunes that ensued. The whole country became the reward of the merciless enemies of this House who spared no one, particularly such as were connected with him by blood or marriage. After the confiscation of my family inheritance in favour of Sir Arthur Chichester my family and I were obliged to live in disguise a mean, wretched vagabond life. My wife sunk and due to her afflictions she left this world for a better one on the twelfth of December, 1637. She left me at her death with five children . . .

However, Seán's grandson Cahir (1639–1714) received some land in Co. Cavan from Charles II in compensation for the devastation of Inishowen. This was in the parish of Enniskean. Cahir therefore supported the Stuarts and became a major in the army of James II. After the Treaty of Limerick, he was forced to leave with his regiment, first to serve in the Irish Brigade of France, and then to Spain, where he achieved the rank of lieutenant-general in the Irish Brigade of the Spanish army.

Cahir's grandson John (1743–84) had remained in Ireland living the underground life to which the Gaelic nobility were reduced under the Penal Laws. His brother Henry (1745–96) had studied at the Sorbonne in Paris. He was ordained and eventually became Vicar-General for the Diocese of Meath. This was a highly dangerous position under the Penal Laws. John's sons, young, ambitious men, unable to abide the constraints of the English Penal Laws, decided to leave the country. Their uncle, Henry, had educated his three nephews – Henry (1776–1803), John (1777–1847) and Clinton Dillon (1778–1805). They applied to become officers in the Royal Spanish Navy which was then open only to members of the Spanish nobility. Ironically, the Ulster King of Arms, Sir Chichester Fortescue, supported by the Lord Lieutenant, the Earl of Westmoreland, and Lord Hobbard, certified the ancient genealogy and noble rank of the three young men, and indeed, fourteen bishops, an archbishop, the Irish officers of the Ultonia (Ulster) Regiment of the Irish Brigade of the Spanish army, and the Irish residents in Cadiz, all certified the nobility of their rank in Gaelic Ireland.

John and Clinton Dillon served as cadets in the Ultonia Regiment while Henry went to sea immediately. He died at sea in 1803 and is buried at Vera Cruz, Mexico. Clinton Dillon O'Dogherty also died at sea serving in the corvette *Batidor*, in 1805, being buried in Havana, Cuba. In 1797, he had captured an English corvette and, in 1804, personally led the boarding party which captured the English frigate *Enriqueta* in the River Plate. On the death of Henry, John became the founder of the O'Dogherty family in Spain. He participated in many sea battles and achieved fame for his part in the battle of Puente Sampayo (1809) during the Napoleonic Wars. In this battle, he commanded Spanish troops defending Vigo against the invading French forces. He married Maria Josefa Macedo, whose father was shot by the French.

John's grandson Ramon (1835–1902) served in the Spanish navy and saw action in Cuba, Santo Domingo and Mexico, and was decorated several times. He spent a few years in Ireland and made a legal attempt to get recognition of his title and claims to his family's confiscated Irish estates. The matter came before the Queen's Bench and the *Weekly Report* of 8 April 1871 reported the pedigree of his family. However, while the English administration had grown more liberal, it had certainly not become liberal enough to officially recognise a Gaelic title nor consider the return of confiscated estates.

Ramon's son Pascual (1886–1964) also entered the Spanish navy but showed a talent for mathematics. He founded a School of Mathematics in San Fernando (Cadiz). A street was named after him there following his death.

Pascual had two sons: Ramon, born in 1919, is the current Ó Dochartaigh. He was educated at the Universities of Cadiz and Madrid and he is a doctor of medicine, specialising in biopathology. He is also a corresponding member of the Royal Academy of Medicine of Palma de Mallorca, a Fellow of the Royal Academy of San Romualdo of Letters, Arts and Sciences, Deputy General Visitor of the Supreme Council of the Royal Institution of Knights Hospitaller of St John the Baptist. His tanist is his son Ramon, born in 1959, who is a graduate in law from the University of Madrid.

In 1978 Ramon's brother Rear-Admiral Pascual O'Dogherty, a Spanish naval architect, was invited to Ireland to attend the cultural festival called *Cuirt Ailigh* (court of Aileach) organised by the people of Inishowen. This led to an active relationship between the chief and the people of the peninsula through the medium of his brother, who speaks fluent English. Because of this, the Standing Council of Irish Chiefs and Chieftains bend their rules slightly to allow Admiral O'Dogherty to represent his brother and his tanist on the council. The strict rule is that only the chief or his tanist may attend meetings. The Admiral has written a history of the O'Dogherty chiefs of Inishowen in English.

In July 1990 there was an O'Dogherty clan gathering, and Ó Dochartaigh was invited to attend. During the proceedings he was ceremonially installed at the ancient inaugural stone in Belmont House, Derry, in the manner of his ancestors. The year was a special occasion in that the Chief Herald of Ireland had finally given 'courtesy recognition' to his title. The Ó Dochartaigh had issued a statement in Irish and in English in which he sought a more active role for those bearing Gaelic titles.

During the inauguration ceremony, in which Ó Dochartaigh received the traditional white willow wand of office, he was also handed the sword of his ancestor Caothaoir Ruadh Ó Dochartaigh, killed in the battle at Doon in 1608. The sword was kept in the Guildhall vaults in Derry. The newspapers reported the colourful installation ceremony as being that of the first inauguration of a Gaelic noble in Ulster for four hundred years. They had forgotten The O'Neill of Clanaboy's inauguration at Shane's Castle, Co. Antrim, in 1982. Ó Dochartaigh's ceremony was attended by several hundred visitors from Ireland, the United States, Canada, New Zealand, Australia, Holland, Germany and Spain.

Today, there is a thriving O'Dogherty clan association with a newspaper entitled *Ar nDuthchas*, edited by Pat Dougherty from Inch Isle, Co. Donegal. A major Ó Dochartaigh gathering is planned for July 2000.

The O'Dogherty castle still stands in Magazine Street, Derry, on the site of the original sixteenth-century tower house where the arms of the chief remain engraved on stone above the fireplace in the banquet hall. The castle is now a cultural centre and museum. It was originally built by the lords of Inishowen to protect access to their secluded peninsula.

The Ó Dochartaigh accepts that his title, since the death of Caothaoir Ruadh, has been passed down following the principle of senior son inheritance but realises that it has its base in Brehon law. He is, of course, proud of his Spanish citizenship but 'As a member of the Irish Diaspora, I would be very proud, if it is ever permitted by Irish law, to be given an honorary Irish passport.'

He does not see any significant political role for the old Gaelic aristocracy in a modern Irish Republic but believes that the Standing Council of Irish Chiefs 'should act as a stimulus to the upkeeping of Irish culture, history, language and traditions.' He feels that the holder of an ancient Gaelic title embodies the representation of large numbers of Irish people and 'being the direct descendant of the Irish royalty and nobility . . . in this way, a chief can rally the Irish spirit of all clan members.'

III
THE O'DONEL,
Prince of Tirconnell
(Ó Domhnaill Thir Conaill)

The O'Donel princely house of Tirconnell represents perhaps one of the most historically eminent of the old Gaelic aristocratic families. They descend from Niall of the Nine Hostages as do most of the northern aristocratic families but through his son Conall Gulban, who gave his name to Tir Conaill, the Land of Conall. Conall means 'strong as a wolf'. Conall Gulban was the ancestor of other Donegal families such as the O'Dohertys and O'Gallaghers. As kings of Tirconnell (now Donegal) they were inaugurated on the Rock of Doon, near Letterkenny, and, in Christian times, then proceeded to Kilmacrenan to be blessed by a bishop.

The original name Ó Domhnaill has been Anglicised in many forms from O'Donel to O'Donnell. It is merely a matter of personal choice. The form O'Donel was given by the Genealogical Office in 1944 for the holder of the title and this seems as good an Anglicisation as any.

The current O'Donel is a man of some mystery. He is Father Hugh O'Donnell OFM, born in Dublin in 1940 and educated at the

Presentation College, Glasthule, and University College, Galway. He also studied in Rome where he was ordained a priest in 1965. He has served as a missionary in Zimbabwe for the last twenty years and is a parish priest in Harare.

Although he still allows his entry as chief to go forward in *Who's Who in Ireland* and other directories, such as the *Nobility of Europe*, and has his name on the *Clár na dTaoiseach* (Register of Chiefs), he declines to take any interest in the obligations that go with his title, does not attend meetings of the Standing Council, does not answer correspondence on matters related to his title and family, and expresses a general lack of interest in such matters. It has been left to others to promote Clan O'Donel gatherings.

Writing to the author from Rome on 11 May 1998, after much prompting, Father Hugh commented in a brief note: 'I made the decision several years ago not to be drawn into any correspondence on the matter. I have personal and family reasons for that decision.'

Father Hugh's sister, Nuala Ní Dhomhnaill, has argued, on radio and television, for the succession of the title to go to the female line so that she could claim it for herself and her children. This would be totally contrary to the Brehon law of succession as well as primogeniture inheritance. However, the official tanist is Don Leopoldo O'Donnell y Lara, Duke of Tetuan, in Spain. Appearing on an RTÉ programme, hosted by Bibi Bascin, with The O'Neill of Clanaboy and The O'Conor Don, Nuala Ní Dhomhnaill, while accepting that the Duke of Tetuan was the heir apparent, countered: 'In this day and age when women are beginning to take their proper place in society, I cannot see any reason to shift the title three hundred years across the sea to Spain.' She believed that the Duke of Tetuan's title had passed through a female heir, and cited this as a justification for her argument. She was, of course, incorrect and was probably confused because a title of O'Neill Mór, Marques de la Granja, had passed in Spanish law from a female line.

Probably the most famous member of the family was St Colmcille, also known as St Columba, (*c.* 521–97), born at Garton, Donegal. His father was Fedlimid of Tir Conaill, grandson of Conall Gulban. He is regarded as the monastic scribe who wrote the *Cathach*, the famous Latin book of psalms which was carried by the O'Donels into battle as their rallying symbol. The book has survived and is now in the Royal Irish Academy while its fabulous silver shrine is in the National Museum, Dublin. St Adamnán, the Abbot of Iona (626–703) was another member of the family, and he wrote a life of his kinsman. Colmcille founded monasteries at Derry and Durrow, and the *Book of Durrow* (in Trinity College Library) was said to have been written in his own hand. The

Book of Durrow was already venerated as a holy relic as early as the tenth century.

It has been argued that Colmcille was responsible for the first copyright law and ruling in the world. Colmcille went to stay with St Finnan at the Abbey of Maghbhile (Moville, near Newtownards). Finnan possessed a copy of the Gospel of St Martin (of Tours) which Colmcille coveted. Each night, unknown to Finnan, Colmcille went to the abbey library and worked on copying the book. Finnan discovered what he was up to and took him before the court of the High King, Diarmaid Mac Cearbhaill. The judgement was '*Le gach bóin a bóinín, le gach leabhar a leabharín*' (To every cow belongs her calf, so to every book belongs its offspring book). Colmcille, being of a princely family, took exception to the ruling and raised his clan to punish the High King for the judgement. The battle of Cuildremhne (Cooldrevy, in Sligo) in 561 was a victory for the High King. Colmcille was in peril of excommunication and death. But, instead, he was exiled with some of his followers to the kingdom of Dàl Riada in what is now Scotland. He settled on Iona which, under his guidance, became a great ecclesiastical centre from where many Irish missionaries went to convert the pagan Anglo-Saxon kingdoms.

Domhnaill (World Mighty), '*Rex Tir Conail*' won a great victory over the mercenary forces of his foster son Prince Congal Claen at Magh Rath (Moyra) in 637. During a six-day battle, he annihilated Congal's forces. The battle is the subject of an ancient poem which John O'Donovan translated for the Irish Archaeological Society in 1846.

Maeltuanadh son of Domhnaill (990–1010) became the first to use the surname Ua Domhnaill (O'Donel).

Aodh Ruadh Ó Domhnaill (1461–1505) was responsible for building a castle at Donegal which became the stronghold of Manus Ó Domnaill, Prince of Tirconnell (d.1563). Manus was a flamboyant man who dressed in the style of Henry VIII of England. He has been described as 'very much a Renaissance prince'. He was married five times and had nineteen children. He had a great literary talent and wrote love poetry and satiric verse of considerable merit. In 1541 he followed the example of the king of Ulster and surrendered his title to Henry VIII. As with other nobles who surrendered their titles, there was unrest among the *derbhfine* against the legality of the action. Finally, in 1555, his own son Calbhach, Anglicised as Calvagh, and meaning 'Bald', deposed his father and held him as a prisoner at Lifford Castle where he died in 1563. It is said that the ambition of Calbhach to succeed was countered by family support for his half-brother Aodh Dubh who was considered the legitimate tanist. Calbhach was himself captured and imprisoned by the king of Ulster, Shane the Proud, and died in 1566.

It was, therefore, Aodh Dubh who succeeded as Prince of Tirconnell but he surrendered his title and received a knighthood in 1567, the year of Shane the Proud's death. His son was the famous Aodh Ruadh (1571–1602) whose youthful abduction is one of the great romances of Irish history. The English Lord Deputy, Sir John Perrott, seeking to break Irish resistance to the conquest in the north, kidnapped the seventeen-year-old Aodh Ruadh, along with the sons of two other nobles, Donal Ó Gallchobhair, whose father was hereditary marshal of the army of O'Donel, and Aodh Mac Suibhne, son of Mac Suibhne na dTuath. Taking them by boat from Lough Swilly, the English incarcerated them in Dublin Castle.

Here Prince Aodh Ruadh found two sons of Shane the Proud, Henry and Art, who were being held as hostages for their father's good behaviour. On the night of 25 December the three young princes, Aodh Ruadh, and Henry and Art O'Neill, escaped from Dublin Castle, with the help of Aodh Maguire, Prince of Fermanagh. Through one of the coldest winters they trekked across the snow-covered Wicklow Mountains towards Glenmalure, hiding from English patrols. Aodh Ruadh and Art became separated from Henry. Art died from exposure while crossing the mountains. More dead than alive, Aodh Ruadh reached Ballinacor, at the head of Glenmalure, the stronghold of Fiach MacHugh O'Byrne, chief of the O'Byrnes of Wicklow who had been a thorn in the side of the English administration. O'Byrne helped Aodh Ruadh reach the safety of his father's castle in Ballyshannon in Donegal. Aodh Ruadh had, however, suffered the loss of both big toes with frostbite. A few years later, O'Byrne was captured by the new Lord Deputy, Sir William Russell, and instantly beheaded. It is a great saga which has been the subject of novels and even a Walt Disney movie entitled *The Fighting Prince of Donegal*.

On the joyous return of Aodh Ruadh, and recognising the talent of his son and the inspiration his escape had given to the people, Aodh Dubh abdicated in his favour. In 1598 Aodh Ruadh joined his namesake Aodh Ruadh O'Neill, King of Ulster, in his war against England. After their initial triumph at the battle of the Yellow Ford, however, came the reverse at Kinsale. Aodh Ruadh O'Donel immediately went to Spain seeking assistance and was received by Philip III. But in 1602 he suddenly fell ill and died at Simancas. It is clear, from a letter from Sir George Carew to Lord Mountjoy, that a spy in the pay of the English, one James Blake, had poisoned him. O'Donel was thirty-one years old. He was buried with regal honours in the church of the monastery of Valladolid.

Ruaidri Ó Donel (1575–1608), his brother and tanist, had fought alongside Aodh Ruadh during the war, and after the defeat at Kinsale, during his brother's absence in Spain, he had assumed the chiefship. He was not inaugurated until after his brother's death. For a while Ruaidri and O'Conor Sligo banded together in guerrilla warfare against the English but in 1603 when Aodh Ruadh O'Neill surrendered the war was virtually over. In exchange for his surrender Ruaidri was both knighted and given the English title Earl of Tirconnell.

Learning that the English were planning the removal of himself and other 'troublesome' Irish leaders, Ruaidri joined O'Neill, Maguire and other northern Gaelic nobles, leaving Ireland to go into exile. The plan was always to return to free Ireland and never to settle abroad for ever. He died in Rome in 1608, aged only thirty-three, and was buried in the church of San Pietro in Montorio, where Aodh Ruadh O'Neill was buried when he died in 1618.

Ruaidri's son, Hugh Albert, a page to the Infanta of Spain, living in Flanders, was recognised as the Earl of Tirconnell and heir to the chiefship. There are some letters extant from Brussels in which he signs himself, 'Earl of Tirconnell, Baron of Lifford, Lord of Lower Connacht and Sligo, Knight of the Order of Alcantara, Captain of Spanish Artillery in Belgium'. Hugh died in 1642.

There was now the problem of the succession. Although the chiefship was abolished by English law, it was still regarded as important among the people of Donegal. Sir Niall Garbh O'Donnell (1569–1626), Calbhach's grandson, had opposed Aodh Ruadh's election as chief. With some followers, he had installed himself as 'O'Donel' at Kilmacrenan, just north of Letterkenny. Because he was implicated in the O'Dogherty uprising in Derry in 1608 he was taken captive to the Tower of London where he languished and died in 1626. His eldest son was also imprisoned in the Tower and died there. A second son, Manus, was killed at the battle of Benburb in 1646, fighting for Eoghan Ruadh O'Neill.

Hugh O'Donnell (d. 1704) known as 'Balldearg' because of his distinctive red birthmark, left Donegal to join the Spanish army in which he served as a general. He returned to Ireland to serve James II's army but arrived after the defeat of the Boyne. He claimed the title Earl of Tirconnell but James II had other ideas. He had given the title to Richard Talbot (1630–91) of Malahide, Co. Dublin, who had fought against Cromwell in the defence of Drogheda and was a vehement supporter of the Jacobite cause. Talbot came from an 'Old English' family in Ireland. A Catholic himself, he was given command of the army in Ireland and became Viceroy in 1687. In July 1688 he was made Duke of Tirconnell.

However, Balldearg's brother had been appointed Lord Lieutenant of Donegal by James II. Balldearg seemed one to grab the main chance, and he immediately joined the army of William of Orange, demanding, in return for his services, the earldom of Tirconnell. He served William in several missions in Europe but eventually, realising there was no hope of William making him earl, he rejoined the Spanish army, retiring with the rank of major-general. His will was made out in Madrid on 9 April 1674, and he signed it as Earl of Tirconnell. He died in Spain about 1704.

Another member of the family who had studied for the priesthood, becoming a Jesuit Father in Spain, bore his literary ancestor's name, Manus Ó Domhnaill. He attended the University of Salamanca and in 1694 he translated into Irish the *Lunario* of Geronimus Cortès of Valencia, a treatise of medical astrology. It might be significant that Salamanca was the last European university to have a faculty of astrology (as opposed to astronomy) which finally closed in 1770.

After the Treaty of Limerick, Brigadier Daniel O'Donnell went into exile in France taking the *Cathach of St Colmcille* with him. It was placed for safety in a monastery where it was rediscovered in the 1880s. Sir Niall O'Donnell, a descendant of Daniel, claimed it as a badge of their right to be The O'Donel, although this was disputed by other branches of the family. Sir Richard Annesley O'Donnell, 4th Baronet of Newport House, placed the priceless *Cathach* in the Royal Irish Academy.

According to John O'Donovan, Niall Garbh's second son, Manus, killed in 1646, had a son Ruaidri who married an O'Donnell cousin. His son Colonel Manus O'Donnell of Newport House had three sons, one of whom was Hugh O'Donnell of Larkfield, who claimed to be The O'Donel and even called himself 'Earl of Tirconnell'. He died in 1754. His son Conn of Larkfield maintained the Gaelic title and he married Mary O'Donnell, the sister of Sir Neil O'Donnell of Newport (the 1st Baronet). Conn died in 1825 and his eldest son was an Anglican clergyman in Yorkshire, Reverend Constantine O'Donnell, whom John O'Donovan, in 1860, believed to be the rightful claimant to the title.

Father Hugh O'Donnell OFM descends from this line of O'Donnells and is accepted by the Chief Herald of Ireland as The O'Donel. No O'Donnell asked *Thom's Directory* to list a claim in their early 'unofficial' listing of Gaelic titles. However, when the Genealogical Office began to give courtesy recognition to such titles, *Thom's Directory* printed the approved 'chieftainries'. John O'Donel, born 23 May 1894, was listed as succeeding to the title in 1932, and is styled as 'O'Donel of Tirconnell'. He married Ellen Reidlinger of Portsmouth, and Aodh, the Irish form of Hugh, is set down as his heir. Aodh was born on 3 February 1940, at Monkstown, Dublin. John O'Donel was not one of the first Irish chiefs to have his claim recognised by the Genealogical Office and his name does not appear in the *Éire Iris Oifigiúil* of 22 December 1944.

It is obvious that from the early seventeenth century no clear succession was made and no claimant could really justify their title under Brehon law due to the various dynastic arguments within the *derbhfine*. The later claims under primogeniture, under which the title Earl of Tirconnell was claimed, are also arguable. There were too many branches of the family. Leopoldo O'Donnell is the only representative of the family who has shown the author a detailed family tree, drawn up by qualified heraldic genealogists, with other items, showing his line back to the last princes of Tirconnell.

Many O'Donnells fled abroad in what became known as the 'Flight of the Wild Geese'. Major-General Henry, Count O'Donnell was founder of an Austrian branch of the family. His eldest son Count Joseph (1755–1810) became Finance Minister to the Austrian government, steering Austria to economic recovery after Napoleon's victory. His son Joseph (1755–1840) was Minister of Finance to Emperor Francis II and his second son Field Marshal Count Maurice O'Donnell (1780) was father to the famous Major-General Maximilian, Count O'Donnell, aide-de-camp to the Emperor Franz Josef whom he had saved from assassination in 1853. The Austrian Counts O'Donnell von Tirconnell are a continuing line in modern Austria.

Joseph O'Donnell (1722–1800), who became a Lieutenant-General in Spanish service, had two sons. Both Don José and Don Carlos became generals in the army. Don Carlos (1772–1830) became father of one of the most famous O'Donnells – Don Leopoldo (1809–67). He rose in the army to become Field Marshal, 1st Duke of Tetuan, Conde de Lucena, and Visconde de Aliaga. He commanded Spain's successful Moroccan campaign for which he was given his title from Tetuan in Morocco in 1860. He was also Governor of Cuba for a while. He was then appointed Minister for War and President of the Council of Ministers (basically the office of Prime Minister) in 1858. It is also no secret that he was the lover of Queen Isabella II of Spain.

His nephew, also Don Carlos (1834–1903), served as Minister of State and ambassador to the courts of Brussels, Vienna and Lisbon. He became the 2nd Duke of Tetuan as his uncle had no male issue. Carlos's son, Don Juan, who became the 3rd Duke, Count of Lucena and Marques de Altamira as well as Visconde de Aliaga, was General of Cavalry and Minister for War (1864–1928). He became president of the Convention of the Irish Race in Paris in 1919. This convention, encompassing the Irish of the Diaspora as well as from Ireland, endeavoured to get US President Wilson's recognition for Ireland's claim to independence. Ireland's unilateral declaration of independence had been made in January 1919.

Through his line has descended the 6th Duke of Tetuan, Marques de las Salinas, who was born on 19 May 1915. He is accepted in all quarters as heir to the title of O'Donel, Prince of Tirconnell. Although he and his family hold many Spanish titles, the Duke of Tetuan is enthusiastic about his Irish links. In 1956, Eamon de Valéra, as Chancellor of the National University of Ireland, conferred an honorary doctorate on him. He is amazingly active for his age, fascinated by Irish history and the history of his own family. He is proud to be a holder of the Niadh Nask. His son Hugo is also a holder of the honour.

Hugo O'Donnell, Duque de Estrada, Conde de Lucena, Marques de Altamira, trained as a lawyer and is a retired Minister of Marine under King Juan Carlos of Spain. He is also an historian and corresponding member of the Spanish Academy of History.

The lack of interest by the current holder of the title is therefore more than made up for by the enthusiasm of those who will succeed him. In fact, it has been suggested in some quarters that the current O'Donel should follow the Gaelic custom of abdication in favour of a more suitable chief. Aodh Dubh, for example, resigned his title when he realised Aodh Ruadh, his tanist, was better fitted for the duties of chiefship.

The Spanish O'Donnells are a large family. Their influence is all pervasive in Madrid where a principal street bears their name as do shops, commercial houses and even garages. The duke has said: 'Being in my mid-eighties, perhaps I will not inherit the title of my forebears, nor even my son in his lifetime. But one of my grandsons doubtless will. Our family, forced to flee from our native land to maintain our own existence, has never really abandoned Ireland, our patrimony nor our people of Tirconnell. We would sincerely wish to maintain their interest in the ancient Gaelic culture that once made Ireland the cradle of civilisation during the grim, bleak days of the European "Dark Ages".'

IV

THE MAGUIRE,
Prince of Fermanagh
(*de jure* 14th Baron of Enniskillen
in the Jacobite peerage)
(Mag Uidhir Fhear Managh)

The current Maguire, Prince of Fermanagh, traces his descent from Cormac Mac Airt, High King of Ireland (AD 226–28), considered the most learned and wisest of all the pre-Christian kings of Ireland. Cormac has been dismissed by some scholars as a mythical figure as he features as both hero and villain in many of the stories of myth and folklore. Indeed, so much has myth gripped popular consciousness during recent years that Cormac even features in comic strips as well as popular fantasy novels. Yet, if one accepts the ancient Irish genealogies, there is no reason, other than prejudice, to dismiss him or his reputation.

The Maguire princes trace their descent through Colla, the great-grandson of Cormac. The name Mag Uidhir means 'son of Odhar' which is a comparatively rare early name, perhaps being 'dark, sallow or grey-brown'.

Donn Carrach Mag Uidhir (Maguire), King of Fermanagh 1264–1302, earned the accolade among the bards as 'Ireland's most gracious lord'. The current Maguire is twenty-seventh heir male in direct descent from Donn Carrach.

The ancient annals and chronicles of Ireland are filled with praise for the Maguire kings. It is recorded that they gave good government, endowed churches and monasteries, encouraged the arts and defended their kingdom assiduously.

The Maguire kings were patrons of many well-known bards and scholars and were scholars themselves. Cathal Mac Magnus Mhag Uidhir, Archdeacon of Clogher, for example, compiled the famous *Annals of Ulster* in 1498 from earlier records. Nioclás Mhag Uidhir (1460–1512), Bishop of Leighlin, was a leading historian of his day. The personal bards of the Maguires were the Ó hEoghusa (O'Hussey) bards of whom Eochaidh (1570–1617) stands out as chief *ollamh*; he is often regarded as the last of the traditional *ollamhain*. He was certainly one of the two foremost poets of his day, his rival being Tadhg Dall Ó hUiginn. He wrote a famous poem describing the campaign of 1599–1600 during which Aodh (Hugh) Maguire was fighting with Aodh Ruadh O'Neill against the forces of Elizabeth. Eochaidh's brother or cousin was Gille-Bríghde Ó hEoghusa (1575–1614), who had to flee Ireland and entered Louvain as a Franciscan in 1607. His poems are regarded as classics and he was also the author of one of the earliest Irish printed books in Louvain, *Teagasc Críostaidhe* (1611). Printing in the Irish language was generally forbidden under the English administration, so books in Irish – including grammars, dictionaries and theological works – were often printed in France, what is now Belgium, Italy and Spain.

The annals record that Pilib na Tuaigh (Philip of the Battle Axes) who ruled Fermanagh 1363–95, controlled an army as well as a navy which 'never tasted defeat'. His grandson Tomás Óg is noted as having made a pilgrimage to Rome and then to Santiago de Compostella in 1450. He was king of Fermanagh from 1430 to 1471.

The last Maguire recorded as *Rí Fhear Manach* (King of Fermanagh) was Giolla Pádraig Bán (1538–40). From then on the form of 'Prince of Fermanagh' was used. Did the change in title come about because Seán Maguire assisted the English in their war against Shane the Proud, the Maguire overlord? In 1568 Shane the Proud led an army into Fermanagh in revenge and helped to establish Seán Maguire's brother 'Coconaght' as prince. The name was Cú Chonnacht ('Hound of Connacht') much favoured among the Maguires and the O'Reillys in the later Middle Ages. On 1 June 1585 he surrendered to Lord Deputy Perrott. It is noted on that date: 'Surrender by Coconaght Magwyre of Innyskillen, captain of his nation; of the whole country of Fermanagh, alias Magwyre's country, in the province of Ulster, with the intention of its being regranted to him.' Thus Cú Chonnacht was allowed, in January 1586, to retain some of his estate in return for a fee. Pardon was granted to him and members of his family provided Cú Chonnacht agreed to the usual conditions associated with such surrenders. The Maguires had surrendered first the kingship and then the princedom for the title of an English baronet.

Three years later Cú Chonnacht was dead. His son Aodh was made of sterner stuff, and became one of the most famous Maguire princes. It was he who helped Aodh Ruadh O'Donel and the sons of Shane the Proud in their famous escape from Dublin Castle in 1592. Maguire had travelled to Dublin, ostensibly to be knighted in Christchurch Cathedral as part of the surrender process. It was, however, a cover in order to be on hand to plan the escape of the princes.

The Maguire was given command of the Irish cavalry at the battle of the Yellow Ford. He claimed to be the first Irish noble to raise the standard against Elizabeth, having stood alone for two years before O'Neill and O'Donel took the field with him. In January 1596 he wrote to Philip II of Spain:

I was the very first of all in this kingdom, not of my own authority, but through reliance on God's help and your clemency, who had the courage to rouse the Queen of England's wrath. I have incurred infinite losses in consequence, but all these are little account because of your good will towards me . . .

Lord Ernest Hamilton, in his *Elizabethan Ulster: The Irish Rebellion of 1641, with a History of the Events which led up to and succeeded it*, observes that 'Hugh Maguire was incomparably the best military commander among the Chiefs of the North.'

Maguire followed O'Neill south where, in 1600, he is said to have encountered Sir Warham St Leger in combat and been mortally wounded by him, but not before he was able to cleave St Leger's helmet with a massive blow. The death of Aodh or Hugh Maguire was a severe blow for the Irish cause. He was succeeded by his brother Cú Chonnacht as Prince of Femanagh.

Cú Chonnacht was endorsed as The Maguire by his people but the English administration tried to set up a rival leader, Conor Ruadh, who goes disparagingly into Irish history as 'the Queen's Maguire'. He was not, at this time, successful in his claims for the *derbhfine* and people gathered behind Cú Chonnacht.

Cú Chonnacht was certainly no friend to the English administration. The northern Irish princes, having surrendered in 1603, learned that the colonial administration had plans to remove them entirely. The Maguire took the initiative and went to Rouen, in France, where he made arrangements for the potential refugees and purchased a ship, bringing it into Lough Swilly. It was from there that The O'Neill, The O'Donel and The Maguire, with their families and a hundred loyal followers, left Ireland into exile, an event known as 'the Flight of the Earls'. It has been pointed out that more realistically, from an Irish viewpoint, it should be 'the Flight of the Princes'. The current Maguire prefers to call it such and says: 'The Flight of the Princes ranks as one of the most important events in Irish history. Its most immediate effect was the clearing of the way for the agrarian settlement known as the Plantation of Ulster which marked the new era and was the most significant evidence of the passing of Gaelic rule.'

Maguire, Prince of Fermanagh, was received with great favour by Pope Paul V, and given a pension by Philip III, King of Spain. He died in Genoa in 1608 a few days after arriving there. His brother Brian had survived him back in Ireland but caused no trouble with the authorities, merely obtaining a grant of land at Tempo, Co. Fermanagh. He was not considered for the succession.

His cousin Conor Ruadh, chieftain of the Lisnaskea branch, came forward again with his claims. Conor Ruadh had supported the English during the war and for this he was granted 6480 acres around Lisnaskea and a pension of £200 for life. Although, technically, there was no Gaelic title to claim, Conor Ruadh was knighted at Whitehall in 1616. When he died in 1625, his son Brian continued in the English Crown's good opinion and was created Lord Maguire, Baron of Enniskillen. He died in 1633 leaving four sons.

His eldest son, another Conor Ruadh (b. 1612), succeeded as Lord Maguire. Following the terms of surrender of the Irish nobility, he had been educated at Magdalen College, Oxford. He had a son, also a Conor. Surprisingly, this Conor Ruadh, for all his English education and the pro-English stance of his father and grandfather, supported the Irish uprising in 1641.

On 20 October 1641 Conor Ruadh set out on horse for Dublin. He had been charged by Phelim O'Neill with seizing Dublin Castle with his men. The attack was to take place on 23 October. He was due to be joined by Rory O'Moore and Hugh MacMahon and their men. However, the plan was betrayed by an Owen Connolly and the three leaders were arrested while in their beds in the early hours of 23 October. They were held in solitary confinement for eight months in Dublin Castle and then sent in chains to the Tower of London. Hugh MacMahon had already been executed a short time before Maguire was put on public trial. Maguire asserted that he was an Irishman and entitled to fight for his country. He was condemned to be hanged, drawn and quartered. On 20 February 1644 he was taken to Tyburn in London and executed.

A witness, Hugh Bourke, Commissary of the Irish Friars Minors in Germany, disguised among the crowd, wrote this account:

> On February 20, 1644, Baron Maguire to whom the executioner would have shown some favour by leaving him to hang on the gallows until he should be quite dead, and meanwhile the executioner was busy kindling the fire with which his entrails were to be burned after his death, but so inhuman were the officers that they totally denied the Baron the services of one of our Fathers on the scaffold and waited not for the executioner but one of them cut the rope with a halberd and let the Baron drop alive and then called the executioner to open him alive and very ill the executioner did it, the said Baron making resistance with his hand and defending himself with such little strength he had; and such was the cruelty that for sheer compassion the executioner bore not to look upon him in such torment and, to have done with him, speedily handled his knife well and cut his throat.

The title of Baron Maguire of Enniskillen was thereby placed under the subject of attainder.

Lord Maguire's brother Ruaidri commanded the Fermanagh contingents during the 1641 insurrection and was able to drive the English out of the area with the exception of the garrison in Enniskillen. Ruaidri was in command of a thousand troops under Eoghan Ruadh O'Neill at the battle of Benburb in 1646. He was regarded as one of the most able of Irish commanders.

In spite of the fact that the title had been forfeited by an act of attainder, Conor, the son of the executed Lord Maguire of Enniskillen, assumed the title as did his son in turn who died without an heir. The grandson of the 1st Baron, Ruaidri (Rory) Maguire, became a supporter of James II, claiming the title of 5th Baron in spite of the attainder of his grandfather. He took a seat in James II's parliament in Dublin and was appointed Lord Lieutenant of Co. Fermanagh in 1689. James II seems to have had no problem in styling Ruaidri as Lord Maguire of Enniskillen. Ruaidri also raised an infantry regiment, fought at the battle of Aughrim and then fought a rearguard action until going into exile in France. He was proclaimed a traitor by William III and died at the Court of St Germain in France in 1708, aged sixty-seven.

His son Alexander Maguire, known as the 6th Baron of Enniskillen, served as a colonel in the French army and died in 1719 without issue. He was succeeded by his uncle, Philip (the 7th Baron), who had married Mary, a daughter of Sir Phelim O'Neill, the leader of the 1641 uprising. His son, Theophilus (the 8th Baron), on succession, married Margaret, the daughter of O'Donel of Tirconnell. Their son, Alexander, the 9th Baron, who had been born in Ireland, became an officer in the Irish Brigade of the French army, serving first in the Duke of Berwick's regiment and then in the regiment of the famous Thomas Lally. The 9th Baron was created a Knight of the Royal French Order of St Louis, retired from the army in 1763 and died in 1801 in France without issue. He left his entire estate to Comte Justin MacCarthy Reagh of Toulouse.

There was now some question as to the successor of the princely line of the Maguires.

A cadet line of Maguires had been founded in Austria in the eighteenth century by John Maguire, born at Ballymacelligott, Co. Kerry. He became a lieutenant-general in the Austrian service in 1751, was awarded the Grand Cross of the Order of Maria Theresa and given the title Graf von Enniskillen. He died in 1767. It was thought this line might have a claim on the title for a while.

In 1834, however, the famous antiquarian, John O'Donovan, while visiting Fermanagh, found a hardware merchant in Enniskillen called Thomas Maguire. He claimed to be not only The Maguire, Prince of Fermanagh, but Baron Enniskillen. O'Donovan wrote cynically to a friend: 'He is a hardware merchant and, like shopkeepers in general, void of patriotic feeling. Indeed it is hard to expect that any man in his situation of life could take any interest in historical research.'

However, Thomas Maguire possessed several things which supported his claims, including the will of the first Lord Maguire of Enniskillen written in the Tower of London in 1644 before his execution. O'Donovan examined the documents and wrote on 18 November 1834 (the letter is held in Linenhall Library, Belfast): 'Thomas Maguire of Enniskillen is now The Maguire, as descending from the brother of Conor, who was created Baron of Enniskillen by Queen Elizabeth.' Apart from the glaring mistake, for the title Baron of Enniskillen was not created by Elizabeth, O'Donovan had traced the line from Brian, the third brother of the first Lord Maguire of Enniskillen. However, more genealogical research would have revealed that the senior line actually descended from another brother, Tomás, who was older than Brian.

The heir male after the 9th Baron was in fact William Maguire (d. 1870), the fifth in descent from Tomás. The family lived in Belfast and had become Protestants. William's father, Daniel Maguire (1760–98), had joined the Lisnaskea Volunteer Company and held the rank of lieutenant. His insignia and belt buckle are still held by the family. He was present at the 'Monster Review' of the Fermanagh Volunteers at Maguiresbridge. Many of the Volunteers, unappeased by the reforms being enacted in the early 1790s, joined the United Irishmen. Daniel Maguire was one of them and was killed during the battle of Antrim on 7 June 1798, when Henry Joy McCracken tried to capture Antrim Town for the republicans.

Daniel's son William, a miniature of whom survives, showing his Maguire flaming red hair which was why so many had the nickname Ruadh, died in 1870. He was succeeded by his grandson Robert who had married a Catholic, Rose Morrison, in 1875. Their younger son, James, was raised a Catholic and educated at St Malachy's College in Belfast. He died in 1937 and his son Anthony succeeded him. Anthony died in 1985, leaving one child, Harriett, who had married Thomas Donal, The MacCarthy Mór, Prince of Desmond, father of the current MacCarthy Mór.

With Anthony's death, his brother Terence James became The Maguire, Prince of Fermanagh and *de jure* 14th Lord Maguire of Enniskillen, in the Jacobite peerage, although it is a title he does not particularly wish to claim. Born in Belfast in 1924, he is also a Knight of the Companionate of Merit of the Military and Hospitaller Order of St Lazarus of Jerusalem as well as holder of the Niadh Nask. His title was given 'courtesy recognition' by the Chief Herald of Ireland in 1990.

The Maguire is a Fellow of the Institute of Chartered Secretaries and Administrators, although now a retired company director. He lives in Dublin but is widely travelled, especially through China, to whose people and culture he admits an attachment. He is patron of the Maguire Clan Society and chairman of the Clan Maguire Trust.

One of his principal interests has been the Maguire Chalices. As kings of Fermanagh, the Maguires were famous for their endowments to churches and they presented precious chalices to many churches and religious communities. One of the earliest that survives dates back to 1493 and is now in the National Museum of Antiquities of Scotland. The inscription reads, in translation, 'Katherine, daughter of Neill, wife of John Maguire, Prince of Fermanagh, caused me to be made in the year of the Lord 1493.' The Maguire has become an expert on his family chalices and has lectured both in Ireland and abroad on the subject as well as being the author of *Historic Maguire Chalices*. The unique chalices bear testimony to the skills of the Irish craftsmen in gold, silver, copper and wood as well as being of monumental importance.

The Maguire is shortly to publish a study on his family history on which he has been working for some time. Married to Patricia Haslam, he has two daughters, Denise and Patricia, and his tanist is a cousin, although previously he gave some thought to the intricacies of female inheritance under Brehon law. He recognises that the old Gaelic title can only be meaningful if passed down under Brehon law and he is conscious that his title should proceed under such laws.

It was The Maguire whose energies created the Standing Council of Irish Chiefs and Chieftains in 1990.

I strongly believe that we should have some say in the future of Ireland, not politically but certainly culturally and economically, as we are, whether we like it or not, the representatives of the Old Gaelic Order and represent a very large number of people world-wide.

He feels that there should be Senate seats available. 'Were I a younger man I would certainly enter politics for that is where the action is.' He continues:

Over the past twelve years or so I have endeavoured to play a cultural role in the Republic. It was my great privilege and honour to call together, for the first time since Kinsale (1601–2), the Irish chiefs (October 5, 1991) at Aras an Uachtaráin [the Irish President's residence]. I have been told by my good friend O'Neill of Clanaboy, that when we formed our Standing Council, after the 'Gathering', it was the 19th Council in our Irish history, the first recorded Council was when the High King Muirchertach Mac Ercae mac Eóghain formed a Council c.AD 515. It was my great honour to have been elected the first chairman of the Standing Council . . .

He is a staunch supporter of efforts to expand a knowledge of Gaelic Ireland and maintains:

The Irish language is of the greatest importance within our culture and I fully support the ideal of a bilingual Irish people . . . at the present our Council is promoting the Irish language through Cork University where it is offering a prize (finance) for an essay in Irish on an Irish event.

Although he is a Catholic, The Maguire is quite firm that 'no church should have a special position within our state, although I recognise that the Catholic Church has played the most prominent role in our Irish history. This Ireland of ours is now, without doubt, a secular state, and it is also evident that the Catholic Church does not hold any special position.'

The Maguire has been one of the most energetic of the generation of chiefs who have attempted to raise awareness among Irish people as to the aspects of their Gaelic history that tend to be overlooked in modern interpretations of that past.

11

The Kingdom of Leinster

The name Leinster derives from the Irish Laighin to which the Norse added *stadr* (place) in the ninth century. Today, it is the second largest of the four provinces of Ireland, encompassing 7850 square miles. It consists of the counties of Carlow, Dublin, Kildare, Kilkenny, Laois, Longford, Louth, Meath, Offaly, Westmeath and Wicklow. However, in its original form, the counties of Meath and Westmeath and parts of Dublin and Offaly were not included. They formed the middle kingdom of Midhe. Leinster occupies the middle and south-eastern portion of the island.

Leinster has two origin stories. One is that it received its name from Laighne Lethan-glas, a Nemedian who settled in Ireland before the sons of Míle Easpain. The second is that it is named after a host of Gaulish Celts who settled there having accompanied the exiled prince, Labraid Loingsech, when he returned home to overthrow his uncle, Cobhthach Caol, in the fourth century BC. The Gauls were said to have used a broad pointed spear called a *laighen* because of its blue-green colour. The story is told in *Orgain Denna Ríg* (Destruction of Dind Ríg). *Lebor na Nua-chonghbhála*, popularly known as the 'Book of Leinster', written at Glendalough about 1150 under the authority of Bishop Fionn Mac Gormain, dates these events to 307 BC.

Like the Uí Néill of the north and the Uí Briúin of Connacht, the royal dynasty of Leinster traces its line back to Eremon, son of Míle Easpain. It was Ughaine Mór, fifty-ninth successor to Míle, listed as king of Ireland *c.* 331 BC but given a rather fanciful and anachronistic reputation by medieval storytellers, who was the grandfather of Labraid Loingsech.

The royal dynasty of Leinster became known as the Uí Cheinnselaig from Énna Cennsalach, listed as ninety-second in descent from Míle

Easpain, whose son Crimthann (d. AD 483) was, therefore, the first of the Uí Cheinnselaig. The genealogies of the family in written form survive from the beginning of the seventh century with no fewer than three *forsundud* or genealogical praise poems written under the patronage of the Leinster kings.

From earliest times there were two main royal residences in Leinster. Most famous is the fourteen-acre site of the hill-fort of Dún Ailinne, Hill of Allen, near Kilcullen, Co. Kildare. This appears in the stories of the Fianna, the bodyguards of the High King, and their leader Fionn mac Cumhail. The stories relate that Fionn's father, Cumal, was leader of the Clanna Baoiscne and a king of Leinster. The second royal site is Dind Ríg, on the banks of the Barrow, Co. Carlow, associated with the story of Labraid Loingsech. However, the Uí Cheinnselaig dynasty made their court at the site of the alder trees (Fearna), now called Ferns.

Every Irish child, if they have heard of only one Irish king, will probably name Dermot MacMorrough of Hy Kinsella (Diarmuid Mac Murchadha Uí Cheinnselaig), King of Leinster and the Foreigners. 'Putrid while living, damned when dead' is the popular description. It was he who, being driven from his kingdom by the O'Conors and O'Ruaircs, travelled to France in search of the Angevin emperor, Henry II, and secured what he fondly thought was mercenary help from the Norman barons to win back his kingdom. He thereby precipitated the Norman invasion of Ireland.

Few other Irish kings are so reviled or have had so much written about them. While one cannot argue with the results of his action, the more one examines the reasons behind Dermot's invitation to the Normans, the more one can sympathise with him. His story has been exceptionally and sympathetically told by Nicholas Furlong.

Dermot was born in 1110, the third son of the then king of Leinster, Donnchadh Mac Murchadha (MacMorrough). His father and one of his brothers died in battle in 1115 while the other, Énna Mac Murchadha, became king of Leinster but died unexpectedly in Wexford in 1126.

Dermot MacMorrough had barely reached the age of choice when his *derbhfine* gathered at the royal residence at Ferns and he was elected king. It has been argued that he was only sixteen but the Brehon law regarding the age of choice, *aimsir togu*, was strict. No one could hold any office or inherit unless they were of age. Furlong believes that Dermot has been overly vilified. His achievements are forgotten, his patronage of the arts and his political acumen have all been subsumed by his reputation as the first great Irish traitor who betrayed his country to a ruthless foreign enemy. However, it has to be pointed out that he did live with two wives simultaneously, was responsible for the rape of an abbess and eloped with the wife of Tigernán Ó Ruairc, King of Breifne.

Dermot's kingdom had been under threat for nearly a century from the centralising ideas of the O'Brien High Kings and then from the O'Conors. Their aggressive policies had made the Leinster kings turn to military alliances, not only with other Irish kingdoms but with the Danes; the latter resulted in the battle at Clontarf in 1014.

In order to protect the kingdom, which had been raided by the O'Conor High King and his allies, Dermot left Ireland in order to seek military aid from the Normans. We have seen in Chapter 1 how he persuaded Strongbow to invade. In 1170 Strongbow captured Waterford and married Dermot's daughter Aoife. Dermot died at Ferns in 1171, according to the *Annals of the Four Masters*, 'without a will, without penance, without unction, as his evil deeds deserved.'

Henry II, realising his liege men were now doing rather well in Ireland, arrived with his own army on 17 October 1171 in Waterford. Henry received the submission of Strongbow at Waterford, who assured him of his continued oath of fealty, and so was promptly granted the lordship of the kingdom of Leinster, with the exception of Dublin, Wexford and Waterford and a coastal strip south of Dublin to Arklow. The rightful king of Leinster, Domhnall Caermanach (1171–75) was already in arms against Strongbow and the Normans. So was the High King, Ruaidri Ua Conchobhair. Henry spent the next six months campaigning in Ireland and thus laid the foundations of what became English rule there and the start of over eight hundred years of conflict between Ireland and England.

Leinster was the first of the Irish kingdoms to fall to Norman domination. In spite of the aspiration of their motto '*Siothcháin agus Fairsinge*' (Peace and Plenty) the Leinster kings fought on against the conquerors. Domhnall was slain in 1175. Over a hundred years later, in 1281, a successor, King Mortough MacMorrough Kavanagh, was slain at Arklow. Little had changed in that time. It seems incredible, but in spite of the Normans' early conquest and occupation, as well as the proximity of the Anglo-Norman colonies which occupied several towns in the former kingdom, the MacMorrough Kavanagh kings survived and managed to maintain the allegiance of their people in the war against the Normans. Norman influence remained confined mainly to the port towns.

By the start of the fourteenth century the entire kingdom of Leinster had seen a revival of its fortunes and many of the old Norman barons, who had settled on estates there, families such as de Clare, de Valence and Bigod, had become extinct or moved off. In 1324 Donall Mac Art MacMorrough had been elected king of Leinster and installed to the acclaim of the entire kingdom. He was eventually captured and imprisoned in Dublin Castle, escaped but was slain in 1347.

One successful Leinster king at this time was Art Mór Mac Airt (1375–1417) who is recorded as restoring the fortunes of the kingdom on a scale not unworthy of its pre-Norman days. Art even had annual tribute paid to him by the English colonists. Irish writers extolled King Art as courageous, liberal and hospitable. He married a Norman, Elizabeth Veele, whose estates were then seized by the English who claimed that she had forfeited them by her marriage.

Richard II was said to have concluded an agreement with King Art in 1395 restoring his wife's lands and conferring a knighthood on him. However, the breaking of the agreement by Richard's administrators saw Art start hostilities against the English. In 1399 Richard II arrived back in Ireland with an army. Jean Creton witnessed a meeting between Richard II's emissary, the Earl of Gloucester, and King Art.[1] He describes him as a fine, large man, marvellously agile, stern and riding on a very swift horse of great value. The discourse lasted some time and led to no agreement. Gloucester demanded Art's surrender to Richard II to which he is reported to have replied: 'I am a rightful king in Ireland, and it is unjust to deprive me of what is my land, by conquest.' In fact, King Art demanded that Richard II withdraw from his kingdom.

Richard had apparently paled with anger on hearing King Art's response and offered a hundred marks for the Irish king alive or dead. He swore that he would burn him out of his woods. King Art conducted a war of attrition on the English and, being a good general, refused to enter a major battle on unfavourable conditions. Frustrated, and marching back to Waterford, unable to counter the guerrilla tactics of the Irish king, Richard II found grim news awaiting him. His rival, Henry Bolingbroke, Duke of Derby had returned from exile and raised a rebellion against him. Richard II, regarded as the last of the Plantagenet kings of England, sailed home on 13 August 1399, only to surrender to Henry six days later at Flint. After an imprisonment in the Tower of London, he abdicated and Bolingbroke became Henry IV, the first king of the house of Lancaster. Richard is said to have met his death by starvation at Pontefract Castle, in Yorkshire.

King Art now entered into negotiations with the new English king. Sir John Stanley was appointed Lord Deputy in Ireland. Stanley was so great a favourite with Henry IV that he rose to become 'King' of a Gaelic kingdom himself. In 1405 Henry gave him the Isle of Man: 'Sir John Stanley, King of Mann and the Isles and by the best of the Commons of the Isle of Mann.' The Stanley dynasty lasted, with a few interruptions, until the kingship, which had been changed into a lordship during Henry

VIII's time, was sold to the English Crown in 1765. In March 1400, however, John Stanley reported to his master that King Art was 'the most dreaded enemy of the English in Leinster'. King Art was so influential that Owain Glyn Dŵr (Owen Glendower), trying to restore an independent Welsh kingdom, wrote to King Art for aid. Glendower's independent Wales finally collapsed the year before King Art died in 1417.

As Edmund Curtis observes of the kingdom of Leinster:

> . . . all the country went back to the old race. It was made clear how fatally the Normans had erred in taking over only the richer lands for settlement, and in leaving vast tracts of the hinterland to the Irish, from which in due time they emerged triumphantly.

'The MacMorrough Menace', as the English called the independently minded kings of Leinster, was giving such a check to the plans of the colonists that it was felt something had to be done. Sir John de Grey decided that Donnchadh mac Airt Mhóir MacMorrough, who had been a hostage of the English, should be returned and set up as king 'on certain terms'. But within a year after his release Donnchadh was in arms against England raiding and exacting tribute. King Henry IV finally signed a treaty with him, agreeing to pay Donnchadh an annual tribute of eighty marks for the land under English occupation.

In spite of its proximity both to the ports of access from England, Waterford and Wexford, and to the Dublin Pale, as well as the consideration that Leinster was the first kingdom in which the Normans settled, the Leinster kings held their kingdom until 1603. There seems no record of surrenders until the reign of Caothaoir Mac Airt who became king of Leinster in 1547. He is recorded as initially being in the forefront of the war against the new Tudor administration. Letters patent show that many of his followers did surrender and received pardons before the king himself. It is a point of interest that Caothaoir was married to Alicia, daughter of Gerald Óg FitzGerald, 9th Earl of Kildare, who had been Lord Deputy but died in the Tower of London in 1534 suspected of treason. On 8 February 1553, during the reign of Edward VI, Caothaoir Mac Airt of Leinster came forward and surrendered his kingdom. All he received in return was a barony. He was to be Baron of Ballyanne (Ballian according to the Fiant) in Wexford.

The records of succession show that Caothaoir was regarded as king of Leinster for less than a year after his surrender. He was deposed or abdicated, and in 1558 his son Dermot was claiming to be the new Baron Ballyanne by application to Philip and Mary while another son Morrough, called Morgan, was claiming to have succeeded his father as the Baron of

'Conellelyn' (Coolnaleen, Co. Wexford). Morrough and another brother, 'Keant' Kavanagh, had been imprisoned as hostages for Caothaoir's good behaviour at the time he had surrendered. It was yet another son, Bryan, who is recorded as succeeding his father as head of this branch of the family, although, significantly not as king of Leinster, and rising up against the English.

Murchadh Mac Muiris Kavanagh of Coolnaleen, Co. Wexford, appears as successor to Caothaoir as king of Leinster. There was some confusion as to whether Murchadh was Caothaoir's son, for he is described as *Mac Muiris* (son of Muiris). Yet we are told that he became Baron of Coolnaleen in 1554, the year of his accession to the throne. This is the same title as the one applied for by Morrough, Caothaoir's son, as belonging to his father. Have the English bureaucrats merely confused the matter in their records through lack of knowledge of Irish and Irish patronymics?

I believe we are talking about two different people because the letters patent refer to Murchadh Mac Muiris's family as of 'the sept and company of Donell Reagh Cavanagh' who was his grandfather. Murchadh Mac Muiris, having been regarded as king of Leinster between 1554 and 1557, was deposed or abdicated, and died in November 1622. Did the fact that he accepted the title of Baron of Coolnaleen cause his *derbhfine* to depose him?

In 1557, the son of Murchadh Mac Muiris, Criomthann, Anglicised as Crephon in English records, became king of Leinster. Criomthann is listed as king of Leinster until 1582. It becomes significant that, in 1581, several pardons were issued for 'Crephon m'Mortagh Kavanagh's people'. On 23 July, Criomthann was deemed to be principal captain 'of the sept and company of Donell Reogh Cavanagh . . . with power upon warning from the seneschal or sheriff of Co. Wexford, to assemble the gentlemen and freeholders of the sept and all others inhabiting their countries, and to govern them according to the laws of the realm'.

There is no record of any further Leinster kings until the start of Aodh Ruadh O'Neill's attempt to drive out the English in 1595. Domhnall Spáinneach Mac Donnchadha, whose name indicated that he had been in exile in Spain, was accepted as king. Domhnall is listed as a grandson of Caothaoir Mac Airt which would appear to mean that he married his first cousin Elinor, daughter of his uncle Brian Mac Caothaoir. Domhnall commanded the Leinster men, fighting against Elizabeth's forces, but after the defeat at Kinsale and surrender of O'Neill, he accepted that his situation was untenable. In 1603 he abdicated his kingship, significantly refusing to surrender his title on behalf of his heirs and successors nor abandon his royal prerogatives, demonstrating that he acknowledged he could not do so under Brehon law. He retired with his wife to Clonmullen where his death was recorded in 1632.

I
THE MACMORROUGH KAVANAGH,
Prince of Leinster
(Mac Murchadha Caomhánach)

The current MacMorrough Kavanagh, Prince of Leinster, succeeded his father in 1962 at the age of twenty-two and is now a retired oil engineer dividing his time between his house in Florida, United States, and another in Pembroke, Wales. He is planning to move to Ireland shortly. His line stems from a younger son of Morgan Kavanagh, The MacMorrough Kavanagh of Borris (1668–1720). This was Hervey Kavanagh of Bally-hale, Co. Kilkenny (d. 1740).

The line of the MacMorrough Kavanagh princes of Leinster had descended through Brian, the son of Caothaoir Mac Airt, who became known as The MacMorrough of Borris and Poulmonty. His eldest son was Morgan MacBryan Kavanagh (1566–1636) who married a daughter of Lord Mountgarret, thus making sure he had a good political link with the new colonial order.

The line proceeded by senior son inheritance.

Thomas Kavanagh, The MacMorrough of Borris (1767–99) became Member of Parliament for Kilkenny City and subsequently for Carlow, in the Irish parliament just before the Union of Ireland with the United Kingdom of Great Britain.

A later generation of the family also entered politics in the person of Arthur Kavanagh, The MacMorrough of Borris (1831–89). He was born without arms and legs, only rudimentary stumps, but he showed great resolution in his youth and learnt to ride, shoot, fish and become a fair painter, using his stumps with extraordinary dexterity. He rode to hounds strapped to a chair saddle and even took fences in his stride. His eldest brother, Thomas, was his companion in travels to India, Russia and Persia, and he took part in a tiger hunt.

Returning to Ireland in 1853 he succeeded Thomas, who had died in Australia, to the family estates and to the title. He married his cousin, Frances Mary Forde-Leathley. He was energetic and rebuilt the villages of Borris and Ballyragget and subsidised the local railway from Borris to Bagenalstown. Although the family were by now firmly Anglican in religion and he opposed the disestablishment of the Church of Ireland, he had the New Ross poorhouse provided with a Catholic chapel, the first of its kind in Ireland.

He became High Sheriff of Co. Kilkenny in 1856 and of Co. Carlow in 1857 and was a Unionist Member of Parliament for Co. Wexford in 1866–68 and for Co. Carlow in 1868–80. He was made a Privy Councillor for Ireland in 1886. Surprisingly, he supported the Land Act of 1870 which showed him out of step with most Unionists and Conservatives. He was, of course, a Justice of the Peace. As an enthusiastic and experienced yachtsman he sailed his own yacht and in 1865 he published *The Cruise of the RYS Evan*, an account of a cruise along the Albanian coast. He died at his London town house in Chelsea in 1889 and his body was returned to Borris for burial.

He had several children, his third son being General Sir Toler Mac-Morrough (1864–1950) who served in the British army during the second South African War (1899–1902), in which he won the Distinguished Service Order. For services in World War I, he was knighted twice and received several foreign awards. It was his elder brother, the Rt. Hon. Walter MacMorrough Kavanagh (1856–1922), who took the title. He had been educated at Eton and Christ Church, Oxford, and took a commission in the 5th Battalion of the Royal Irish Rifles. He left the army as a captain and followed his father into politics but as a Liberal. He was High Sheriff of Co. Kilkenny in 1884 and Co. Wexford in 1893, and a Justice of the Peace. He became Member of Parliament for Carlow in 1908–10. He was also appointed a Privy Councillor. In 1917 he became the representative for Carlow County Council, sitting as a Nationalist, in the Irish Convention of 1917–18. He died in July 1922, as Ireland struggled towards independent statehood.

His son, Major Arthur MacMorrough Kavanagh (1888–1953), became The MacMorrough of Borris. Educated at Eton and Sandhurst, he was commissioned in the 7th Queen's Own Hussars and won the Military Cross. Major Arthur MacMorrough of Borris died without male issue but with four daughters. The eldest daughter Joane, born in 1915, married twice. Her first marriage was to Gerald, Marquess of Kildare, and only child of the 7th Duke of Leinster, by whom she had issue. The marriage was dissolved in 1946. Her second marriage was to Lieutenant-Colonel Archibald Macalpine-Downie of Appin. Her son by this marriage, Archibald Macalpine-Downie, became a jockey. He assumed the name Mac-Morrough Kavanagh by deed poll, and settled at the family estate at Borris. When his grandfather died on 3 December 1953, he could not, of course, succeed to the title either in Brehon law or in English law.

When Major Arthur MacMorrough Kavanagh's title had been recognised, his heir was given as his brother Sir Dermot. With Irish independence there came another of those ironies that beset Irish history. The lineal descendant of the kings of the first Irish kingdom to be invaded and occupied, Colonel Sir Dermot MacMorrough, became Equerry to George VI of England, Crown Equerry and Extra Equerry to Elizabeth II. He died in 1958.

The title, as the family followed inheritance by the senior male heir, technically passed to Sir Dermot between December 1953 and the time of his own death on 27 May 1958. Sir Dermot made no claims and his only child was a daughter. The next senior branch of the family had already applied to the Chief Herald of Ireland to have their pedigree confirmed.

This was the Ballyhale line started by Hervey Kavanagh, the son of Morgan, The MacMorrough Kavanagh (b. 1688) and his second wife. Hervey (d. 1740) had a son Morgan Kavanagh of Ballyhale (d. 1817) who had married Lady Frances Butler and the name Butler has subsequently occurred as a name in the family. In 1875 Morgan Butler Kavanagh (1845–82) married Katie Shine. Their son Morgan Butler Kavanagh (1876–1919) was born in Dublin and educated at Clongowes Wood College, Co. Kildare. Aged twenty, he decided to go to Australia but eventually settled in India as a journalist. His income was apparently augmented by a private allowance from his family. He married in Melbourne in 1906. With the threat of war, he returned to Ireland via the United States where, in February 1914, his son William Butler Kavanagh was born in Springfield, Massachusetts. During 1914–1918 Morgan served in the British forces. After the war, he returned to India and died shortly after arriving in 1919.

William's mother was Isabella McKenzie Young, and she and her five-year-old son went to her family's native Scotland to live. William was educated in St Andrews University and became a chartered civil engineer, finally settling in Pembroke in South Wales. He became Pembroke Borough Surveyor and in 1939 married Elise Addis. After the death of his cousin Arthur in 1953, and knowing that Arthur's brother Sir Dermot was elderly and without male heirs, William decided to submit his claim to be MacMorrough Kavanagh to Gerard Slevin, Chief Herald of Ireland.

Following the death of Sir Dermot in 1958, the Chief Herald formally confirmed William's pedigree and gave 'courtesy recognition' to him as MacMorrough Kavanagh, with the right to own and use his arms, on 2 January 1959.

William died in 1962 and was succeeded by his son, also William Butler Kavanagh. He had been born on 9 February 1944, in Pembroke, and educated locally, attending Shenstone College before entering the oil industry. He married Margaret Phillips, and his sons are Simon (b. 1967) and William (b. 1974). Simon, who has been appointed his tanist, is also a professional engineer following a career in the oil industry. William retired from the oil business and divides his time between Florida and Wales. With his sons, who are learning Irish, he is working on a book on the family history. The MacMorrough Kavanagh, his tanist and his younger son are Niadh Nask.

We saw in Chapter 6 how the Genealogical Office took forty years to place the family's name on the Register of Chiefs. It was not until 1998 that the Chief Herald eventually agreed to remedy the matter, although without explaining or apologising for the situation which had been allowed to develop. In January 1999 The MacMorrough Kavanagh applied to join the Standing Council of Irish Chiefs and Chieftains.

The MacMorrough Kavanagh admits that his family's claim to the title is based on being the senior surviving line of the royal house but he is aware that Brehon law does not exclude such a claim. He admits that his knowledge of international law is insufficient to take any authoritative stand on the matter.

It seems that the recognition of chiefship accorded in Brehon law may also be interpreted within European law. Therefore this allows for a chiefship to be recognised from the senior line of a family, by the senior member or members of that family. It is my present understanding that within my family, recognition of my own chiefship, as successor to my father, gains recognition on this basis.

With his sons learning Irish, and plans to relocate his main residence to Ireland, and applications underway for Irish passports, The MacMorrough Kavanagh is keen to play a full part as a member of the old Gaelic aristocracy:

Having been brought up in Wales, where the issue of language is an important facet in the cultural identity of the people, I can entirely sympathise with the problems encountered in Ireland today when trying to promote the use of the Gaelic language in daily life. Although English has become the international language used between nations to communicate, the identity of a nation may be more fully expressed within its own language. My sons are endeavouring to learn the Irish language, partly as an aid to their studies, but also the more they learn about their own history, the more determined they are to participate in its future. Language has its part to play in their endeavours, as they wish to spend an increasing amount of time in Ireland pursuing their studies.

In is only during the past year that The MacMorrough Kavanagh has started to become interested in gaining a higher profile for his dynasty and working with other surviving members of the Irish aristocracy. He had previously been disillusioned by the problems encountered at the Genealogical Office, but the recent acceptance of his existence has given him and his family impetus to become more involved.

'It is my hope that with the recognition of The MacMorrough Kavanagh and the ancient royal house of Leinster . . . we may then act as a catalyst for others with similar interests.' Those interests, he stresses, are to take any opportunity that allows the promotion of the culture and heritage of Ireland. 'I have always endeavoured to promote the cultural and historical background through which the chiefs hold their titles and will continue to do so.'

II
THE O'MORCHOE
of Oulartleigh and Monamolin
(Ó Morchoe)

This cadet line of the princely house of the royal dynasty of the Uí Cheinnselaig takes its name from Murchadha, as does Morrough, but in this instance it is Anglicised as Murphy. It is generally thought that the branch started out from the descendants of Morrough, a brother of King Dermot MacMorrough. However, Alfred Smyth, in *Celtic Leinster*, believes that the split goes further back to the Murchadha who was a grandson of Fedlimid son of Énna Cennselach; his branch became the Uí Felmeda which appears, in some annals, as the original designation of O'Morchoe chieftains in the sixteenth century.

The 9th Earl of Kildare, when Lord Deputy in 1518, demanded taxes from 'The M'Morrow country at Oulartleigh' (the name comes from *abhallort*, an apple orchard). On 10 May 1536 Donal Mór O'Morchoe of Oulartleigh entered into an agreement with the Lord Deputy, Leonard Grey, that he would hold his country with feudal dues to Henry VIII if the English king maintained him in his 'lordship'. In keeping with the surrender agreements, Donal O'Morchoe changed his name to the Anglicised form of Daniel Murphy and adopted the Anglican religion. This was even before the demands for the surrender of Gaelic titles in 1541. 'Daniel Murphy' and his descendants lived quietly at Oulartleigh but when the English administration were sorting out what they called 'defective titles' in 1618, Brian Murphy (O'Morchoe) was made to agree to a deed of entail and the lands went to his son in trust. However, all the lands were forfeited because of the family's participation in the 1641 Irish uprising.

In more liberal times in the late nineteenth century Arthur Mac-Murrough Murphy (1835–1918) decided to assert the title abolished by English law over four hundred years previously and call himself O'Morchoe of Oulartleigh. Indeed, the family in 1892 commissioned H. Farnham Burke, Somerset Herald, to draw up their pedigree

Arthur's eldest son, Reverend Thomas Arthur MacMurrough Murphy (1864–1921), a graduate of Trinity College, Dublin, went further than his father, resuming the surname of O'Morchoe by deed poll in 1895. He was an Anglican minister and rector of Kilternan, Co. Dublin. He was fascinated by historical issues and became a member of the Royal Society of Antiquaries of Ireland and the Royal Dublin Society, served on the Dublin County Committee of Agriculture and Technical Instruction, and was on the Board of Education as well as being a member of the General Synod of the Church of Ireland.

He seemed confused between his enthusiasm to re-establish the use of Gaelic titles, including his own, and his loyalty to the English Crown. In 1904 he published a booklet, *The Succession of the Chiefs of Ireland*. In this he argued eloquently for the English Crown to recognise the old Gaelic titles. But he was not knowledgeable about Brehon law and thought tanistry was merely a transitional stage between election by the *derbhfine* and primogeniture descent. He also believed that the Tudor policy was not to *abolish* Gaelic titles, in spite of the evidence to the contrary. For entirely the wrong reasons, he argued:

> That the representatives of the former Chiefs at the present day are justified and within their rights in assuming the titles of their ancestors is supported by the numerous precedents quoted, in which the Crown [of England] recognises the titles of native nobility in countries which have come under British rule.

He referred to an official list from 1515 of the Irish nobles and their titles as a list of the 'Chief Captains of Ireland'. This roll, he felt, was a starting point for gathering evidence to judge claims. He believed a list of chiefs should be drawn up and registered in the office of the Ulster King of Arms.

> Once the right to the use of titles shall have been determined by the official act of the Crown, it becomes only a question of the proof of

the claimant's pedigree that he is the lineal male representative of the last recognised Chief. To determine the right to the use of the titles rests with the Crown as the Fountain of Honour; and although the titles have been recognised by courtesy at the Royal and Viceregal Courts, yet the absence of any official act either to determine the right to their use or to accord them a definite precedent, as in the cause of the Maltese Nobles, leaves the matter in an unsatisfactory state, which only the Crown can settle.

When he died on 18 November 1921, he had seen that the English Crown was already becoming a matter of little importance in most of the country.

His eldest son Arthur, b. 1892, educated at St Andrew's College, Dublin, and Trinity College, Dublin, joined the Leinster Regiment in 1914, serving as aide-de-camp to Major-General the Hon. Edward Montagu Stewart Wortley. He held various military posts, ending his career as Commissioner of Police on the Gold Coast in 1934. He served on the British General Staff at the War Office in 1940. He died in 1966 and was succeeded by his brother.

Nial Creagh O'Morchoe (1895–1970) was also educated at St Andrew's College and was commissioned into the Leinster Regiment in 1914. Mentioned in dispatches and then serving in India, Colonel O'Morchoe commanded the 4th Battalion of the 15th Punjab Regiment from 1939 to 1941. He served in Iraq, Persia and India until 1946 and retired in 1947. He married Jesse Elizabeth Joly, the daughter of Charles Jasper Joly, the Astronomer Royal of Ireland. He died in 1970, leaving two sons.

The current O'Morchoe, David Niall Creagh O'Morchoe (b. 17 May 1928), the elder son, followed the military tradition of his immediate family. He is a former major-general of the British army. Commissioned in the Royal Irish Fusiliers in 1948, having been educated in St Columba's College, Dublin, and the Royal Military Academy of Sandhurst, he commanded the 1st Battalion of the regiment 1967/8 and saw service in the Middle East, north-west Europe, Kenya and Oman. He was Director of Staff at the Camberley Staff College in 1969 and the Royal College of Defence Studies in 1972. He commanded the Sultan of Oman's Land Forces, retiring in 1979 with an MBE and CB. He is now a farmer in Co. Wexford, his ancestral territory.

Married to Margaret Jane Brewitt of Cork, he has two sons and two daughters. His heir is Dermot Arthur, born on 11 August 1956, who was also educated at St Columba's College; he is a horticulturist.

The current O'Morchoe sees the holding of an old Gaelic title 'as important solely as being of great historic interest. The rest of Ireland is so ignorant and ill-educated about the current chiefs that I think that the idea of representation in the Senate or other state bodies would be a non-starter and not understood. Collectively we have no political role, particularly as there are so few of us who are able to trace our ancestry to the days when chiefs had power.'

He sees his role as a chief as being to create an interest in Gaelic heritage, and supports the teaching of Irish. He learnt the Irish language at school and hopes that his grandchildren will continue to speak it. He supports various cultural activities.

As a member of the Church of Ireland he does not agree with the state giving special recognition to one particular religious denomination.

He has been chairman of the Standing Council of Chiefs and Chieftains, taking over from Maguire, Prince of Fermanagh, from 1994 to 1998.

III

THE FOX
(An Sionnach)

Douglas John Fox runs a delicatessen shop in Mildura, Victoria, Australia. The surname has an English appearance and, as such, excites little attention or interest among the majority of his customers. Very few of them realise that he is entitled to be called The Fox, Chief of the Name, nor that he is given 'courtesy recognition' by the Chief Herald of Ireland as heir male and direct descendant of a line of princes and petty kings whose genealogies claim to go back to Eremon, son of Míle Easpain, a thousand years before Christ. Even if one finds the pre-Christian genealogies unreliable, Douglas Fox is still a direct descendant of Niall of the Nine Hostages.

It should be pointed out, of course, that not all Irish Foxes are descendants from the family who took the nickname Sionnach (Fox) as their surname in the eleventh century. Many who bear the surname Fox are of English settler families, so care has to be taken with lineage. When the name Sionnach was translated to its English equivalent Fox in the sixteenth century, it may be said that the princely family, in spite of their ancient Gaelic lineage, quickly accepted the conquest, changing their religion, language and name to become part of the New English Order in Ireland. The Foxes have the unenviable place in Irish history as the first Gaelic nobles that we know of to completely Anglicise themselves.

Yet there is no questioning the ancient Gaelic pedigree of The Fox.

Niall Naoi-Ghiallach was the eponymous ancestor of the Uí Néill, the family which was to dominate in many of the kingdoms of Ireland. Ancient Irish literature gives a detailed, although accepted as mythological, account of his career.

Of Niall's sons, Maine established one of the southern Uí Néill dynasties. He is recorded as dying in AD 440 having founded the kingship of Tethbae (sometimes Anglicised as Teffia), a territory covering modern Co. Longford and Co. Westmeath.

The descendants of Maine are referred to until after the Norman invasion as 'kings of Tethbae'. Sometime before the eleventh century, the dynasty took as their surname Ó Catharnaigh (O'Kearney or Carney), from one of the kings of Tethbae named Catharnaigh. In 1084 the annals record that Tadhg Ó Catharnaigh was nicknamed An Sionnach (The Fox) because of his wily ways. He was killed with one of his sons that year by King Maelseachlin Ó Melaghlin in a battle, and thereafter his descendants added the nickname as a patronymic. An Sionnach became chief of the Clann Catharnaigh.

The influence of the family as providing kings of Tethbae eventually waned. Tairrdelbach Ua Conchobhair, the High King, partitioned the kingdom in 1140, giving Westmeath to Donogh MacMorrough Ó Melaghlin and East Meath to Tigernán Ó Ruairc of Breifne. Nevertheless, we find the annalists and chroniclers still referring to An Sionnach as 'kings of Tethbae' as late as 1234 when Néill An Sionnach was reported killed in a skirmish. In 1400 Donogh An Sionnach was referred to as 'lord of the country of Moyntir, and by right prince of the country of Tethbae'.

By 1526 there was another change. An Sionnach, who had been fairly independent princes, were now referred to as merely chiefs. They and their followers were seen as vassals to The Mac Eochagáin (MacEgan). From rulers of a petty kingdom they had been reduced to princes and then to lords of a small clan territory, known as 'the country of An Sionnach', which was centred in the barony of Kilcoursey.

In 1541, it appears that An Sionnach and his clan initially resisted the conquest. On 13 June 1558 Sir Henry Radcliffe was given a commission to enter into negotiation with The Fox, as the English now called An Sionnach, translating the name rather than merely Anglicising it as happened elsewhere. The commission also gave Sir Henry permission to accept his surrender and, if he did not do so, to 'punish with fire and sword'.

On 1 April 1559 the Tudor administration in Ireland granted a pardon to Brassell (Breasail) Shennaghe (An Sionnach) 'alias The Fox', 'chief of his nation', and his wife, sons and members of his clan. On 8 November 1565 they were granted 'English liberties'. Breasail's pardon was further confirmed on 8 October 1567. From now on, the title An Sionnach was dropped and the English translation The Fox was always used. The original name still appears, however, in the motto of the arms of the family, '*Sionnach Aboo!*' (The Fox For Ever!).

On 26 June 1591, with the English conquests continuing, we find the administration issuing a grant to Hubert Fox *Gentleman* as seneschal of Fox's County called 'Mointerragan' in King's County (Co. Offaly) 'to hold during good behaviour'. On 1 March 1599 Hubert Fox of Lehinch, in the barony of Kilcoursey, King's County, surrendered all manors and baronies to the Tudor administration. On 4 April 1600, under a letter patent of 29 January, a portion of lands was regranted back to Hubert as 'seneschal' and he was allowed to hold a monthly court baron and a court leet twice a year. By the same letter, Hubert was granted a pension of five shillings sterling a day for life. This was an extraordinary sum for the period and one wonders what exactly Hubert had done to earn it from the conquerors.

Hubert, The Fox, was succeeded by his nephew but he died within a few months. Against the background of the wars, there is, alas, no record of where and how these members of the Fox family met their deaths. The succession went to Brassil (d. 1629) and he was succeeded by Hubert of Kilcoursey. This Hubert appears as a supporter of the Irish uprising in 1641 and the establishment of the Irish Confederate Parliament in Kilkenny. With the reconquest by England, the great part of his estates granted during the Tudor conquests was confiscated and given to the Earl of Cavan.

From now on The Fox became a title secretly passed down within the family. The family had become Irish Protestant petty gentry who produced doctors, army officers, even an inspector of the Royal Irish Constabulary, and whose daughters tended to marry regularly into the Anglican clergy.

The Reverend Matthew Maine Fox, the rector of Galtrim, Co. Meath, was the eldest son of James Fox, The Fox of Foxbrooke and Galtrim House, Co. Meath (1773–1850). He was succeeded by his grandson James George Hubert as The Fox (1842–1919). James George Hubert began his career as an officer in the 5th Royal Irish Lancers. He became a Justice of the Peace for Co. Tipperary and his first marriage was to the daughter of the Anglican rector of Rathconrath, Co. Westmeath. His second wife was the daughter of George Ogle Moore, Member of Parliament for the City of Dublin. His eldest son Brabazon Hubert Maine (1868) succeeded to the title in 1930 on his father's death. Brabazon was a major in the Royal Irish Rifles. He married the daughter of Colonel William Le Mottée of Fermoy, Co. Cork, and his son was Niall Arthur Hubert Fox (b. 1897). Niall succeeded to the title and died in 1959 in Cork without issue.

In tracing the next in line to the title, the family went back to James Fox, The Fox of Foxbrooke and Galtrim House. His third son James D'Arcy had married Sara Tarrant of Mallow, Co. Cork, in 1835 and emigrated to New Zealand in 1863. When he died in 1876, he left a son named Brassil (1844–1913) who settled in New South Wales, Australia. His son James George (1873–1957) married, and it was his third son who now aspired to the title The Fox.

With the death of Niall Arthur Hubert Fox, the seat of The Fox changed to Koorlong, Victoria, Australia, when John William Fox succeeded to the title. John was a poultry farmer, born in Tempy and educated at Gipson State School. He was born on 22 August 1916, married Margaret Frances Wilson in 1939 and had five children, a daughter and four sons.

Today, John, of course, is elderly, and, since the death of his wife in 1997, takes no interest in his ancestral heritage. It was therefore decided, early in 1998, that the family resort to the Brehon way of doing things and with the approval of the family (*derbhfine*), John's eldest son and tanist, Douglas John, born on 23 August 1942, assumed the title and duties of The Fox. Douglas was born in Mildura and went to St Joseph's College there. The family is Catholic, a strange twist as the Irish branch had become Anglican in Tudor times. The Foxes changed back to Catholics through the influence of their distaff side. Douglas is married to Marjorie Adeline and has four children; his son Garry John (b. 1964) became tanist.

Douglas John is a small businessman, running his delicatessen shop in Mildura, and does not seem overly enthusiastic about his role as a lineal heir to the Gaelic title he holds. The new Fox freely admits that he has little knowledge of matters Irish although he 'would like to see the preservation of the Irish language'. The Fox and his family are decidedly Australian and are happy to be so. Neither his father, John William, nor Douglas John has ever attempted to take his seat on the Standing Council of Irish Chiefs and Chieftains.

In fact, Douglas John admits, they have never visited Ireland nor is he involved in any Irish cultural endeavours in Australia. However, he does feel that, as the bearer of an Irish title, he would like to hold an Irish passport if the law allowed it; and, business concerns willing, he would like to make a trip to the land of his origins. At the same time, he seems not to be impressed by the 'courtesy recognition' of his title by the Chief

Herald of Ireland, nor by the fact that his banner hangs in the Heraldic Museum in Dublin, nor, indeed, that the ancient genealogies of Ireland give him a generation by generation lineage back to Adam! The concerns of the current holder of the title The Fox, sometime kings and princes of Tethbae, are running his 'deli' in Mildura and the welfare of his immediate Australian family rather than the wider concerns of his Irish clan.

PART THREE

Rank and Merit

12

Gaelic Knights

'There is merit without rank but there is no rank without some merit,' wrote the Duc François de la Rochefoucauld in 1665. It is an observation that most of the kings of Ireland would have agreed with. The Brehon law of succession clearly places merit before heredity. A king, even a minor chief, had to merit his position by his ability and did not take office purely because he was the eldest son of his father. Similarly, the kings and nobles were the patrons of the arts and learning. An *ollamh* was treated as of princely rank. An *ollamh* of law or poetry was even considered the equal of a king at the court; he, or she, for both were equal under the law, could speak before the king at a council and give their advice. They could cross boundaries from one kingdom to another and command respect wherever they were. This high status reflects the preoccupation of Gaelic society with merit and the honour which must be accorded to it.

In ancient Irish society each person had an honour price, and that for a king was precisely the same as that for his chief bishop and his chief Brehon or professor of law. A petty king was on the same level as bishops, lawyers and poets. Tanists were marginally higher than other classes of poets, chief architects, doctors, smiths and musicians. When we compare the value accorded to such professions in other European cultures even in medieval times, we can see the essential meritocracy of Gaelic Ireland.

It is often claimed that the idea of knighthoods, chivalric orders and honours was not introduced to Ireland until after the Anglo-Norman invasion of the twelfth century. This is incorrect. Such a system was already in place arising out of the ancient Celtic practice of admitting those most worthy into élite warrior groups. A parallel in Hindu culture, where the warrior caste was known as *kshatriya*, demonstrates its Indo-European roots.

There are several orders of élite warrior corps mentioned in the sagas and chronicles of ancient Ireland. Perhaps the best known were the Ulster Red Branch Knights or the Craobh Ruadh. They emerge in the Ulster Cycle of myths and especially in the famous epic *Táin Bó Cualigne* (Cattle Raid of Cooley) which has been compared with the *Iliad*. Its date of origin is uncertain; scholars have identified it as being handed down in oral form probably from the La Tène period *c.*500 BC. The first reference to it in a written form occurs in the seventh century. The earliest complete surviving texts are found in the eleventh-century *Leabhar na hUidhre* (Book of the Dun Cow) and the twelfth-century *Leabhar na Nuaconghbhála Laighnech* (Book of Leinster).

The Red Branch Knights were represented only in the service of the kings of Ulster. Few scholars have been able to come up with a satisfactory reason why they were so called but Thomas O'Rahillly, one of the leading experts in this field, believed, from the epigraphic evidence, that they were actually called Craobh Rígh (Royal Branch) and the transformation into Craobh Ruadh was the fault of a lazy scribe.

In 1993 it was announced that The O'Conor Don, on the advice of an American who believed himself to be an expert in these matters, had instigated a chivalric confraternity to be known as the Chompanach na Craoibhe Ríoga (Companions of the Red Branch). It was pointed out that the Red Branch was an Ulster military élite and the stories concerning them clearly demonstrate them fighting against the monarchy of Connacht and not for it! It would have been as illogical for the Roman emperors to have established an order of 'Gaesatae', the Celtic military élite who fought the Roman legions so vigorously. The O'Conor Don was persuaded to cancel the plan. In 1995 he considered the establishment of 'The Noble and Equestrian Order of the Collar of Ériu', to reward outstanding contributions in Irish culture, in the arts, literature, science, medicine and philanthropy. This was also cancelled after some consideration. It would, it seemed, be hard to justify the creation of a chivalric order which had no historic basis nor continuity.

Contemporary with the Ulster knights were the Degad, or Clana Deagha, who appeared in Munster, the Clanna Baoiscne of Leinster, and Gamanrad or Gamhanrhide of Connacht. The Degad, however, were revealed by Eugene O'Curry not to be native to Munster but a group of Ulster warriors who had been banished to Munster to serve their exiled prince Cú Roi Mac Daire. There was also the Fianna, famous in the Fenian Cycle of tales of Fionn Mac Cumhail (sometimes Anglicised as Finn MacCool). The Fianna were bodyguards of the High Kings recruited from the Clan Baoiscne of Leinster and the Clan Morna and their headquarters were on the Hill of Allen in Kildare. When the Irish

Republican Brotherhood was formed in 1858 they adopted the name Fenians. The word *fianna* has become the modern Irish term for soldiers as in the political party Fianna Fáil (Soldiers of Destiny). The Fenian Cycle is one of the largest body of stories in early Irish literature and the stories are basically set during the reign of Cormac Mac Airt in the third century.

There is another fascinating trace of an élite Irish warrior group who were called the Ríglach. In the *Metrical Dindsenchus*, the *Betha Colmáin maic Lúachain* and the text of the *Táin Bó Cuailgne*, as given in the 'Book of Leinster', the word Ríglach is used to denote a high-ranking warrior élite. With the root *ríg* (royal), it is clearly a royal bodyguard. The Middle Irish glossators had difficulty understanding the concept behind the word and glossed it as 'veterans' (warriors) and from 'veterans' it degenerated in use over the centuries to being merely 'old people'.

The clue to the ancient Ríglach seems to lie in a common Indo-European root by a comparison to the warrior caste of northern India, the Rajputs. The name derives from *raj* (king) and *putrá* (sons). This group became a tribe, 'The Sons of Kings', who all claimed to be descended from the original *kshatriya* – the élite bodyguards to the kings presumably recruited from the king's family to ensure personal loyalty. The Rajputs made the principality of Rajputana in north-west India into a powerful state in the seventh century AD but had to submit to the Mughals in the seventeenth century and finally agreed a treaty with the English Crown in the nineteenth century.

There are several ancient Continental and British Celtic tribes described by classical writers as 'kings' or descendants of kings, whose names end in the element '*riges*'. Might it be that the Ríglach of ancient Ireland, clearly an important and distinctive group in the early references, were the equivalent of their fellow Indo-Europeans, the Rajputs of India? Were they also 'the sons of kings' and did some awareness of this survive in folk tradition, explaining the popular Irish notion that 'we are all kings' sons'?

It is clear, then, that there were élite warriors who were honoured by the kings. But did the practice develop as it did in other parts of Europe?

An English jurist and legal antiquarian, John Sladen (1584–1654) was disarmingly candid when he stated that the Irish had an 'ancient custom of knighthood before they received manners of English civility'.[1] When Richard II was in Ireland in 1395, one of his advisers asked the Leinster King Art and his nobles 'if they would not gladly receive the order of knighthood and that the King of England should make them knights according to the usage of France and England and other countries. They answered him how they were knights already and that sufficed for them.

I asked where they were made knights, and how, and when? They answered that at the age of seven years they were made knights in Ireland, and that a King maketh his son a Knight...'[2] The person recounting this conversation was Enrique de Castile, and he might have misheard the numeral for *seven* was when a boy went to be educated and *seventeen* was the age of maturity when he was entitled to take his role in society.

All these bodies of Gaelic élite warriors and knights have now passed into oblivion except one.

The Niadh Nask developed from the old warrior guard of the Munster kings. Originally called the Nasc Niadh, it actually indicated a gold necklet and would have originated from the famous gold torcs which ancient Celtic warriors wore around their necks. *Nasc* meant a chain or collar worn around the neck and *Nia(dh)* was a champion. In English it became known as the Military Order of the Golden Chain.

It survives today because it was a dynastic order at the personal disposal of the head of the royal house of Munster. Today, as the Niadh Nask, it continues as a nobiliary fraternity but it is not an order of chivalry or knighthood and admission is not restricted to persons of Irish descent. It undertakes charitable work and in particular the relief of suffering amongst the very young and elderly.

In July 1984 it was recognised as a valid dynastic and nobiliary association by the International Commission for Orders of Chivalry. It has been recognised by other European royal dynasties and by many heraldic authorities, such as the Heralds of South Africa (1983), Canada (1984), United States (1986) and Spain (1998). An *International Niadh Nask Journal* is published twice yearly for holders of the honour, who include two former Prime Ministers of the Irish Republic. A detailed history of the order was published as *Links in a Golden Chain*, edited by The Count of Clandermond.

The ancient texts attribute the foundation of the Niadh Nask to King Muinheamhoin in 681 BC. According to the *Annals of Clonmacnoise*: 'Mownemon [Muinheamhoin] was the first king that ever devised a golden chain fit to be worn about men's necks ... He reigned five years and then died. He was of the sept of Munster.'

The great Irish historian Séthrún Céitinn (*c.* 1580–*c.*1644) in his famous *Foras Feasa ar Éireann* (History of Ireland), relates how an unlawful claimant to the High Kingship forced his way into the palace at Tara:

... a learned druid came into his presence and said to him that it was not lawful for him to violate the *geasa* [prohibition laws] of Tara; 'for it is one of its *geasa*,' he said, 'that no king should settle down in Tara with a view to assuming the sovereignty of Ireland till he should first

wear the Nasc Niadh round his neck'. This was the same as to say
that he should have received the degree of Knight of Chivalry. For as
the Knight of Chivalry is called Miles Torquatus, so also *Nia Naisc* is
applied in Irish to the champion who wore a *nasc* or chain round his
neck. For *nia* means 'champion' or 'valiant' man and *nasc* means 'a
chain'.

According to Céitinn the spurious claimant immediately relinquished his
demand to be recognised as king.

Comte O'Kelly d'Aughrim stated:

After the quality of noble, and that of king, the first and only title of
honour in use among the Milesians of ancient Ireland was knight,
called in their language Niadh Nask, or even Eques Torquatus, with
a golden chain which was worn about the neck. This Order was instituted by King Muinheamhoin: one had to be a Niadh Nask, or Knight
of the Golden Chain, to aspire to the Monarchy of Ireland.[3]

Anthony Marmion agreed:

There were five Equestrian orders: the first of these was the Neagh
Nase [*sic*], or Knights of the Golden Collar, instituted by King Muin-
hamhoin, one of the ancient Milesian Kings, which derived from the
golden chain worn about the neck like the golden collar of the Roman
knights. This order was peculiar to the blood royal, and none could
be a candidate for the monarchy without being admitted to it . . .[4]

Patrick Weston Joyce says:

There was an order of chivalry the distinguishing mark of which was
what was called *nasc-niad* (champion's ring or collar; *nia* gen. *niad*, a
trenfer or champion). Neither the order – nor of course the decoration
– was conferred except it was won on the field of battle; and the person
who won the *nasc niad* was called *Nia Naisc* 'champion of the collar'
(like the English 'Knight of the Garter'), and also *ridire gaisge*, or
'knight of valour'. This collar, according to Keating (Céitinn), was
worn around the neck.[5]

The Niadh Nask is mentioned in many ancient works especially those
emanating from Munster, such as *Caithreim Chelleachain Chaisil*, commissioned by King Cormac III of Munster *c.* 1130. In *The Vision of
Tnugdal*, the story of a knight of Cashel written at Ratisbon in 1149 by

an Irish monk, Marcus of Munster, the knight could only have been a Niadh Nask at that time.

The Niadh Nask continued to exist long after the conquest and destruction of the territory of the kingdom of Munster and then of Desmond.

The poet Aodhagan Ó Rathaille (Anglicised as Egan Rahilly, 1670–1728), of a family long in the service of The MacCarthy Mór, referred to the Niadh Nask in one of his elegies. He hails Gerard FitzGerald, son of the Knight of Glin, thus:

> Nasc Nia of all Connello, without fault
> Nasc Nia of Glin
> a sore wound to his friends;
> Nasc Nia of Dingle, I utter not lies;
> Nasc Nia of defence with his flock.

The surviving portrait of Donal IX (d. 1596) shows him wearing the emblem of the order around his neck. A portrait of O'Sullivan Beare, as Conde de Berehaven, painted in Spain and now in Maynooth, shows him wearing the ribbon of the Niadh Nask entwined in a golden chain with a Spanish order. The curious cross of the Niadh Nask seems to have its origin in a solar emblem rather than in a Christian one. Numerous other artefacts, swords and ceremonial daggers have survived bearing this emblem. In fact one of the earliest Niadh Nask crosses dates from the third century AD.

The evidence shows that the dynastic order continued to be bestowed by the MacCarthy Mórs of the Muskerry branch of the MacCarthys after they had been driven into exile in France. Abbé MacGeoghegan, who was a close friend of Robert, 5th Earl Clancarthy, then head of the Niadh Nask, wrote in 1758, 'The knights of this order, like the Roman knights, wore chains of gold around their necks.' In the 1768 edition of an Irish-English dictionary the Niadh Nask are still known and are identified as a nobiliary order.[6] The order's 'In Memoria Roll' of holders of the order dates from 1811. It is of interest that one of the first non-Irish names on this Roll is that of His Highness Sidi El Hadj Moulay Abdeslam Ben Alarbi, Grand Sheruf d'Ouazzane (1840–91) who was awarded the Niadh Nask in 1877.

When Sir Charles MacCarthy, Governor-General of Senegal and Lieutenant-Governor of Sierra Leone, was killed during the Ashantee uprising in 1824, he was carrying a dirk with the emblem of the Niadh Nask, made by a local craftsman. It remains in the possession of the current MacCarthy Mór.

When Pol, 7th Duc de Clancarthy wrote to the *Cork Historical and*

Archaeological Journal in 1907, he stated clearly that the MacCarthys were 'knights after the ancient Irish fashion'. In the 1890s he admitted the then O'Neill, Prince of Clanaboy to the order.

The bestowal of the Niadh Nask has, therefore, continued without interruption through the various MacCarthy Mórs, as heads of the Eóghanacht dynasty, to the present day. Among the notables on whom the order was bestowed by Thomas Donal, MacCarthy Mór (1905–47) was HM Queen Geraldine of the Albanians, and HH Prince Xhehal, brother to HM King Zog.

Lieutenant-Colonel Baron O'Kelly de Conejera had been serving on the International Commission for Orders of Chivalry since 1981 and had been interested in references to the ancient history of the Niadh Nask. When he began his research into the pre-chivalric Gaelic royal order he was not even aware that a representative of the Eóghanacht dynasty still lived. He approached the then Chief Herald of Ireland, Gerard Slevin, who informed him that the house of MacCarthy Mór was still extant. He identified the current MacCarthy Mór as the genuine holder of the title nearly eight years before Slevin's successor in the office of Chief Herald gave 'courtesy recognition' to him.

Having contacted MacCarthy Mór, Baron O'Kelly was even more astonished to discover the evidence of continued bestowal of the honour. He invited MacCarthy Mór to submit this evidence to the International Commission for Orders of Chivalry, emphasising that the burden of proving the continuity of the Niadh Nask to that international body of experts lay with MacCarthy Mór rather than the Commission. These proofs were submitted and at the Commission's Plenary Session, held in Washington, DC in the summer of 1984, the Niadh Nask was recognised and duly placed on their register. However, because of the uniqueness of the order, a new category had to be created and it was described as a 'Nobiliary Association'.

The late Rt. Hon. Lord Borthwick of that Ilk (d. 1996), a president of the commission, wrote:

The Niadh Nask is without doubt one of the most ancient nobiliary honours in the world, if not the most ancient! Its origins are shrouded in the mists of time. According to Gaelic historians writing in the fifteenth century, it was founded almost a thousand years before the birth of Christ! Whether this is true or not we cannot say, but it is evident that the order is at least pre-Chivalric in origin if not pre-Christian.

... When, in 1984, after several years of scrutiny, the International Commission for Orders of Chivalry recognised the Niadh Nask or

Military Order of the Golden Chain, as a perfectly valid and legal Dynastic Honour of the ancient Irish Royal House of Munster, under the Chiefship of The MacCarthy Mór, Prince of Desmond, it had to devise the entirely new category of 'Other Nobiliary Bodies' to list it under, not because it was 'less important' than the great and ancient Dynastic Orders of Chivalry, but because it was even more ancient in its origins!

In his preface to *The 1996 Membership Roll of the Niadh Nask*, Lord Borthwick pointed out:

The Roll itself is a testimony to the validity of the Niadh Nask and the Order's fidelity to its Gaelic origins, for whilst it is a nobiliary Order it does not define 'nobility' in the narrow genealogical sense but adheres to the Celtic definition whereby military officers, doctors, religious and Ollamhs (professors and other graduates) are considered of 'equal' rank. Similarly as a pre-Christian Order The Niadh Nask has no sectarian qualification. This is perhaps most eloquently illustrated by reference to the membership of the First Division which lists simultaneously as members His Holiness Patriarch Diodorus I, Greek Orthodox Patriarch of Jerusalem, and His Majesty King Leka I of the Albanians, the only Muslim Sovereign in Europe!

The current membership roll includes representatives of several other religions.

One might have expected that with the weight of evidence, there would have been no question about the existence of the Niadh Nask, especially in an Irish context where two Prime Ministers of the state, Charles Haughey and Albert Reynolds, have been pleased to accept the ancient order. Charles Haughey accepted the order while he was in office. But, as mentioned in Chapter 6, as part of what appears to be a deliberate campaign to undermine the good name of the current MacCarthy Mór, the subject of the Niadh Nask was seized upon. MacCarthy Mór dismisses the campaign as being 'chiefly conducted by Anglophile Hibernophobes who detest the very concept of a Gaelic aristocracy'. Four claims were publicly made: 1. that there was no historical evidence for knighthood existing in Gaelic Ireland; 2. that there were no historical references to the Niadh Nask; 3. that in consequence the conferral of the order by MacCarthy Mór was illicit and unjustified; and 4. that even had such an order existed in the past it had been abolished by the Constitution of the Irish Republic.

Once such claims had been made public, the matter had to be faced in a legal battle.

The MacCarthy Mór took legal action against Professor Marco Horak for making these allegations public, having ordered him to desist from asserting them in public or in private. As we have seen, the action took place in the Italian courts. The judgement on this matter formed the second of the two judgements and was issued in June 1998. The court found:

> It is proven that knighthood existed as a rank in Gaelic Ireland before the advent of the Anglo-Normans in 1169 and accordingly that The Niadh Nask, or Military Order of the Golden Chain, existed and, according to documentary evidence, was established by King Muinheamhoin who has been proven to be the direct ancestor of the Eóghanacht Kings of Munster and specifically of the Royal House of MacCarthy Mór; that the Office of Grand Master or Hereditary Head of the Niadh Nask [in Italian: *Ufficio di Gran Maestro e Capo Ereditario del Niadh Nask*] is inalienably vested in the Chieftainship of the Royal House of MacCarthy Mór as a Dynastic honour of non-Chivalric knighthood [in Italian: *Ordine Dinastico di natura non Cavalleresca*], so that The Niadh Nask must be considered in International Law as a Dynastic honour of the Royal House of Munster, which lawfully exists as a nobiliary body corporate and politic being so recognised by various States and by the International Commission for Orders of Chivalry.

The existence of the Niadh Nask and the right of The MacCarthy Mór to bestow it were now made absolutely clear in law.

13

A Future for Gaelic Aristocracy?

To reiterate the Introduction of this book, this has been a study of a much neglected area of Irish history. No assessment of Irish history can ever be complete without a consideration of the history of the families who ruled in Ireland for at least two thousand years prior to the English Tudor conquests.

The pedigrees of those Gaelic aristocrats who are represented on the Standing Council of Irish Chiefs and Chieftains are not in doubt. These pedigrees are as old as the written word in Ireland, if not older, and stem from a number of genealogies dating back as early as the seventh century AD, but most surviving from twelfth-century books and annals.

What seems to be a matter of contention is whether the current chiefs have the right to hold their Gaelic titles and under what legal criteria they may do so. This problem has been discussed in detail in the early chapters of this work and the opinion of international scholars and jurists is one that I share, that any recognition by the modern Irish state can only follow the precedents and rulings of international law in this matter.

Whether these survivors of the ancient kings and nobles of Ireland, the oldest traceable aristocracy in Europe, now have any role to play in the modern Irish state is a matter for debate and, in the end, depends both on the members of that aristocracy and on the decisions of the Irish state. It was Napoleon Bonaparte who observed: 'The practical policy of a [republican] government is to make use of aristocracy, but under the forms and in the spirit of democracy.' Admittedly, Napoleon had his own agenda to pursue although he did make this point after abolishing the teetering French Republic and making himself emperor.

Eversheds Professor of International Law, Anthony Carty, not only believes that the Irish state should give 'courtesy recognition' to the holders of Gaelic titles under the Brehon law of succession, as clearly supported by international law, but he feels that the Irish Constitution should be amended to give recognition to the heads of these families. He writes (letter dated 9 February 1999):

> I believe there should be some formal recognition in the Irish Constitution of the world which was lost by the violence of Irish history, i.e. the violence done to Ireland, particularly in the sixteenth and seventeenth centuries. That should find reflection in the present Constitution, for instance in a place for at least some of the old Irish Houses in the Irish Senate through election from among themselves.

Some individual members of the Standing Council agree with Carty and consider they should be given a political role within the modern state. Whether an allocation of seats in the Seanad Éireann (Irish Senate) needs a constitutional change is arguable. The Irish Prime Minister can, constitutionally, appoint members of the Senate by nomination. In 1998 there were eleven Prime Minister's nominees sitting in the Senate. There is no reason why the heads of the royal dynasties might not be appointed in such a manner, sitting as independents, and using their expertise under Article 18 in the areas of the national language, culture, literature, art and education.

The Standing Council of Irish Chiefs and Chieftains, reflecting the individual concerns of its members, does envisage its primary function as being the promotion of Gaelic culture, of an awareness of history and of tourism, especially through the Irish Diaspora with the interest in clan gatherings. The Council already presents, through the University College of Cork, an annual prize for writing in the Irish language.

However, to sit in the Senate one is required to be a citizen. Not all the members of these Gaelic noble families are Irish citizens for they have been in exile too long. The O'Neill of Clanaboy, for example, is a Portuguese citizen. His family have been exiled since the seventeenth century. Like others, he does not automatically qualify for an Irish passport or citizenship rights. However, the Minister of Justice (writing to the author on 28 May 1998) has explained that he has the power to dispense with the standard conditions of granting citizenship, under the Irish Nationality and Citizenship Acts of 1956 and 1986, in certain circumstances 'including where the applicant is of Irish descent or Irish association'.

> It is therefore open to anyone who feels that they have sufficiently strong Irish associations to make a case to the Minister that he exercise this exception on their behalf and, from time to time, individuals

are successful in this regard. You will appreciate, however, that the association would have to be exceptional to warrant the Minister waiving the specified statutory requirements. Having regard to the very significant numbers of people who might be able to claim Irish origins, the Minister is unlikely to consider ancestry alone as being sufficient and it would certainly not be equitable to discriminate in favour of those who are descended from particular families.

In other words, being a direct descendant of Irish kings and High Kings who reigned in Ireland for two thousand years or more, of a family who was forced into exile during the English conquests, is not regarded as being an 'exceptional' circumstance to claim an 'Irish association' by the office of the current Irish Minister for Justice. One has to bear in mind that the Ministry was sensitive at this time after media revelations of passports being supplied to foreign citizens for cash payments when there was patently no 'Irish association' at all to justify the granting of them, not even the qualification of residency.

MacCarthy Mór comes close to agreeing with the Minister, though for entirely different reasons. He believes that the holding of an *Irish* passport has nothing to do with being *Gaelic*.

Another idea has been proposed to the modern Irish state. Many of the old castles, manors and estates, owned by the Gaelic aristocracy and confiscated during the conquests of the sixteenth and seventeenth centuries, are now the property of the Irish state. Most of the properties are owned by departments which eventually come under the direction of the Ministry of Arts, Heritage, Gaeltacht and Islands. Only The O'Brien still lives on his family's original Dromoland estate although his family sold Dromoland Castle in the 1980s.

It has been suggested that in an attempt to encourage tourism the current holder of a royal title could be given an apartment in his family's old castle or manor, free of rent and expenses, in return for a degree of involvement in promoting the site. In Britain, the fact that many 'ancient families' are still in residence in their stately homes has proved a great attraction. How much better it would be, some have argued, for Bord Fáilte to promote visits to castles and manors that are not simply empty shells in which kings or High Kings once lived centuries ago, but have the modern-day heir in residence. The increase in tourism and the resulting interest in Irish history and culture would make any outlay on such apartments pay for itself if, in fact, extra financial outlay was even needed. The state already has to maintain these properties. The Irish state, in fact, already give grants to Anglo-Irish peers for the upkeep of their stately homes.

The MacCarthy Mór reports that he discussed the matter informally with Irish President Mary Robinson and Prime Minister John Bruton. President Robinson failed to grasp the point and felt that the state could hardly 'dispossess countless smallholders to benefit a handful of people'. MacCarthy Mór agreed with her but pointed out that there was no question of 'smallholders' being involved as the properties in question were state-owned. In the case of Muckross, once a seat of the MacCarthys, it was a National Park estate. 'I asked her if the state could feel confident in owning a property donated to it by the American Bourne-Vincent family which, in turn, had purchased it from the Herberts who obtained it by fraud during the Penal period.' He also pointed out that in the European former communist states, as a gesture of reconciliation some confiscated property was being restored.

The idea also received scant enthusiasm at the Ministry of Heritage. When asked to comment on it, the Ministry curiously asked the Chief Herald, Brendan O'Donoghue, to state its policy in this area. In a letter to the author dated 15 April 1998, he stated:

Property rights are fully protected and guaranteed by the Constitution, and the Courts are there to vindicate those rights. There are no proposals, and unlikely ever to be any proposals, to vest additional property rights on particular classes of citizens or other persons by references to circumstances that may have prevailed in the past. It should also be borne in mind, of course, that the ownership of the castles and estates to which you refer may have been passed, in full accordance with law, over the centuries, to persons other than to whom titles passed.

This, again, was not addressing the actual question. It is probable that such suggestions would meet with some incomprehension when the Irish state has not even been able to agree to give 'courtesy recognition' to Gaelic titles as titles in accordance with international precedent and usages but sought to describe them as 'designations'.

As we have seen, during the period 1541–1610 all Gaelic titles, as well as the native Irish legal system, were abolished and made 'utterly extinct' under English common law and statute law which, along with the English language and customs, were forced on the Irish people by military conquest.

The policy was to recreate the country in the English image. The Irish aristocracy, from kings downward, were to be forced to surrender their titles and territories, to accept English titles from the English kings, and to have the clan territories they controlled under the restrictions of Brehon law regranted to them in part to be tenants under English feudal law. As kingship was an electoral as well as an hereditary office, and as the king was not a feudal monarch with complete ownership of the land, it was an impossibility for a king to agree to this change of social system against the will of his family and people. He simply did not have such rights under the Irish law. Some Irish aristocrats did surrender and internal dynastic wars immediately commenced, weakening the Irish defence against England and allowing the English forces to move in and seize territories during the internecine struggles that had been created. Where the Irish held out with a degree of unity, a vicious campaign of military conquest was pursued creating near deserts in the once affluent kingdoms.

When an Irish state re-emerged in 1922, the state had, for convenience' sake, adopted the English legal system, the most important aspect of which – for the surviving Gaelic aristocracy – was the principle of inheritance by the eldest male heir.

When in 1943 the Irish state started to give 'courtesy recognition' to the surviving chiefly houses, the state announced that recognition of their legitimacy could only be based on the inherited English law of primogeniture. This caused immediate criticism from historians and Gaelic scholars and even from some of the chiefly houses themselves. Having been abolished in both statute and common law, no Gaelic titles can exist in modern times under those laws which had been adopted by the emerging Irish state.

Gaelic titles, it was also pointed out, could only exist by an acknowledgement that the laws of the conquerors, enacted by *force majeure* and not by the will of the people, were invalid. They did not, therefore, abolish those titles nor the dynastic laws of succession in the perception of the people. Indeed, this idea is reflected in the very assertion by the Irish people, by force of arms, generation after generation since the Tudor conquests, of the illegality of England's presence in Ireland. This has always been the *raison d'être* and the justification of Irish military uprisings against English rule, as clearly demonstrated in the various insurgent proclamations culminating in the Irish Declaration of Independence on 21 January 1919.

The first great problem to be resolved for the chiefly houses, therefore, is the one arising from the initial mistake of policy in 1943 which we have previously discussed. The Standing Council of Irish Chiefs and Chieftains has declared that the titles stem from the Brehon law system and that the dynastic laws of succession cannot be retrospectively altered. In seeking to force a change in those successional laws, the modern Irish state can only be seen as acting in an illegal fashion. It also brings itself into a ridiculous position by declaring that it will only give 'courtesy recognition' to Gaelic titles if they are claimed within the parameters of the legal system which has 'utterly abolished' the same titles.

International law argues that such titles can only exist through the maintenance of the native laws of inheritance applying before the conquest of the state. It further argues that no 'successor state' can arbitrarily and retrospectively change those laws of inheritance.

Therefore, international law is quite clear that without a recognition of the Brehon law of succession, no claimant to a Gaelic title has the authority to use it. Even if their genealogies prove their direct antecedents to the last established holder of that title, before the title was abolished during the conquests, they can be 'recognised' only as lineal descendants and not as holders of any title. The title is not transmitted by primogeniture and therefore cannot be claimed by primogeniture. A Gaelic title is the 'ideal property' of the family, and remains at the disposal and bestowal only of the family as prescribed by dynastic law, and cannot be devised, bestowed nor conferred by any authority outside the family, whether it exercises heraldic or state jurisdiction. Even if the Irish state refuses to allow 'courtesy recognition' to the Gaelic aristocracy, they and their titles will continue to exist so long as they are handed down by the *derbhfine* of each house.

The question whether the Gaelic aristocrats have any relevance in the modern world, and the modern Irish Republic, is yet another matter. Could the Standing Council of Irish Chiefs and Chieftains have a similar role in Ireland to that of the Standing Council of Scottish Chiefs in Scotland? Was Irish Prime Minister Eamon de Valéra really serious in 1937 when he examined the idea of installing a direct descendant of the High King Brían Bóroimhe as 'Prince President' under the new Irish Constitution?

There are now twenty heads of Gaelic aristocratic houses given 'courtesy recognition'. This does not mean that there are only twenty heads of aristocratic families who have survived the centuries of repression, maintaining the right to their ancient titles. Several claims have been submitted to the Chief Herald of Ireland or to the Standing Council, which, under its constitution, has its own Committee of Privileges; this can grant recognition to such claimants irrespective of the Irish Genealogical Office. Claims for recognition of the titles The O'Dignan, The O'Dowd, The O'Gara and The O'Neill Mór have been submitted to one or other of these bodies. However, as recognition took eight years in one case and the publication of actual recognition four decades in another, the families examined in this book are confined to those who have been acknowledged by both the Standing Council and the Chief Herald, with the exception of The O'Neill Mór, as yet unacknowledged but intricately linked to the fortunes of the entire O'Neill family.

The Heraldic Adviser to the Council, Gerard Crotty, explains the basis for those claiming Gaelic titles:

> When the Office registers a chief or chieftain the act is one of recognition only, not of creation. This recognition is by courtesy only, and therefore a recognised chief is in a position hardly differing from the holder of a foreign title, though the courtesy has been *formally* accorded to him.
>
> This is an important point in connection with those chiefs whose families have allowed the use of the title to lapse. In such cases, the newly resumed title is not a new creation. The underlying concept must be one of continuity. There are no *new* chiefs. The title must be deemed to have been vested *de jure* in all their intervening predecessors from the time of the last acknowledged holder before the period of dormancy began.

This volume, then, has not simply been a study of several extraordinary family histories; nor merely the story of their loss of power as the ruling Gaelic élite of Ireland and their subsequent struggle for survival; likewise it is not a voyeuristic examination of current lifestyles of families who had their origin in the primeval beginnings of an archaic Celtic society, whose lineages were claimed as ancient even at the time of the birth of Christ.

It may be all those things . . . but more.

It is the story of the attempted destruction of a venerable civilisation and culture; the near eradication of a language, social concepts and an ancient law system. In many respects, the current conflicts of the chiefly houses over the manner of their recognition by the modern Irish state may, sadly, perhaps be seen as the last dying kicks of a cultural incompatibility; the final destruction of what was one of the most vibrant, artistic and philosophical of European cultures; the final twilight of three thousand years of cultural continuum. Or are they, one might wonder, the initial pangs of a rebirth?

Notes

Foreword

1. Dinneen, P.S. and O'Donoghue, T., eds, *The Poems of Egan O'Rahilly*, Irish Text Society, 1965, vol. 3, p. 11, 'The Ruin that Befell the Great Families of Erin'.
2. Ibid., 'On the Death of Muirchertach O'Griffin', p. 97.
3. Ibid., 'The Ruin that Befell...', p. 11.
4. Ibid., 'The Wounds of the Land of Fodla', p. 5.
5. Ibid., 'The Ruin that Befell...', p. 11.
6. Ibid., 'On the Death of O'Callaghan', p. 71.
7. Ibid., 'On Removing to Duibhneacham beside Tonn Toime in Kerry', p. 27.
8. MacCarthy Mór, King Donal IX, 'A Sorrowful Vision has Deceived me', ante 1596.
9. Lyons, F.S.L., *Ireland Since the Famine*, Dublin, 1973, pp. 370-1.

Chapter One: The Gaelic Aristocracy

1. *Uber die Aelteste irische Dichtung*, Berlin, 1913.
2. *Land Tenure in Ireland*, 1889.
3. Edmund Curtis, *A History of Medieval Ireland*, 1923.
4. Ibid.
5. Mike Ashley, *British Monarchy*, 1998.
6. State Papers, Henry VIII, II, 1-31.
7. Ibid., II, 162-3.
8. Ibid. III, 48.
9. Ibid. II, 480.
10. Ibid. III, 140.

11. Letters and Papers, Henry VIII, XVI, No. 755, and Calendar of Carew MSS, III, 523.
12. State Papers, Henry VIII, III, 304-5.

Chapter Two: Gaelic Dynastic Laws of Succession

1. *Early Irish Laws and Institutions*, p. 97.
2. 'Irish Regnal Succession: a reappraisal', *Studia Hibernica*, No. 11, 1971.
3. 'The Heir Apparent in Irish and Welsh Law', *Celtica*, Vol. IX, 1971.
4. *The Brehon Laws: a legal handbook*, 1896.
5. Gearóid MacNiocaill, 'The Interaction of Laws' in *The English in Medieval Ireland*, ed. James Lydon, Royal Irish Academy, Dublin, 1984.

Chapter Three: The 'Utter Abolition' of Gaelic Titles

1. Cal. Pat Rolls, ed. Morrin I, 81.
2. State Papers, Henry VIII, III, 332-4.
3. Cal. Carew MSS I, 245-6.

Chapter Four: The Struggle for Survival

1. Trans. S. O'Grady, *Catalogue of Irish MSS in the British Museum*, p. 473.
2. Calendar of State Papers, Ireland, 1509-73, pp. 289-312.
3. State Papers, Henry VIII, Ireland, II, 288.
4. *O'Brien of Thomond: The O'Briens in Irish history 1500-1865*, p. 19.
5. Calender of State Papers, Ireland, 1509-73, pp. 509-11, 515.
6. Richard Bagwell, *Ireland under the Tudors*, 1885-90, Vol. III, p. 105.
7. John Murphy, *Ireland, Industrial, Political and Social*, p. 255.

Chapter Five: 'Extinct For Ever'?

1. *The Cromwellian Settlement of Ireland*, p. lxxii.
2. *Daniel O'Connell*, Cork University Press, 1929.
3. In the Introduction to Eugene O'Curry, *On the Manners and Customs of the Ancient Irish*, 1873.
4. Thomas Matthews, *The O'Neills of Ulster*, p. 348.
5. *Arthur Griffith and Non-Violent Sinn Féin*, Dublin, 1974.
6. *The Irish Republic*, 1937.

Chapter Six: 'Courtesy Recognition': A Conflict of Perceptions

1. Charles Lysaght, *Edward MacLysaght 1887-1986*, National Library of Ireland, 1988, p. 20.
2. 'The Irish Chieftainries', *Burke's Introduction to Irish Ancestry*, London, 1976, pp. 454-6.
3. *Aspects of Irish Genealogy*, ed. M.D. Evans, Dublin, 1996.

Chapter Seven: The Kingdom of Munster (Desmond)

(I)   1. In *Miscellaneous Irish Annals*, ed. Séamus O hInnse.
        2. 'Desmond: the early years and the career of Cormac MacCarthy'.
        3. *History of Medieval Ireland*.
(IV)   1. *Dánta Shéfraidh Uí Dhonnhadha an Ghleanna*, ed. Pádraig Ua Duinnín, Dublin, 1902.
(VII)   1. *Geheimauftrag Irland*, Hamburg, 1961.
        2. Joseph T. Carroll, *Ireland in the War Years 1939-1945*, 1975.

Chapter Eight: The Kingdom of Munster (Thomond)

(I)   1. *The O'Briens of Thomond*.
        2. *These My Friends and Forebears: the O'Briens of Dromoland*.

Chapter Nine: The Kingdom of Connacht

(I)   1. *The History and Heritage of the Royal O'Connors*.
(IV)   1. Hist. MSS Comm. Cecil MSS 3-4, No. 32, p. 509, National Library of Ireland.

Chapter Ten: The Kingdom of Ulster

(I)   1. *The Birth of Ulster*, 1936.

Chapter Eleven: The Kingdom of Leinster

1. *Histoire du Roi d'Angleterre Richard*.

Chapter Twelve: Gaelic Knights

1. *Titles of Honour*, London, 1614.
2. *Froissart's Chronicle*, ed. G. C. MacCanley, London, 1904.
3. *Essai Historique sur Irlande*, Brussels, 1837.
4. *The Ancient and Modern History of the Maritime Ports of Ireland*.
5. *A Social History of Ancient Ireland*.
6. *Focalóir Gaoidhilge-Saxs Bhéarla* compiled by John O'Brien, Bishop of Cloyne, printed in Paris by Nicolas-Francis Valleyre.

Acknowledgements

I would like to express my gratitude to the people without whose co-operation, warm hospitality and assistance this book would not have been possible – to the members of the *Buanchomhairle Thaoisgh Éireann*, the Standing Council of Irish Chiefs and Chieftains, both collectively and individually, whom I list below:

MacCarthy Mór, Prince of Desmond; MacDermot, Prince of Coolavin; Maguire, Prince of Fermanagh; MacGillycuddy of the Reeks; O'Brien, Prince of Thomond; O'Callaghan; O'Carroll of Ely; O'Conor Don, Prince of Connacht and his tanist, Desmond O'Conor; Ó Dochartaigh of Inis Eóghain and his representative and brother Rear-Admiral Pascual O'Dogherty; The O'Donoghue of the Glens; the tanist of The O'Donel of Tirconnell, Don Leopoldo O'Donnell, Duque de Tetuan; O'Donovan; the late Philip, The O'Grady and his successor, the current O'Grady; O'Kelly of Gallagh and Tycooly; O'Long of Garranelongy; O'Morchoe; O'Neill, Prince of Clanaboy; and the O'Ruairc, Prince of Breifne.

The MacMorrough Kavanagh, Prince of Leinster, and his tanist, Simon MacMurrough Kavanagh, had not taken seats on the Council at the time of publication, but are due to. I am most grateful to them both for their help and co-operation.

I am also appreciative of the replies given by The O'Neill Mór, Don Carlos O'Neill y Castrillo, Marques de la Granja y del Norte y de Villaverde de San Isidro, Conde de Benagiar.

I express my thanks and appreciation to the Chevalier Gerard Crotty, formerly Hon. Secretary to, and now Heraldic Adviser of, the Standing Council of Irish Chiefs and Chieftains for his support, co-operation and advice.

Special thanks have to be accorded my indefatigable researcher, Mrs Elizabeth Murray.

[307]

Further appreciation must be tended to Mary Aylward for her linguistic assistance; Anthony Carty, Eversheds Professor of International Law, University of Derby; the Count of Clandermond; Collette Ellison, Executive Secretary of the Royal Society of Antiquaries of Ireland; Dr Tommy Graham, Trinity College, Dublin; Terry McBride (Irish and Reference Department) of the Linen Hall Library, Belfast; Hubert Cheeshyre, former Norroy and Ulster King of Arms and now Clarenceux King of Arms; Rosemary MacGillycuddy of Baltimore, Co. Cork; Maurice McCann; Professor Brían Ó Cuív who, although retired from the Dublin Institute for Advanced Studies, was still willing to deal with obscure questions, and his son, Eamon Ó Cuív, Minister of State Department of Arts, Heritage, Gaeltacht and Islands, and his cousin and departmental head, Minister Síle de Valéra, for consideration of my questions; Brendan O'Donoghue, Chief Herald of Ireland; John O'Donoghue TD, Minister of Justice; Seán Ó Ceallaigh BA, LLB, of Phibsboro, Dublin; Colonel Philip O'Grady of Askeaton, Co. Limerick; Donall Ó Luanaigh, Keeper (Collections), National Library of Ireland; Kevin O'Toole, secretary of Clann Ua Tuathail; my Spanish interpreter, Francis H. Westwood; Thomas Woodcock, Norroy and Ulster King of Arms; Dr Margaret Tierney, chairperson of Clans of Ireland Ltd.

I would also like to thank MacCarthy Mór for agreeing to write a foreword to this study, in which he raises several polemics. I invited him to do so not only as an Irish prince but as the Standing Council's leading expert on matters of heraldry and genealogy. Needless to say, these views, as well as the views of the individual members of the Standing Council given in this book, are not necessarily shared by the author.

Finally, last but by no means least, warmest thanks and appreciation to my wife Dorothy, for her encouragement and advice, for some practical and tenacious research assistance in a couple of difficult areas, and, above all, for just being there!

Bibliography

Specialist Bibliography on Brehon Law

ANCIENT LAWS OF IRELAND, 6 vols, Stationery Office, Dublin, 1865-1901.

BINCHY, D.A. 'The linguistic and historical value of the Old Irish law tracts', *Proceedings of the British Academy*, vol 29 (1943).

BINCHY, D.A, *Celtic and Anglo-Saxon Kingship*, (O'Donnell Lecture for 1967/8), Clarendon Press, Oxford, 1970.

BINCHY, D.A. 'Some Celtic legal terms', *Celtica* 3 (1956).

BINCHY, D.A. ed. *Crith Gablach* (Medieval and Modern Irish Series, vol xi) Stationery Office, Dublin, 1941.

BINCHY, D.A. 'Irish History and Law II', *Studia Hibernica* 16, 1976.

BINCHY, D.A. 'Ancient Irish Law' *The Irish Jurist*, Dublin, 1966.

BINCHY, D.A. *Corpus Iuris Hibernici*, 6 vols, Dublin, 1966.

BRYANT, SOPHIE. *Liberty, Order and Law Under Native Irish Rule*, Harding and More Ltd, London, 1923.

CHARLES-EDWARDS, T.M. *Early Irish and Welsh Kinship*, Clarendon Press, Oxford, 1993.

CHARLES-EDWARD, T.M. 'The Heir-Apparent in Irish and Welsh Law' *Celtica*, 9, Dublin Institute for Advanced Studies, 1971.

GERRIETS, MARILYN. 'The King as Judge in Early Ireland', *Celtica*, Dublin Institute for Advanced Studies, 1988.

GINNELL, LAURENCE. *The Brehon Laws: A Legal Handbook*, T. Fisher Unwin, London, 1894.

HOGAN, JAMES. 'The Irish Law of Kingship: With Special Reference to Aileach and Cenél Eoghain', *Proceedings of the Royal Irish Academy*, Vol XL, Hodges, Figgis & Co, Dublin, 1931-1932.

JASKI, BURT. *Early Irish Kingship and Succession*, Four Courts Press, Dublin, 2000.

KELLY, FERGUS. *A Guide to Early Irish Law*, Dublin Institute for Advanced Studies, Dublin, 1988. (Early Irish Law Series, Vol.III).

MACNEILL, EOIN, *Early Irish Laws and Institutions*, Burns, Oates and Washington, Dublin, 1935.

MACNEILL, EOIN. 'The Irish Law of Dynastic Succession', *Irish Historical Studies* 8 (1919).

MAC NIOCAILL, GEARÓID. 'The Interaction of Laws', pp 105-117, in *The English in Medieval Ireland*, ed. James Lydon, Royal Irish Academy, Dublin, 1984.

MAC NIOCAILL, GEARÓID. 'The Heir-Designate in Early Medieval Law', *The Irish Jurist*, iii, Dublin (1964).

NICHOLLS, KENNETH W. *Land, Law and Society in Sixteenth Century Ireland* (O'Donnell Lecture) May, 1976, University College, Cork. (pamphlet)

Ó CORRÁIN, DONCHADH. 'Irish Regnal Succession: A Reappraisal', *Studia Hibernica*, No 11, Coláiste Phádraig, Dublin, 1971.

THURNEYSEN, R.; Power, Nancy; Dillon, Myles; Mulchrone, Kathleen; Binchy, D.A.; Knock, August; Ryan, John. *Studies in Early Irish Law*, Royal Irish Academy, Dublin, 1936.

Select General Bibliography

AITCHISON, N.B. *Armagh and the Royal Centres in Early Medieval Ireland*, Boydell & Brewer, Suffolk, 1994.

ASHLEY, MIKE. *British Monarchs: The Complete Genealogy, Gazetteer and Biographical Encyclopedia of the Kings and Queens of Britain*, Robinson, London, 1998.

BLAKE-FOSTER, CHARLES FRENCH. *The Irish Chieftains: or A Struggle for the Crown*, McGlashen, Dublin, 1871.

BOURKE (DE BÚRCA), ÉAMONN. *Burke, Bourke & De Burgh People and Places*, Edmund Bourke and Ballinakella Press, Clare, 1995.

BOURKE, MARCUS. *The O'Rahilly*, Anvil Books, Kerry, 1967.

BRALY, DAVID. *Uí Néill: A History of Western Civilisation's Oldest Family*, America Media Co, USA, 1976.

BREIFNE, *Journal of the Breifne Historical Society* 12 vols. 1966-1984, Cavan.

BURKE'S IRISH FAMILY RECORDS, Preface by Hugh Montgomery Massingberd, Burke's Peerage, London, 1976.

BURKE, SIR BERNARD. *A Genealogical and Heraldic History of the Land Gentry of Ireland*, revised by A.C. Fox-Davies, Harrison, London, 1912.

BUTLER, WILLIAM F.T, *Gleanings from Irish History*, Longman, London, 1925.

BYRNE, JOHN FRANCIS, *Irish Kings and High Kings*, Batsford, London, 1973.

CALLANAN, MARTIN. *Records of Four Tipperary Septs. The O'Kennedys,*

O'Dwyers, O'Mulryans and O'Meaghers, JAG Publishing, Shannon, 1995.

CANNY, NICHOLAS. *The Elizabethan Conquest of Ireland, A Pattern Established*, Harvester Press, 1976.

CARNEY, JAMES, ed. *A Genealogical History of the O'Reillys* (written in the eighteenth century by Eoghan Ó Raghallaigh), Institute for Advanced Studies, Dublin, 1959.

CASTANET, J. *Mémorial Historique et généalogique de la maison O'Neill de Tyrone et de Claneboy*, Bergerac, 1899.

CLANDERMOND, THE COUNT OF. 'Gaelic Feudalism and the Kingdom of Desmond', *The Augustan Omnibus* 14, Vol XXX, 1993.

CLANDERMOND, THE COUNT OF. *Three Centuries of Niadh Nask Bookplates.* Foreword by The MacCarthy Mór, Prince of Desmond, The Black Eagle Press (Co. Antrim, Ireland) for the Niadh Nask, 1997.

CLANDERMOND, THE COUNT OF, ed. *Links in a Golden Chain: a Collection of Essays on the History of the Niadh Nask or The Military Order of the Golden Chain.* Foreword by Peter Berresford Ellis, Gryfons Publishers, Arkansas, for The Royal Eóghanacht Society, 1998.

CLANDERMOND, THE COUNT OF, ed. *A New Book of Rights: a complete transcript of the legal verdicts handed down by the courts of the Republic of Italy concerning the heraldic rights, status and prerogative of The MacCarthy Mór, Prince of Desmond, Chief of the Name and Arms and Head of the Eóghanacht Royal House of Munster & etc.*, Gryfons Publishers, Arkansas, USA, for the Royal Eóghanacht Society, 1998.

CLIFFORD O'DONOVAN, P. *The Irish in France*, De Beauvoir, London, 1990.

COLLINS, JOHN T. 'The Longs of Muskerry & Kinalea', *Journal of Cork Historical and Archaeological Society*, Vol LI, No 173, January–June, 1946.

CONE, POLLY, ed. *Treasures of Early Irish Art 1500 BC to 1500 AD (from the collections of the National Museum of Ireland)*, Royal Irish Academy and Trinity College, Dublin, The Metropolitan Museum of Art, New York, 1977.

CONNELLY, RICHARD F. *Irish Family History: An Historical and Genealogical Account of the Gaedhals, from the earliest period to the present time & etc.*, Tallon, Dublin, 2 vols, 1864/5.

CORKERY, DANIEL. *The Hidden Ireland*, M.H. Gill, Dublin, 1924.

CROTTY, GERARD. 'Chiefs of the Name', in *Aspects of Irish Genealogy*, ed. M.D. Evans, Dublin, 1996.

CUNNINGHAM, BERNADETTE. 'The Composition of Connacht in the lordships of Clanricade and Thomond 1577-1641', *Irish Historical Studies*, Vol XXIV No 93, May, 1984.

CURTIS, EDMUND. *A History of Medieval Ireland from 1086 to 1532*, Maunsel and Roberts, 1923.

CURTIS, EDMUND. *Richard II in Ireland 1394-95 and the Submission of the Irish Chiefs*, Oxford University Press, 1927.

CURTIS, EDMUND, MCDOWELL, R.B. *Irish Historical Documents 1172-1922*, Methuen, London, 1943.

D'ANGERVILLE, COUNT, ed. *The Royal, Peerage and Nobility of Europe* (Annuaire de la Noblesse de France), International Edition in English, founded 1843. Monte Carlo, Monaco, 1997.

DE BLACAM, AODH. *Gaelic Literature Surveyed*, Talbot Press, Dublin, 1929.

DILLON, MYLES. *The Cycle of the Kings*, Oxford University Press, 1946.

DILLON, MYLES. 'The Hindu Act of Truth in Celtic Tradition', *Modern Philology*, Vol XLIV, No 3, February, 1947.

DILLON, MYLES, ed. *Lebor na Cert* (The Books of Rights), Irish Text Society, London, 1962.

DILLON, MYLES. *Celt and Hindu* (pamphlet), University College, Dublin, 1973.

DILLON, MYLES. *Celts and Aryans: Survivals of Indo-European Speech and Society*, Indian Institute of Advanced Study, Simla, 1975.

DOBBS, MARGARET C. 'The Ben Shenchus', *Revue Celtique*, Paris, Vols XLVII (1930), XLVIII (1931) and XLIX (1932). A translation and commentary on the *Banshenchus* (History of Irishwomen).

DOHERTY, MURRAY. *The O'Doherty Historic Trail*, Guildhall Press, Derry, 1985.

DUHALLOW, THE LORD OF. *Gaelic Titles and Forms of Address*, Irish Genealogical Foundation, Kansas, USA, 1990 (second ed. 1997).

ELENCO DE GRANDEZAS Y TITULOS NOBILIARIOS ESPAÑOLES, 1997 Edicion de la Revista, Hilalguia, Madrid, 1997.

ELLIS, PETER BERRESFORD. *Hell or Connaught! The Cromwellian Colonisation of Ireland, 1652-1660*, Hamish Hamilton, London, 1975.

FIANTS; *The Irish Fiants of the Tudor Sovereigns*, new introduction by Kenneth Nicholls, preface by Thomás G.O. Cannann, 4 vols 1521-1603, Eamonn de Burca for Edmund Burke Publisher, 1994 (limited edition).

FLANAGHAN, M.T. *Irish Society, Anglo-Norman Settlers, Angevin Kingship*, Oxford University Press, 1989.

FURLONG, NICHOLAS. *Dermot, King of Leinster and the Foreigners*, Anvil Books, Kerry, 1973.

GENEALOGICAL ATLAS OF IRELAND, David E. Gardner, Derek Harland and Frank Smith, Stevenson's Genealogical Centre, Utah, USA, 1972.

GENEALOGICAL HISTORY OF THE MILESIAN FAMILIES OF IRELAND, 3 parts. Herald Artists Ltd., Dublin, 1968.

GLEESON, REV. JOHN. *History of the Ely O'Carroll: Territory of Ancient Ormond*, Roberts, Kilkenny, 1982.

GREHAN, IDA. *Irish Family Names*, Johnston, London, 1973.

GRENHAM, JOHN. *Clans and Families of Ireland: the heritage and heraldry of Irish Clans and Families*, Gill and Macmillan, Dublin, 1993.

GWYNN, DENIS. *The O'Gorman Mahon: Duelist, Adventurer and Politician*, Jarrolds, London, 1934.

HAMILTON, HANS CLAUDE. *Calendar of the State Papers Relating to Ireland of the Reign of Elizabeth 1574-1585*, Longman for HMSO, London 1867.

HAYDEN, M. and MOONAN, G. *A Short History of the Irish People*, London, 1921.

HAYES, RICHARD. *Ireland and Irishmen in the French Revolution*. Preface by Hilaire Belloc, Benn, London, 1932.

HAYES, RICHARD. *Irish Swordsmen of France*, M.H. Gill, Dublin 1934.

HAYES, RICHARD. *Biographical Dictionary of Irishmen in France*, M.H. Gill, Dublin, 1949.

HENNESSY, MAURICE, *The Wild Geese: The Irish Soldier in Exile*, Sidgwick and Jackson, London, 1973.

JEFFERIES, HENRY ALAN. 'Desmond: The Early Years & the career of Cormac Mac Carthy', *Journal of the Cork Historical and Archaeological Society*, LXXXVIII No 247 (Jan-Dec, 1983).

JEFFERIES, HENRY ALAN. 'Desmond Before the Norman Invasion: A political study', *Journal of the Cork Historical and Archaeological Society*. Vol LXXXIX No 248 (Jan-Dec, 1984).

JENNINGS, BRENDAN, ed. *Wild Geese in Spanish Flanders 1582-1700*, Dublin Stationery Office, 1964.

JOYCE, PATRICK WESTON. *A Social History of Ancient Ireland*, 2 vols, Longman, London, 1903.

KAVANAGH, ART, and MURPHY, RORY. *The Wexford Gentry: Irish Family Names*, Bunclody, 1994.

KEATING, GEOFFREY (Séthrún Céitinn *c.*1580–*c.*1644). *Foras Feasa ar Éirinn* (The History of Ireland), 4 vols, Irish Text Society, London, 1902, 1907, 1908, 1914 (reprinted in 1987 with separate Foreword by Dr Breandán Ó Buachalla).

KILFEATHER, T.P. *Graveyard of the Spanish Armada*, Anvil Books, Kerry, 1967.

LYDON, JAMES, ed. *Law and Disorder in Thirteenth Century Ireland: The Dublin Parliament of 1297*, Four Courts Press, Dulin, 1997.

MACALISTER, R.A.S., ed. *Book of MacCarthaigh Riabhach, otherwise the Book of Lismore*, Collotype facsimile, Dublin Stationery Office, Dublin, 1941.

MACCARTHY CLAN SOCIETY. *Clan MacCarthy Gathering* (booklet) printed by the Society, Kanturk, Co. Cork, September, 1992.

MACCARTHY, DAN and BREEN, AIDEEN. 'Astronomical Observations in the Irish Annals and their Motivation', *Peritia*, Journal of the Medieval Academy of Ireland, Vol II, 1997.

MACCARTHY CLAN SOCIETY. *The Last King: Donal IX MacCarthy Mór, King of Desmond and the Two Munsters, 1558-1596*, The MacCarthy Clan Society, Kanturk, Co. Cork, 1996.

MACCARTHY MÓR, SAMUEL TRANT MCCARTHY. *The MacCarthys of Munster: The Story of a Great Irish Sept* (first published by The Dundalgen

Press, 1922); a facsimile edition with an Introduction and Commentary by The MacCarthy Mór, Prince of Desmond, Gryfons Publishers, Arkansas, USA, 1997.

MACCARTHY MÓR, THE, PRINCE OF DESMOND. *Historical Essays on the Kingdom of Munster*, The Irish Genealogical Foundation, Missouri, USA, 1994.

MACCARTHY MOR, THE, PRINCE OF DESMOND. *Ulster's Office 1552-1800: A History of the Irish Office of Arms from the Tudor Plantations to the Act of Union*; with a foreword by John P.B. Brooke-Little, Clarenceux King of Arms, Gryfons Publishers, Arkansas, 1996.

MACCARTHY MÓR, THE, PRINCE OF DESMOND, with CLANDERMOND, THE COUNT OF. *An Irish Miscellany: Essays Heraldic, Historical and Genealogical*, Gryfons Publishers, Arkansas, USA, 1998.

MACDERMOT, BETTY. *Ó Ruairc of Breifne*, Drumlin Publications, Manorhamilton, Leitrim, 1990.

MACDERMOT, DERMOT. *MacDermot of Moylurg: The Story of a Connacht Family*, Drumlin Publications, Manorhamilton, Leitrim, 1996.

MACGEOGHEGAN, ABBÉ JAMES. *Histoire d'Irlande*, Paris, 1758 (Eng. trs. P.O'Kelly, Dublin, 1844).

MACGILLYCUDDY, ROSEMARY BROWNLOW. *A Short History of the Clan MacGillycuddy*, MacGillycuddy Press, Blackrock, Dublin, 1901.

MACHALE, CONOR. *Annals of the Clan Egan*, MacHale, Enniscrone, 1990.

MACHALE, CONOR. *The O'Dubhda Family History*, MacHale, Enniscrone, 1990.

MCKENNA, LAMBERT, ed. *The Book of Magauran, Leabhar Méig Shamhradháin (with genealogical chart)*, Institute for Advanced Studies, Dublin, 1947.

MCKENNA, LAMBERT, ed. *The Book of O'Hara, Leabhar Ó hEaghra, (written by Cormac Ó hEadhra, d. 1612)*, Institute for Advanced Studies, Dublin, 1951.

MACLYSAGHT, EDWARD. *Irish Families, their Names, Arms and Origins*, Allen Figgis, Dublin, 1971.

MACLYSAGHT, EDWARD. *More Irish Families (with essay on Irish 'chieftainries')*, Irish Academic Press, Dublin, 1982.

MACMAHON, NOEL, ed. *Here I Am, Here I stay! Marshal MacMahon 1808-1893*, Ballinakella Press, Clare, 1993.

MACNEILL, EOIN. *Phrases of Irish History* (orig. Dublin, 1919), M.H. Gill, Dublin, 1968 (reprint).

MACNEILL, MÁIRE. *Máire Rua, Lady of Leamaneh*, Ballinakella Press, Clare, 1990.

MADDEN, THOMAS MORE. *Genealogical, Historical and Family Records of the O'Maddens of Hy-Many and their descendants*, Powell, Dublin, 1894.

MAGAN, WILLIAM UMMA-MORE. *The Story of an Irish Family (The Magans)*, Element Books, Wiltshire, 1983.

MAGUIRE OF FERMANAGH, THE. *Historic Maguire Chalices*, Fermanagh District Council, 1996.

MARMION, ANTHONY. *The Ancient and Modern History of the Maritime Ports of Ireland*, London, 1858.

MATHEWS, THOMAS. *The O'Neills of Ulster: their history and genealogy*, Introduction by Francis Joseph Biggar. Sealy, Bryers & Walker, Dublin, 1903. 3 vols.

MATHEWS, ANTHONY. *Origins of the O'Kellys and a History of the Sept*, pp. for Mathews, Dublin, 1970.

MATHEWS, ANTHONY. *Origin of the O'Rourkes and a History of the Sept*, pp. for Mathews, Dublin, 1970.

MAXWELL, CONSTANTIA. *Irish History from Contemporary Sources (1509-1610)*, George Allen and Unwin, London, 1923.

MONTGOMERY-MASSINGBERD, HUGH, ed. *Burke's Introduction to Irish Ancestry*, Burke's Peerage, London, 1976.

MOODY, T.W., MARTIN, F.X. and BYRNE, F.J. *A New History of Ireland*, Vol.IX, Maps, Genealogies and Lists, A Companion to Irish History, Part II (Royal Irish Academy, 10 vols), Oxford University Press, 1984.

MORGAN, HIRAM. *Tyrone's Rebellion*, The Royal Historical Society, Boydell Press, Suffolk, 1993.

MORLEY, HENRY. *Ireland Under Elizabeth and James the First*, George Routledge, London, 1890 (containing the works of Edmund Spenser, Sir John Davies and Fynes Moryson on Ireland).

MULLEN, REV. T.H. and MULLEN, REV. J.E. *The Ulster Clans O'Mullen, O'Kane and O'Mellan*, B.N.L., Belfast, 1966.

MURPHY, REV. DENIS. *The Life of Hugh Roe O'Donnell, Prince of Tirconnell (1586-1602) by Lughaidh O'Clery, trs & notes from Cugory O'Clery's Irish Mss in the Royal Irish Academy*, Fallon, Dublin, 1895.

MURPHY, JOHN. *Ireland, Industrial, Political and Social*, Longman, Green and Co, London, 1870.

MURPHY, JOHN A. *Justin MacCarthy, Lord Mountcashel, Commander of the first Irish Brigade in France*, Cork University Press, Cork, 1958. New edition published by the Royal Eóghanacht Society, Clonmel, with a foreword by MacCarthy Mór, Prince of Desmond, 1999.

NASH, PIERS O'CONOR. *The History and Heritage of the Royal O'Conors*, Purcell Print, Boyle, 1990.

NEILL, KATHLEEN. *O'Neill Commemorative Journal of the first International Gathering of the Clan, June 20-27, 1982* (containing three essays on the O'Neill family history by Sir Iain Moncrieffe of that Ilk), Irish Genealogical Association, Dunmurry, Belfast, 1982.

NEWMAN, T.C. *Brian Boru, King of Ireland*, Dublin, 1983.

NICHOLLS, KENNETH. *Gaelic and Gaelicised Ireland in the Middle Ages*, Gill and Macmillan, Dublin, 1972.

O'BRIEN CLAN ASSOCIATION. *The Royal O'Briens – A Tribute*, Dromoland, Clare, 1992.

O'BRIEN, HON. DONOUGH. *History of the O'Briens from Brían Bóroimhe AD 1000 to AD 1945*, B.T. Batsford, London, 1949.

O'BRIEN, GRANIA. *These My Friends and Forebears: The O'Briens of Dromoland*. Ballinakella Press, Co. Clare, n.d.

O'BRIEN, IVAR. *O'Brien of Thomond: The O'Briens in Irish History 1500-1865*, Phillimore, Chichester, 1986.

O'BRIEN, LUCIUS. *Case of the Rt. Hon. Lucius, Lord Inchiquin in the Peerage of Ireland on his claiming the right to vote at the election of the representative Peers for Ireland, 1861*, Walmsley, London, 1861.

O'BRIEN, MAUREEN CONCANNON. *The Story of the Concannons*, Clan Publications, Dublin, 1990.

O'BRIEN, M.A. *Corpus Genealogiarum Hiberniae*, Dublin, 1962 (vol.1).

O'CARROLL ROBERTSON, JUNE. *A Long Way from Tipperary: The Carrolls of Lissenhall and Tulla*, Images Publishing, Upton-upon-Severn, England, 1994.

Ó CIANÁIN, TADHG. *The Flight of the Earls*, M.H. Gill, Dublin, 1916.

O'CONNOR, PATRICK. *The Royal O'Connors of Connaught*, Old House Press, Swinford, Co. Mayo, 1997.

O'CONOR, MATTHEW. *The History of Irish Catholics*, Dublin, 1813.

O'CONOR, RODERIC. *An Historical & Genealogical Memoir of the O'Connors, Kings of Connaught and their Descendants*, McGlashan and Gill, Dublin, 1861.

Ó CRONÍN, DÁIBHÍ. *Early Medieval Ireland AD 400-1200*, (Longman History of Ireland), Longman, London, 1995.

Ó CUÍV, BRÍAN ed. *Seven Centuries of Irish Learning AD 1000-1700*, Stationery Office, Dublin, 1961.

O CUÍV, BRÍAN. 'A Sixteenth Century Political Poem', *Éigse* XV (1973-4).

Ó DALAIGH, AONGHUS RUADH, trs by James Mangan. *The Tribes of Ireland: A Satire*, ed. John O'Donovan, Dublin, 1852.

O'DONOGHUE, JOHN. *Historical Memoir of the O'Briens*, Hodges Smith & Co, Dublin, 1860.

O'DONOGHUE, ROD. *O'Donoghue People and Places*, Ballinakella Press, Clare, 1999.

O'DONOVAN, JOHN. 'The O'Donnells in Exile', series in *O'Duffy's Hibernian Magazine*, Dublin, Nos 1-7, June-December 1860.

O'DONOVAN, JOHN. *The O'Conors of Connaught: an historical memoir... with additions from the state papers and public records by Charles Owen, O'Conor Don*, Hodges Figgis, Dublin, 1891.

O'DONOVAN, JOHN. ed. *Tribes and Customs of Hy-Many (published from The Book of Lecan)*, Tower Books, Cork, 1976.

O'DUGAN, JOHN. *The Kings of the Race of Eibhear: A Chronological Poem* (bilingual text of *Ríogha níl Eibhir* by Seán Mór Ó Dubhagáin, d.*c.* 1372.), Commentary and Appendices by The MacCarthy Mór, Prince of Desmond, Foreword by Peter Berresford Ellis, Royal Eóghanacht Society Publication, Clonmel, 1999.

O'DWYER, SIR MICHAEL. *The O'Dwyers of Kilnamanagh: the history of an Irish Sept*, John Murray, London, 1933.

'O'H, E.' *The O'Reillys of Templemills, Celbridge and a pedigree from the old Irish mss & etc.*, M.W. O'Reilly, Moorefield, Dundrum, Co. Dublin, 1941.

O'HART, JOHN. *Irish Pedigrees: or the Origin and Stem of the Irish Nation*, 2 vols, Duffy, Dublin, 1887-88.

O'HART, JOHN. *The Irish and Anglo-Irish Gentry*, introduced by Edward MacLysaght, Irish University Press, Shannon, 1969.

Ó HINNSE, SÉAMUS (ed. & trs.). *Miscellaneous Irish Annals: AD 1114-1437*, Dublin, 1947 (including The MacCarthy's Book).

O'KEEFE, J.C., H. AND A.J. *Record of the O'Keefe Family of Co. Cork*, Cork, 1927.

O'KELLY D'AUGHRIM, COMTE. *Essai Historique sur l'Irlande*, Brussels, 1837.

O'LONG, THE (DENIS C. LONG). *A history of the Longs*, pamphlet No 1, Canovee Historical and Archaeological Society, n.d.

O'MAHONY, REV. CANON JOHN. *A History of the O'Mahony Septs of Kinelmeky and Ivagha*, Crookstown, Co. Cork, n.d.

O'MEAGHER, J.C. *Some Historical Notices of the O'Meaghers of Okerrin*, London, 1886.

O'MORCHOE, REV. THOMAS. *The Succession of the Chiefs of Ireland*, Ormond Printing, Dublin, 1904.

O'NEILL, SÉAN. *O'Neill People and Places*, Ballinakella Press, Clare, 1991.

'OLLAMH'. *The Story of Shane O'Neill: Hereditary Prince of Ulster Surnamed 'An Diomais' or The Proud*, Sealy, Dublin, n.d.

O'RAHILLY, THOMAS F. *Early Irish History and Mythology*, Dublin Institute for Advanced Studies, Dublin, 1946.

O'REILLY, I.J. *The History of the Breifne O'Reilly*. Vantage Press, New York, 1976.

ORPEN, GODDARD HENRY. *The Song of Dermot and the Earl*, (from Carew Mss No 596, Archiespiscopal Library, Lambeth Palace, ed., trs and notes), Clarendon Press, Oxford, 1892.

O'TOOLE, JOHN. *The O'Tooles, ancient lords of Powerscourt* (Feracualan, Fertie and Imale, with some notice of Feagh Mac Hugh O'Byrne, Chief of Clan Ranelagh), Sullivan, Dublin, n.d.

POINTE DE VUE (Paris), series of articles: July 14, 1992 to August 8, 1992. The Maguire (July 14, 1992); MacCarthy Mór (July 21, 1992); O'Brien (July 28, 1992); O'Neill of Clanaboy (August 1, 1992); O'Conor Don (August 8, 1992),

POWER, PATRICK C. *A Literary History of Ireland*, Mercier Press, Cork, 1969

PRENDERGAST, JOHN P. *The Cromwellian Settlement of Ireland*, Longman, Green & Co, London, 1865.

QUIEN ES QUIEN EN ESPANA, Editorial Campillo S.L., Edicion 1996 (Madrid).

ROCHE, RICHARD. *The Norman Invasion of Ireland*, Anvill Books, Kerry, 1970.

ROYAL EOGHANACHT SOCIETY. *Cashel '96: The Quatercentenary of the death of King Donal IX, MacCarthy Mór, 1596-1996*. Royal Eóghanacht Society, Clonmel, 1996 (commemoration book with pictures of the quatercentary commemoration ceremonies).

RUSSELL, C.W. and PRENDERGAST, JOHN P. *Calendar of the State Papers Relating to Ireland of the Reign of James I, 1606-1608*, Longman & Co, London, 1874.

SIMMS, KATHARINE. 'The O'Hanlon, O'Neill and Anglo-Normans in 13th Century Armagh', *Seanchas Ard Macha* (pp 70-90), Vol. IX, 1978.

SIMMS, KATHARINE. *From Kings to Warlords: The Changing Political Structure of Gaelic Ireland in the Later Middle Ages*, The Boydell Press, Suffolk, 1987.

SOMERVILLE-LARGE, PETER. *From Bantry Bay to Leitrim: A Journey in Search of O'Sullivan Beare*, Victor Gollancz, London, 1974.

SULLIVAN, T.D. *Bantry, Berehaven and The O'Sullivan Sept*, Tower Books, Cork, 1978.

TAYLOR, J.F. *Owen Roe O'Neill*, Fisher and Unwin, London, 1906.

UA CRONÍN, RISTEARD O'DEA. *Ua Déaghaidh: The Story of a Rebel Clan*, Ballinakella Press, Clare, 1992.

UA DUINNÍN, AN ATHAIr PÁDRAIG. *The Maguires of Fermanagh*, M.H. Gill, Dublin, 1917.

VON DASSANOWSKY, DR ROBERT. 'The Gaelic Royal Houses of Ireland', *Monarchy*, December, 1998.

WALPOLE, C.G. *A Short History of the Kingdom of Ireland*, London, 1885.

WALSH, MICHELINE KERNEY. *Destruction By Peace: Hugh O'Neill After Kinsale*, Cumann Seanchais Ard Mhaca, Armagh, 1986.

WALSH, MICHELINE KERNEY. *The MacDonnels of Antrim and on the Continent*, Dublin, 1960.

WALSH, MICHELINE KERNEY. *Hugh O'Neill, Prince of Ulster, An Exile of Ireland*, Four Courts Press, 1996.

WALSH, FATHER PAUL. *The Will and Family of Hugh O'Neill, Earl of Tyrone* (with an appendix of genealogies), Sign of the Three Candles, Dublin, 1930.

WALSH, FATHER PAUL. *Irish Chiefs and Leaders* (Maguires, O'Reillys, MacSweeneys, MacDonnells, Bissets, Gallagher, MacGeoghegan, O'Molloys and Kirbys of Munster), ed. Colm Ó Lochlainn, Sign of the Three Candles, Dublin, 1960.

WALSH, FATHER PAUL. *Irish Men of Learning* (O'Duigenan, O'Maolconaire,

O'Curnín, Mac an Bhaird, Mac Firbisigh), ed. Colm Ó Lochlainn, Sign of the Three Candles, Dublin, 1947.

WARE, SIR JAMES. *The Antiquities and History of Ireland*, London, 1705.

WATKINS, CALVERT. 'Indo European Metrics in Archaic Irish Verse', *Celtica* Vol VI, 1963.

WEIR, HUGH W.L. *O'Connor People and Places*, Ballinakella, Clare, 1994.

WEIR, HUGH W.L. *O'Brien People and Places*, Ballinakella, Clare, 1994.

WEIR, H.W.L. ed. *Ireland: A Thousand Kings*, Ballinakella, Clare, 1998

WHITE, REV. P. *History of Clare and the Dalcassian Clans of Tipperary, Limerick and Galway*, M.H. Gill, Dublin, 1893.

WILLIAMS, J. *History of the Name O'Neill*, Mercier Press, Dublin, 1978.

WILLIAMS, J.D. *History of the Name MacCarthy*, Mercier Press, Dublin, 1978.

WILLIAMS, J.D. *History of the Name O'Kelly*, Mercier Press, Dublin, 1977.

WILLIAMS, J.D. *History of the Name O'Brien*, Mercier Press, Dublin, 1977.

YOUNGS, SUSAN, ed. *The Work of Angels: Masterpieces of Celtic Metalwork, 6th-9th Centuries AD*, British Museum Publications, in association with National Museum of Ireland, 1989.

Some Unpublished Manuscripts

I was particularly grateful to be allowed access to many unpublished sources, MSS and letters, too numerous to be listed here. I would, however, like to acknowledge the following:

MACCARTHY. 'Généalogie de la Royale et Serenissime Maison de MacCarthy' compiled by Sir Isaac Heard, Norroy King of Arms, and Ralph Bigland, Clarenceux King of Arms of England for Justin MacCarthy, c. 1760. Ownership vested in The MacCarthy Mór, Prince of Desmond, original on permanent loan to Cashel Heritage Museum.

METCALF, SIR AUBREY. 'History of the Descendants of Richard, The Mac-Gillycuddy of the Reeks (1826-1866) by his grandson. 1957', duplicated and distributed by MacGillycuddy Clan Society.

O'DOGHERTY, REAR-ADMIRAL PASCUAL. 'The Genealogy of the O'Doghertys; Chiefs of Inish-Owen', unpublished MS, together with cuttings and other material.

O'DONOVAN, THE. 'Letters of Dr John O'Donovan to Morgan William O'Donovan', Vols 1 (1841-43), 2 (1843-1854) and 3 (1855-1861), privately held by The O'Donovan.

O'DONNELL DUKE OF TETUAN. 'The O'Donell Pedigree', commissioned by the Duques of Tetuan, Spain, in the possession of the Duque de Tetuan y Lara.

Index

Charles II, 73, 74, 123, 139, 153, 158,
181, 237, 238, 248
Edward I, 28
Edward II, 28
Edward VI, 49, 60, 64, 271
Edward VII, 204
Elizabeth I, 23, 47, 49, 50, 53, 58–9, 60,
62, 84, 121, 123, 152, 157, 176, 177,
178, 196–7, 201, 207, 232–3, 260
George IV, 82
George V, 204
George VI, 90, 275
Henry IV, 29, 270, 271
Henry VII, 137
Henry VIII, 29–33, 35, 44, 45, 56, 57–9,
63, 84, 133, 138, 174–5, 232, 247, 253
James I, 53, 5–6, 68, 70–2, 139, 152, 201
James II, 74, 75, 123–5, 139, 140, 144,
153, 158, 161, 178, 207, 214, 240, 248,
255, 263
John, 195
Mary, 49, 55, 60, 176
Richard I, 27
Richard II, 29, 199, 270, 289
see also Angevin Empire
English law and Ireland, 5, 6, 28, 40, 41, 45,
46, 55, 64, 70, 71, 87, 103, 104, 139,
175, 176, 209
English titles in Ireland, 54, 55
Ennis, Sir John, 148
Eniskillen, Barons, 128, 258, 262, 264
Alexander (6th Baron), 263
Alexander (9th Baron), 263
Philip (7th Baron), 263
Ruaidri, 263
Theophilus (8th Baron), 263
see also Maguire of Fermanagh, The
Eochaidh Feidhlioch, High King, 42
Eóghanacht dynasty, 1, 16, 17, 18, 19, 39,
49, 65, 89, 102, 103, 112, 113, 115,
122, 125, 133, 151, 156, 160, 293
and Brian Boru, 169–70
Carrthach (d.1045), 114
Cellachán Mac Buadacháin (d.954), 116
Chaisil branch, 114
Coirpre Luachra, 142
Cormac II Mac Cuileannáin (836–908),
39, 115
Donnchadh II mac Ceallacháin Caisil
(d.963), 169
Eóghan Mór (d.192), 113, 114, 160, 168
Locha Léin, 142
Maelmuad mac Brían, 113, 169

and O'Briens, 168–71
see also MacCarthy Mór, The; Munster,
Kingdom of
Eremon, 17, 43, 112, 113, 226, 227, 267,
280
Essex, Earls of, 200–1
Robert, 233, 234
Walter, 233
Étain, Princess of Desmond, 43, 119, 120

Falls, Cyril, 238
Feinius Farsaidh, 113, 227
Fenians, 147–8, 288, 289
Fianna, the, 288–9
Fianna Fáil, 90, 102, 184, 210, 289
Fine Gael, 164, 216
Finnan, Saint, 253
Fionn mac Cumhail, 268, 288
FitzDermot, John, 157
see also O'Long of Garranelong, The
FitzGerald, family, 28, 32, 49, 120, 121, 173,
174
Daniel, 159
Gerald, 137, 174, 292
Gerald Óg, 271
Honora, 48
James, 174, 176
Maurice, 212
Thomas, 232
see also Desmond, Earls of; Kildare, Earls
of
Fitzgibbon, Edmund (the White Knight),
133
FitzGilbert, Richard, Earl of Pembroke
('Strongbow'), 21, 50, 269
FitzHenry, Mylor, 194
FitzThomas, John, 119
FitzWalter, Theobald, 136; see also Butler
FitzWilliam
Lord Justice, 52, 176
William, 221, 247
'Flight of the Earls', 201, 234, 261
'Flight of the Wild Geese', 1, 257
Flynn, Pádraig, TD, 102
Fox, The (An Sionnach), 65, 95, 280–4
arms, 282
Brabazon Hubert Maine (1868), 282–3
Brassell, 281–2
current see Douglas John
Donogh, 281
Douglas John (b. 1942), 280, 283–4
Garry John (b.1964), 283
Hubert, 282